H

W9-ASR-669

Hickory Flat Public Library
2740 East Cherokee Drive
Canton, Georgia 30115

The Collector
of
Dying Breaths

**Center Point
Large Print**

Also by M. J. Rose and available from
Center Point Large Print:

The Book of Lost Fragrances
Seduction

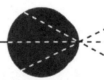

**This Large Print Book carries the
Seal of Approval of N.A.V.H.**

The Collector of Dying Breaths

M. J. ROSE

CENTER POINT LARGE PRINT
THORNDIKE, MAINE

This Center Point Large Print edition
is published in the year 2014 by arrangement with
Atria Books, a division of Simon & Schuster, Inc.

The text of this Large Print edition is unabridged.
In other aspects, this book may vary
from the original edition.
Printed in the United States of America
on permanent paper.
Set in 16-point Times New Roman type.

ISBN: 978-1-62899-118-5

Library of Congress Cataloging-in-Publication Data

Rose, M. J., 1953–
The collector of dying breaths : a novel of suspense / M. J. Rose. —
Center Point Large Print edition.
pages ; cm
Summary: "This gothic tale zigzags from the violent days of Catherine
de Medici's court to twenty-first-century France. Set in the forest of
Fontainebleau, crisscrossing the lines between the past and the present,
this mesmerizing tale of passion and obsession illuminates the true path
to immortality: the legacies we leave behind."—Provided by publisher.
ISBN 978-1-62899-118-5 (library binding : alk. paper)
1. Immortality—Fiction. 2. Large type books. I. Title.
PS3568.O76386C66 2014b
813'.54—dc23
                                                                2014007831

The author Mark Slouka once
gave writers this advice:

1. Trust a few, necessary voices.

2. Try, as much as possible, to avoid torturing
these brave souls with your own insecurities.

3. Shut up and write.

With gratitude, this book is dedicated to
the two brave souls I'm sure I do torture:
Steve Berry and Douglas Clegg.

"You may think me superstitious, if you will, and foolish; but indeed, I am more than half convinced that he had, in truth, an abnormal gift, and a sense, something—I know not what—that in the guise of wall and door offered him an outlet, a secret and peculiar passage of escape into another and altogether more beautiful world."

H. G. WELLS,
"THE DOOR IN THE WALL," 1911

Chapter 1

MARCH 1, 1573
BARBIZON, FRANCE

Written for my son to read upon my death, from his father, René le Florentin, perfumer to Catherine de Medici, Queen Mother.

It is with irony now, forty years later, to think that if I had not been called a murderer on the most frightening night of my life, there might not be any perfume in Paris today. And that scent—to which I gave my all and which gave me all the power and riches I could have hoped for—is at the heart of why now it is *I* who call myself a murderer.

It is one thing to fall in love with a rose and its deep rich scent. Once the blood-red flower blooms, browns and decays and its smell has dissipated, you can pluck another rose about to bloom. But to fall in love with a woman after a lifetime of not knowing love? In the browning of your own days? Ah, that is to invite disaster. That is to invite heartbreak.

The château is cold tonight, but my skin burns. My blood flows hot. Who knew that yearning alone could heat a man so? That only memories could set him on fire? I feel this pen in my fingers, the feather's smoothness, and I imagine it is Isabeau's hair.

I close my eyes and see her standing before me.

Isabeau! Exuberant, tender, dazzling. And mine. I see her sapphire eyes twinkling. Her thick mane of hair like a blanket for me to hide in.

I whisper to her and ask her to undress for me slowly, in that way she had. And she does. In the dream she does. She strips bare, slowly, slowly, of everything but her gloves, cream kid gloves that stretch above her elbows. Her silken skin gleams in the candlelight, golden and smooth, smelling of exotic flowers. Gardenias and camellias and roses, scents that emanate from within. This is her secret and mine. Isabeau had a garden inside of her body. Flowers where other women had organs. Her own natural perfume richer and more luxurious than anything I ever could have created and bottled.

In this dream, Isabeau never takes off her gloves. Night after night, I beseech her to strip all the way for me, but she just smiles. *Not yet, René. Not yet.* And then she reaches out with one gloved finger and traces her name on my skin. *One day, René. Once you have found the elixir.*

I dream this asleep. And hear it, awake, in the wind. Her promise.

Once you have found the elixir.

I lie there, sweating into my nightshirt. Trembling from the memories.

There was something about the way the bell rang that first day she came to my shop. Its tone was different, almost tentative, as if it wasn't sure it should be ringing at all. Now, looking back, were the fates warning me? How cruel of those witches to give me love at that moment—after a lifetime of holding it back.

But I will have my revenge on them. I, Renato Bianco, known as René le Florentin, will figure out how to reanimate a dying breath and so wreak havoc for their folly. So help me God, this I will work at until I have no more of my own breath in my body.

Winter is upon us now, and it is quiet here in the woods and forests of Fontainebleau. The days stretch before me, an endless vista of foggy mornings and chilly evenings and dark nights devoted to one thing and one thing only: my experiments. If I cannot succeed with them, I cannot, I will not, go on with my life.

It was one man who heard the bell ring to the shop and opened the door, and another who closed it. That was how long it took for Isabeau to alter me. And it is the me who is altered who has this need for revenge on the crones who have done this to me.

Let me tell you first about the man who heard the bell.

Chapter 2

MARCH 2, 1573
BARBIZON, FRANCE

When I close my eyes, I can still see the laboratory as it was, shrouded in shadow. The light hurt Dom Serapino's eyes, and so I would only ignite a very few candles—enough to see what I was doing. Their flames danced, mocking the solemnity of the occasion. Their burning added to the scent in the windowless cell, which was sweet with Serapino's favorite incense—a combination of rosemary, angelica, lavender, and frankincense.

Dom Serapino, the monk I was apprenticed to, had been suffering for weeks and had begged me to help him leave this world and travel to the next. Heaven, he was certain, would welcome him. Had he not spent his life creating wonderful-smelling potions and healing balms and tonics? Had he not been devout?

I watched the shallow rise and fall of his chest. Listened to the rattle of his breath. As his student, I had memorized all his instructions. I had seen him perform this duty but had never done it myself.

His quest was to capture a person's last elusive exhalation, to collect his dying breath, then to release it into another living body and reanimate that soul. To bring it back from the dead.

What was he? A necromancer? A magician? An alchemist? Serapino would accept no title but that of monk.

"René," he would say, "that is all I am. A humble monk using the gifts nature offers."

In the last few years, Serapino had devised a method to capture those dying breaths. Now it was up to me to use the contraption the way I had seen him use it so many times on other monks once his tonics and balms had lost their capacity for healing and death was inevitable.

The iron rack, the length of two hands, had spaces in it for a dozen openmouthed bottles; nearby corks were at the ready. The job of the collector was to judge when the end was near and then start filling one bottle after another with breaths, stopping them one after the next. It was only the last one that mattered, but there was no way to guess which that would be.

Sometimes the end took so long in coming that I was given the task of rinsing the bottles out with wine so Serapino could reuse them and start from the beginning again. Filling one bottle after another.

But that final night, I had no helper. My master was dying. I'd arranged three sets of collection bottles. Thirty-six chances to capture Serapino's final breath. Then—later, much later—I might complete his alchemical research and find the elixir to mix with the breath and perhaps one day bring him back to life.

Serapino hadn't opened his eyes for several minutes. I knew enough about the potion I'd administered to know that he wouldn't open them again. His death was only moments away. The draught had been far more powerful than it needed to be, but that was what he'd asked for. He wanted no half measures and no mistakes. Serapino was ready for the end and didn't care that some considered it a sin.

The pain of the disease eating his bones was too great a burden.

"Surely God did not put herbs and flowers, even these, on the earth if he didn't want us to use them," he said. "The greater sin would be not to use those gifts."

And now I was listening to his breaths, counting how long between each. They were coming further apart. And then he began to move his lips. No sound emanated from between them. Was he praying? Asking God for forgiveness? For help? For a benediction? I tried to read the words as he formed them. Struggled to make sense of the way his mouth moved.

It was my name he spoke—not the name of his God, but my name. What was he trying to say?

What was there left to say? I had known him since I was brought to the monastery, fourteen years before, when I was but three years old and an orphan. And it was Serapino who, when I was seven, had taken me as his apprentice, befriended me and given me a profession.

He mouthed my name again. And then managed a hoarse whisper. "René . . . the bees . . ."

I was so caught up in trying to understand that I forgot my task and stopped capturing his breaths. What was he saying? Was this the poison talking or had he in these last hours made some connection that he wanted to share?

"Bees?" I asked.

But there was no response.

I remembered with a start that I had a job to do and followed the instructions Serapino had taught me before he became ill.

"Make sure you move quickly, René. Be careful not to let the atmosphere in the room corrupt the breath."

I lifted a bottle to his lips, captured his breath, and then shoved a cork in its glass neck.

That night, with tears streaming down my cheeks, I corked the tenth vial. Then, I held the eleventh up and waited. Waited. Counted. Waited. His chest did not move. Still I waited.

I had known this moment would come, of course, yet still I was somehow unprepared. I wasn't even aware that I had dropped the eleventh bottle till I heard it crash on the stone floor and shatter.

I threw myself on his still form and wept into the monk's rough robes.

For the first time in memory, I was alone.

How long did I weep that night over the body of my protector, mentor and friend? An hour? Two? At some point I reached out and took the tenth bottle and held it. Held what had been Serapino's last breath.

Serapino had been my all. I could not imagine how to go on living without him on this earth.

As I sat beside his deathbed, I vowed never again to love so much, to be so vulnerable to loss.

I do not know how many minutes or even hours passed, but after a time I became aware of footsteps. Clutching my treasure in my fist, I turned from the still body to see who approached.

How had news of the alchemist's passing traveled? It was still the dead of night. No one had been in the laboratory with us. Serapino had been sick a long time, and no one expected him at midnight prayers, so his absence could not have been a warning. Yet there in the thick shadows under the ancient stone archway stood Dom Beneto, the abbot, long taper in hand, taking in the scene. He glanced from Serapino's body to me. His unearthly black eyes did not blink. There was no compassion in them. No sympathy on his ancient face.

He walked over to the body, placed his long pale fingers on my mentor's neck and leaned down.

From where I stood it appeared Dom Beneto was kissing the dead monk. Rage rose in me. How dare he? I took a step, prepared to grab him and pull him back. But Beneto retreated on his own.

"I smell bitter almonds," he said and looked back at me.

Since the 1220s the Dominicans had been creating herbal remedies, creams and balms renowned for their properties. Every monk at the monastery of Santa Maria Novella was equipped to sniff out hundreds of scents.

"You poisoned him," Dom Beneto said.

I can still see the candles' shadows rising and falling on the walls like specters come to witness the death as the friar's shocking words echoed in that grim chamber.

While I lived in the monastery, I was at home in the city of Florence. Weekly, I traveled outside the sacred walls to interact with the people who bought our wares. I made scents for the daughter of Lorenzo de' Medici, Duke of Urbino and often visited the palace where Catherine lived. I knew the world well and was hardly naive. But the last thing I expected to hear in that moment of grief and despair was Dom Beneto's accusation and his charge.

"You have committed an unspeakable act, René

Bianco. I am placing you under arrest. We will try you here in the monastery."

"Dom Beneto, it was Serapino's wish."

"Do not lie to me."

"Brother Serapino created the formula for the potion himself. He drank it himself."

"He was too ill to make a potion."

"Before he fell so ill."

"And how did he get it into his hands? He has not had the energy to leave his bed for weeks."

"Well, yes, I . . . I . . . handed it to him, but—"

"So you admit your deed," he said, interrupting.

"I was just doing what he asked of me. He was in such pain, Dom Beneto. What was I to do? Refuse him?"

"So say you! How do I know you haven't been poisoning him all along? His illness has come upon him suddenly enough. He was a healthy man five weeks ago and you alone had much to gain by his passing."

Beneto waved his arm around the laboratory. His candle illuminated the hundreds of glass bottles filled with potions and elixirs, essences and remedies. The light flickered over the brass scales, the mixers and measuring cups on Serapino's worktable. Those he studied to make up the salves and lotions and scents as well as the notebooks wherein he kept the formulas he'd created and the ones he was working on.

"Chief apothecary of the monastery is a title

worth killing a man for. Isn't that what you have been aiming for all along? Has not Brother Serapino talked about your ambition?"

"I would never have done such a thing." It was a feeble defense. But what else could I say? I was unprepared. Even now I don't know what I might have offered that would have changed Beneto's mind. Because I wasn't really who he was accusing that night. It was Serapino who he was damning.

"His was not the work of God and I will not allow it to be continued!" Beneto shouted at me. "I ordered Serapino to stop these experiments!"

Reaching out, he shoved the rack of captured breaths to the floor. An explosion of breaking glass echoed in the small chamber as bottle after bottle fell and shattered on the stone floor. The noise was so loud and the scent so overpowering I glanced over at Serapino to see if the melee had roused him, forgetting for the moment that he had died.

Bottles were still falling, still breaking. I watched the continuing destruction of all our work. "No!" I moaned and knelt down to . . . what? The mess was too great. The demolition too complete. Hundreds of scents were escaping into the air. Stinking as they mixed together.

"Get up," Beneto shouted. "Leave all that alone."

Then, crunching more glass under the weight of his body, he walked past me and over to

Serapino's table. Reaching for my master's notebook, Beneto opened it, held the candle close, wax dripping on the pages, and read.

All was quiet for a few moments, then: "Did he not heed any of my warnings?" he asked, looking up at me. "How long has he been disobeying me?"

When I didn't answer, Beneto took two steps toward me, grabbed me by the collar of my shirt. I was decades younger and stronger, but he was the abbot. I could not fight back.

"How long?"

But I could refuse to answer. And I did. Infuriated, Beneto shoved me away. It took such a great effort that he stumbled, bumped into the deathbed and fell. The impact jostled Serapino's body. One of Serapino's hands fell from his side off the cot and onto Beneto's shoulder.

The abbot screamed like a frightened little girl.

Struggling to his feet, he brushed off his robes. Then, glaring at me, he made his way back to the desk. After searching through Serapino's things for a moment, Beneto grabbed a ring of keys and pocketed them. Then he riffled through the books. Ignoring those that were written by others, he separated out Serapino's notebooks. When he'd gathered all four that he found, he turned back to me.

"There will be a trial, René Bianco. You will stand for the crime of killing Brother Serapino with poison. Until that time, you will remain here.

Pray for your soul, you miserable liar. Because no one else will be praying for it. You have robbed the monastery of one of its treasured monks. That deed will not go unpunished."

Then, before I realized what he was doing, he walked to the door, pulled it closed and locked it from the outside.

I rushed to the door, but I was too late. Grief had dulled my reflexes. I was imprisoned in the laboratory with the body of Brother Serapino. There were bits of glass everywhere. Liquid spills. The smell was now an ugly combination of too many essences that had no business being mixed together. All augmented with the odor of death. Precious books lay soaking in the mess on the floor, being ruined while I watched.

But I wasn't thinking about that.

I'd been charged with a job by Serapino—to discover the secret of reanimating dying breaths. I had promised him I would achieve that goal. But to succeed I would have to escape with two items.

Beneto may have thought he had erased all traces of my master's work.

But the notebook holding the unfinished formula I needed was hidden under a loose stone in the floor. Serapino never trusted anyone but me with it. And in my hand was something I'd been clutching when Beneto barged into the cell, the bottle I'd never let go of, the bottle that held Serapino's dying breath.

Chapter 3

"Go to Melinoe Cypros in Barbizon . . ." Despite how weak he was, Robbie's voice was insistent. "Collect my books . . . our grandfather's books . . . Ask her to show you . . ." His voice drifted off. His eyes fluttered closed.

Had he fallen asleep again? Jac L'Etoile didn't know, so she did what she had been doing for days: she watched and waited. After almost ten minutes, just as she was about to go get the nurse they'd hired, Robbie reopened his eyes and resumed the conversation as if no time had passed at all. Perhaps for him it hadn't. For her it had been interminable. Every moment of his illness had been.

How was it possible that her baby brother, who weeks ago had celebrated his thirtieth birthday in perfect health, could suddenly be so sick?

Robbie ran the family perfume business on his own, practiced meditation daily with Zen masters, hosted fetes that were the talk of Paris, and was on the board of one of the foremost fragrance museums in the world.

22

The man in the bed could barely string more than two or three sentences together.

"You need to finish my work with her . . ." he said haltingly, then stopped.

What work was Robbie doing in Barbizon? And with whom? He seemed to think he'd explained it to her, but he hadn't. And she didn't want to press him.

"You have the talent to . . . You doubt yourself, Jac. Don't." Every word came out on the edge of a ragged and labored breath. He closed his eyes once more.

Although he was two years her junior, Robbie had always been there to help her. Was the wiser of them, who, since childhood, had calmed her and showed her the way. The Zen sage who reminded her that the path would reveal itself if she was only patient. Now, at his most vulnerable, even if nothing he was saying made sense, he was still trying to teach her.

This time he was quiet for so long, Jac was certain he had fallen asleep. She fingered the thin scarlet cord tied around her left wrist. There were things Jac should do, calls to make, family to inform, papers to take care of, but she didn't get up. Couldn't leave Robbie's sickbed. There was nowhere she wanted to be but with him. To be with her brother while he fought this disease that the doctors didn't understand and couldn't control.

"Why are the drapes pulled?" Robbie asked ten minutes later, suddenly awake and smiling, more energetic than he had been all day. "People always pull the drapes and keep the lights dim when someone is dying. Open the window . . . I want to smell . . . the garden."

"You aren't—" She couldn't even say the word.

"I am." The burst of energy was spent. His voice was fainter already. "It will get easier to accept, Jac." He fastened his eyes on her. "I promise it will."

As Jac unbolted the mullioned windows and looked out at the damp February day, she wished that there were more flowers blooming for him. And then felt the sting of tears. She took a deep breath. No. She would not cry, not yet. There would be all the time in the world to miss him later, if the worst happened.

But it wouldn't. They would figure out what was wrong with him. The doctors would find a drug to administer in time. They had to.

Turning back, she forced a smile to match Robbie's.

Her brother, who was so fit and handsome, was drastically withering and aging while everything around him had stayed the same. The bedroom, which he'd always called his "cabinet of curiosities," still seemed a magical Ali Baba's cave of delights, full of collected treasures from his extensive travels. On the bed stand was a miniature jade laughing Buddha, an amethyst geode, Tibetan prayer beads and three antique perfume bottles—two glass with silver overlay, one gold with porcelain inlays. Books were stacked in piles on the floor. African sculptures, snow globes, vintage telescopes and kaleidoscopes, Victorian flower arrangements under glass domes and framed butterflies filled shelves. Prints and photographs covered the walls. Robbie was a dreamer and a scientist. An artist and an explorer. And all those aspects of his life were on display here.

"Every L'Etoile perfumer since the mid-1700s has died in this house," he said with great effort. "I like keeping tradition."

"Robbie, the doctors are going to figure out what's wrong and cure it."

"Hope so . . . but it doesn't seem likely . . ." The effort to communicate was draining him, and he paused. "Need to prepare you."

She shook her head, all ability to speak suddenly deserting her.

"Listen." He reached for her and took her hand. But the effort exhausted him, and for the next few moments they sat in silence. His fingers resting on hers. Hers on his. How cold his skin was!

Finally he spoke: "You have to go to Melinoe Cypros . . . in Barbizon."

Did he know he was repeating himself?

"She's extravagant . . . sad and extreme." Pause.

25

"All she has, Jac, are her collections. Rooms and rooms of antiques and artifacts she's spent a lifetime amassing."

He stopped again. Took several more of those arduous breaths. Robbie's heart was so weak that he couldn't walk across the room anymore. Most of the time he even needed help to sit up. He slept twenty hours a day. Ate nothing. His liver had stopped functioning. His skin was a pale yellow. Once the doctors at the hospital had told him they had run every test there was and still didn't know what was causing his illness or what to do for him anymore, he'd asked if he could go home. Nurses were hired, and he'd returned to Rue des Saints-Pères.

Only then had he called Jac. She was on location, filming an episode of her cable TV show, *Mythfinders*, in Greece. He'd been in the hospital, he said, and missed her. She was instantly on alert and worried, but he lied, assuring her that he was all right. Just wanted to know when she'd be coming. Jac had a little less than three days of shooting left, but she offered to shut down production. No, he'd insisted, she should finish up.

He sounded tired, but otherwise she had no reason to suspect it was any more serious than he'd explained. It made sense that he'd be anxious for her to come back. They were both unmarried and both currently unattached. Their mother had died years before. Their father had Alzheimer's and was lost to them. Of course if Robbie was ill, he'd want her there while he recuperated. They were each other's closest family, each other's best friend.

Even with her overactive imagination and tendency to worry, Jac hadn't guessed that at thirty years of age, her brother, Robbie, had returned home to die.

"Do you want some ice chips?" she asked. It was what he was living on now—ice and the IV drip that forced nutrients and glucose into his frail body.

"I need to tell you about Melinoe and the job I started . . ." Robbie began to cough again. It was a long and ruthless bout. When he put a tissue to his mouth, Jac saw a red stain blossom on it like a rose.

She stood up. "I'm going to get the nurse."

He shook his head. Fought the cough to try and speak, but lost.

Jac stepped next door. Once a guest room in the family mansion, it was now the nurses' station.

"He can't stop coughing," Jac said in an alarmed voice.

The nurse went to attend to Robbie.

Jac didn't follow. Not yet. She leaned against the wall in the hallway of the second story of the house where she had grown up. Where her grandparents had lived. And her great-grandparents.

And all the generations before them. There were windows here that faced the landscaped courtyard and offered a view of the darkened workshop. So many L'Etoiles had lived and worked here. And now it was just her and Robbie. Only the two of them.

When they were young, their father had built them a miniature perfumer's organ, just like the grand one where generations of L'Etoiles had sat and created the house's great creations. Shaped very much like the full-size organ, it had three shelves filled with amber bottles of essences, absolutes and scented oils. Everything a perfumer needed. For hours, she and Robbie played a game of their own invention, trying to capture concepts in fragrance. They made the Scent of Loyalty, the Scent of Lies, the Scent of Us Forever, the Scent of Rain and the Scent of Loneliness.

Robbie had claimed the Scent of Us Forever—with its combination of cinnamon, carnation, jasmine, patchouli and a little pepper—as his signature and always wore the spicy perfume. He said he'd been inspired by the tricks they played on each other and their parents and grandparents. The mysterious fragrance suggested getting in trouble. Going where they weren't supposed to. Doing dangerous things in the name of adventure. It was an homage to the two of them against the world. Against their mother, whose manic-depressive moods were a constant source of anxiety for each of them. Against their father, who never seemed to be able to make a success of anything and had put the House of L'Etoile into debt.

Robbie's awful coughing had finally stopped. The nurse came out and told Jac that her brother was sleeping, and she should get something to eat, then try to nap and get some rest.

Jac had another idea. She might not be able to mix any magic in, but a fresh version of the Scent of Us Forever might cheer Robbie up. She walked to the end of the hall, down the steps, through the French doors in the living room and outside into the courtyard. Here she and Robbie had built forts and played elaborate games of hide-and-seek. It was chilly and damp today, but in the spring the garden would be scented by roses, lilacs and hyacinths—*jacinthe*, the flower she was named after. Now there were only green aromas mixed in with the smell of wet tree bark.

She'd meant to go directly across to the workshop, but instead she walked between the two boxwood pyramids and into the labyrinth.

Here two-hundred-year-old cypresses were pruned into impenetrable walls. So tall a man couldn't see over them. The puzzle of warrens and dead ends was so complicated anyone without prior knowledge of how to navigate the maze was lost. But Jac and Robbie knew the route by heart.

At the maze's center, two stone sphinxes waited for her. Once in a fit of laughter, she and Robbie had named them Pain and Chocolat—after their favorite breakfast croissant.

Centered between the sphinxes was a stone bench. Jac sat. This had been her sanctuary as a girl. Where she fled to escape an angry parent or nanny, this green room was her hiding place. Here she was safe from everyone but Robbie. And she never minded when he came to keep her company.

Jac felt tears threatening again. Knew they wouldn't help. Forced herself to hold them back. She inhaled the sharp, clean smell, braced herself and stood.

The ambient light from the courtyard illuminated the workshop. Robbie had taken sick more than two weeks ago, so it had been at least that long since the room had been ventilated. The air was heavy with a particular mélange of aromas that she knew so well. Each perfume studio had its own signature combination of smells created by the predominant notes that house or that nose gravitated to.

These smells, here in the workshop, signified *home* to Jac in a way nothing else did—for both good and bad.

This was where she'd sat at her grandfather's feet and learned the art of mixing perfumes. Where he'd read to her, teaching her about mythology and history and magic. Where her father had spun his tales about the imaginary future he wanted them all to have. Where she and

Robbie had played with their own fragrances. And where she'd spent much of the last ten months working with Robbie on a series of scents based on nineteenth-century formulas created by Fantine L'Etoile, the first and only other female perfumer in the family's history.

After their mother's suicide when Jac was fourteen, she'd been sent to a Jungian clinic in Switzerland for a year. Afterward, seemingly cured of the hallucinations that had plagued her, she'd gone to live with her aunt and uncle in New York City. Robbie had remained here in Paris with their father. Through the years, brother and sister had remained close no matter how far apart they were. Remained each other's constants. This last year, working side by side, they'd become even closer.

Jac sat down at the organ. Closed her eyes. Conjured the Scent of Us Forever. Then she began to gather the ingredients. Cinnamon, jasmine, patchouli . . . all the individual notes that Robbie had combined to suggest the mischievousness of their childhood with the mystery of their future.

As Jac mixed, the relief of doing something other than watching Robbie suffer soothed her. With each new essence she dripped into the bottle, the perfume grew, assuming greater complexity. She was lost in it. Floated on it. Disappeared into it.

Often a perfume smells slightly different on

whoever is wearing it, but the Scent of Us Forever reacted drastically differently on Jac's skin than on Robbie's. If you smelled them each wearing it, you'd never think it was the same. Related—but unique to each of them.

"Like us," Robbie had said when they'd first noticed it.

Returning to her brother's sickroom, bottle in hand, Jac found him still sleeping. She put the mixture on the dresser and turned to go.

"Jac?" Robbie's voice, once deep and musical, was thin and frayed now.

She went to his side.

"What you do . . . the past-life memories you have . . . you know they are real," he said. "Don't you?"

She shrugged, refusing to commit.

"With everything that's happened to you, are you still a skeptic?"

Suddenly Robbie reminded her of their father. The dreamer.

Jac sighed. The last thing she wanted to do was fight with him now, and she told him so. But he didn't back down. Despite how ill he was, he raised himself up on his elbow and looked into her eyes.

"You won't ever find any peace until you accept . . . there's more than just . . . just the here and now. Souls live on. As long as we need them. As long as we love them."

A new fit of coughing silenced him. Jac got a glass of water and held it while he took tiny sips. Then, instead of lying back and resting, he started again. "You can access deeper memories than the rest of us. You've proved it . . . You need to use it to . . ." He stopped to catch his breath and then drank more of the water.

"Robbie, you need to rest and—"

He interrupted. "So many things still to tell you. There *is* magic—it's what we call something we don't understand. Don't dismiss it, Jac . . . please. Accept it, all right?"

Even with interruptions, the speech had exhausted him. He fell back against the pillows.

"All right. I can tap into past-life memories."

"But you don't believe it. You still think you might be crazy. I can hear it in your voice. Why, Jac?"

"I don't know," she said, and it was the truth.

Jac hated herself for not being able to convince him that she believed him and give him some peace. Why was it still so damn hard for her to accept she had access to past-life memories? She'd found proof her brain wasn't manufacturing hallucinations. Why still doubt what she had lived?

Over the last couple of years, Jac, Robbie and her mentor, the reincarnationist Dr. Malachai Samuels, had amassed evidence of her ability. She'd made discoveries she couldn't have guessed at. And not just memories that came from what appeared to be her own past. Sometimes she'd be able to remember other people's memories too. A rare and unusual talent, Malachai had told her.

Robbie's question was the right one. Why couldn't she believe it? Didn't karma teach us that we repeat the past over and over until we get it right? If her memories of her own previous incarnations were accurate, then time after time her lives had been heartbreaking and ended tragically. She'd never moved on. Each repeated the same horror. She was stuck in a karmic nightmare. If she could accept that, then maybe she could move on and—

"What we don't know is so much greater than what we do know." Robbie was looking at her. "Isn't it exciting?" For a moment her brother's ravaged face lit up with a glimmer of curiosity. Then the cough returned. His beautiful eyes filled with tears. His emaciated chest heaved.

Jac waited. Robbie's hacking subsided. He took a shallow breath. And then another. Finally he pleaded: "I need you to understand."

"I do." She was determined to give him what he asked for.

"There's no end. No beginning. Only the infinite passion of life. The past . . . present . . . the future coexist. My body—this envelope—will die, but not the essence of me—not my soul." He smiled.

"You won't have to miss me. I'll be all around you." He paused. "This is so much harder for me because you are in pain. Don't you see? You don't need to be."

She nodded, not trusting herself to speak.

He coughed again and again. Drained of all energy, he closed his eyes. After a moment, one tear escaped and slid down his cheek.

Jac dug her knuckles into her mouth to stop her sobs from erupting.

Robbie fell asleep again, this time deeply. For the next few hours Jac came and went, checking on him. At five in the afternoon, she found him awake again and gave him the new bottle of scent she'd mixed.

"Thank you." He smiled. "Will you put some on me? And then I have to finish telling you what I was doing. What I want you to finish for me."

She opened the small vial, wet her fingers and touched her brother's neck on the right side and then the left and ran her fingers through his thick auburn hair that was the same color as hers. He had always been so lovely. With finer features and heart-shaped lips, Robbie had always been the more beautiful of the two of them. She was handsome, resembling the women in Pre-Raphaelite paintings with strong bones and wide shoulders.

Robbie breathed in the scent so deeply she thought he was going to set off a fresh coughing fit. But he didn't. He just smiled at her and said: "Us forever, right, Jac?"

And as it turned out, that was the last thing her brother ever said to her.

Chapter 4

Jac was in her brother's bedroom when their cousin arrived on Sunday morning. Luc L'Etoile had driven up from Grasse on Friday night when Robbie had slipped into a coma.

"Jac, you have to get up now," Luc said.

She had not moved from the chair beside Robbie's bed since the nurse had woken her up to tell her Robbie was dead. Had not looked away from his still, quiet face at all.

"Doesn't he look like he is sleeping?" she asked Luc.

"Yes, darling, but he isn't." Luc pulled up a chair and sat down beside her. "Days ago Robbie called and told me how he wanted everything handled," he said, "so let me see to it while you take a nap. Nurse said you barely slept last night. The next few days are going to be trying, so you need to rest."

After even more effort on Luc's part, Jac finally agreed to leave Robbie's bedside. She was sure she'd never be able to sleep, but for the rest of that afternoon and for most of the next few days that was all she really did. Meanwhile Luc arranged for the cremation, invited guests to the memorial and hired caterers and florists and musicians. All to Robbie's specifications. And then on Wednesday, it was Luc who hosted the celebration downstairs in the formal rooms of the house—the memorial Robbie had requested instead of a funeral.

That morning Jac showered and then dressed in a simple black sheath with black pumps, her grandmother's pearls and the watch she always wore, her mother's. Ready far too early, she sat in her rocking chair and stared out her window at the courtyard with its barren trees and sleeping flower beds. She heard the first guest arrive. Was aware from the growing noise level that more guests had gathered. Finally it was time for her to go downstairs. But she couldn't. Instead she rocked back and forth in the antique rocker, staring at the naked tree branches swaying in the March wind. At some point Luc knocked on her door and told her everyone was there and waiting for her. In a quiet voice, she told him to start without her. That she'd come down soon.

But she never did. She never left her room. Never stopped staring at the lonely courtyard. Jac didn't want to hear them eulogize her brother. Didn't want to interact with the people who'd offer her condolences and try to reassure her with all kinds of meaningless platitudes.

Robbie had promised he wouldn't leave, and he'd never broken a promise to her before. Maybe if she just waited, stayed in that rocker long enough, he'd come back to her.

That evening, when the house was finally still and quiet, Jac attempted to meditate herself into one of the hallucinations that had plagued her since childhood. These fugue states took her out of the present and into dreams of unknown origin where she was someone else, living another life in another time.

If she could go there now, she could escape the pain of missing her brother for just a while. She longed to disappear into someone else's life, someone else's history, and get some relief from this unrelenting loss.

She closed her eyes. Slowed her breathing. Imagined a dot of light between her eyes. Her third eye. Focused on the place ancient mystics believed was the portal to altered states.

Jac waited for the warm air and infusion of scents that accompanied what Malachai called "memory lurches." But she couldn't summon one any better than she could prevent one when it came unbidden.

On the Monday following Robbie's funeral, Jac began attending to business. In the morning she dealt with the bank and at noon sat down for lunch with Luc, his two brothers, George and Marcel, as well as Monsieur Corlaine, the family solicitor. It was the first meal she'd shared with anyone since her brother had died.

Jac had asked the cook to make a simple lunch of cold soup, roast chicken and salad with a fruit tart for dessert. Just choosing the menu had been an arduous effort. Even the most mundane tasks were suddenly more difficult.

She met her guests in the living room, where navy silk jacquard curtains with white stars and moons and gold suns draped windows that looked out onto the courtyard. Created in the early 1900s for her great-great-great-grandparents, the motif was repeated all over the formal downstairs rooms. There were gold stars painted on the night-sky-blue ceiling. Astrological signs woven into the gold carpet. The furniture was a mix of pieces from different eras arranged artfully. Classic but comfortable.

As she was about to lead everyone into the dining room, Jac's cell phone rang. Glancing at the LED screen, she asked her guests if they would mind waiting a moment. The call was from Detective Marcher of the Paris police department.

Almost two years before, a journalist had come to the L'Etoile workshop to interview Robbie about a new perfume line. Robbie quickly realized the reporter wasn't who he purported to be. He knew nothing about the industry. Robbie guessed the man was there to steal fragments of ancient Egyptian pottery that Robbie had found, artifacts that contained a clue to a fragrance formula that might enable people to access their past lives.

Through the ages mystics had used incense to access memories of previous lives, including Tibetan monks, who believed each new Dalai Lama was a reincarnation of the previous one. If there was a fragrance to aid in regressions, it could be a powerful weapon. A memory tool could help Tibetans foil China's efforts to control who became the next Buddhist leader. China had incentive to prevent Tibetans from getting the formula.

Being a practicing Buddhist, Robbie deduced the Chinese had sent an operative to steal the potential reincarnation aid.

So he'd played along with the charade until he was able to trick the impostor into smelling a toxic essence designed to cause him to pass out. Then Robbie planned to call the police and get help.

But what Robbie couldn't have known was that the thief was an asthmatic; the fumes caused an attack that led to his death. Robbie fled in order to protect the pottery shards, but his disappearance suggested the possibility that Robbie had committed murder.

Marcher was called in. Eventually Robbie's name was cleared. Though it was proved he had acted in self-defense, her brother still had precipitated the death of a Triad member. Detective Marcher had warned them at that time that the powerful Chinese Mafia might seek revenge.

Over the next year and a half nothing suspicious had occurred. Then Robbie got sick. The doctors couldn't find any reason for why his body was failing, and failing so quickly. That's when Jac had called the detective, and he'd begun looking into the possibility of a connection. Several times he'd reported in, but without any information. The last time he'd called was to offer condolences.

"Mademoiselle L'Etoile, would it be possible to see you this afternoon?" he asked now.

This task too would be a welcome distraction, and she agreed to a time and then returned to the dining room.

The purpose of today's luncheon was to plan for the future. The House of L'Etoile didn't have a second in command. Jac and her brother owned the company jointly, but Robbie had been running it on his own. When they'd first inherited it, Jac and Robbie, having no heirs of their own, had decided they'd each leave their respective shares to their three cousins to ensure the company stayed in the family. At the time it had seemed a decision for the faraway future. It was impossible to Jac that future was now.

She went into the dining room to rejoin her cousins. "I've heard the rift between our grand-fathers was over a perfume," Jac said as she poured wine for her cousins. She really only knew a few facts—that in 1941 the House of L'Etoile had been owned by Jac's grandfather and his brother, Pierre L'Etoile. After a falling-out, Pierre sold his share of his firm to Jac's grandfather, moved to Grasse and started his own company. Playing on the family name, L'Etoile—which meant "star"—Pierre called his firm Luna Parfums.

"A perfume and a woman," Marcel L'Etoile said as he buttered a piece of a roll. "Our grandfather was seeing a woman he was very much in love with. So of course he created a perfume for her. And of course she always wore it. One day he ran into her in the street, it was a day when they had no assignation planned, and she was wearing a different perfume. One that Pierre knew all too well. He'd watched your grandfather create it for a supposed wealthy client. The discovery that they were both in love with the same woman destroyed the brothers' relationship, and ultimately Charles bought Pierre out."

"Who was the woman?" Jac asked.

"Your grandmother," Luc said with a rueful smile. "She'd met Pierre first and liked him well enough. But when she met Charles, she fell in love."

"She was seeing them both?" Jac pictured her grandmother in the photographs of when she was young. Lovely with almond-shaped eyes and high cheekbones, the very essence of chic. Even as an older woman, Grand-mère was a bit of a flirt in that utterly charming way French women had. Jac remembered being at the beach in the South of France with her grandmother and Robbie when a gentleman—

Her cousin Luc was talking to her. Jac came out of her reverie and asked him to repeat himself.

"We don't want you to feel obligated to the House of L'Etoile. If you want to sell us your shares of the company, we've discussed it and we would be interested."

"I'm not sure how I want to arrange my life right now," she said. And she wasn't. In New York she had an apartment and a successful career as a mythologist with a cable show that examined the origins of myths. It was on hiatus now, and she had until June to decide whether or not to sign another contract. In Paris she had this house and the family business. She'd spent all her time off this year with Robbie, being a full-time perfumer for the first time in her life, and she'd loved it. But how much of that feeling came from working with Robbie?

"I don't want to sell my shares." She shook her head. That would be akin to voluntarily amputating a limb.

"We're glad about that," Luc said warmly. "We don't think that would be the right direction for the company."

"Neither did your brother," the lawyer interjected. "Robbie's wish was that you take a leave

43

of absence from your job in New York and run L'Etoile with your cousins for at least two years."

It was like Robbie to advise.

"We can discuss having an office in New York if you preferred to work from the States," George suggested.

Jac had rarely seen her cousins in the last twenty years until recently because she'd spent so little time in France. And now she was surprised how easy it was to be with them. They had the classic L'Etoile family features—mahogany hair, aquiline nose, light-green eyes—that reminded her of her father, her grandfather and her brother.

"Robbie hoped you might all merge the running of both perfume companies," the lawyer said. "He outlined a scenario that he thought would work."

Jac nodded. It made sense. "I like that idea. While our grandfathers might have had their problems, we don't." She looked at her cousins. "Your fragrances are wonderful, and Luna seems to be well run. It would be a much stronger company if both halves were reunited."

For the next hour they discussed Robbie's suggestions about how the merger might be financially arranged. Jac thought her brother would be pleased by the solutions they chose.

She felt an odd peacefulness. A cessation from the grief. Almost as if the last week and a half had been a bad dream and Robbie was just in the workshop and about to join them any moment.

Once she'd even turned around, thinking she heard his footsteps, but there was, of course, no one there.

At four o'clock one meeting ended and another began. Jac greeted Detective Marcher and ushered him into the L'Etoile workshop. The detective looked tired, and Jac offered him coffee. While she waited for the water to boil, she filled the French press with ground espresso beans. The smell of coffee was always welcome here. It cut through the mélange of scents that hovered in the air. Coffee beans were to a perfumer like the lemon sorbet a gourmand eats between courses or the crackers wine tasters munch between flights. When a nose was building a fragrance, it was important to stop and cleanse the olfactory palate.

"We have the preliminary results of the autopsy," Marcher said

She was surprised. "An autopsy? I hadn't realized, but of course . . ."

"I'm sorry. I know how painful this is for you, Jac."

"Thank you." She nodded.

Marcher's face seemed to bear an aspect of perpetual melancholy, as if all the years he'd been on the job and all he'd witnessed had worn him down. More than once Jac had wondered if, when he was with his wife and family, the expression in his face lightened and his shoulders lifted. She hoped so.

It occurred to her now that her own expression was dark too. Since Robbie's death, whenever she caught a glimpse of herself in the mirror, she didn't quite recognize the lost soul who glanced back.

Jac poured coffee into two white porcelain espresso cups and brought them over to where Marcher was sitting.

He sipped the coffee. Smiled at her. "This is excellent. Thank you."

She nodded. To her it was hot and distracting, and that was enough for now. Both her sense of smell and taste seemed dulled since Robbie had died. Grief had numbed her.

"Would you mind turning that on?" He pointed to Robbie's stereo system.

Jac was startled by the request but turned it on. Beethoven's *Eroica* Symphony filled the air. The last time she'd heard it was when they'd been here working on a new fragrance. This was the music her brother had chosen. How many of these *last time* moments would she have to endure?

"Based on the rapid onset of organ failure and how healthy your brother was prior to the attack, they still suspect poison."

"But the doctors tested his blood for poisons when he was in the hospital and didn't find anything."

"And they still haven't."

"So how is that possible?"

"Certain poisons clear the system after a particular amount of time. The complication here is that even so, there's no known poison that presents in the manner of Robbie's reaction." He shook his head. "I'm sorry, I know uncertainty isn't helpful. The bottom line is they don't know the root cause yet, but poison remains the most logical answer. Especially because, being a perfumer, your brother was always working with foreign substances and could have easily inhaled or ingested something that he reacted to this way."

"An accidental death then?" she asked.

"No, Jac, not necessarily accidental. Someone might have come to see him and asked him to smell some new fragrance, sold him something tainted. Perhaps switched one of his ingredients with an exotic substance."

Marcher gestured to the eighteenth-century perfumer's organ that took up a full quarter of the room. Where every nose in the L'Etoile family had composed fragrances, drop by drop. Lined up on three tiers were more than five hundred bottles filled with essences and absolutes of flowers, plants, spices, woods and chemicals.

"With your permission, we need the lab to come in and take samples of all these ingredients."

"Of course."

"If it's not a substance typically used in perfume making and we can't prove that your brother purchased it, that will suggest foul play. And in the meantime, I don't want you using any of these ingredients."

She told Marcher she had mixed up a fragrance just before Robbie died. And she was fine.

"All right, but don't mix up any more until the lab runs their tests. Okay?"

Jac nodded.

Marcher drank more of his coffee. The antique cup's gold rim glinted in the light. Limoges from the late eighteenth century was very valuable. Once she'd asked Robbie if they should be using it as everyday china.

"Never put treasures away in a cabinet," he'd said. *"You need to surround yourself with beauty, be aware of it and enjoy it—allow your soul to feed on it—gorge on it."*

"So the case isn't closed." Jac had expected this visit to be the detective's last.

"No, not closed, not at all," Marcher said and placed the tiny cup in the saucer.

"Would you like more?" Jac asked.

"Yes, perhaps I would."

She brought the French press over to where he was sitting and poured more of the fragrant brew.

"These findings have me most concerned," he said as he watched her, "because if it was poison, then your brother's death mimics the pseudo journalist François Lee's."

Jac shivered at hearing the name of the man who had died here almost two years ago.

"And I don't like coincidences," Marcher said.

In the midst of pouring herself more coffee, Jac looked up quickly, and a drop spilled onto the desk. She reached for a cloth—there was always a stack of them nearby in the workshop. L'Etoiles sprayed their creations on cloth to test them, not on the cheaper paper strips so many perfumers used.

The coffee leeched into white cotton, staining it.

"Robbie didn't believe in coincidences either," Jac mused as she wiped up the rest of the spill. "He always told me—"

The now familiar threat of tears stung her eyes, and she felt her throat constrict. Crying, especially in front of Marcher, was not an option.

The detective sat farther forward in his chair and put his hand on her arm. "Jac, my concern now is for you."

"I don't understand."

"One of the most powerful crime syndicates in the world lost one of its members because of your brother, and the episode didn't just involve Robbie but—"

"It involved me too," Jac interrupted. Even though she'd had help from her ex-lover Griffin North, Jac had been the one to save her brother by exposing the spies.

She and Marcher were both silent for a moment.

"I don't want to scare you, but we need to take precautions," he said finally.

"Except you are scaring me." Some part of her was surprised she could feel enough to be scared.

"It's unlikely you are a target, but until we know more about your brother's death, I'd like to have someone watching the house and discreetly following you when you go out. Logic tells me that if there was a vendetta, it was with Robbie—" Marcher stopped talking. He was looking out into the courtyard and frowning. Jac followed his glance.

"Ah, you see our ghost," she said.

"I doubt that. But I did think I saw a man out there."

"No, it's just the shadow of a very old tree to the right of that hedge. Robbie and I used to call it our ghost. In certain light, it appears to be a man."

Marcher got up, walked to the window and peered out.

The wind was blowing. Branches swaying. Some dried, dead leaves scurried across the paths.

The gardens had been planted by the first L'Etoile, who had bought the property in the 1770s. Several generations had grown flowers here that perfumed the air with scents not smelled anywhere else in Paris: rare hybrid roses that had bloomed only here for the last two hundred years.

Jac scanned the barren bushes now. In two months they would be heavy with the deep blood-red roses that her mother had always said smelled like sex.

It was just a trick of light, a play of shadow. It wasn't a ghost out in the garden. That was only what she and Robbie had called the odd phenomenon.

Except today it really did look like one.

His curiosity satisfied, Marcher returned to the settee.

"I like to err on the side of being too careful. Organized crime groups do not lose their soldiers lightly. Especially one of François Lee's standing. If this was retribution, I want to know the score is now settled."

"So what is your plan?" She turned away from the optical illusion in the courtyard and looked at Marcher.

"I am going to continue to work the case and find out what happened to your brother. And make sure that whatever it was, it doesn't happen to you."

Chapter 5

MARCH 11, 1573
BARBIZON, FRANCE

The place where you have willingly worked all of your life takes on very different dimensions and sensibilities when you are imprisoned there. For seven days I was locked inside my mentor's laboratory, under arrest pending a trial.

Brother Serapino had told me over and over that he longed for death the way a thirsty man yearns for water. That the pain was too much to bear. It is horrible to see a loved one suffering. I thought that I too would find relief once he was gone, knowing that he was no longer in agony.

But in truth I had no idea how it would feel. I had not been apart for him for a single day in more than ten years. I slept in an alcove in the laboratory steps away from his cell. I ate with him. Studied with him. Only when I bathed or relieved myself was I alone. Now he was truly gone, and my loneliness pressed down on me in the darkness of the cell. I shed tears until I had none left. Then I tried to pray. But prayer had never been of much solace to me. I did not truly believe. I had seen too much suffering in my short life. While many of the brothers around me espoused blind faith, Serapino did not.

My mentor felt blessed by the bounty of the garden that allowed him to create the lotions, potions, elixirs and waters that were so coveted both in and out of the monastery. He dutifully went to Mass every morning and matins every afternoon and awoke in the middle of every night to join the others in supplication in the chapel. But once he was back in the laboratory, there was never talk of God. Never prayers. His work was his all. It fed him and energized him and kept him curious. That was what he had imbued me with. His true belief was his faith in alchemy.

And so, alone in the laboratory in those hours after his death, I had no branch to reach for, no promise of solace waiting if only I could dive deeper into prayer and contemplation. Instead I sunk deeper and deeper into the muck and mire of mourning.

When the door opened the morning after Serapino's death, five monks entered the cell: three to remove Serapino's body and two to stand watch over me and make sure I didn't try to— what? Run? Overpower them? What did they think I was going to do? It was in fact their suspicion that ignited my imagination. If they thought me so capable of escaping that I needed watching, then perhaps I was.

Serapino used to tell me that he could see cunning and determination in my eyes and talked to me about using my intelligence for good and not evil. As I grew older, I questioned him about what he thought me capable of. He smiled that secret smile he had, put his hand on my shoulder. "Every man has two souls," he said. And he was watching mine wage a battle with each other. "You are strong, René. Tragedy has tempered you. Your determination can be either your salvation or your ruin. Go after what you want, but not ruthlessly. Explore the ramifications. Pay attention to cause and effect. Weigh your actions against your desires. It's critical you understand."

But I didn't. How was I any different than he was? How was I any more cunning?

I didn't know. Not then. Not yet. But as they prepared to remove Serapino's body, I called upon that part of me that he had warned me about and began to plan.

Brother Leo put his hands under Serapino's arms. Brother Pietro took him by the feet. Brother Alferius supervised. On his count, the other two lifted the body and carried it gently out toward the door.

Brother Michael, who I knew well and who had often worked with Serapino and me in the garden, looked down on me with sympathetic eyes. "René Bianco, the friar has requested I explain what is going to happen."

"I was only doing what Serapino asked," I protested. "You saw how ill he was. You know he was eager for his time to come."

I had never pleaded before.

Michael shook his head. "I'm sorry." He held out his hands, palms up, in supplication. "You'll stay here in this cell until the abbot is ready for the trial."

"When will that be?"

"No more than a fortnight. There's never been an inquisition here in his time. He needs to prepare."

"But I have to be allowed out to go to the service for Brother Serapino. I must be at his internment." When I grabbed the hem of Michael's rough brown robe, Brother Pius stepped forward, yanked my hands loose and shoved me backward, sending me tumbling.

"They can't bury him without allowing me to say good-bye," I begged.

But hearing my own voice, seeing the look of pity on Michael's face, I was ashamed. Sniveling on the stone floor. Whining like a child. It awakened anger in me.

I didn't want compassion or sympathy. I was René Bianco, Brother Serapino's apprentice. I already excelled at creating perfumes and potions. Hadn't I created the scented water that Catherine de Medici used exclusively? Hadn't I created the fragrant water that Alessandro de Medici traveled with?

Slowly, I rose to my feet.

"This is not right or just. You both know it. And I will make sure that all the brothers know it." My voice was calmer now. "Brother Michael, will you please tell the abbot that I request permission to attend the funeral services of Brother Serapino? I am an innocent man who has neither been tried nor proven guilty, so it seems inhumane to prevent me from paying my respects as my mentor prepares to enter the kingdom of heaven."

Slowly, a plan began to emerge in my mind. The fact was, I was not a monk. Had taken no vows. I was a free man who had willingly stayed here to work with Serapino. If I could escape the monastery during the funeral, there were ways a young man could hide in a city as big as Florence. All I needed was to get out of this cell.

"The abbot was clear: you will not be allowed to leave here until the day of your trial."

Calculating how best to play this, I bowed my head. "I beg you to tell the abbot how grief-stricken I am and how much this kindness would mean to me."

They left and soon I heard the far-off chanting that accompanied Serapino to his resting place in the catacomb beneath the basilica of Santa Maria Novella.

As I tried to envision the ceremony, it suddenly occurred to me: If they believed I was guilty, then Brother Serapino could not have taken his own life. Not committed the ultimate sin in the eyes of the Lord. And they could still bury him in hallowed ground. Even if I was innocent in the brothers' eyes, even if some of them believed me, I was the scapegoat; they needed to sentence me to eternal damnation and protect the holy sanctity and reputation of the monastery.

Such was the power and the glory of the church. Such was the duplicity of these holy men who claimed to care about the human soul but were no less selfish than the princes and noblemen outside the stone walls.

It was two hours after the chanting ended when the key turned in the lock. With a creak the door opened. Two monks stayed at the door, blocking any attempt I might make to escape. One walked inside.

Brother Michael was carrying a wooden tray with a loaf of bread, a jug of water, a wedge of cheese and a meager bunch of grapes. My rations for the next twenty-four hours.

His soft brown eyes were heavy with sorrow as he put the tray down on the table and then from his pocket removed a candle stub. I could smell smoke still clinging to it. He held it out.

"I have candles aplenty," I said, gesturing to the shelves of supplies in the laboratory.

Or were they going to strip the laboratory of supplies and leave me with just this?

"No, this is not for light," he whispered. "We buried your mentor this afternoon, and this is the candle I held during the Mass. When it was time to pass by the body and pay our respects, this was the candle I used to drop wax on his lips to seal his soul so it would be delivered intact to God. I thought you would like to have it."

Stunned by his compassion, I took the candle from his hand. Unable to speak, I looked at the well where the wax had melted and dripped onto Serapino's lips. They didn't know they hadn't sealed his soul inside his body with that last rite. I had his soul in the glass vial that was strapped to my chest. And somehow I would escape this prison and learn how to free it and bring my Serapino back to life.

Chapter 6

THE PRESENT
FRIDAY, MARCH 14
PARIS, FRANCE

During those last days, while Jac sat with her brother as he lay dying, he asked her to write down some things he wanted her to do when he was gone. Now, two weeks after Robbie's death, she opened her notebook and read down the list. Most items were bequests of art and antiques that Robbie owned and wished her to give away.

The first was a perfume bottle in the shape of a rose that Robbie wanted given to his friend and fellow perfumer Dmitri Distas. Next a Tibetan prayer necklace he wanted given to Mark Solage, who had been his lover for years and had remained his friend. Jac smiled, thinking about how Robbie's lovers always remained his friends. One of the wondrous things about her brother was his ability to bring people into his life, care for them and keep them close.

Number three was for Malachai.

"I want to give him something special," Robbie had said. *"My jade Buddha. That's something he'd like."*

And he would. Dr. Malachai Samuels was the therapist who had helped Jac out of her childhood crisis and had continued to watch over her. He and Robbie had gotten to know each other well over the years and shared a deep belief in reincarnation.

Jac's eyes rested on the fourth item, a bequest for Griffin North.

Griffin. Her first lover and first love and one of Robbie's closest friends. Griffin, whose imprint she wore on her very soul. She remembered the horrific accident almost two years ago. He had almost died saving her. How still and pale he'd looked lying in the hospital bed. Hour after hour, he remained unconscious, his breaths so shallow, his color so bad, the only way she knew he was still alive was by staring at the machines recording his vital signs. She remembered how it had felt to sit beside him, holding his limp, unresponsive hand. It seemed impossible that these were the same fingers that could set off sparks when he touched her skin.

Over and over she wondered how she would be able to live if he died, knowing his death was her fault.

Griffin had come to Paris to work with Robbie on the translation of the ancient Egyptian pottery he'd found. During that brief time, she and Griffin had reunited, and her strange and awful fugue states had started up again. Jac experienced two sets of hallucinations—or, as Robbie and Malachai believed, past-life regressions. In both, each of the men she'd seen in her visions had died tragically because of the love they had for a woman.

If Jac was having hallucinations, it didn't matter—but if she accepted Robbie and Malachai's interpretation of her memory lurches, *she* was the incarnation of those women and Griffin was the men.

She hadn't wanted to give the theory any credence until Griffin had almost died while saving her life.

Once he'd gotten out of the hospital, she became obsessed by the idea that she'd almost been responsible for his death. She didn't really want to believe in reincarnation, but what if her brother and Malachai and thousands of years of traditions were right? What if reincarnation was real? She could not be responsible for Griffin's death a third time. She had to give him up.

She told him it was because she was worried about the effects of his impending divorce on his six-year-old daughter. Jac encouraged him to try and save his marriage.

Weeks after he left, Jac discovered she was pregnant. Even before she'd figured out what to do about it, or how to tell Griffin, she miscarried. She never told him. What was the point? He was where he belonged. Safe in New York with his wife and his child.

She hadn't been in contact with him since.

Griffin had called the day before Robbie's memorial service, but she hadn't talked to him. He'd called the day after the service and the day after that. She hadn't returned any of his calls, and finally he'd stopped trying. What was there to say? What was there to hear? Everyone had said everything to her already and nothing made any difference.

Jac returned to the list. Knowing Robbie, she wondered if there was some meaning in the order of the things he'd asked of her. Did he want her to visit or speak to these people as they appeared? She continued reading down. She came to the last item.

10. Call Melinoe Cypros/Barbizon.

Yes, she'd forgotten about this till now. On his deathbed, Robbie had pressed Jac to go retrieve the books he'd taken there from their own library here in Paris.

Barbizon was only an hour-and-a-half drive out of Paris. Suddenly the idea of going away was attractive. She wasn't sure if it was losing Robbie—the one constant in her life—or Marcher's concern, or a combination of both, but Jac hadn't been comfortable since the detective's visit. It might be good to get away and escape her extended family's well-meaning but overwhelming kindnesses for a day or two.

It was also a chance to escape from the silver box containing her brother's ashes, which she'd hidden away in the armoire in Robbie's bedroom. Even there, in a room she never entered, behind a closed door, they haunted her. She needed to find a resting place for them—but then she'd have to let him go. Accept that he really was gone. And she couldn't do that yet.

Jac called ahead and made arrangements with the contact her brother had given her—Serge Grise—to come to Barbizon the next morning. She also called a hotel in town and booked a room for that evening.

In the garage downstairs, the sight of Robbie's car gave her a fresh pang. He'd bought and restored the sleek 1964 silver Mercedes when he was eighteen, and had never owned another car. This vehicle was one of the few things that tested his Zen-like attitude toward objects. He adored it and fussed over it and worried about every scratch.

She opened the door. His smell overwhelmed her. Intense and powerful. As if he'd just gotten out of the car himself. Jac tossed her overnight bag on the back seat, slipped inside, and adjusted the seat to fit her shorter frame. She put her hands on the wheel and caressed the smooth wood. Suddenly she sensed Robbie, right there beside her.

She listened, sure he was going to talk to her,

and when she felt the air beside her vibrate a little, she shivered. Instead of upsetting her, it made her comfortable to think that she wasn't quite alone. With a relief she hadn't felt for weeks, she put the key in the ignition and started up her beautiful brother's beautiful car.

Driving away from Paris was liberating. As if she were leaving part of her intolerable sadness behind her. No matter that she was venturing out to collect Robbie's belongings—the freedom of the road was invigorating. As soon as she was out of the city proper and driving through the countryside, she opened all the windows and let the damp early spring air in.

After an hour she reached her destination. The "village of painters," as Barbizon was known, consisted of a long curving street lined with gray stone buildings and ancient trees. A bit bleak on this March day, but still charming. It seemed time had not touched the town. Jac imagined it had looked exactly like this in the early nineteenth century when a group of painters rebelling against the Romantic movement came here to form an art colony. They availed themselves of the wondrous forest of Fontainebleau, where they worked from nature—a hallmark of their movement.

It was before lunch and there weren't many people on the street, so Jac could imagine that when she did see the villagers they were going to be dressed in nineteenth-century garb.

"No wonder you were so enchanted with this place," she said out loud, unconsciously, to Robbie. She wondered if that was a bad sign, and then decided it didn't matter. She wanted to talk to him. It made her less sad to think he was hovering and could hear her.

Jac reached the end of the road and the inn. After checking in, she spent a quiet afternoon exploring the town and then having a simple dinner of salad and coq au vin in one of the small restaurants lining the street. It was filled with locals who were treated more like family by the host than guests. The atmosphere was easygoing and the food was delicious, and Jac felt less lonely here than she had at home. She was used to being away, on her own, traveling in search of mythological stories to tell. Used to being by herself.

In the morning, following the directions Serge Grise had given her, she turned out of the inn, onto the main street and then turned right, then left and then, after another stretch, came to the next turnoff. The town disappeared, and she began driving through the woods. Twice she passed a gate but never saw any houses. After another ten minutes she came to the stone well Serge had given her as a landmark. She turned right and took that road almost a kilometer until she reached a set of ornate gates decorated with a coat of arms featuring roses, fleurs-de-lis, a flag and a shield.

She rolled down the window and pressed the intercom button.

"Qui est là?" a disembodied female voice asked.

"Jac L'Etoile."

"Entrez."

The gate opened. In the distance the château came into view. Planted in the middle of the woods, it was encircled by a moat, complete with an old-fashioned drawbridge.

Jac was surprised how familiar the château looked, from the elaborately carved limestone facade to the multiple towers and chimneys gracefully rising out of the slate roofs and into the clouds.

Only the woods seemed wrong. They were too close to the house.

Why did she think she'd seen this place before? She'd never been to Barbizon. Had Robbie described it? She didn't think so. Perhaps there was a famous landscape that featured the château that she'd seen. She'd ask the owner.

As she approached the driveway, Jac thought she saw a man in period dress—a tunic and leggings—and sporting long hair. Then the clouds shifted and she realized there wasn't anyone there at all. It must have been light playing on one of the columns flanking the front door. No one was waiting for her. It was just her imagination.

Chapter 7

The door was opened by a tall, broad-shouldered man.

"I'm Serge Grise," he said and held out his hand.

He wore corduroy pants and a matching turtle-neck sweater. His hair was thick and chocolate brown.

Jac let go of the possibility this was the man she'd seen in the shadows and took in Serge's face. He had slightly sad eyes. Strong cheekbones and a well-attenuated chin. The way his features came together was provocative and handsome.

"I hope you found us all right?" His English carried a French accent.

"Yes, perfect directions."

He hesitated and then said, "I'm so very sorry about your brother. While he was working here, we spent quite a bit of time getting to know each other, and I came to like him very much."

Jac nodded. Watched his face. Observed him instead of listened. She didn't like to hear other people talk about Robbie. It forced her to think about him being gone. When no one mentioned him, she could pretend that he was off on another of his treks through the mountains in Tibet and that they'd meet back in Paris, at home, soon.

"I've been reading about Buddhism because of Robbie. It's struck a real chord with me."

Something about how Serge said her brother's name made Jac wonder how close he and Robbie had been. Her brother always said he fell in love with people and then noticed what sex they were. It didn't matter to Jac if this man and Robbie had been together—quite the opposite. Anyone who had been close to him, she wanted to keep close to her. She'd made a list of all his friends who got in touch with condolences. As if each had a small piece of him and by amassing their names she could one day rebuild him.

"We talked about me going with him on his next retreat. I've always rejected formal religion, but when Robbie spoke about his Buddhism, it was so appealing." He gestured to the grand hall filled with elaborate decorations. "Though this is quite the opposite of a Buddhist retreat," he said with a laugh. "We live here in excess."

"It's very beautiful excess," Jac said.

And it was. The green marble floor, antique tapestries on the wall, heavy brass chandeliers glowing with soft light, and opulent vases of fragrant flowers were all in perfect harmony with one another. The great room to the right and the glimpse of the library all looked exquisitely decorated. Jac loved old houses, castles, ruins, cemeteries, burial sites, anything left behind in the quake of the passage of time.

Behind them, a white stone staircase, shaped like a double helix, rose toward the upper floors. Jac had seen a similar one, which legend said was designed by Leonardo da Vinci himself, at the Château de Chambord. There two separate staircases intertwined and rose three floors without meeting.

"It's magical," she said.

"Yes," Serge said. "We've had experts examine them, and these stairs are in direct proportion to those at Chambord—just about thirty percent smaller."

"That means this building goes back to the fifteenth century?"

"The original structure. With some additions and many renovations along the way. We still aren't finished. I've been working on the reconstruction here for three years. The most extensive job I've ever undertaken. And one of the most complicated. There were so many mistakes to undo before we even could start restoring."

"So you're an architect?"

"I am."

"Robbie mentioned you, actually. He told me that as a preservationist you were a perfectionist. He was very impressed with the house."

Serge smiled, and Jac saw melancholy change his eyes, making them smaller for the moment. She couldn't be sure how close they had become, but there was no question Serge had cared about her brother.

"Did you find Robbie? Did you hire him?"

"No. Melinoe, my stepsister, brought him in. I believe that a mutual friend of theirs, Malachai Samuels, introduced them."

She was taken aback. Robbie had never told her how he came to accept this commission. Malachai? She knew so little about what Robbie was doing here. All he'd said was he was working on an experiment with Melinoe. Did it have something to do with reincarnation? Was Melinoe Cypros another disciple of Malachai Samuels?

No, Robbie, Jac said to herself. Whatever you started here, it isn't something I have any interest in finishing.

"I don't want to take you away from your work. I'm happy to just pack up Robbie's things and be on my way."

"Not at all. From what Robbie told me, I'm sure you'd be interested in seeing the house and some of the ruins on the grounds. Melinoe and I were hoping you'd stay and have lunch with us. Are you free?"

Jac was torn. She wouldn't have minded going on the tour—the house fascinated her. But at the same time she was uncomfortable about staying now that she knew of Melinoe's interest in the one subject Jac wanted to avoid.

"Robbie often said that he wanted to bring you

up here so you could see some of the older areas we've discovered. Can I show you around now? Then after lunch you can collect his things."

Jac's fascination won out. If the conversation turned to past-life theory, she thought, *I'll just not engage.*

Serge led her down the main hall and into the living room. Everywhere Jac looked were multiples. The sign of an avid collector. There were not two Foo dogs on the mantel as one would expect, but six. There were four Fabergé eggs on an end table on one side of the couch.

Jac had of course heard of Melinoe; it was difficult not to have heard of her. The only daughter of a Greek shipping magnate who'd died when Melinoe was in her teens, she was still called the "Billionaire Orphan" by the press, even though she was now middle-aged.

Jac marveled at a grouping of a dozen architectural prints on the south wall. Palladian, she was certain. A Renoir hung over the grand fireplace. Two smaller ones on either side of the couch. Four van Gogh drawings of flowers, graphite on paper under glass, graced the north wall. One Aubusson rug covered the parquet floor under the couch; another Aubusson lay under the grand Bösendorfer piano near the windows. Scattered across its ebony surface were six Fabergé enamel frames set with semiprecious and precious stones. The photographs inside were all of a young girl with an older man. Jac guessed it was Melinoe with her father.

Alexander Cypros had been a renowned collector, and clearly his daughter had not only inherited his possessions but also his passions. A fashion icon, she was often on the international best-dressed lists and referred to as an eccentric for her outrageous costumes. Nothing was too outré or bizarre for Melinoe's taste. When she was young, she'd been one of Yves Saint Laurent's muses. She started more trends than she followed.

Now, being here, surrounded by the spoils of her fabulous fortune, Jac was even less surprised that Melinoe had charmed Robbie. He appreciated beauty, and clearly so did this collector. It wasn't the value of these objects that struck Jac, but rather how exquisite each and every one was. Not just another drawing, but one that brought out the very essence of what made van Gogh such a master—and to have several of such quality. It was astonishing.

"We didn't have to do much work here. This floor—the main rooms—had been altered the least over the centuries," Serge said.

As he led her through a dining room, another drawing room, down hallways, she was in awe of all she saw. It was like being in a small museum. At the same time it was exhausting. Jac's eyes were too full. She couldn't take in the nuances of the pieces any longer.

They had reached the kitchen area.

"This is the only part of the house where Melinoe and I argued. She wanted it taken back to a true fifteenth-century kitchen. It would have been quite a conversation piece, but cooking here would have tried any chef. Modernism won. But there are several details I kept."

The floor's ancient marble tiles had been repaired but showed their age. The beams were scarred with dark burn marks and wormholes. The walls were made of thick plaster and crackled like a Renaissance oil painting.

"We've used some unusual methods to bring the room back to what it was, and then sealed it that way to prevent further destruction while allowing the look of it to stay," Serge explained.

"I think it's wonderful."

"Do you like to cook?"

"Not much, actually." She laughed. "But something about this kitchen is very inviting."

"Your brother said the same thing."

She felt a fresh stab of missing Robbie. "He loved to cook," she said.

Serge nodded. "I know. He cooked for us several times. One evening Melinoe had a grand fete, and Robbie made us an amazing Moroccan tagine. He also made some French classics that were better than I've ever had in a restaurant."

"He made his onion soup, then?" Jac asked.

"Yes!"

"It's our great-grandmother's recipe. We have a handwritten book of them. It wasn't the most precise recipe, but it was always perfect." She recited it. " 'One onion for every person. One knob of butter for every onion. Caramelize the onions. Then add one ladle of veal stock and one of white wine for every person and let it cook while you take care of the bread.' "

Serge laughed. "As long as you know what a knob of butter is, you're fine."

"No one ever did quite know. But Robbie was so good with intuiting measurements. It showed in his perfumes as well, of course." Jac had wandered to the windows and looked out.

"That's our vegetable garden," Serge said. "With all this land, the wildlife, the sheep and the barn, the house is fairly self-sufficient."

She turned around and noticed a door in the corner of the room. There was nothing special about it. Just a wooden door with a black glass doorknob, but something about it made her ask Serge what it led to.

"The cellar."

"Could I see?"

He looked at her as if it was a strange request—and it probably was. So she told him more about her job. And how, as a mythologist, she researched old stories and tried to find their fountainhead. "I seem always drawn to the lower level," she said. "Caves, cellars, crypts, tunnels . . . Over time we build up and over cities. The most interesting places are often those buried beneath our feet. Digging down, you find the past."

"Well, there's not much past down here," he said as he led her toward a narrow staircase. The steps were marble, chipped and worn. The wooden handrail smooth but gouged in several places.

"The servants lived here, below the house. We use it for storage now. It would be an awful place to ask someone to sleep."

They walked through a long hallway off of which was one small room after another. At the end they came to an iron door with a large keyhole.

"And through there?" Jac felt a stirring of excitement. The door was ancient. Certainly more than five hundred years old. Clearly this part of the house was the least restored.

"I'll show you." From his pocket Serge pulled out a key ring.

Jac was surprised that the door was locked. The skeleton key turned in the mechanism and creaked in a very particular way. Hearing the sound, Jac thought it sounded familiar. Often when she sensed something might have happened before, Jac obsessed over it, trying to figure it out and understand it.

"Don't worry about what it all means, just live in the moment," Robbie would tell her. *"When you need to know more, it will reveal itself to you."*

But Jac didn't like not knowing, wondering, feeling lost, imagining what the past foretold and what the future might be. She and Robbie weren't alike that way. *"My beautiful dreamer,"* their mother had called her son. Jac had her feet on the ground. Even if that ground was deep down in the earth. Which was where they were heading now.

They were descending another staircase. This one was stone and spiral and even more narrow. Twisting, tortured steps turning on one another. The air was colder, and Jac shivered.

"Here we are," Serge said as he turned on an overhead light—the only modern object in this ancient space. "This is the deepest part of the house. Where they kept wine and cold storage. The temperature never rises above twelve degrees Celsius."

They stepped into the large cellar. The stone floor was cracked and splintered. The ceiling was all beamed and so low that Serge had to stoop. There were empty niches equipped with hooks lining the north wall. The west wall was outfitted with shelves filled with dusty bottles. Dark glass, covered with cobwebs, glistened in the lamplight. Jac guessed this wasn't where they kept their drinkable wine. There were so many cobwebs in the corners it was obvious no one could keep up with cleaning. As soon as the webs were swept away, the spiders would spin them again at night. It was like her family's cellar in Paris, which was not this elaborate or large but just as deep underground.

Suddenly Jac became aware of the scent. She expected to smell earth and mold, but instead was hit with a whole cacophony of wonderful fragrances—flowers and spices, most familiar but some unusual and unknown.

The air, almost freezing a moment ago, was warming and swirling around her. It was the same dreaded sensation she'd had since she was a little girl that foreshadowed the oncoming fugue state. And that, for the last twenty-two months, presaged what Malachai Samuels was certain were memories from her previous lives or other people's lives.

Oh no. Not here. No matter what was coming— a hallucination or a past-life regression—Jac didn't want it.

Malachai had taught her a series of quick exercises to keep her in the moment and block a memory lurch, and she practiced them now. The first rule was to get to a window for fresh air. Down here that was impossible. She started on the rest of the list . . . Inhale to the count of four . . . then hold to the count of four . . . then exhale to the count of four . . . then hold to the count of four. Concentrate on each number as you count . . . two . . . three . . . four . . . then focus on where you are. Feel what is under your fingers. What you are standing on. Look at your watch. Focus. In the dim light, she stared at it and forced herself to speak.

"What do you know about this space?" she asked Serge.

If he talked and if she focused on listening, she might be able to keep herself centered on his words and stave off the attack. And she had to stave it off. She hadn't had an episode for over a year. She'd been getting better and better at preventing them. It was crucial she not give in.

Jac rolled the scarlet cord tied around her left wrist between her fingers, the connection that kept her tethered to her own time and place during memory lurches. More than a talisman, it was her anchor to the present. Robbie had called the bracelet her lifeline when she'd told him about the weaver on the Isle of Jersey who'd made it. Jac had been collecting bits of thread and ribbon all her life, and had felt an instant kinship with the artist Eva Gaspard, who'd given the bracelet to her.

Part of a mystic kabbalist tradition, it was called a *roite bindele*, Eva had said, and warded off misfortune and the evil eye. Jac had felt as if she'd been looking for it all her life.

She ran her finger down its silken length now. The concept of the evil eye went back over five thousand years to ancient Babylon. Every culture had its version. What was so fascinating about studying mythology was discovering how many stories and symbols were the same through the centuries and across cultures. Since she'd been wearing the bracelet, Jac often dreamed of Moira, the goddess of fate. She saw her weaving her beautiful silks in shimmering colors—gold, silver, aqua, cobalt, purple, rose. All of the threads seemed thin—too thin—to be strong. But they were. In her dreams, Moira sat cutting those threads, weeping, singing. Jac even remembered the first line of her song: *We are the keeper of the threads.*

Jac tried to focus on the silken thread. On her breathing. On the present. No matter that Robbie thought she was blessed to have memory lurches. As Malachai knew, her ability to see past her own time was a curse. No one is meant to remember so many of their past lives. Each of hers was fraught with pain and sadness and the inestimable loss of a man she'd loved and watched die because of her. There was enough in the present to cope with. But to deal with all the sadness of all your lives? Of others' lives? She could drown in their wake if she wasn't careful.

Chapter 8

MARCH 14, 1573
BARBIZON, FRANCE

Ten days of living in one locked room. Ten days of carefully slicing pages out of the notebook that Serapino had stitched together himself. Ten days of hiding the notebook back under the stone every time I heard a creak and then removing it again. Ten days of sewing page after page of that thick vellum to the inside of my rough-hewn shirt. Of accidentally pricking my finger with the needle and being forced to wait until the blood coagulated before I could continue for fear I would stain those precious manuscript pages. Ten days of listening for the sound of footsteps to make certain I was not interrupted in my task.

Even though Brother Michael and the two other monks came at the same hour every day—before their midday high Mass—I lived in fear that one day they would come earlier and interrupt me. What would they do if they found me with Serapino's notebook? Confiscate it and bring it to the abbot? And then surely my trial would include both thievery and heresy for the work that Serapino had undertaken. The goal of capturing the soul in a dying breath so that it could be resurrected through alchemy was as heretical as saying a Black Mass.

Yes, it is true. Under God's roof, Serapino had become a man who wanted to break God's rules. And I had been his helper. We feared not the wrath of an omniscient being but rather that time would run out before we could figure a formula. And we had been right.

The evening before the trial, I finished sewing the vellum pages into my shirt. The same candles that had illuminated Serapino's passing were now only a finger high. I had burned three weeks' worth in half that time. But I'd succeeded in my task. Only the leather binding had proved too thick to save.

The most important part of my escape plan had also been the most difficult. Mixing potions is complicated. Perfumes do not have to be precise, but poisons do. If the scent of orange blossoms is slightly too strong or too weak in a fragrance, someone might notice, but no one would be affected. But too many grains of the same powdered foxglove seeds that can help cure an ailing man can also kill him.

No, the potion I was making was not intended to kill, just to overwhelm. I had no desire to leave dead monks in my wake, only sleeping ones I could run from. This particular remedy required time to seep and become fully integrated. I needed it to be as strong and powerful as possible, without being fatal, and to work quickly.

During his lifetime at the monastery, Serapino had collected every herb, spice, flower essence, tree bark, metal, oil, pit and nut that could be grown in Italy or bought in Florence from the traders who came from other lands.

Often, I'd accompanied him when he ventured out to the markets by the Arno. We'd wander through the aisles of merchants, inspecting their goods, purchasing items that he needed to replenish or obtaining new ingredients that had arrived from far-off lands. Once he took ill, he sent me alone to the markets, and for the first time I practiced the art of haggling with the merchants, in the end getting even better prices from them than Serapino had.

As I followed his formula, which I intended to use to overcome my guards, I thought carefully about when I should try my escape. Before the trial? Or let it take place and, if I was found guilty, then make my exit?

I tried to calculate which would be easiest, but there was no way to judge. I had no one to ask. No one to confide in. The loneliness in the cell was overwhelming.

In the dark, at night, while I pushed the needle in and out of the hemp and into the vellum, as I dripped single drops of liquid into beakers, I went over and over my options, planning, calculating, trying to come up with the best plan.

I was able to remember the lessons Serapino had taught me and apply them. And one of the most important of those was to always keep your own secrets and silence. Never reveal any more than you have to. Watch and listen.

And so for ten days that was what I did. I watched and I listened. When the monks came to my cell, I was careful to study their body language, the way they looked at me, and to listen to what they said outside my door before they entered and after they left.

I had been told that the trial would be on a Tuesday. But on Monday when they came with my daily rations, none of the monks would make eye contact with me. Even Brother Michael, who usually asked after me and gave me some news about what was going on in the monastery, was silent. They came in, left the bread and water, cheese and fruit, and then departed.

What was going on? What had changed? I had no way of finding out. But I decided to prepare myself in case.

I had fashioned a holder for Serapino's breath out of thick cord that I'd made into a belt of sorts. I wrapped it about my naked waist. The bottle was a small thing—no longer or thicker than my forefinger—so it was easy enough to secure and hide.

Over that I wore the shirt with the vellum book sewn inside of it.

I took the bottle of the sleeping water I'd prepared and shoved that into my pocket along with a handful of rags.

In the early afternoon they returned.

This was the first time other than the day of Serapino's funeral that they'd come twice.

"Your trial is today, René," Michael said.

"Not tomorrow?"

"No. And the abbot is waiting. I have prayed for a good outcome."

This time he met my eyes, and I believed he meant it.

Caught up in that moment, I suddenly realized I'd lost the chance I'd been hoping for. This was when I should have opened the bottle and pushed the cloth up to his face when the others were not looking and then catch them by surprise. I'd been foolish. Touched by his words, I was unprepared.

The pain of Serapino's passing had turned me soft and overly emotional. I would not survive this way. I needed strength, not tears.

The monks had me walk in front of them from the laboratory to the refectory, where the trial had been set up. It was the first such event at Santa Maria Novella. No infraction had ever been so great that a tribunal had been convened. But suspicion of murder was a serious matter. Protecting the name of the most revered apothecary in Florence was of grave importance to the reputation of the monastery and its pharmacy.

I'd never been in that room when food was not being served. Instead of the smells of hot dishes and fresh bread, the sweet smell of the gardens infused the air that wafted in through the open casements flanking the south wall.

The abbot and the two most senior monks in the monastery were in the same seats where they sat for meals at the long dining table. The beautiful slab of cherrywood, smoothed from years of use, was empty, and to my eyes looked naked. Out of context, you can see things anew and learn them better.

To the right of the abbot was the archbishop of Florence, Niccolò Ridolfi. This dour-faced man, with a protruding forehead and thin lips, was the reason we'd had to wait for the trial to begin. My life was proceeding according to his schedule.

The brothers who'd brought me to the refectory now escorted me to the table and offered me a chair facing my accusers and judge. Behind me other tables were filled with the members of the monastery. It seemed everyone was present.

"We are not here to condemn you without giving you a chance to explain yourself, René Bianco," the abbot began.

My stomach began to ache. Sweat started to drip down my neck. I felt my bowels liquefy. I had spent so much time planning on how to escape and what to take with me, but I had not thought very much about the trial itself. I knew about civilian trials, but how did monks conduct such things?

"We are men of God and mercy," Beneto said. "Please describe the events that led up to the passing of Brother Serapino."

"He was very ill . . ." I started in halting words.

"Yes," Beneto said, almost encouraging me.

I searched his face. Today he looked almost benign. I didn't see the accusation I'd viewed that night in the laboratory when he came so soon after Serapino had died.

"Go on," Beneto prompted.

"He had been ill for months. He grew weaker and weaker and was in constant pain."

"The same illness that befell Brother Adamo during last winter," said Brother Jacimo, the librarian, who sat on the other side of Beneto. He was an ancient man, at least eighty years old, with a keen mind. Serapino had always spoken well of Jacimo, and I hoped that would bode well for me. He had been of very noble birth—but a seventh son with no hope of inheriting any of his father's estate.

"Yes, that's right." Beneto looked at me. "Is there a connection there? That they both had the same illness?"

I didn't know what, if anything, Jacimo knew

about Serapino's experiments. I had thought no one other than I knew about the collection of dying breaths that Serapino had amassed, but I might have been wrong.

My mentor visited with each monk as he lay on his deathbed and offered solace and succor along with a syrup that he claimed made death less painful. Prepared with ground and liquefied grains of seeds from the poppy, it offered dreams of the next world to those about to leave this one. But that was not all he did while attending the dying men. Serapino also collected their breaths so he had samples to work with.

If Jacimo mentioned any of this, a search of Serapino's workplace might reveal the items I was hiding, and that would be a catastrophe.

Again, I thought of the lesson Serapino had taught me: Always keep your own secrets and silence. Never reveal any more than you have to. Watch and listen more than you speak.

"No, I don't know of a connection, Father," I said.

The abbot spoke to Jacimo now: "Are you satisfied with his answer?"

"Yes," Jacimo said. "Brother Adamo died slowly of a disease of the heart that I do not believe was contagious. Something not uncommon in the elderly. I was just making an observation."

"And so, René Bianco, your mentor was growing more and more sickly?" The abbot returned to the previous line of questioning.

"Yes, and as the pain became more intolerable and the syrup offered less relief, he spoke to me about hastening his death."

"And why would he do that? He was a man of God. We do not hasten death. We wait for God to take us."

I was about to speak when I realized the hopelessness of the position I was in. If I told them what Serapino believed and what he'd desired, I would be painting the picture of a true heretic. I would be betraying him. At the same time, the only way I might go free was to tell that truth.

"He thought such suffering was not necessary." I chose each word carefully. Maybe I could make an argument that was based on the science Serapino practiced. "With all the formulas and elixirs he prepared, he knew that there were some that could bring about peace sooner."

"Elixirs or poisons?" the archbishop asked.

"Elixirs," I answered.

"But elixirs that were poisonous?"

"Yes," I said in a lowered voice.

"And Serapino mixed these poisons?"

"Yes. In smaller doses, some were cures."

"And one of these poisons is made from almonds?" asked Beneto.

"Yes," I answered.

"And that is what I smelled on Brother Serapino's breath."

"Yes."

I couldn't tell if I was making things any better or worse. He was throwing the questions at me quickly, and I didn't have much time to think through the case he was building.

"And this particular poison, was it something Serapino made often?"

"Yes, he kept it on supply, in the laboratory."

"He made it?"

"Yes."

"And did you, in the past, ever help him to make it?"

"Yes, I assisted in all things in the laboratory."

"So you know how to make it also?"

I had stepped into the first trap. It was too late to figure out how to get out of it. "Yes."

"So you might have made the particular dose that killed Serapino yourself? In fact, didn't you mix it? Is that not what you told me that night?"

"Yes, I did mix it. Serapino asked me to."

"When did Brother Serapino take the poison?"

"Several hours before he died."

"But he was weak, was he not? He had not come to meals in over three weeks. Had not left the laboratory to come to a single Mass."

"Yes, he was weak."

"So if he could not come to Mass, a man of the cloth who lived his life for God, how could he get up off his sickbed and get a vial of poison?" Beneto asked.

I could have argued that the same energy was not required to walk five steps as to travel the length of the monastery.

"Serapino asked me to give it to him."

"And you obeyed him."

"Yes."

"Knowing that he was asking you to help him die."

"Yes."

"Did you try to talk him out of that?"

"At first, yes, I did."

"You did? Why is that?"

"I cared for Brother Serapino. He is the only family I have known. He is my teacher. I . . . I . . ."

"But in the end he convinced you?"

"The pain convinced me," I said. My voice was low.

"You decided to play God?"

"No. I would never do such a thing. Brother Serapino asked me to give him the poison."

"You swear that you gave him the poison because he asked for it?" Beneto asked.

"Yes."

"Not because you were tired of being his apprentice? Not because you wanted to take over the apothecary?"

So this was what was at the heart of the inquiry.

"No."

"But that is what would likely happen, is it not? You are the most knowledgeable of all of us. You are in a position to use what you have learned to gain power here."

"I was satisfied working with Serapino. I had nothing to gain by having him die."

"Unless he was holding you back. Unless he was keeping you from grander ambitions. You have been an apprentice far longer than is customary. Isn't that true?"

It was true. Serapino had kept me an apprentice longer than I thought was right. There had been some rancor between us over how far and how fast I was progressing.

"There are some of us here who have heard arguments between the two of you to that effect. You wanted more than Serapino was willing to give you. You were greedy for power, René Bianco, were you not?"

"Those were just conversations, Friar. Two men arguing about ideas. I would never want to hasten his death for my own benefit."

"Look at the evidence. We have heard the fights between you about how you wanted more responsibility in the pharmacy. You knew how to make the poisonous bitter almond paste. You were alone with him day and night for weeks with no one to witness your actions. And we know, because we have all taken the same oath and love the same Lord, that Serapino would not break the sacraments in the last hours of his life. So close to heaven to risk entry by disobeying a major rule?"

"No!" I leapt up, stepped forward and pounded my hands on the table. "He was in terrible pain. Serapino said God would not have made these herbs and flowers and nuts capable of such things if he did not intend for us to use them. He said that God did not make the rules that men impose upon one another in his name—"

"Heresy!" The abbot screamed and stood, pointing his finger at me. All the hatred in his heart visible on his face. How could I have been so stupid? This was not about burying Serapino in hallowed ground. I alone in that hall knew what I was really on trial for. Years before Beneto had wanted Serapino to be his lover. I had heard the abbot proposition him. Had heard Serapino rebuff him and then listened as Beneto threatened to remove him from his position overseeing the apothecary if he uttered one word of his proposition to anyone. And then, as the abbot left my mentor's room, he noticed me huddled on my pallet. He'd forgotten I slept just outside Serapino's cell. Hatred flashed in his eyes. He'd been mortified in front of an apprentice.

I finally understood. This trial, my demise, was Beneto's revenge.

He was conferring with the archbishop and the librarian. The room was silent. Everyone waited to hear the verdict.

It was the archbishop who spoke. "I declare you guilty, René Bianco. Since you are not a religious man, we cannot charge you. Therefore we will turn you over to the government of Florence and they will mete out your fate."

The abbot addressed the monks who had escorted me into the rectory: "Take René Bianco to the laboratory and lock him up again until the chief magistrate from the city arrives later this afternoon," Beneto said.

And then, with a smile that he was trying so very hard to hide playing on his lips, he gazed at me and offered a benediction.

"May God have mercy on you, René Bianco. I fear you are going to need it."

Chapter 9

THE PRESENT
FRIDAY, MARCH 14
BARBIZON, FRANCE

Jac never lost focus on the space she was in. Only minutes had passed, but a story had begun unfolding in her mind, and she'd become aware of another layer of time. She knew—because it had happened to her many times before—that she'd just experienced an impossibility. She wished she could still convince herself that these manifestations were an abnormality of her brain, some story-telling psychotic episode. Madness would be a relief. But she knew better because she'd discovered the tales that spun out, these fragments of someone else's life, were in fact provable. The people she saw and heard had lived. She'd researched them. And when she couldn't find proof of them—because they'd lived too long ago—she'd found other details in the story, confirming she wasn't imagining it.

Putting her hands on the edge of one of the shelves, she let her mind settle. She'd seen a man in clothes that suggested a long-lost era. Bent over a table, by the light of a candle, he was mixing a formula. Measuring out drops from small amber bottles that gleamed in the light. Was he blending perfume? Medicine? Intent on his task, he didn't look up, never blinked, his lips pursed.

"Are you all right?" Serge asked. "You didn't seem to hear me just now. I asked if you wanted to pick out a bottle of a wine for lunch."

Jac knew from previous episodes that what seemed like hours to her had passed in only seconds in real time.

"Sorry. I was just stunned by all this. There must be a thousand bottles of wine here."

"Yes, and worth a small fortune. The whole collection came with the house actually. Part of the estate sale. Melinoe hasn't even gotten around to having it appraised. Over here"—he pointed to one set of shelves—"some bottles even date back to the time of the French Revolution. Worthy of a museum. Would you like to see one?"

"How amazing. Of course."

He pulled out a bottle and handed it to her gingerly.

The unlabeled bottle was handblown and much more squat than she'd expected. The glass was a dark, dull green, and Jac could see there was still liquid inside.

"How is it possible it was all left here?" Jac was already wondering if there were other items left in the house from the 1700s. Perfumes perhaps?

"The house is like a time capsule into past centuries. It was in the same family for the last two hundred and fifty years. That's one of the reasons Melinoe bought it."

"What do you mean?" Jac asked as she handed the bottle back to him.

"There were collections here she wanted to own. The house was just the way to get at them." His laugh was slightly off-key. "Shall you pick your bottle and go upstairs? It's not that pleasant down here. Too damp. Red or white?"

She chose red, and he showed her to a section of the racks. Jac inspected the bottles, taking too much time, she knew. But the scene she'd seen a moment ago shimmered here still.

He led her away and she followed, but hesitantly. At the door she turned and looked back.

Serge was talking, and she refocused.

"But it wasn't just the collections. Melinoe's always been attracted to buildings with legends attached to them. The first project we worked on was a castle in Germany not far from one of Ludwig's masterpieces. That took four years to renovate. From there it was a convent in the Languedoc. After that it was a palazzo in Venice. She's especially drawn to anything that's remained relatively untouched over the years. Somewhat intact but falling apart is fine."

It was a perfect description of how she felt—somewhat intact but falling apart. In need of renovation. Jac had the odd thought that, upon meeting her, Melinoe might see that and want to restore her too.

"Have you always worked for her?" she asked.

Jac and Serge had reached the upper hallway.

"No. I was on my own for a few years after I graduated, and then she bought her first castle . . ."

They rounded the corner.

"But we've really always been together." The dulcet and almost childish voice was coming from the hallway. Jac could hear the woman before she saw her and had a moment to try and place the accent—if anything, she sounded British. The voice had been so sweet, so young. Then the woman who had spoken stepped out of the shadows, and Jac was taken aback. The voice didn't fit the sparkling creature who came forward, bejeweled hand extended.

"I'm Melinoe Cypros. Welcome to La Belle Fleur. I'm sorry it's under such sad circumstances." She smiled kindly at Jac, showing pointy little eyeteeth. Suddenly, instead of just self-assured, she looked almost predatory. Then the moment passed.

Melinoe had jet-black hair with white wings framing a pale, heart-shaped face. Her cat-round eyes were light gray and heavily fringed with dark lashes. Ancient eyes that looked haunted. Her lips were painted a deep red, the only color on her face. She exuded so much energy, Jac didn't realize at first how petite she really was.

Robbie must have admired Melinoe for her style. From the simple black knee-length cashmere shift to the black high-heeled suede boots that disappeared under the dress, her clothes were obviously couture. Her three-inch-wide heavy belt looked to be an authentic Elizabethan silver-and-jewel-encrusted treasure. It glowed with large pearls, square sapphires and round rubies as dragons chased one another around her waist.

Dozens of hammered white-gold bracelets encircled her wrists. And there were stacks of rings on all of her fingers except for her thumbs. Bands of diamonds, set in what Jac guessed was platinum, piled one on top of another. Her earlobes sparkled with large square-cut diamond solitaires. It would have been too much jewelry for anyone else—especially someone so small—

but Melinoe wore it all like armor, and it somehow worked.

As Jac stepped closer to take Melinoe's outstretched hand, she recognized the fragrance her hostess wore and was flattered and a bit surprised that it was one of the House of L'Etoile's signature scents. Rouge. The heavy damask-rose-and-honey scent was, of all her grandfather's creations, Jac's favorite too.

Melinoe cupped both Jac's hands in hers. "I really am so sorry about Robbie," she said in her almost little-girl voice, her words slow with sadness. "I can't imagine how lost you must be. He spoke so much about you and how close you were."

Melinoe was holding her hand too long.

"You know, you remind me of Robbie," Melinoe said.

Jac never liked being touched by strangers, and the embrace, coupled by the still lingering memory of the vision she'd had in the cellar, was making her uncomfortable.

"I'm sorry," Melinoe said, dropping Jac's hand. Had she sensed her discomfort? "I know how intrusive other people's condolences can be. And yet here I am subjecting you to mine."

Jac liked her then for understanding something so complex. Saw for a moment what Robbie must have seen. A woman who had been orphaned when she was only sixteen who had turned herself into an icon and devoted her time to a worthy—eccentric, but very Zen—quest.

"Now, let's have lunch," Melinoe said as she led them into the dining room, where a round table was set with gleaming silver, china and crystal. In the center was a bowl of white roses and ivy. Tiny droplets of water, like diamonds, sparkled on some of the rose petals. Jac didn't doubt they'd been placed there on purpose. She was certain there was nothing in this house that was not designed for its impact and theatrics.

As Serge poured the wine, Melinoe said, "You and your brother went through so much together, Jac. He told us all about the criminal he accidentally poisoned and how you saved him when the Chinese went after him for revenge."

Jac was surprised that Robbie had shared the story with Serge and Melinoe. He must have gotten very close to them.

"Yes, it was a frightening time. And the police still aren't quite certain that it's all behind us."

Melinoe raised her eyes, but it was Serge who asked: "What do you mean?"

Jac shrugged. Now she wished she hadn't said anything, but it was too late. "If it turns out Robbie was poisoned, which is a possibility, the Chinese mafia are the only people who would have a motive. Revenge . . ."

"How horrible for you," Serge said.

"Would you be in danger too?" Melinoe asked.

"You were responsible for their agents going to prison, yes?"

"Yes, but the police don't think it's likely," Jac said.

Jac had left Paris to get away from the surveillance, so very much on purpose she changed the subject. "This is a very beautiful room. Extraordinarily so," she said, eyeing the oil paintings. Still lifes by old masters. Fruits, vegetables, flowers so real they glistened with the same luminosity as the roses in the middle of the table. Melinoe had hung the paintings in groupings to cover the walls. But every one of the more than three dozen deserved a wall of its own.

"Thank you," Melinoe said.

"Do you know a lot about the history of the château?" Jac asked.

Then, as they sipped the rich red wine and spooned hot asparagus soup with Parmesan croutons, Melinoe told Jac a bit about the house and how she had come to buy it.

"The château was built in the fourteenth century but then rebuilt into what you see in the early sixteenth century by Francis I, King of France, for one of his mistresses. It's amazing to think of it but when he ascended the throne, France was bereft of great art. There wasn't a single piece of important sculpture in the country. He commissioned paintings and sculpture from all the masters of the age, including Andrea del Sarto, Benvenuto Cellini, Giulio Romano, and he even arranged for Leonardo da Vinci to come and live in France in the later part of his life. During his reign, Francis built up a great collection, the bedrock of what is now in the treasured Louvre. But in his lifetime, some of that great art was here . . ." Her voice trailed off wistfully.

It was always easier to talk about the impersonal past, and Jac was relieved to listen to Melinoe recounting what history she knew about the house. The rough edge of tension Jac had been feeling because of the vision she'd had in the cellar was fading.

"Being so close to Fontainebleau, where Francis summered, we believe that he spent quite a bit of time here. After he died, the château remained in the royal family until 1570, when Catherine gifted the house to a favored member of her retinue, her perfumer, René Bianco. He was known as René le Florentin since he'd traveled with her from Florence to Paris when she was fourteen and came to marry the prince."

Jac had heard of René le Florentin. Very little was known about him, but he was credited with bringing perfume to France.

"The château was quite a fitting gift considering its name—La Belle Fleur," Melinoe continued. "Probably for its extensive gardens. René retired here but never stopped working on what really mattered to him—and he spent the rest of his life conducting experiments here."

Jac's anxiety returned. A perfumer had lived in this château? She hadn't done any research before coming. Usually she dug deep when she visited someplace new, but she wasn't here professionally. Just to collect Robbie's notes and the family books. But now all she could think about was the hallucination she'd had in the cellar. Yes, that could have easily been a sixteenth-century man working in his laboratory. Hadn't she seen the beakers and old alembics, those antique vessels connected by a tube used for distilling liquids? So what had happened?

Had Robbie told her that René le Florentin had lived here and she'd been too upset to focus on it? He'd been so ill. She'd been so worried. If he had mentioned it, that would explain what she'd seen. It would have been her imagination playing tricks on her in the dark, damp vault under the house. Taking an unconscious bit of knowledge and weaving a story out of it.

But she knew Robbie hadn't told her. She feared the image she'd seen of a man bent over a table, working on his formulas, had been some sort of memory lurch.

Jac had stopped hearing what Melinoe was saying. Now she refocused and listened.

". . . which wasn't very unusual. René le Florentin had an illegitimate son he'd acknowledged, Pierre, who was also a perfumer. He lived here with his father and inherited the château next. It then remained in the Florentin family for many generations until it was sold to a wealthy nobleman in the 1700s. Miraculously that family retained it until 2009, when I bought it. The gentleman who sold it to me had never lived here. He'd inherited La Belle Fleur from a great-aunt who lived in Switzerland. No one had actually been in residence in more than fifty years, and it had become an albatross. The owner sold most of its valuable collections at auction but left some surprising things behind, like the wine in the cellar. It was worth a fortune." Melinoe shrugged, as if she didn't quite understand his laziness.

"What an amazing history," Jac said.

"Isn't it? There are mentions of the château in Queen Margaret's sixteenth-century diary. Apparently both Catherine and her daughter came here several times when they were staying at Fontainebleau to visit with René."

Jac was feeling overwhelmed by the story Melinoe was still telling.

"René was credited with single-handedly bringing the art of perfume to France from Florence and the monastery of Santa Maria Novella. Your brother was very familiar with his legacy. But his personal life is a mystery. Historians haven't discovered much about him . . ."

Jac was thinking that René le Florentin had once sat in this very room.

"René is quite shrouded by the past. It's been a very frustrating treasure hunt," Melinoe said.

"Treasure hunts often are," Jac said. "I make my living searching for that one new tiny clue to explain a whole concept, and more often than not . . . never find it."

"I bought the house because of René le Florentin and his work. Did your brother tell you?"

"No, he didn't tell me very much . . . By the time I got to Paris, Robbie was . . . He didn't have much energy . . ."

There was quiet for a few moments.

"Serge, could I have some more wine?" Melinoe asked as the maid came out and took away the soup bowls.

Serge stood and went to Melinoe's side. As he poured with his right hand, she put her hand on his left arm. It was an intimate gesture and struck Jac as unusual because it didn't seem familial but rather seductive.

"Jac, do you want more?" Serge asked after topping off Melinoe's glass.

"No, I'm fine, thank you." She still had half a glass.

"Robbie didn't tell you about René's work?" Melinoe asked.

"No. Robbie wasn't able to tell me much. Just that he was working for you on a fragrance project."

Was there subtext to the look Melinoe gave Serge? Was Jac imagining more to the glance than there was?

"Well, it appears René was not only creating beautiful perfumes for Catherine de Medici. What he was doing was much more amazing. But instead of telling you, why don't I show you. Let's go to Robbie's laboratory."

Chapter 10

As Serge and Melinoe led Jac through a maze of hallways, Jac steeled herself for what new fresh hell of memories she might encounter in her brother's workroom.

"This used to be an office that belonged to the head of the household staff," Serge explained as he opened the door.

The modestly sized room was painted a warm cream color and was clearly set up to be an office. The two windows faced north and looked out into a dark, shadowy copse of trees. What had once been a desk was now a makeshift perfumer's organ with over a hundred amber bottles of essences and absolutes.

Jac felt herself tearing up and dug her fingers into her palms. A pain to distract her from a worse pain.

Yes, there was no question. This was Robbie's purview. The books were piled on the floor around the desk the same way he stacked them at home. There in the corner was the ever-present dish of Robbie's favorite brand of peppermints from a store on Rue Mouffetard in Paris, and on the windowsill a glass bowl of lemons—the olfactory palate cleanser he preferred over the ubiquitous coffee beans.

Jac shut her eyes and breathed in. The scents that mingled here were slightly familiar, but they didn't remind her of the workshop at the L'Etoile mansion. There the mélange of smells was informed by the strong rose, carnation and cinnamon base that was the Etoilinade, the signature of every one of her family's fragrances. The same way Guerlain's Guerlinade of vanilla and amber was part of their signature. Her family's was spice; Guerlain's was sweet. "Let them put vanilla in everything," Jac's grandfather always said of his rival. "I won't turn our perfume into candy in order to increase sales." And indeed, despite L'Etoile being the more sophisticated house, it never came close to reaching the worldwide acclaim of its rival. And it probably was because it was missing that sweet element Guerlain offered.

What was *this* aroma? Jac wasn't sure she could identify it, even though she was certain she'd smelled it before. She needed to get closer to it.

Jac had an excellent nose, as they called it in the business. Normally she could remember and identify a scent even if she'd only smelled it once before. So how was this one familiar yet unidentifiable?

Jac sat at the table—where Robbie had sat—leaned in, and inhaled more deeply. As she did, she noticed the black-and-gold box of Mariage Frères tea that her brother favored. She closed her eyes. Missing him was a constant, and sometimes, like now, the ache went so deep she thought she must be hollow inside.

Robbie had tethered her. Without him, without knowing he was somewhere on earth, she worried she might float off. Until her brother died, Jac hadn't realized how few people there were who she cared about or who cared about her. Even though he was only one person, their relationship took the place of many. But with him gone . . .

Jac opened her eyes and forced her focus back to the desk. There were several open books she recognized from their home in Paris. She stopped trying to identify the scent—which was proving impossible to dissect. These books were why she was here—to retrieve them and Robbie's notes.

Closing one book, she put it in the corner. Stacked another on top of it.

"I should have packed it all up and sent it back to Paris so you wouldn't have had to make the trip," Melinoe apologized.

That was true, Jac thought. Why hadn't she?

"Except I wanted you to see what your brother was working on."

So it had been a conscious decision. Jac turned away from the desk to the mistress of the house. "Why is that?"

"I wanted to ask you if you would consider taking up his quest."

Jac immediately shook her head. "No, I don't think so."

"But you haven't even considered it."

"There's nothing to consider. I'm a mythologist, not a perfumer."

"Your brother said you were a perfumer as well and had been working with him. He told me about the fragrances you and he were developing."

"My show airs for only twelve episodes a year, so during the downtime I was working with Robbie . . . but I'm not a scent scientist, I have no formal training . . . His fascinations are not mine . . ."

"Are you on hiatus now?" Melinoe asked. There was something in her voice Jac hadn't heard up till now. Almost a challenge. Jac wasn't sure she understood why.

"Yes, I was in Greece, finishing up the last episode, when Robbie took ill."

"So you are free now?"

It wasn't any of her business, Jac thought. Yes, after Robbie died, Jac should have gone back to

New York to edit next season's shows. Instead she and her editor had been working online because Jac just didn't want to leave France. When her mother died, she couldn't wait to get away, but this was different. The memories and reminders of Robbie didn't overwhelm her—instead they cosseted her, comforted her. While she felt hollow and sad, she also felt Robbie was still with her. She was almost sure of it. And she was afraid if she left France, she'd leave him behind.

"What were you shooting in Greece?" Serge asked.

Jac wasn't sure if he was curious or trying to cover the tension Jac's refusal had engendered.

"A series about the Fates. Trying to find the origins for the myths of the three women."

"Interesting," Melinoe said. She looked at Serge and smiled as if they had a secret this had reminded them of. "You know my father was a student of mythology. That's how I got my name."

"I was surprised when I heard it. It's very unusual," Jac said.

Melinoe fingered the stack of rings on her ring finger. One was much thicker than the others and heavily engraved.

"Yes . . ." Melinoe said. "A rarely-heard-of minor goddess. Melinoe, the goddess of ghosts. Imagine giving that name to a child? But then he wasn't an average man." She paused and then with a laugh added: "And I wasn't an average child."

"Have you ever been an average anything?" Serge asked, also with a laugh.

"Did you grow up together?" Jac asked, including Serge in the question.

"No," he answered. "My mother married Melinoe's father when I was seventeen and she was sixteen."

Melinoe glanced at him, and something unsaid passed between them. Jac sensed a wave of sadness coming from Melinoe. Comfort coming from Serge in return. Then Melinoe squared her shoulders as if she was trying to shake off her melancholy, and her eyes returned to Jac.

"I inherited my father's love of collecting. And all of his collections. Which I've added to. There are collectors who make arrangements for their life's work to be kept intact after they die. But do you know how often their wishes are upheld? The enormous sums of money it takes to ensure that a collection is not disbanded? We don't even have full records of some of the most important collections in history. Emperor Rudolf had one of the greatest in the world, and we only know a few hundred paintings, jewels, curiosities and other works of art that he owned. I can't think about all this being broken up. I must be with it always!"

Jac sensed Melinoe's passion might have an edge of hysteria. Her objects were lovely and fascinating, but she spoke as if they were children.

"That's why your brother's work was so important to me. Jac, René le Florentin's true life's work was finding the formula to capture and reanimate a dying breath. Your brother was trying to figure out René's formula."

Jac was trying to listen but was too confused. The morning after Robbie's death, before his nurse had left, she'd come to see Jac. She had something to show her, she'd said.

Apparently Robbie had taught the nurse how to capture his breath in test tubes and made her promise to try and catch his last exhalation. The nurse gave Jac a box containing a half dozen corked tubes.

"The one with the blue X was his last one," she'd said as she pointed.

"Did my brother tell you why he wanted you to do this?" Jac asked.

The nurse shook her head.

Jac had been so overwhelmed with sadness and shock, she hadn't thought much about why Robbie had made such an odd request. She'd assumed it had something to do with thinking he'd been poisoned . . . that he wanted his breath analyzed.

"If there is a way to reanimate a soul," Melinoe was saying, "a way to force a reincarnation if you will—then I could be reunited with my collection. My stewardship of all these wonders would continue from one lifetime to the next." Her eyes were shining. Her face was slightly flushed. She looked almost possessed.

Melinoe couldn't be serious. Did she truly think this was possible? Was all this effort so she could come back to be with her collection?

Melinoe walked to the armoire in the corner of the room. Took a key chain out of her pocket and unlocked the cabinet. Then she flung open the doors.

"Come look," she invited Jac.

Inside were twelve antique, slightly battered bell-shaped silver domes about ten inches high and five inches wide at the base, with rings at the top. Jac had never seen anything like them.

"There has always been a legend about a purported alchemical solution to reanimate dying breaths into new souls, but there was nothing to go by until these came up for auction at Sotheby's in London. Actually, it was a friend of your brother's and an old friend of mine who found them. I'd been helping fund his research, and he wanted me to purchase them for his foundation."

"You mean Malachai Samuels?"

Melinoe nodded. "Yes, so you know him too?"

"I do." Jac was relieved Robbie obviously hadn't told Melinoe anything about her history.

"Once I knew this collection existed, I had to own it. I needed to solve the mystery of how reanimation worked so I could use it myself. The bells had come from this château, and after I found out that René le Florentin had spent his last years here, with his son, working on a method to galvanize these breaths, I approached the owner and offered him more than he was asking for the house. It wasn't romantic foolishness. It was very likely there might be something here that would help us learn about the process. Something tangible . . . If René lived here—maybe if I lived here . . ." She shook her head as if she was refuting something she'd thought of. "There is something magical about this château. How long it's stood here relatively undisturbed. How few changes have been made to the building. How much of it is now the same as it was then. Barbizon is a town out of time, and so is René's château. And when your brother agreed to come and work on my puzzle, I felt sure we'd find the solution."

"Can I see those?" Jac asked, gesturing to the bells.

Melinoe carefully removed one of the domes. Underneath was a bottle about seven inches high made of thick pale-blue glass. Inside was a thin layer of something dark. She tipped the bottle. The residue didn't move. Wasn't liquid. Wasn't even viscous.

"Do you know what this is?" Jac asked.

"We know the bottle is from the sixteenth century. We've guessed, and your brother concurred, it's someone's dying breath mixed with some kind of elixir or potion."

Amazed, Jac stared at the dark sludge. Then she took the proffered covering from Melinoe. Clearly very old, the metal surface was deeply engraved and from the look of the tarnish appeared to be silver. The writing looked like a combination of Latin and Hebrew. There were Egyptian and Syrian symbols. Roman and Greek numbers.

"What do all these inscriptions say? Is this the formula?" Jac asked.

"We didn't get that far. Your brother was working on the translations with someone, but whoever it was hadn't finished. I'd like to get the results. I had agreed to pay for them."

Jac nodded. Felt a slight clench in her stomach. She could guess who Robbie had gone to for translations of the arcane inscriptions. The last time he'd needed help like this, he'd gone straight to Griffin.

"Do you think you could at least be able to find out who he hired?" Melinoe asked.

"I can try," Jac said. "Are all the inscriptions on all the covers the same?" she asked.

"There's some repetition, but most of what's written on each bell is unique," Melinoe said.

Jac picked up the second bell and then the third. Beneath each was another of the same pale-blue bottles.

"We had the glass tested. The bottles date back

to the mid-sixteenth century. We believe they were part of René le Florentin's collection."

Jac removed the fourth silver bell. Beneath it was . . . nothing.

"What happened?"

"There are two missing. One was lost before I bought the collection. Your brother broke that one by accident." Melinoe shook her head; the incident was obviously still bothering her.

"I'm sure Robbie was careful." Jac wasn't certain why she was defending her brother.

"Yes, I know he was," Melinoe said.

Jac continued to inspect the inscriptions. Robbie had clearly been fascinated with the idea of what these bottles contained and the concept they represented. And he had done his best to bequeath his interest in it to her.

"What is it? You were shaking your head," Melinoe asked.

"Nothing really." She put the bell down. "Other than these measuring tools, ingredients and books—is there anything else of Robbie's?"

Melinoe pushed the door back a little. A navy sweater was hanging there. Thick cashmere, hooded. Jac recognized it and took it off the hook. Robbie had so many sweaters just like this. Once he found a style he liked, he stockpiled it. There had been a hunter green one on the back of his chair in the workshop at home. As she held the sweater, Robbie's smell rose up and surrounded her. Jac knew that the olfactory center in the brain was next to the memory center. There was a scientific reason for scent and memory to be connected. But for her it was more exaggerated. And now, suddenly, in front of these strangers, not quite in the room, not quite in her mind, she heard her brother's voice.

I haven't left you. I won't leave you.

For years, Jac's mother had talked to her from the grave whenever she visited her at the family mausoleum in Sleepy Hollow Cemetery in upstate New York.

Hearing her mother's voice was just one of the reasons Jac was never quite sure she was completely sane. The hallucinations she'd had since she was a child were another. When they multiplied after her mother's death, Jac's father had taken her to a myriad of doctors. One finally determined the manifestation was caused by a bad synapse in her brain. She'd seen the MRI on her father's desk with the doctor's notes attached. Read the words and studied the picture. Jac was fourteen. Old enough to understand that in her brain, in the area where the disease was usually found, she had a cluster of malformed cells. What the doctor wrote proved she didn't suffer from an overactive imagination but from an illness. There was no cure, but there were psycho-pharmacological drugs that could prevent the hallucinations. But there were side effects. Jac felt as if she were living behind a wall. Soon, the world dulled. She became lethargic.

That's when her grandmother insisted Jac be sent to the Blixer Rath clinic in Switzerland. A Jungian institution where Malachai Samuels was one of the therapists. This "last resort," as her father had called it, was run by disciples of Carl Jung, who believed many so-called "brain diseases" could be cured with the healing of the soul. Like his mentor, Charles Blixer said the psyche required mythic and spiritual exploration before medications.

The traditional medical community was openly hostile to this holistic, soul-centered approach. But it helped Jac. During her nine months in the clinic she was exposed to in-depth analytic therapy designed to strengthen her own healing abilities. In order to understand the symbolism of her dreams and drawings done after deep medi-tative sessions, in order to translate her symptoms and recognize any possible synchronistic events in her life that might have a deeper meaning, Jac had to learn the universal language of the soul. What Jung called mythology. And the man who taught her that language and spoke it with her was Dr. Malachai Samuels.

On leave from his practice at the Phoenix Foundation, Malachai was at Blixer Rath as a Jungian therapist, not as a reincarnationist. He never talked to any of his patients about possible past-life episodes. Only years later, reading a magazine article about Malachai, did Jac realize he'd been at the clinic investigating his theory that a high percentage of schizophrenics were misdiagnosed and suffering from past-life memory crises.

Jac folded Robbie's navy sweater and put it into a cardboard box Serge provided. Then, book by book, she packed up. Melinoe's phone rang, and she left the room to take the call.

Outside, a steady rain fell, and the moat that Jac could see through the window was so full the water was spilling over onto the mossy bank.

She shivered.

"Are you cold?" Serge asked.

"A little."

"The sweater?"

Jac picked it up. No reason not to put it on. It would keep her warm. Her brother wasn't a tall man. Not very broad either. The sweater would only be a bit big. But she couldn't. She didn't want to smell him that intensely.

"Do you have any newspaper? I need to wrap up the bottles of ingredients so they don't break."

Serge left the room to get some. Jac was alone. She went back to the window and looked out again. The shadows were heavy. There was no way to sense how deep the woods were. She wondered how often Robbie had stood here and looked out. Jac suddenly saw it darken. She saw trees falling and branches breaking in some kind of violent storm. How could the rain have gotten so much worse so quickly? But even as she watched, the view changed again and she was seeing it as she had before. The felled branches and trunks were covered with moss and lichen. They weren't falling anew. She'd seen the view from a different perspective. Had imagined what it had looked like years ago. Not hard to do when your mind is so ready to play tricks on you anyway. Her imagination was both her heaven and her hell. And right now all she wanted to do was finish packing up and get back to Paris before she had to indulge it anymore.

When Melinoe and Serge returned, he was carrying two rolls of paper towels. Jac began to wrap the bottles, tightening the cap on each one.

"Do you share your brother's belief system?" Melinoe asked. "Are you a Buddhist also?"

Jac shook her head. "No, I'm afraid I don't believe in anyone—sorry—anything." The slip of the tongue had been embarrassing but true. In these last weeks Jac had become aware how little faith she had in anyone. Even Robbie had left her. Abandoned her the way her mother had, the way their father had.

"So you don't believe someone's dying breath could contain his soul?" Melinoe asked.

"No."

"But your brother thought it could."

"Yes, I know that now. He had his nurse collect his dying breath."

Jac didn't know why she'd revealed that to a stranger.

"I wondered if he might."

"Why?"

"He was so taken with the idea. We'd talked about it at length," Melinoe said.

Jac was almost finished putting the bottles in the box.

"My brother was a dreamer. Like my father. And like my mother until the dreams broke her."

"And you?"

Jac shrugged. "I'm not my brother."

"But you are a perfumer. And, he told me once, a far better one than he was. He was convinced that the solution to the dying breaths would have something to do with scent and essences. He said that alchemy and medicine and scent were closely aligned until the nineteenth century and that he'd done a lot of research suggesting there were ancient ingredients that might have held secrets we've become too sophisticated to trust."

"Yes, that sounds exactly like my Robbie."

"If he's right and if you have his dying breath, then perhaps you should rethink your decision. Wouldn't it be worth a few weeks of your life to find out if it's true?"

Chapter 11

MARCH 17, 1573
BARBIZON, FRANCE

Time passes slowly in hell. A young man turns bitter in prison. A personality is forged. You change when you live in rancid darkness, forced to inhale the stench of your own body mixed with the stink of the years. When your only companions are monstrous rats and insects. When all you hear is silence.

Every hour was the enemy. Every minute pushed against my sanity. I believe I spent most of my jailed hours hallucinating. Now, I do not remember enough about them to recount how I passed them all. I know I slept because my nightmares clung to my mind through my waking hours.

When I was lucid, I tried to live in my memory. Starting from my earliest days, I worked at recounting everything in an attempt to keep my mind active. For the very first time I remembered moments that I did not know I had access to. I saw my mother—even though up to my days in jail I had never been able to recall her face. How much she looked like one of the women in the frescoes in the chapel at Santa Maria. A pale, thin woman so clearly heaven bound. How long had she been sick? Of that I'm not sure, but in my cell I was able to pull up the distant memory of her speaking to me as she walked me to the monastery on the day she left me there. It was a moment that had never surfaced before but floated to me out of the empty darkness of the prison. And in the dark I wept for her. My young mother whose name I do not know to this day.

I could recall the scene of her standing before the monks and telling them that she had been married to a dead soldier whose name was René Bianco. And that was the reason the monks took me. My father was the cousin of one of the monks. I was related to a Dominican brother. Yes, there in the dungeon I worked out all the fragments of memory. My father's cousin was the one who took me in. He was the calligrapher who worked in the library. I had always known that I first was taught by Brother Silvius, but I'd never before remembered the connection. I was with Silvius for my first few years, but he was frustrated by my inability to master the finer points of penmanship. As good as I was, he said, I would never be good enough. So when I was seven, Serapino, who had watched me work in the garden, took me. He sensed that I had an affinity for being an herbalist.

Some days, though, were filled with insanity. I couldn't remember where I was. A prison? An infirmary? Beneath the river? In a cave in the mountains? A lion who stalked my cell spoke in a language I could not understand. A mule appeared and offered escape, except when I tried to pull myself onto him, I found I could not move my legs or my arms. A large bird of prey often circled me, staring with beady eyes, waiting, I was sure, for me to be still long enough for him to take a bite out of my flesh.

The worst of it was that I could find no escape. In my saner moments, I often took out the packet of poison pills from Serapino's laboratory and sewn into my shirt along with the vellum pages. I would examine it. Contemplate what to do. Swallow them now before I heard my sentence? Or wait? Was there any chance of reprieve? Or would the next stage of my journey be even worse than this one?

I was not a seer. Like many of the monks in the convent I was suspicious of men who looked into mirrors or bowls of water and claimed to foresee the future. Indeed they were heretics who went against God. But then so was Serapino, who believed that he could bring back the dead. I had no premonition about my future. No hint of what was to befall me.

I wanted to take the bitter almond pills and end this hell. All reality was steeped in fantasy, and fantasy was nothing but one horror after another.

What kept me from killing myself was a smell.

I had the pills in my hand, ready to end the torture of the hours that did not pass and the fear that did not abate. I had seen Serapino die not two weeks before, and the peace that he found at the very end beckoned. I did not believe I would ever have the chance to work on his formulas, even as they chafed my skin beneath my shirt. I would never see him or speak to him again in this world. Why not hasten the time when I could?

And then I smelled a familiar odor of lemon, orange blossom and bergamot. A scent I had created in the laboratory at Santa Maria Novella! The fragrance I had made expressly for the daughter of the dead Duke of Urbino.

Catherine's scent.

The infirmary had been famous for more than three hundred years, dispensing balms and healing waters, poultices and creams. The Dominican brothers were known through all the city-states for their cures. And once Serapino had taken over the pharmacy and begun experimenting with scented waters, our customers often purchased perfumes as well. Serapino's products for the toilette became as popular as his medicines.

Most days I worked in the pharmacy, selling wares while Serapino kept more to the laboratory, overseeing the novices who pressed the flowers and herbs, dried the leaves, ground the seeds and nuts. So the first time Catherine came to Santa Maria, I waited on her and her chaperone.

I did not know who she was that first day, but the charming dark-haired girl exuded strength and power. She had a pale, rounded face and lithe figure. But it was her brilliant and sad eyes that captivated me. I knew right away—though I don't know how—that like me she was an orphan. Losing your family at a young age changes the way you look at the world. Your eyes are always searching for family long gone. For people who will never reappear.

Approaching, I asked what I might help her with. She'd come for soaps, she said, and I showed her the bars with pressed violets that we had just created. All expression of melancholy vanished from her now delighted face as she examined the soap, sniffing at it and asking me how we molded it. I explained the process to her, surprised at how interested she was in what I described.

"Did you make it yourself?" she asked.

"Yes." I nodded, for I had.

"And you make the scented waters too?"

"Some of them, yes, I do." This was a lie. I helped Serapino, but I had not yet worked on a fragrance on my own.

She cocked her head to one side. Then leaned forward as if to tell me a secret. "I've always wanted a scent that would be mine and no one else's. Would it be possible for you to create such a thing?"

"Of course. We take orders all the time. What

kind of scents do you like?" I asked and began to open bottles and let her sniff at different essences to learn her taste.

She didn't like incense. Wasn't fond of cinnamon. Didn't appreciate sandalwood. She gravitated to the flower absolutes. Rose. Jasmine. Iris. I noted her reactions and then promised that in a week's time I would have a fragrance for her.

"Would you bring it to the palazzo?" she asked. "As soon as it's ready?" Her face was alight with pleasure. And I felt heady with the idea that I had put it there. Not sexual excitement. This was different. There was no stirring in my loins for the young girl—though I had plenty of feelings for other girls I'd seen on my excursions out of the monastery or for women who'd come to the pharmacy.

This girl didn't stir me. But she intrigued me. She made me curious.

"The name of the palazzo?" I asked.

"The Villa de Medici," she answered.

I believed my fate had just been sealed. I had been invited to create a scent for one of the noblest families in Florence!

Serapino agreed that the fragrance for this maiden would be my own maiden voyage. And so I set to making a scent for the young girl who had never had one made for her before but who, at the age of thirteen, was already at the center of so much political intrigue and gossip.

As I worked, I recalled all the stories I'd heard about her and her lineage.

I would have guessed my awe would have prevented me from doing a good job—but quite the opposite. It was as if suddenly I found my voice. The challenge energized me. I became enamored of the process of mixing perfume in a way that I had not known I was capable. Something in me was born that week. A desire to create. To paint a portrait with scent. And mixed in with that was the realization that becoming an artisan might elevate me. Tantalizing fruit hung from the trees I envisioned during those days. Wealth. Power. Stature. I smelled it in the mixture.

I had chosen the ingredients carefully. Orange blossom for innocence. Lemon for purity. Roses for beauty. And bergamot—it not only smelled wonderful, but the peel of the green fruit helped cure sadness. Just the right addition to the scent.

And so with the flask of perfume I'd created, I took off the next day for the Villa de Medici, only to find the young duchess was not there. Instead of leaving my merchandise, I waited.

After about an hour a manservant came to speak with me. "The duchess has returned. Please come with me," he said and led me out of the kitchen.

The walk through the palace made me swoon. The monastery was a rich one, with marble floors and gilt decorations. There were fine frescoes everywhere, and money had not been spared to make it comfortable and exalted. But the palace made it look like a shamble. The gold was dazzling. The rugs and porcelain, the tile work and fabrics, were like nothing I had ever seen.

Catherine's rooms were as sumptuous as the rest of the palace. After she greeted me, she offered me a seat, treating me more like an equal than a merchant.

"Would you like some wine?" she asked.

I nodded and watched her pour the deep-red liquid into fine glass goblets. Everywhere I looked was something to see. I reached out to touch a curtain, to caress a table skirt. I had never been inside such a grand house. Why hadn't I grown up in a palace like this? Why had fate given me the life of an apprentice and this girl the life of a princess?

Catherine, astute as she was even at thirteen, ever curious and defying convention by talking to someone of a much lower status, asked me about my time in the monastery and my beginnings. When I told her of my orphanage, her eyes misted with tears, and she took my hand.

"René, we are sister and brother in sadness." And then she told me of how her mother had died, then her father, and how she had lost her most beloved aunt. Now there were rumors that her uncle was fixing a marriage for her.

When she opened the bottle I had brought, she was tentative at first. In time I would learn that was her personality. Cautious, then passionate.

Tipping the bottle over, she wet her fingers with the perfume and then rubbed it at her temples, neck and hands.

Then she closed her eyes and breathed in.

Though you would not think so to look at her now in her dour black clothes and severely pulled-back gray hair, Catherine is a sensualist. She has always delighted in smells and sights and tastes and touches and reveled in beauty. Has she not created more and more beauty and left examples of it in her wake?

"I shall wear no other scent for as long as I live," she said to me in a solemn voice.

"I'm pleased you like it," I told her.

"Then what is wrong? I can see that your expression doesn't match your words."

"If you never wear another scent, then I can't create other scents for you."

She laughed. "Clever René. You have barely sold me this one and already you are vying to sell me more." She cocked her head and examined me. "You're more than an apprentice at the monastery, aren't you?"

"I don't know what you mean, my lady."

"You have ambition, don't you?" She said it as if she had never expected it of me.

For a moment I was stunned into silence because I had never realized it of myself. But she was right. I did have ambition. That was the fire I felt. That was what made me wake up in the morning earlier than even the monks and race out into the garden to see what had bloomed. It was ambition that made me scour the spice market, smelling every dark and mysterious concoction I could find. What made me haunt the cellars of the laboratory, sniffing at bottles of scents and potions, some of which dated back more than three hundred years. It was ambition that made me different than Serapino and must have been what he feared in me when he looked at me that way he had.

"Yes," I said, and with my declaration took one step closer to my future. "I do have ambition."

"Then I shall help you realize it," she said, laughing as if we were embarking on a game. Opening a velvet purse hanging off the belt around her waist, she pulled out a gold ducat and gave it to me. "A new scent every month, Master Perfumer. But always this one shall be my favorite. What is its name?"

"Water of the Duchess."

It was that scent I smelled in the dungeon that day as I held the poison pills in my hand. The duchess's favorite wafting toward me, over the stench, under the stink. I smelled Catherine.

I was certain I was hallucinating again. I identified orange blossoms and lemon and bergamot and roses. Yes, it was only right that if I was to lose my mind I could at least dwell in the fantasy world of scents that I loved. There were worse fates than to die smelling something beautiful.

I was ready to take the pills. I could accept that this was my end, though I was surprised a bit that all men who were about to depart this earth were ushered out on the clouds of a sweet-smelling aroma. I was happy that the thing I loved the most—scent—would be part of dying.

"René Bianco!"

So I was hearing voices now in my madness? A familiar voice from the other side to greet me in the next world?

"You are a horrible sight!"

Was it someone I knew who had passed over? No! It was not someone who had died. I knew this voice. I opened my eyes.

Catherine de Medici stood before me. Fourteen years old and full of determination and outrage. "I'm leaving for Paris in ten days' time, and you are to come with me. I'm going to need my perfumer there in that barbaric city."

Chapter 12

THE PRESENT
FRIDAY, MARCH 14
PARIS, FRANCE

Back home, Jac returned her grandfather's books to the shelves in the library. Filling in the empty spaces felt restorative, and when she was done, she surveyed the wall. Books always gave her solace. Especially these. There were some volumes dating back to the seventeenth century that she knew belonged in a national library. But she and Robbie both felt that even if it was selfish to keep them home, they wanted them here, the magnificent collection created by her great-grandfather and her grandfather complete.

Jac played a game she hadn't since she was little, not taking any books out, just running fingers down the lines of books. Catching a word in a title here, another word there. As if she could absorb their knowledge by touch. She loved to feel the smooth leather and paper, the grooves where one ended and the next began, the incised letters on some of the more elaborate leather covers.

There were volumes on magic and alchemy and

medicine since in so many cultures and eras scent was used for far more than perfume. There were books here that listed mysterious ingredients now extinct that supposedly had magical properties. Sometimes when she and Robbie were mixing up their new potions as kids, they would try some of the odd or curious ingredients in these books. Once she collected rainwater outside in the garden under the rosebushes because a book said that it would make a more fragrant eau de toilette base. Fascinated with the scientific aspect of scent, Robbie had tried cat urine after reading that in ancient Egypt it had been considered a sacred ingredient.

Once the books were restored, Jac took Robbie's notes out of the box and put them on his desk. She wanted to read them . . . would read them . . . but not yet. There was company business she had to attend to first. Luc was waiting for her to sign some papers so they could begin the full integration of the two companies. As she scribbled her signature on contract after contract, her sense of well-being about the continuation of the House of L'Etoile grew.

She could have made a lot of money if she had sold her part ownership to a conglomerate, but the House of L'Etoile had been family-owned since 1774. She couldn't be the one to bring an end to that long, long era. Now the company's future was ensured for her lifetime and probably her cousins' children's lifetimes since among them they had six children, three of whom were already working in the business.

At five o'clock, Jac finished all the work that had been waiting for her. Shut the computer down and turned off the lights in the office. Before she left the workshop, she always sprayed scent. Now she lingered, searching the shelves, looking at the familiar bottles for the wonderful wisteria scent that Robbie had made her for her last birthday.

Wisteria was an impossible scent to bottle since the true essence of the flower couldn't be extracted directly. Like lily of the valley and lilac, the fragile flowers crumbled when exposed to the heat of the effleurage process. Robbie had told her he'd worked on and off for two years trying different combinations of other ingredients, building a formula that would imitate the intoxicating scent.

And he'd done it.

Octavian, a friend of Jac's who had a perfume blog, had once described the wisteria's scent as peppery, sweet and green with a distinctive smoke-phenolic note. He'd said when the flowers are in full bloom they have a hint of burnt vanilla that gives the scent a sweet edge.

Robbie's formula contained twenty-two different ingredients that combined and melded to create the perfume that he'd called Jac's Dream.

And as she sprayed it on, she thought of her

brother, smiled and felt the tears threaten. The ache was still fresh enough to throb.

Jac looked around. Robbie's things were everywhere. His sweater on the back of the chair. A canister of his favorite tea by the electric kettle. The Zen singing bowl sitting on his desk. The Chinese calligraphy that he'd begun collecting in the last eighteen months—all of flowers—hung on the walls. She didn't want the reminders to go away. Was glad for them. But they were a tease. She just wanted him to come back. Wanted more of those moments she'd had in the car and at the château when she'd felt him with her. She knew it would never be the way it was when he was alive. But she hoped some part of him could stay with her.

She opened the doors to the garden.

Robbie had added a great granite laughing Buddha in the courtyard and placed it so that every morning the sun shone on his grin. But the sun wasn't out today. It was cloudy, chilly and damp. Just as well, she thought. She wasn't ready for spring. For the lovely colors of the flowers and hopeful blossoms. She wanted it to keep raining. For the dark to come early. For the evening sky to be dull. Robbie was gone. Her life shouldn't have any color.

Through the garden, on the other side, she opened the matching French doors and entered the living quarters of the house. She walked through the formal rooms to the kitchen, where she found a bottle of Sancerre. She poured herself a glass and took it into the living room, turned on the stereo, and then sat down on one of the couches and opened the book she'd been reading for the last few days. Or trying to read. She'd get through only a few pages and then realize how little she'd actually absorbed. It wasn't the book. She'd read other books by Gabriel García Márquez. And Robbie had told her that this one, *Love in the Time of Cholera*, was his favorite. But she couldn't focus.

The music, jazz from the '30s, wafted through the room, and she rode the waves of the melancholy moodiness. Robbie didn't like jazz as much as she did. He loved opera, which she didn't like at all. She couldn't stand knowing there were words being sung that she didn't understand. She wanted to know what every one of them meant.

Understanding what was going on around her mattered to Jac. She didn't like the unexplained or unexplored. It was what made some of the issues in her life that much more complicated—like what had happened between her and Griffin. They'd begun a dance that had ended unexpectedly and for reasons that still confused her.

They'd met when she was a senior in high school. She'd smelled his scent before she saw him. A scent that reached out, pulled her in and promised stories. Its ingredients included lemon, honey and musk. Rich florals and animalic accords that blended together to create a particular fragrance that for her would always be associated with Griffin. With their time together. With wonder. With falling in love. With a cessation of loneliness. And then with anger and grief.

Long after they'd broken up, she still scanned tables at flea markets and auctions on eBay, buying up even half-empty bottles. In the recesses of the armoire in her bedroom, she had a cache of eight bottles of his signature scent. But even in sealed packaging, even in the dark, cologne evaporated. Like moments in life.

They'd seen each other all through college and graduate school. Then, just when they finally had the chance to live together, he left her. He'd said it was because he couldn't bear that she would always be disappointed in him . . . that he wasn't as smart or talented as she believed him to be and he'd never live up to her expectations.

He'd left when they were just past the budding stage of their love. His abrupt departure never gave it a chance to fully bloom and then decay— if that's what was going to happen—of its own accord.

She'd survived, even though at times she was certain she wouldn't. Even though one night she'd sat in the bathtub, staring at a razor blade and thinking about what would happen if she just . . .

Although she couldn't forget him, and never let

another man in the way she'd let Griffin in, she'd built up a solid satisfying life for herself. Until eighteen months ago when Griffin had come back in the midst of the worst crisis she'd ever faced and was there to help her save Robbie in Paris. And then—just like that—he was gone, and she was alone again.

But she'd still had her brother.

Jac picked up the phone and dialed a number in New York City. Malachai Samuels answered on the second ring, saying hello in his mellifluous voice. She pictured her mentor and friend in his office, surrounded by his antique card collections, books and objets d'art.

"Am I catching you between sessions?" she asked, knowing that Malachai saw patients during the afternoons.

"My next appointment isn't for another half hour. How are you?" he asked in a concerned voice, and she felt cosseted. They could argue and had, but Malachai knew her better than anyone—even Robbie in many ways.

They spoke of his work and hers, and she told him about her business decision to bring her extended family into the House of L'Etoile and how it was working out.

"That all sounds wonderful, but it's not why you called. Are you having a hard time in France on your own? Do you think you might be happier here in New York again?"

"I don't know. Sometimes. But then the idea of leaving seems much worse."

"That's because you feel more connected to Robbie's memories there. It's where you spent your time with him. You were never here with him."

She took a sip of the wine and listened to him offer advice in a smooth voice.

"Jac, take your time. It's important to be where you feel closest to Robbie right now. And his soul is there, in Paris, in that house, in the workshop."

"You mean that as a metaphor?"

"What? That his soul is in the house?"

"Yes."

"No . . . I mean it literally . . . I believe that often when someone leaves so suddenly his or her soul remains for a while to ease the passage from grief to acceptance for those left behind."

"That's all?"

Malachai laughed. "Well, it's a fairly large concept, but yes. Why?"

"Because . . . he didn't tell you about . . . Did he tell you what he was working on before he died?"

"I hadn't spoken to him for a few months, so no."

That made sense. Robbie only knew the reincarnationist through Jac, and while the two men shared a very deep and abiding belief in past-life theory, they were not close the way Jac and Malachai were.

"What is this about, Jac?"

She took a breath and dove into the beginning of the story. "You do know a woman named Melinoe Cypros, don't you?"

Malachai remained silent. Ever enigmatic. Revealing so little. But Jac thought she'd heard an intake of breath on the other end of the phone.

"She said she knew you."

"You met her?" he asked.

"Yes. Because of Robbie. He'd been working for her right up to the time he died. She told me that she met Robbie through you. Is that true?"

In all the years Jac had known Malachai, and she had known him since she was fourteen, he had never revealed very much about his personal life. Oh, certainly there were anecdotes about childhood, or his years studying psychology at Oxford, or conversations about his likes and dislikes. She knew he was closest to his aunt, Beryl Talmage, who ran the Phoenix Foundation with him. And Jac understood that Malachai's father was still alive at ninety-two and living in England and that they were estranged. But she didn't know if he'd ever been married. If he lived with anyone. If there was someone, he was very discreet about her, for he never brought her to dinners or mentioned her. Malachai had been alone in his country home when she'd visited there eight months ago.

At the same time Malachai never seemed like the kind of man who was celibate. He was too much of a sensualist for that. So Jac had always assumed there were women here and there but that ultimately Malachai had chosen to live alone.

She'd gotten the sense from Melinoe that she and Malachai had been close. Perhaps even lovers. Was that true? She certainly seemed like someone he might be interested in. Both collectors, both eccentric. Both elegant and sophisticated. Both fascinated with the shadows and secrets that hid just beyond our reach.

"Yes, it's true. I knew Melinoe. Why, Jac?"

And so Jac told him about the dying breaths project Robbie had been working on, that he'd intimated he thought she should complete.

"That collection was supposed to be mine," Malachai said in a low voice.

Jac was startled by the vehemence and anger in the seven words.

"What do you mean, yours?"

Malachai sighed, as if he was loathe to talk about it.

"She was interested in reincarnation and came to New York to talk to me."

"When was this?"

"Five and a half years ago."

Very specific, Jac thought. "And?"

There was silence on the other end. Jac wondered if Malachai was remembering or just not certain he wanted to continue.

"She was a highly knowledgeable amateur. As

you know, since you've met her, she's immensely wealthy. She began to contribute large sums to fund our archaeological projects and research. In fact she was invited to serve on the foundation's board of directors . . . Melinoe was very much committed to aiding us to find memory tools that might enable people to access their past lives . . ." He trailed off.

Jac took another long sip of her wine while she waited for Malachai to resume. She pictured him at his desk, picking up one of his exquisite objets d'art, as he often did, and contemplating it. He had a collection of jeweled creatures arranged at the base of the Daffodil Tiffany lamp that sat to his left. His favorite was a jadeite frog with ruby eyes. She'd held it once, and it was cool to the touch and soothing.

"And you were close?" Jac asked, nudging him toward a revelation.

He ignored her question but continued speaking.

"About three years ago, I found out about a collection of very curious objects coming up for auction at Sotheby's. According to the legends engraved on their silver coverings—the parts that could actually be deciphered—they were the property of Catherine de Medici's perfumer and were his collection of last breaths—including the breaths of the queen's husband, son and other members of her family. They had been found in a château in Barbizon. The first time in modern history that anything had ever surfaced that went back to the alchemical breath experiments that were done in the Renaissance."

Jac knew from the edge in his voice he was becoming more distressed as the story progressed.

"I told Melinoe about them. When we flew to England together to see the collection and examine it, we were both fascinated. Obsessed if you will. Drunk on the possibilities that there were still breaths in the bottles and instructions on the silver coverings. And that if we could decipher them, there might be a way to . . . I went to the auction. I was bidding on behalf of the foundation to acquire the collection. The foundation's money is not my own. The board of directors—which included Melinoe—had voted on a very generous sum to enable me to buy the breaths. Well above the estimate of $60,000. We all thought that was enough. No one even knew if the breaths were still in the bottles. So what were we even buying? What was the collection really worth? What's a dream worth? It was all legend . . . all myth."

"Well, you don't have to tell me how seductive a myth is. What was the estimate?"

"The estimate was $35,000 to $50,000 because of the workmanship of the silver cases that covered each bottle and the connection to Catherine de Medici. No one took the legend very seriously."

"But it had been authenticated? It must have been for Sotheby's to be handling it."

"Yes, the glass and the silver had been dated to 1550 to 1575. It was authentic all right. Just authentic what?"

"So how much did they go for?"

Malachai didn't give her a simple answer. But then she shouldn't have expected one. Simplicity and Malachai didn't go together.

"I went to the auction alone. Melinoe had other business and told me she was certain I'd get the collection—that no one would want it as much as we did. There were quite a few people bidding at first. After all, the pieces were associated with a queen of France. I hadn't planned on entering the bidding till it got close to my limit—I didn't want to drive up my own price. But once it reached $30,000, it was just me and a private bidder on the telephone."

Jac had been to quite a few auctions and could picture the scene, with the auctioneer at the podium and a grouping of auction house employees fielding bids on the phones to the right. Telephone bidders were always a dramatic and mysterious part of an auction.

"What happened?"

"The bidding landed at $60,000. It was with a bidder on the phone. I should have stopped, but I was too far gone by that point. I had convinced myself we would discover something of great importance from the collection. I had to have it. So I decided to add some of my own money to the foundation's sum. The bidder and I were now locked in a game of one-upmanship. I went to $65,000. The telephone bidder went to $70,000. And so it continued until we had reached $250,000. I was going to have to liquidate part of my retirement fund. But I didn't care anymore. I had to have the silver bells and the bottles for the promises they held. And the fact that someone else wanted them as much as I did only made me more convinced that they would reveal something astounding."

"How far did you go?" Jac was fascinated seeing this side of him.

"I bid $300,000, and then the person on the phone bid $1.85 million. A very significant amount."

"Wow. That's a crazy jump. But why was it significant?"

"It was $25,000 more than my portfolio plus the foundation's $60,000. Exactly and to the penny out of my reach. And not by five or ten thousand dollars that I might have been able to raise but by enough that I really had to stop."

"I see."

Malachai was silent on the other end.

Jac finished the story for him. "She knew how much you were worth because you were lovers. She was the other bidder, wasn't she? It was Melinoe who bought the collection out from under you."

Chapter 13

Jac had never heard Malachai sound vulnerable before, but talking about Melinoe seemed to unnerve him. He was at the same time wounded and angry. And even wistful. Was he still mourning the loss of the collection—or the woman who stole it from him?

"She is without heart. Without honor. Utterly selfish. Why are you asking me about her?"

"She told me it was through you that she had heard about Robbie."

"Yes, but it would have been back a while. I haven't talked to Melinoe or seen her since the night after the auction."

"Did you accuse her of what you suspected? That she had been the bidder on the phone?"

"Yes, of course. That night, at dinner. And she laughed at me. She has a very curious laugh. It's very childlike. There are aspects of her that have never quite grown up. As if part of her had been frozen at the time of her father's death. Do you know about that?"

Jac knew only the broad strokes of the story. So Malachai told her.

"Melinoe's father had a butterfly house and spent hours there taking care of the plants, cataloging the butterflies. She said he always played music in there. Mostly opera, which he loved, especially the Italian grand dramas. When she came home from school, she would always go directly there, and they would spend an hour together. No matter who he was married to, and he had married four times, that hour after school was time she and her father spent alone.

"When she went in that day, Verdi's *Il Trovatore* was playing. This tragic opera was one of her father's favorites. She walked through the heavy green foliage toward the back, where he had a grouping of chairs and a workbench and where she often found him repotting a plant or making notes.

"He was sitting in a chair, his head down. *Sleeping,* she thought. And then she noticed there were odd designs on his face and hands. And on his khaki pants. And on the floor around him. A small red pattern made up of tiny red dots. No, not red dots. They were butterfly feet. The butterflies had gotten into something red, and everywhere they'd landed they'd left a stamp. As she watched, a monarch approached her father and landed on his chest, then flew a few feet, landed on a leaf, then flew off, leaving the mark.

"Melinoe looked back at her father. He had been wearing a navy T-shirt so she hadn't seen the stain at first, but now she did. She also saw that there was a slash on his neck, a gaping wound still bleeding. She ran to him. Shook him. Shouted at him over the music. Touched his face. In her growing panic she never remembered those next minutes with him, but she said it took her a long time to realize or accept that he was dead. And then she noticed that behind her father, partially obscured by a group of potted palms and other foliage, there were two more bloody bodies: her stepmother, Lynda, and Serge. Melinoe tried to rouse them too but couldn't. By then she was covered in her father's blood, and when she ran toward the greenhouse exit to get help, she added her own bloody prints to those of the butterflies. Her hands and face—from where she tried to wipe away her tears—were stained too. When she ran into the house—incoherent with panic—the housekeeper thought she had been hurt. For a few minutes, she'd tried to tend to her until she understood what Melinoe was saying.

"It was a murder-suicide. Serge's mother, who had severe emotional issues, came to believe her new husband of eight months, Melinoe's father, was trying to seduce Serge. In a rage she attacked Cypros with a knife. Serge tried to intervene and was hurt. When Lynda saw her son bleeding out, she assumed she'd killed him and then killed herself.

"There were many who cheered Cypros's death because he'd been ruthless and uncaring in business. He often bought up companies and stripped them of their employees as he merged them into larger entities. If economies required people lose their jobs—so be it, he always said. Cypros presented a cold exterior. But to Melinoe, he'd been warm and loving. Trying to be twice the parent since she'd lost her mother at such a young age. Her 'Poppa,' she used to call him."

Malachai had paused, then continued. "Serge's wound would have been fatal had Melinoe not saved his life by finding him when she did. And so at sixteen she and Serge, who was a year older, became orphans and formed a deep and complicated bond.

"I could tell from the way Melinoe told me the story, from how she talked about her life pre-accident and post, that she integrated her father's personality into her own. I think what attracted me to her at first was her coldness. She seemed so impervious. It was a challenge to the therapist in me. I'd never met anyone as calculating and capable of control. All traits I shared with her, I'm afraid, but she had perfected them. I was in awe of her power over her feelings. Frightened too, I think, to look at her and see myself. I have often thought since then that my need to seduce her, to find some tenderness in her, was a search to find it in myself."

In all the years Jac had known him, Malachai had never revealed himself to her like this. And Jac wondered why he was doing it now.

"You were in love with her," she said.

"I was."

Jac thought that she had never heard two words spoken with so much sadness before. Malachai didn't usually elicit empathy from her—he did now.

"I'm sorry," she whispered into the phone as if she were offering condolences upon hearing that someone had died.

He laughed softly and, understanding the tone in her words, responded.

"I was a fool. But I supposed every man has to play the fool at least once in his life. She is a magnificent narcissist, Jac. A marble statue not quite a woman. I think I believed I could play Pygmalion and, to overuse a cliché, melt the ice in her veins. Instead she turned my blood cold." He was quiet for a moment.

"She's asked me to take over and finish what Robbie started," Jac said. "To work on the collection of breaths and see if I can re-create the elixir that is supposed to be used with them to allow the souls to reincarnate."

"Wouldn't it be something if it could?"

"Do you think it's even possible?"

"I was willing to spend my savings to buy that collection and test the theory. If it is possible to absorb a soul—to host it—to reincarnate some-one—it would be . . . If it's possible we could preserve souls. Not just access them but save them

149

and then reanimate them so people could fully remember their previous lives . . . what an amazing thing that would be." He was breathless. "Are you considering taking on the project?"

"No, but . . ." She hesitated for a moment as she pictured the test tube she'd hidden in her bedroom where no one would stumble on it. She hadn't been able to scatter his ashes—how could she discard the container that might actually contain his soul?

"What?"

"Robbie was so immersed in the work he was doing with Melinoe, he had the nurse who was here with us save his own dying breath," Jac said.

"He did?"

"He did, and I have it . . ." She paused . . . seeing Robbie . . . her beautiful vibrant brother . . . so ill . . . She shook her head trying to make the image disappear. "But don't worry, I'm not going to accept Melinoe's offer."

"I wasn't going to ask you to refuse her," Malachai said.

"You weren't?"

"No, I think you should accept."

Jac was shocked. She'd fully expected him to warn her off the idea. "You're always so worried about me, though. As if I'm one of the figures you collect—that someone might jostle the shelf and break me."

"I'm not worried about you spending time with

her. Melinoe's not a murderer, Jac. She's just a thief."

When she got off the phone, Jac was puzzled. Last year he'd tried to talk her out of taking on a project on the Isle of Jersey for her TV show, but she'd gone anyway. Was Malachai using reverse psychology now so that she wouldn't go? She wouldn't put it past him. As much as she loved him, she wasn't oblivious to the fact that he was manipulative and Machiavellian.

But wouldn't this elixir be critical to his studies? Wouldn't he sacrifice anything to get it?

Now there were two puzzles. What did Malachai really want her to do? And if she went back to Belle Fleur, what was she going to find?

Jac needed to clear her head. She shrugged on a jacket and left the house. It had rained while she was on the phone, so the streets were wet and there was a fresh smell in the air that suggested spring was coming. She stuck her hands in her pockets, walked the two blocks to the Quai Voltaire and then over the bridge and through the entrance to the Louvre. Here kings and queens—including Queen Catherine—had lived for centuries before it was conscripted into a museum. Turning left, she walked into the Tuileries.

It was five thirty and dusk was falling, but Jac wasn't alone. There were people milling about, walking their dogs, strolling with baby carriages or young children. Others hurrying across the park. There was a group of teenagers in soccer clothes, sweaty and high on the excitement of the game they'd obviously just played. And then there were the lovers. She avoided looking at them. Or tried to. But Jac was always drawn to watching lovers in Paris. She believed that it was an homage to the city to declare your love, and that if you lived in Paris and you were in love—whether you were seventeen or seventy—that it was your duty to show your passion. That it gave you entry to a different kind of city. Almost like a magic ticket that allowed you to leave the Paris of traffic and noise and tourists and enter into the city of lights and sights and scents and for a time exist on another plane. Jac had never fallen in love in Paris. But once, for a week, she'd been there with Griffin. When he had come to help Jac find Robbie. They hadn't enacted all the rituals, though. They'd never kissed on the bridge. Never walked hand in hand through the gardens. Hadn't strolled by the Seine at night and listened to strains of "La Vie en Rose" that played on the sightseeing boats cruising the river. They'd never bought one of those silly locks and locked their love on one of the bridges.

Their passion had erupted in the dark. In the few minutes stolen between searching for Robbie, bursts of momentary escape from worry.

By the time Jac reached the allée of chestnut trees, there were fewer people in the park and twilight had descended. She kept walking, hearing the gravel crunch underfoot. All sounds of the traffic were muffled, and there was a stillness in the park that was reassuring. Until she realized someone was following her.

Chapter 14

This area of the Tuileries was deserted. Jac kept moving at a steady pace, hoping the sense someone was following her was all her imagination. She didn't dare turn around. She passed through the outdoor seating areas of two cafés that were open only during the day. Now just empty chairs and tables. She kept walking, not changing her pace. It could just be someone heading in the same direction. But what if it wasn't? What if this was someone from the Chinese Mafia? . . . What if this was her reckoning?

Damn, she was supposed to have let Marcher know when she was coming back so he could have her watched, and she'd forgotten.

She pulled out her cell phone, found Marcher's name on her favorites list and tapped it. Marcher had said it was unlikely the vendetta against her brother would extend to her, but . . .

"Jac? Are you all right?"

"I'm in the Tuileries—"

"You were in Barbizon," he said in surprise. "You were supposed to—" He broke off, suddenly concerned. "What is it?"

She lowered her voice. "I think I'm being followed."

"Where are you exactly?"

She described her location.

"Okay, I'm going to put you on hold, but keep talking as if I'm still here, talk to me as if I'm your mother or your boyfriend . . . inconsequential things, tell me what you did today."

For the next few minutes Jac did as she was told, kept talking about nothing to the silence. And then he was back.

"There is a gendarme less than sixty seconds away across from the Crillon Hotel. Turn right and start to walk toward the Rue de Rivoli exit. Don't hurry and don't stop talking to me. Be animated. I want you to argue with me, fairly loudly."

"What?"

"Please, Jac. If you are being followed, I don't want him to think you've noticed him. So here we go. How dare you question where I was tonight? Argue with me, Jac. Pretend you are fighting with your boyfriend. Accuse me of lying to you."

Jac did as she was told. "You're lying to me," she said, raising her voice slightly.

"I am not. I was at work. You are so suspicious."

"You weren't at the office. I called and your assistant said you had left hours ago."

"She was wrong. Haven't you ever heard of someone being wrong before?"

It was a surreal conversation.

"Are you telling me that you just flat out don't believe me?" Marcher shouted into her ear.

"Yes!" Jac raised her voice too.

"You have to!"

She saw the policeman now—he was only about thirty feet away. She felt the knot of fear inside her begin to unclench, but the adrenaline that was running through her veins didn't stop pumping.

"That's the worst thing to do," Jac said. "Never tell me what I have to do. You just make me want to do the opposite. Don't you understand that?"

In other circumstances Jac would have laughed—it was what she had just been wondering about Malachai. In pretending to have a conversation, she had, out loud, explained one of the guiding principles, right or wrong, of her life. She had always done the opposite of what people expected of her. Everyone had thought she'd be a perfumer, but she became a mythologist. The TV show had been a success and people had expected her to ramp it up and take it to the next level. She'd kept it small. Griffin wanted her to fight for him. She'd walked away. Last year, Malachai begged her not to go to the Isle of Jersey searching for Druid ruins. She decided searching was exactly what she needed to do.

"Go up to the policeman and tell him your

boyfriend is in your house and you are afraid to go home alone," Marcher told her.

She did.

The policeman nodded. "You're all right, Mademoiselle L'Etoile. The man who was walking behind you turned left when you turned right. He's gone now."

Jac looked. There was a woman walking a Maltese dog. A father and son riding bicycles. An elderly man with a cane making his way down the path.

"Jac?" It was Marcher on the phone.

She told him what the policeman had told her.

"Let me speak to him," Marcher said.

Jac handed the policeman the phone. He listened for a few minutes and then handed the phone back to her.

"Officer Passey is going to escort you into the Crillon," Marcher said. "I'm getting in my car now and will pick you up there in twenty minutes. Go to the bar, have a cognac. I'll call when I'm out front."

As Jac walked with the policeman across the street, toward the hotel where she'd once had breakfast with Griffin, she thought it was an odd coincidence that she was feeling just as panicked now as the last time she'd been here. Eighteen months ago they had been trying to find Robbie and keep him safe; now he was gone, and she was the one who might be in danger. Suddenly her fear gave way to anger. Anger that Robbie had died. That she was alone. That she was floundering. That Malachai might be manipulating her. That her life had become all about dreams and visions and sadness and loss and talking to ghosts.

Or had it always been like that?

Jac ordered the cognac. While the bartender poured it into a lovely crystal glass, she played with the scarlet cord tied around her wrist. He placed the glass in front of her. As she took a sip and felt the burn and then the warmth, she examined her surroundings. In the mid-eighteenth century King Louis XV had commissioned this building to house government offices. Benjamin Franklin had concluded the French-American treaty that recognized the Declaration of Independence here. Everywhere in Paris there was history built on history. Nothing ever died. It was transformed and transmuted. Like Robbie had said about people's lives. She wasn't sure if she was remembering him saying it—or if he was whispering it to her again, here in the bar.

Energy can't die, Jac. It can only be transformed. And our souls are energy. So when we die, that spirit that is us is transformed.

Jac wanted to transform. She wanted to stop trying to escape her own past and instead finally face it and fight it and find out what it was and come to terms with it and then move on.

She knew it then. Like it or not, finishing what

157

Robbie had started was something she was going to have to do. It was the only way to truly leave the past and move on, and moving on was the only way she was going to have a life.

Her phone rang a few minutes later, and Jac was surprised to see she'd finished her cognac without realizing it. She left a twenty-euro note on the bar and walked out to the street in front of the hotel.

Marcher was waiting for her in his car.

"You feel okay?" he asked when she was seated with the door shut.

She nodded. "Yes, I'm fine. Did you find the man who was following me?"

"No. I had two men near the park," Marcher said as he pulled out and entered the traffic on the Rue de Rivoli. "One focused on you, the other on the people around you. There were three men and a woman in the vicinity. My officer couldn't identify which of them might have been following you."

"I don't suppose any of them were Chinese?"

"That would be too easy, wouldn't it? If the Triad is actually keeping tabs, the last thing they'd do is use someone identifiable. I don't think it's them. There still hasn't been any chatter that Robbie's death was deliberate."

"But they were pleased that he died."

"They were *appeased* that he died."

Jac shivered. "Robbie didn't mean to hurt that man. It was an accident."

"I know. And they might even know. But the fact is Robbie was responsible for François Lee's death and he was a high-ranking member of the Chinese Mafia."

"As you said yourself, it's not likely that they are after me, is it?"

"No, it's not."

"So I'm just being paranoid."

"I wouldn't say that. You are reacting as you should. But after tomorrow you won't have to. I was going to call you tonight to tell you, but here you are. Tomorrow we are announcing that we are closing the investigation into your brother's death—"

"You can't!" Jac interrupted.

Marcher held up his hand. "We are announcing we are closing it and declaring that we accept that it was death by natural causes—strange causes, but natural causes."

"Even though you don't really believe that?"

"It doesn't matter what I believe. There is no evidence at all that his death was deliberate. There is no evidence that he came in contact with anyone who might have found a way to infect him with what he had. Your perfume workshop was clean."

"Then why are you still unsure?"

Marcher shrugged. "I'm a suspicious man. It's my nature."

They were on the Left Bank now, driving down

Saint-Germain toward the cross street that would take them to the L'Etoile residence.

"What should I do?"

"Go on with your life, Jac. Be cautious but not afraid. We are monitoring the Triad. We have an excellent man on the inside. If we hear anything, you will be the first to know."

"I might leave Paris for a few weeks," she said.

"You don't need to run away."

"I'm not. Robbie left some unfinished business, and I think I'm the one who needs to finish it."

At home, she called Malachai. When he said he thought she was making the right choice, the excitement in his voice was real. Reassured, Jac telephoned Melinoe, telling her that she was accepting her offer and making plans to drive down the next day.

And then she decided she needed to make a second call—in spite of all her misgivings and cowardice. If she was going to take on Robbie's work, she needed all available information.

Jac's fingers started to tremble when she scrolled down the list of names in her phone. Her insides started to flutter. She tapped the call button, and when she heard his voice on the other end, she felt a rush of heat.

"Griffin, it's Jac."

"Hello." His deep velvety voice that sluiced through her like warm honey. Damn. Just hearing

him always did this to her. Despite everything—
her mourning, her fear, her anger—she felt the
first stirrings of arousal. Just from his voice. Just
from hearing him say hello. Would she ever break
the spell this man had over her? Ever figure out
what subterranean connection there was between
them? How could he turn on the switch in her
brain that sent her endorphins rushing, made her
breasts tingle and her womb throb all with just a
hello?

"Jac?"

She realized she hadn't spoken.

"I'm sorry. Did I disturb you?"

"No, I'm just sitting here on the couch,
reading."

"You're home? I didn't mean to bother you at
home." Jac felt her cheeks flush. The last thing
she'd wanted to do was call him at home. She'd
thought it was his office number she'd called. Was
his wife next to him? Was he sitting with his
daughter? She felt ill. She'd never allowed herself
to imagine this scene, and now she had intruded
on it.

"I thought you'd be at work. It's only three in
the afternoon."

"Actually it's nine at night."

She was confused. "Where are you?" For a
second she wondered if he were somewhere in
Paris. That he'd known she was going to need him
and had already come to her. Magical thinking,

she knew, but they used to be like that with each other. She'd often just have to think of him calling and he'd call. The connection between them had scared him, but to her it had been proof of the rightness of their connection.

"I'm in Egypt."

"I—I assumed you were in New York."

"I haven't been in New York in a while."

She was surprised to hear that. When she'd last seen him, he'd said he only went on digs during the fall and winter because it wasn't good for his marriage or his daughter for him to spend more time than that away.

"Have you all moved to Egypt?" Jac knew she was asking more questions than she should, but she couldn't stop herself.

"No. Therese and Elsie are in New York."

Jac couldn't bring herself to ask the next logical question. Had the reconciliation failed? If she asked and he said yes, she'd have to deal with that, and she wasn't sure she could.

She had always wanted to be with him—more than anyone she had ever met in her life. Felt that she belonged with him in a way that defied all logic. She was embarrassed by how much she had longed for him and how much of her life she'd spent fantasizing about him. Hated him for how deeply he had gotten inside her head and, to use a most apt cliché, under her skin. Griffin had imprinted himself on her. She'd discovered her sexuality with him. He was her first lover, her only real love.

The first time they'd been together, she was seventeen. They'd been in her bedroom in her aunt's house. Dusk was turning to night. After they'd made love, he'd told her the story about the two halves of Plato's whole.

"Humans were originally created with four arms, four legs and a head with two faces. Fearing their power, Zeus split them into two separate parts, condemning them to spend their lives in search of their other halves. We're each other's halves . . ." he'd said.

"Âmes Sœurs." She'd translated the phrase from French. "Soul mates," she whispered.

That picture was replaced by a more recent image of Griffin on a stretcher, being rushed into the hospital in Paris. Blood dripping from his fingers, leaving a trail on the sidewalk. His voice interrupted her thoughts.

"Jac, are you all right? I've called and called since Robbie's died. I wanted to talk to you."

"I know. I'm sorry. I couldn't . . . Listen, I have a favor to ask you," she said, not wanting to stay on the phone longer than she had to. It was just too damn painful.

"Anything."

Were all the implications she thought she heard in that one word really there? Or was it her wishful thinking? Her heart beat harder. Be with

163

me, she wanted to blurt out. But instead she told him, in unemotional, even-toned words, why she had called.

"Were you helping Robbie translate some inscriptions? Do you have them?"

"I was and I do."

"Great. I've decided that I need to finish what he started and I need to know what the writings say. I need to be the one to do this before the woman who owns them brings someone else in to do it."

"I'd already started working on them but stopped when . . . Robbie got sick. Let me get back to them. Where are you? How can I reach you?"

And so it begins, she thought. Yet again, we are connected by Robbie. Almost, Jac thought, as if Robbie had planned this reunion between her and Griffin as he lay dying so that she would have to reach out to the only person who might actually offer some solace and healing.

But if Robbie had forgotten, she hadn't. Griffin was also the one person she shouldn't have anything to do with. She was poison for him.

Chapter 15

THE PRESENT
WEDNESDAY, MARCH 19
BARBIZON, FRANCE

"We're putting you in a different suite than the one your brother had," Serge said as he led Jac up the château's grand staircase.

"Thank you," Jac said. "That's very thoughtful."

Actually Jac would have much preferred to stay at the inn in town and drive up to the château every day, but René le Florentin had lived here in these rooms, walked these halls, looked out at this view. And she felt she should forgo her need for privacy to absorb as much of the atmosphere of this place as she could while she worked on the collection.

"Here we are." Serge opened the door into a soft lemon-colored sitting room decorated in pale-yellow silk and light blue-and-yellow curtains that pooled on the thick carpet. A beautiful bouquet of yellow tulips and blue delphiniums graced the desk. Large windows looked out on a small lake surrounded by forest. One door led to a black-and-white-marbled bathroom. A second door opened into a bedroom.

"I'll let you settle in. I'll be downstairs in the library if you need anything," Serge said and left the room, shutting the door quietly after him.

The bedroom contained a curtained king-size bed and a window seat filled with pale blue-and-yellow needlepoint pillows. A perfect place to curl up and read, Jac thought, though she didn't think there would be much time for doing that. Her stay didn't have an end date, but Jac had packed for no more than a week.

Barbizon was certainly within commuting distance to Paris—an hour each way without traffic—and it would be easy enough to drive home if she needed anything. But she didn't want to go before the week was up. Jac needed a break from her paranoid fantasies that Robbie had been killed and that his killer was now after her. The episode in the park, she now thought, after several days of deliberation, had to be her imagination on overdrive. But as she unpacked, she could still remember her fear. She was too susceptible. Too fragile. She needed some distraction. She hadn't felt her brother's presence in Paris. And that had bothered her too. The last time she'd sensed him was here. And that was another reason to come back.

Jac opened her suitcase. The first thing she took out was a travel candle and lit it. This was her ritual whenever she arrived at a new place. Infusing her surroundings with the scent of

166

L'Etoile's signature Noir settled her. As the fragrance filled the corners and seeped into the fabrics, it transformed a strange room into a familiar one. With so little constancy in her life, and so much of her family gone, now more than ever, scent was important.

She sniffed the air and returned to unpacking. Jac hung up black jeans and a black skirt. Her grandmother's vintage black Chanel jacket—which went everywhere with her and was the most versatile piece of clothing she owned.

The bouclé jacket, with the gold chain stitched into the hem to make sure the jacket hung correctly, was her staple and signature.

"Always buy the very best, Jac, even if it means buying far less. Trust me, you'll treasure each piece if it is a classic and well made," Grand-mère had told her.

Smoothing out a black cashmere sweater and then refolding it, Jac thought about how much of her style came from her grandmother. How little from Audrey, her mother, who'd never abandoned the hippie look of her American youth and never adapted to French fashion.

Done with unpacking, Jac went downstairs to the room Robbie had turned into a workroom. She'd brought all the books and papers back with her and now rearranged them on the desk.

Once that was completed, she sat down at the makeshift perfumer's organ Robbie had created and scanned the four dozen bottles of essences and absolutes. And then her eyes rested on the armoire. Melinoe had given Jac the key, and now she opened it and looked at the dozen silver bells. Each with its odd combination of letters and symbols.

She shivered with excitement and knew this was just what Robbie must have felt at the prospect of solving this puzzle. Yes, it was an astonishing proposition made even more complex by the mechanics of the concept. If there was a formula to reanimating the breaths, how would it work? Would the soul of the departed become one with the person who inhaled the breath? Or did you have to find an infant in which to implant the soul?

The Renaissance perfumer must have made notes—every perfumer did. Somewhere René had to have left behind a record of what he was doing . . . what he was thinking.

Melinoe said none of her research had yielded any specifics, and she had been counting on Robbie's intuitive skills and the translations.

How far had Robbie gotten in his understanding of the process?

Jac had not yet read Robbie's notes, though she'd brought them home with her. She'd sat in the studio, his notebook in her hands. Stared down at it. Examined it. But had been frightened to open it and see his handwriting. She was too worried that it would bring on a fresh spate of missing him.

That was before she'd decided to come here and try to finish what he'd begun. Now she had no choice. She had to know where his experiments had started, where they'd taken him and where he'd left off.

Robbie's handwriting slanted to the right and was difficult to read. Her brother, who was so aware of beauty, wrote with a spidery, narrow hand. His style was very similar to their father's. Jac wondered if his handwriting was inherited or if Robbie had copied it—emulating him just the way Jac had changed her handwriting completely in the tenth grade to emulate her English teacher Mrs. Wein.

Rather than being upset, she felt closer to Robbie and missed him less as she read through his first two pages of notes. He'd listed the ingredients he'd brought to La Belle Fleur with notations about the history of each and when it had been introduced to perfume making. Clearly, he'd been attempting to re-create a laboratory from the Middle Ages. Most of the items were familiar and still used. Sandalwood, spikenard, frankincense, myrrh, violet, mint, civet, rose, lavender and musk. A few were more obscure like white poppy and black poppy, goose blood and sap from a cherry tree.

But there were no ideas as to what to do with them or how an elixir might work. Had Robbie only gotten as far as reading ancient texts about sixteenth-century perfumers while waiting for Griffin's translations? She couldn't call and ask him and felt a flurry of frustration that there was so little to go on and anger that his notes were so spare.

She got up and inspected the bells. Lifting the first, she exposed the pale-blue bottle. That wasn't what interested her now. It was the bell she wanted to understand. Running her fingers over the symbols, she wondered if this was nothing but another Voynich manuscript. The centuries-old book had been baffling scientists and historians for years. Written in an unknown language, it was, some believed, an ancient code not yet deciphered, while others were convinced it was nothing but a hoax.

Jac studied the symbols, shapes and words, some clearly Greek, Hebrew, or Egyptian, others unrecognizable. The thought that Griffin was working on them now—perhaps at this very moment—made her breathe in sharply.

As an ancient language scholar, he'd be fascinated by these. He was an Egyptologist, an expert on the Book of the Dead, but had an almost supernatural ability with other ancient languages, including the Semitic language of the Akkadians and Babylonians of ancient Mesopotamia as well as Aramaic and the Sumerian and Ugaritic languages.

"Have you settled in?" Melinoe was at the door.

She was wearing a flowing tunic of claret velvet with black leggings and high-heeled suede boots. Stacks of ruby and diamond bands adorned her fingers. Ancient-looking earrings in the shape of exotic birds with ruby eyes hung down past her chin. Her lips were the same color as the tunic. As she crossed the room to see what Jac was doing at the desk, her wrist-fulls of enameled bangle bracelets jingled. The cloud of gardenia-and-pepper perfume that emanated from her was too strong but still incredibly appealing and very sensual.

She moved like a cat, Jac thought. Part Chimera, part Siren, part feline, she could play the heroine in so many of the Greek tragedies Jac had read.

"Yes, my room is lovely. Thank you for the flowers."

Melinoe pulled up a chair and sat down. "I want you to be comfortable here. Anything you need, just ask me or Serge or any of the help." She gestured to the armoire. "*Anything* you need. If you can help unlock the secret to how these work, there's nothing I won't do for you."

"Well, the first step is getting the translations, and I spoke to the man who's working on them, and he's sending me some preliminary findings later today. I was looking through my brother's notes, and there's not much there. Did he tell you anything about the progress he was making?"

"Nothing in particular, no."

"Before Robbie, had you shown the bells to many other people? Did you get any other opinions? Anything in writing?"

She shook her head. "I'm afraid I've been a bit paranoid about them since I bought them. When Sotheby's put them up for sale, they didn't garner much attention and I wanted to keep it that way." She paused, then leaned forward, as if she were going to share a secret with Jac. "Do you believe in signs?"

Jac flashed on Malachai. He always insisted that there were no coincidences. That everything that seemed to be coincidental was really a sign of synchronicity. Her brother believed that too. "I don't think I do, but Robbie certainly did."

"I have an aunt who is an astrologer . . ." Melinoe said. "She's been reading my cards all my life, and I've always followed her advice. My father didn't. If he had, he might not have died . . ." Melinoe paused. She was worrying the heavy gold snake ring on her right forefinger. Jac had noticed the jeweled serpent with its glinting ruby eyes the first time she'd been at the château too.

Melinoe continued: "It was my aunt who told me not to try to solve the puzzle of the bell jars until I was able to buy this house and move in. She said I would not be able to find the answers I was looking for anywhere but here and only when I was ready to hear them."

Jac had studied the ancient skill of reading charts and the lives of the great astrologers throughout history. She'd seen amazing monuments at Stonehenge and on the Isle of Jersey, and others scattered through the rest of the United Kingdom and the Middle East. These mystic arts were as old as recorded time and still today, no one completely understood them.

"And so you were able to refrain from doing any research until you bought, then renovated the house? Until you finally moved in? What patience," Jac asked.

Melinoe smiled, her two pointy eyeteeth giving her that slightly feral and ferocious look. She nodded toward the silver bell in Jac's hands. "You know that in ancient Greece the belief that the soul passes from body to body in one life after another dates back to an Orphic sect?"

Jac nodded. "Yes, and that Pythagoras followed their teachings and developed them even further."

"My family traces our roots to that sect."

Jac was fascinated. "How amazing that you can follow it back that far."

"I have a collection of ancient Greek sculpture, pottery and jewels that has been passed down from generation to generation, for over four thousand years. Surely I could be patient for four more."

Jac smiled. "Is the collection here?" she asked. She was itching to see it.

"Everything but this one piece of jewelry is in Greece . . ." She held out her hand. "If you'd like to examine the whole collection, I'd be happy to show you when we are done here in France. I read your book. There might be a story you'd want to tell based on what you find."

"Is it on display? In a museum?"

"No, it's in my villa."

Jac had a hundred questions. "I'd love to talk to you about it more."

"So would I. One of the things that makes me so pleased about you being here is not just that you are going to continue on with Robbie's work but that you are also a mythologist. I have a lot to discuss with you. Serge and I are hoping that you'll take your meals with us—even though you are more than welcome to have them brought to your room. In the evenings we often screen movies. Sometimes I have soirees, and friends come. I want you to feel free to join in all the festivities. Not feel as if you are an employee; you are our guest."

"That's very gracious of you." Jac was a loner, but she was also curious and smart enough to know that psychologically it wasn't a good idea for her to isolate herself now. She needed to be around people and stay busy. Continuing her brother's work might have been questionable to some—immersing herself in his world only kept him front and center in her mind—but she knew that she would be less despondent if she was busy doing what he wanted her to do.

And so Jac ate lunch that afternoon with Melinoe and Serge. The three of them all sat at one end of the table. Like his sister, Serge was well educated, and Jac found herself enjoying the conversation more than she'd expected. Despite that, there was something about the dynamic between the two of them that struck her as odd. What was she responding to? What was it about them? There was nothing obvious.

They appeared to be very different from each other. Melinoe spoke with a British accent, was exaggerated and theatrical, excessive and sensual, dark and mysterious. A pale woman with mother-of-pearl skin and the accessories and accoutrements of a modern-day princess.

Serge's accent was French, and he was quite gracious, charming and intellectual. But not as grand as his stepsister.

Yet they both seemed damaged. Jac assumed it was the tragedy they'd survived. She could almost imagine that she could see faint cracks where they each had been glued back together, and it was along those fault lines the two of them came together in order to survive.

After lunch, Melinoe retired to her office, and Serge asked Jac if she wanted to take a walk. "To see the grounds. In case you want to set off on your own, I thought you might like to know where you are."

She said she would, and he further asked if she rode. She said she did but wasn't well trained. Serge assured her that their mares were gentle, and she agreed to go on horseback. In the stable he pointed out Melinoe's horse, a large white stallion with the same self-assured look in his eye as his mistress had.

"He looks powerful and not altogether kind," she said.

"Good call. She named him Ares, and he lives up to his name."

"The Greek god of war, violence and courage."

Serge nodded in the horse's direction. "If anyone but Melinoe rides him, he's a monster. She's never broken a horse, but she manages to control them no matter what their temperament."

There was a tone of compassion in his voice. For Melinoe? Or, Jac wondered, for the horse?

Serge helped Jac mount the brown mare named Pandora, and then mounted his own, another white steed who was much gentler looking than his stepsister's horse. More beautiful too. He introduced her as Psyche.

Jac smiled. "All named for Greek gods and goddesses?"

"All of them," he said and then asked if she needed any reminders on which way to pull on the reins.

"No. I grew up riding with my uncle in Central Park on the weekends when I lived in New York. And we still go occasionally. I just meant I wasn't an expert."

"Okay then, let me show you the best part of La Belle Fleur," he said and took off at a gentle gallop.

They crossed a large emerald-green field, passed an apple orchard filled with trees whose trunks and limbs were ancient and gnarled, and then took a trail that wound deep into thick woods. It smelled so green and resinous Jac reacted instantly. This was a scent of mystery and magic to her, and had been since she was a child and their grandfather took her and Robbie to Médoc, where the family had a country home in the midst of a forest.

"It's about nine kilometers straight across to Fontainebleau castle," Serge was saying. "Two hundred and eighty square kilometers of woods."

Jac pulled back from her memories to return to the present.

"Five times the size of Manhattan," she said.

"Except, unlike your island, this forest is virtually uninhabited. Have you ever been here before?"

"No, but I've always meant to come and see it. I haven't spent a lot of time in France since I was a teenager."

"I thought you grew up in Paris."

"Until I was fourteen. And then I moved to New York."

"But Robbie talked about being a teenager in Paris." Serge was confused.

"After our mother killed herself . . ."

"Yes, I remember now, Robbie told me," Serge said sympathetically.

"I had some problems," Jac acknowledged, "and it seemed that New York, without all the memories, was a healthier environment for me. Robbie stayed in Paris."

"You say it as if it wasn't the right choice. Didn't you want to go?"

"I wanted to very much. I'm just not sure now that it was the best way to deal with the situation."

"Because it was running away?"

"That's what Robbie used to say," Jac said.

"Robbie and I talked a lot when he was here. He was worried about you. He said he wanted you to learn to stay in the moment."

Jac was angry at her brother. Probably for the first time since he'd died. If he wanted to be so open about his own life, that was fine, but she never liked it when he talked to other people about her.

"He said that he always wondered whether, if you'd stayed in Paris, you might have worked out your mother's death in a manner that was more beneficial."

Jac didn't say anything. She really wasn't sure how to respond. Before she could figure it out, he continued.

"Your brother loved you more than anyone . . ." Serge said. Hesitated. Then continued. "In the most wonderful way."

Jac wasn't angry anymore. Rather she was ineffably moved. For a few moments they rode on together in silence. And then, as if it were a refrain from a song repeating over and over in her mind, she heard his words again.

In the most wonderful way.

When *wouldn't* loving your sister—or your stepsister—be wonderful?

The horses approached a gigantic boulder.

"Let's stop here. I'd like to show you this," Serge said as he pulled his reins, and Jac followed.

They dismounted and approached the rounded stone that was easily twice as tall as she was.

"This is one of the famous Bleau boulders," he said.

Jac reached out to touch the rough stone that climbers came from all over to tackle.

Back on their horses, as they continued on, Serge told the history of the magical forest. "Until the mid-nineteenth century the area was virtually unmapped. Kings and noblemen hunted here, of course, but rumors and legends kept most people at bay. Even criminals who escaped from nearby prisons were frightened of what they might find and stayed away."

"Is it haunted? Are there monsters?" Jac asked.

"The legend I heard was about a monster—a giant predator who lived here and guarded his domain. As a result the forest and its thousands of caves remained untouched and uncharted for centuries."

"But some of them have been explored more recently—haven't I read that?"

"Yes, and the historians found prehistoric drawings dating back thirty thousand years."

"Do you know where those are?"

"I do. Melinoe is funding some of the ongoing archaeological research on a cave that's filled with cuneiforms that no one has been able to decipher yet. Some are simple lines etched into sandstone rock. Others are much more complex markings that suggest men who lived here were writing far before the year 3300 BCE, when man supposedly invented writing in Sumer."

Jac was fascinated. By the stories. By the purple shadows and dark-green leaves. By the loamy scents and the twists on the bridle path that suddenly revealed idyllic settings. She was familiar with how this forest had inspired first the Barbizon school of painters and later photographers. Had they defied the unfriendly spirits hiding here? Or just been oblivious to the spirits trying to chase them away? They couldn't have ignored the tension she was feeling in these woods. Their work was so tranquil. Or was she sensing what those artists had not?

"It's lovely, isn't it?" Serge asked as they rounded a corner and came upon a stream, some smaller boulders, and a copse of beech trees.

"Beautiful but disturbing."

"Really? Why do you find it disturbing?"

"I'm not sure."

But she was afraid she did have an idea of what was bothering her. It was the waves of an episode coming at her as if out of the darkest part of the forest. The metallic smell that presaged a hallucination seeping out of the bark on the trees.

Jac immediately went into survival mode, following her sanity commandments.

Silently, she intoned them now.

Take long, concentrated breaths. Count . . . two . . . three . . . four.

Jac inhaled. Counted . . . two . . . three . . . four. Did it again. And again.

Give yourself a task.

She tried to identify and name the trees and shrubs they were passing. Scotch pine. European beech. Juniper.

Take deep breaths. Concentrate.

It wasn't working . . . She was seeing a kind of double exposure . . . the present forest and a shimmer behind it; a parade of ghosts who'd passed through, from kings to princesses to peasants.

"Jac?"

"There's so much history here," she managed. "And sometimes I find the history of a place can be overwhelming." She hoped he'd accept her explanation. It was still an effort to focus, but she concentrated on the horse trotting beneath her. On a shaft of light breaking through tree branches. On Serge's profile.

It was working. The episode was passing.

She was surprised to realize Serge was talking, and she'd missed the first part of what he'd said. But she listened now.

". . . and I once saw an art gallery installation where the artist had painted flat cardboard cutouts of all the people who had walked in and out of the room in the last six months. You had to traverse through narrow paths between the facsimiles of the hundreds who had come and gone. It was a visual history of the room. All those people who had left nothing of themselves but the fact of their presence."

"That's exactly what I'm sensing—I wouldn't be surprised to see a nobleman from another century ride past us."

"I'm sure you could guess this given her other interests, but Melinoe is fascinated with time warps," he said.

There it was again . . . that timbre in his voice that fitted the way he had looked at Melinoe—no, gazed at her. Up till now Jac had thought it was awe. But now she guessed that it was lust. She heard it so clearly now in his tone. It was in every syllable of how he spoke her name. His voice deepened around the word, which slid out as if he were forming it carefully, feeling every syllable with his tongue.

Jac looked over at him. At how his hands caressed the leather reins. How his thighs strained against his pants. He was a vital, sensuous man. What was he doing living with Melinoe in a château in Barbizon?

"Do you live here all the time?" she asked.

"No, we travel quite a bit. There's a manor house outside of London, a house in Marrakesh, an apartment in New York City and a yacht that spends most of its time in Saint-Tropez. And of course the villa in Greece, Melinoe's father's family home."

"Do you have a big family?" She hoped she didn't sound as if she was prying.

"No. Just the two of us."

"Melinoe never had children?"

"Several marriages, but no children." Then he laughed, almost cruelly. "Her husbands were poor saps. None lasted long."

"Why's that?"

"They couldn't in the end, any of them, accept her conditions."

"That sounds ominous."

"I suppose it is. Some people think Melinoe is

a psychic vampire. Do you know the term? It's someone who sucks people dry, exhausts them emotionally. She has a knack for making men think she's inviting them on the adventure of their lifetimes." He laughed again. "I suppose it was ego . . . but each of her husbands thought he was the one who could tame her. She led them to believe that—to trap them. In the end, none of them lasted more than a couple of years. And when they left, each was quite damaged." He said that last part with sympathy.

No, Jac thought, it was more than sympathy; it was empathy.

"You make her sound like a character out of a nineteenth-century novel."

"You've met her—does that surprise you? Melinoe is not one woman. She is not one color. She's part of every era, every time. There is no one like her."

Jac felt his passion. His words, coming at her in the gloom of the forest, were somehow arousing her. Not that she wanted Serge, but she wanted a man to talk about her that way.

"Have you ever been married?" she asked.

"I've never left Melinoe."

It was a non sequitur. It didn't answer the question. Or maybe it did.

They had reached a large outcropping of rocks that appeared to form the entrance to a cave when Jac's horse let out a long whinny and stopped.

Following suit, Serge's horse did also. The two beasts stood pawing the ground and snorting.

"What is it?" Jac asked.

"I don't know. The horses don't seem to want to pass by these rocks."

"No, they don't. Should we see what's inside?"

Jac felt the pull of the rocks, of the entrance to the cave. She dismounted and tied the reins to a nearby tree. At the opening to the cave she peered in.

"I think this is one of the Neolithic sites you told me about. There are carvings in the wall. Odd shapes and symbols." She peered at them. Some were older than others. The very ancient ones were indecipherable, but there were pentagrams she recognized.

He got off his horse, tied her up and joined Jac.

Together the two stepped inside. The air was cooler here. She sniffed it. Rotten eggs. Reaching out, she traced the carvings with her fingers. Some were cut deeper into the stone than others, but all their edges were smooth. Jac had been on enough digs to know what she was feeling.

"Even the most recent etchings go back at least five hundred years," she said.

Taking another few steps, she went deeper into the cave. The scent grew stronger. The darkness became forbidding.

Jac was thinking about the pentagrams. Five hundred years ago royals had spent summers at

Fontainebleau, moving their whole court for a few months until they depleted the food and supplies in that castle and then moving on to the next. Catherine de Medici had been among them. And she was rumored to have dabbled in black magic.

The scent of sulfur was overwhelming now. It was a putrid smell often associated with the devil. Jac felt the all too familiar waving as air moved around her. What had happened in this cave?

Behind them, one of the horses whinnied again. Then snorted. The other joined in.

She and Serge both turned in time to see his horse jerk away with such force she broke the branch her reins were tied to and took off.

"What the hell?" Serge said as Jac's horse followed suit. He ran off after the horses but gave up quickly.

"They're too fast," he said as he returned. His face was flushed and he looked annoyed.

"I wonder if the sulfur frightened them? It has a lot of strange properties," Jac said.

"Do you use it in perfume?"

"No. It was sometimes incorporated into skin creams but never proved effective," Jac said. "Its most popular usage was in black magic to create protection and aid in breaking spells. They say the devil smells of sulfur."

"Maybe that's who scared away our ride back to the château." Serge smiled at her and then took out his phone. "Let me send a boy from the stables out looking for them. Do you want to walk back—we're only about a half hour away—or do you want someone to come get us with more horses?"

Jac had been looking back, toward the cave, thinking about the malevolence she'd sensed emanating from deep inside. "Sure, we can walk . . . That's fine."

He finished with his call, then looked around. "It shouldn't be hard to get back. Once I figure out . . ." He peered to the right, then to the left. "I have to admit I'm a little turned around and not sure where we are, but it can't be too far. We were headed south and followed a fairly straight path . . . We just need to make sure we're heading north . . ."

Jac pulled her phone out of her jeans pocket. "I have a compass on here." She clicked on the application. "Don't worry. I get lost a lot, but never stay lost for long."

But that wasn't really true, she thought. She'd lost part of herself when Griffin first left, and she'd never really found it again.

Chapter 16

"Would you like a glass of wine?" Serge asked when they returned to the château.

Much to Jac's relief, it had been a leisurely walk without anymore disturbing occurrences. Her experience at the mouth of the cave had been unnerving to say the least.

She said that would be perfect.

"Feel like experimenting? I was thinking of visiting the cellar and picking something unusual."

Remembering the first time she'd seen the cellar and smelled its provocative and curious scent, she asked if she could accompany him.

"I'd be happy for the company," he said.

They went down the narrow marble staircase that led from the kitchen to the underground rooms. As they approached the wine cellar, Jac could smell it. Inside the musty ancient room, she inhaled, trying to pinpoint the direction of the scent. The odor was emanating from a section of shelves to the right of center against the back wall.

As Jac walked toward the shelves, her mind flashed on Griffin. But why here? Why now? And then she felt the cold pinpricks of a hallucination coming on. What was down here that triggered them?

The closer she got to the wall, the stronger the sensations. They were pulling her like a magnet to metal. Her curiosity was an actual force. She needed to know what was just hovering on the edges of her mind . . . a story . . . tantalizing her . . . a past that demanded to be discovered. And for only the second time in her life, she didn't fight but invited the images.

Then she saw a familiar man standing just where

Serge was now. Like the two other glimpses she'd had of him, he was once again dressed in dark pantaloons and a tunic shot with gold thread. He smelled like no one Jac had ever smelled. So alluring . . . so seductive . . . a scent that embraced her . . . pulled her closer . . . that made her want just to stand here forever inhaling him.

But when the man reached out toward one of the bottles, his hand went in between spaces. He manipulated something, and the whole shelf of bottles swung out like a door. And inside was . . .

Jac blinked as the room around her came back into focus.

"Are you all right?" Serge asked.

From similar experiences that she'd had since childhood, Jac knew that in reality almost no time had passed. While she felt as if she'd lost minutes—sometimes hours or even days—only seconds had ticked by. In the past she'd asked those around her—her brother, Malachai and Griffin—what they saw when she entered into her fugue states. All they reported was that she'd had a faraway look in her eye and seemed distracted, not always hearing them when they spoke to her.

"Yes, I'm fine." She didn't know him well enough to explain, so she just said, "I had an odd kind of déjà vu."

He nodded. "Your brother told me about that."

Jac was startled. Robbie had talked to Serge about this too?

"You're surprised? I'm sorry. Robbie told me in the context of how difficult it had been for him to watch you suffer and how frustrated he was that he couldn't help you find relief. He was so pleased that you finally seemed to be coming to terms with your abilities. He told me that he hoped one day you'd see it as a real gift—and even pursue it."

In the forest, she had been angry at Robbie for talking about her to someone she didn't even know. But now it was more like being given a gift of flowers. She was hearing Robbie say those words to her from across time and distance.

Jac cleared her throat. "Thank you for telling me," she said.

"He was very special."

She nodded.

Serge was silent for a few seconds. Jac almost reached out for him, so palpable was his sorrow. But then the moment was over. He gestured to the many shelves and extended his hand.

"Reds here, whites here. Champagnes there. What's your pleasure?"

But Jac gravitated to a section he hadn't pointed out. She walked over to the stack of shelves where the very old wines were, and then it was as if someone else took over her hand. She was reaching past the bottles. Stretching behind them to the back wall, where she searched for . . . and felt . . . yes . . . she felt it . . . a knot in the wood. Ordinary.

Nothing you'd notice unless you knew that if you . . . Jac gripped it. Twisted. Nothing happened. She exerted more strength. Twisted it . . . and finally felt the first bit of give. She took her hand out, shook away the pain, and then tried again using all her might. It turned with a loud creak, and she felt the release of the mechanism. Then, with almost no effort, she was able to swing that whole section of the shelves out.

"Incredible. You just discovered a fully functional door!" Serge said.

As she opened it, the faint scent that she'd smelled came pouring out. Light from the cellar illuminated what lay beyond. What appeared to be a Renaissance perfumer's laboratory came into view. As Jac took in the alembics and infusion devices, bottles of essences and measuring tools, she felt a surge of excitement.

The room was perhaps seven feet long and about five feet wide. A narrow closet tucked hidden and locked away from prying eyes.

Behind her Serge exclaimed, "How amazing. Jac, how did you know it was there?"

She shrugged. How to explain? She couldn't. Not really.

"I honestly don't know."

"Can you tell from the tools how old all this is?"

Jac walked into the room, careful not to touch anything. Layers of dust covered everything. She'd seen pristine finds before, and this appeared to be one of them. It had been hundreds of years since anyone had been in here.

"I'd guess sixteenth century. Partially from the tools, but also because it's hidden away. Alchemy and perfume and the poisoner's arts were dangerous occupations in the 1500s," she said. "In the Louvre, René le Florentin had a laboratory that connected to the queen's chambers via a secret staircase. It's well documented. But it's curious he'd have one in his own house. Why would he have to be so cautious here?"

She sat down at the perfumer's organ, with its scarred and worn wood, and felt a presence all around her. Not Robbie, not this time. It was the stranger she'd seen opening the door a few minutes ago. Her guide to this place. A wave of sadness and loss overwhelmed her. Then, just as quickly, scents rose up and soothed her as they engulfed her in their familiarity.

"I've seen drawings of alchemical laboratories like this in a book my grandfather had. Alchemy was at the very crossroads of where magic and science met, the main effort of learned men—and some women—who believed if they could come up with a formula to turn base metals to gold, they could also find the formula for the secret of life . . . for immortality. Many other major discoveries were made while they searched for their holy grail. They found formulas for lifesaving and healthful waters, lotions, elixirs."

Jac examined the floor-to-ceiling shelves at one end of the room. The man who had worked in this laboratory had been a highly evolved perfumer and student of alchemical arts. All the accoutrements were here, alembics in marvelous amoebic shapes, burners, funnels, plates, bottles, tools. Everything in its place as if René le Florentin had just left moments ago.

Jac leaned forward, inspecting a row of bottles, their ingredients written in Latin in a very florid hand.

"How did I not notice this place?" Serge was examining the doorway. "When we were doing the renovation, we inspected the foundations and found them in such good condition we didn't have to do any shoring up. We verified the shelves' reliability by removing wine bottles from random sections. There wasn't any rot at all. Everything checked, and so we went on. So much of the château required work, why create more where none was needed? There was nothing to suggest that there was a false wall on this side."

Jac was only half aware of what he was saying. She'd found a leather-bound book. Worn, cracked and covered with a thick layer of dust. On the cover, in gold leaf, was a complex insignia with flourishes and curlicues, but as she stared at it, the initials "RB" revealed themselves among the decorative coils.

Very carefully, she lifted the cover. Jac was

staring at notes written by René Bianco, also know as René le Florentin. She was looking down at words, numbers and symbols that no one had gazed upon for almost five hundred years.

Chapter 17

MARCH 19, 1573
BARBIZON, FRANCE

Nine years after Catherine rescued me from prison and brought me to France, I was climbing the secret staircase cut into the rock walls of the Louvre palace. I trod each step carefully. It was difficult to navigate those narrow steps even when I was empty-handed. They were slivers of footholds carved in ancient times. How long ago? It was hard to know, but the palace had housed royalty since the year 1055.

From my laboratory on the ground floor, there were thirty-three steps circling up, with a stone handrail also carved out of rock. The angle of the spiral had made me dizzy at first, but I'd learned not to look up or down when I traversed it. Just to keep moving.

The upper landing was no more than an outcropping of rock facing a thick door—rough-hewn on the staircase side, beautifully finished on the other. With the tray that I held, it was impossible to open. Its huge handle was a wrought-iron circle. You needed to pull it out a bit and then twist, and it took both hands. There was barely enough room on the landing for the tray and my feet, but I put my burden down gingerly, opened the door, retrieved the tray and then entered.

The chamber was lit with sweet-smelling candles, Her Highness's favorite. The hearth was lit and flames danced in welcome. I sniffed wine and cakes.

"How good of you to come, René," Catherine said.

I forced a smile. *Merde*! I thought the princess would be alone except for the lady-in-waiting who accompanied her always, but she wasn't. Cosimo Ruggieri sat beside her at a round table in the center of the room. From the expression on Ruggieri's face, the astrologer was no more pleased to see me than I was to see him.

Ruggieri was an unhealthy companion for the princess. A man to be feared. A man who sought power in underhanded ways. And the one man at court who I wanted to destroy.

Catherine smiled back at me, but her expression didn't convey any joy. She looked tired and worn out. Lately there was always sadness in her eyes, but today it even seemed to have fully displaced the determination that usually shone there too.

Nine years ago, I had accompanied Catherine on her magnificent monthlong wedding journey. We made our way from Italy to Marseilles, where she married the second son of Francis, King of France. For the occasion I had created a special perfume from essence of lily of the valley and roses from Turkey. It was a lovely, heady and fresh scent. The lily symbolized her past, the rose her future. Catherine had given me a wedding gift too: the amethyst ring that I wear still. It is a heavy silver piece with a large rectangular cabochon held in place by fleurs-de-lis.

Like my mistress, the ring is not as simple as it appears. Catherine is as wily as she is intelligent. Her book is not the Bible but *The Prince* by Machiavelli. She chose me as her perfumer knowing I was under suspicion of murdering my mentor by administering poison. In fact that day in the cell when she came to save my life so I could accompany her to France, she told me that it was my knowledge of poison as well as my skill as perfumer that she wanted from me: "There might be dangers in France that you can save me from, René."

Catherine was a Medici. She was an Italian. She told me there were people in France who would say she was too dark and evil to marry their prince. She'd understood, even as a young woman, that sometimes you need to seize power. She was already planning how to fight. How to win.

As a Medici, Catherine had cunning flowing in her veins, and during those first nine years in Paris, her astuteness had served her well. But what troubled and pained the princess now could not be solved with cleverness. She was barren. And afraid that if she did not conceive soon the king would annul her marriage and find his son and heir another bride. Since Henry had indeed sired a daughter out of wedlock with a maidservant, the court was rife with rumors that the problem lay with Catherine, not her husband.

My princess had tried every cure at her disposal. She'd had doctors come from all over France. Had tried remedies suggested by midwives and mystics. She'd drunk mule urine and placed cow dung on her private parts. It was a wonder that the Dauphin could even get close to her during those experiments. She'd even had a carpenter drill tiny holes in the floor of a room in the Château de Blois so she could spy on her husband and his mistress, Diane de Poitiers, and watch them copulate to see if there was something that she was not doing correctly.

"Maybe," she had told me, "I don't excite the Dauphin enough. What I saw when I spied upon him was passion he has never showed me. Do you think that could be it?"

I was a man. I had appetites. I knew what excitement she spoke of. I looked at Catherine and her slightly bulging eyes and wondered what she was like when a man lay on top of her. I knew she loved her husband and longed for just half of the affection he showered on his whore, Diane. My heart ached for Catherine. She was my savior, and rather than lord it over me, she had done the opposite by treating me like her equal. She was always the first to talk of our bonds—we were orphans and exiles from Italy; we shared a love of scent and all things beautiful. "When I miss Florence, René, being with you is like being home."

Catherine was good to me. Not only did she have me ensconced in the palace in an esteemed position, but she'd also bought a shop for me on Pont Saint-Michel. There, when she was out of Paris and not in need of my services, I could concoct scents for the nobility and sell my wares. After almost a decade in Paris, I was growing rich.

Of late she had been in constant need of my services. She begged me to come up with ways to entice the prince to her bed, and we had been working for weeks on an aphrodisiac scent. A perfume she would wear that Henry would find irresistible. It was a complicated task. There were potions people talked of that engaged the senses, but I knew it was not flowers that made men hard.

It was the swell of a breast. The pout of a lip. It was looking in someone's eyes and seeing desire reflected back. It was the softness of a woman's body, the silkiness of her flesh. And I knew no perfume alone could excite a man. It was the real scent of a woman that inflamed him. The underneath, between-her-legs scent. That was what I needed to concoct for my lady.

"Come, sit by me," Catherine said.

She patted a chair to her left. Ruggieri was on her right. I took a seat and examined the assortment of objects on the table. What were these oddities?

A milky crystal about the size of my thumb with red occlusions gleamed in the light. Beside it was a series of small glass bottles, each no bigger than my pinkie finger, all filled with a thick viscous red liquid. I could smell it well enough to know that it was blood. On a gold plate lay four curls of hair, each tied and knotted with gold silk thread. Also on the plate were four large iridescent blue-and-green feathers—from what bird I was not certain. I noticed a mother-of-pearl shell holding a small pile of crescent-moon-shaped smaller shells. Or so I thought at first. Upon close inspection I realized I was looking at fingernail clippings. But the sight that made me the most angry and afraid at the same time was the pentagram painted with gold dust in the center of the table. This was the symbol of the black magic Ruggieri practiced. That the court whispered about. That one of Catherine's ladies-in-waiting had told me the princess was turning to in an effort to solve her fertility problems.

And mocking the whole assortment of evil accoutrements were fat votive candles, the same kind as were lit in church. The scent of prayer perfuming this evil air.

"Princess, this is dangerous business," I said, gesturing to the collection.

She shrugged. "I have no choice. I am in trouble now."

What could I say to that? She was right. Nine years without issue. The king, the Dauphin and the court were restless with worry.

"Have you brought your scents?" she asked.

I placed my offerings on the table.

Ignoring me, Ruggieri continued collecting the various objects and stringing them on a piece of silk. In the flickering candlelight, the unpleasant-looking Florentine appeared to be very much what he was—a creature, not a man. Someone connected with other realms. A sorcerer, not a scientist. No matter what he said about the astronomy and astrology that he studied, trying to predict a man's future and saying Black Masses and creating foul-smelling amulets with hair and fingernails was not forward-thinking. He was stuck in the mire of the witches and sorcerers who lived in the world of black magic. And my princess was falling deeper and deeper into his orbit.

If my scents worked, I would be able to woo her away from Ruggieri. If they didn't, I would have to devise another plan to get rid of my rival. For that's what he was. The two of us had been engaged in our struggle since we'd all left Italy together. I appealed to the esoteric and sensual side of Catherine, Ruggieri to the occult and secret side.

At Santa Maria Novella, a visit by Catherine to buy perfumes or pomades would be followed by the monks whispering about the duchessina's ability to see into the future and whether it was a sign of a saint or a heretic. Rumors circulated that since early childhood she'd had portentous dreams. Because she kept the visions to herself and remained a devout Catholic, no one had ever come out and accused her of witchcraft. But she wasn't a foreigner in Italy as she was here in France. Now, one misstep might prove her ruin if she was accused like so many before her had been.

I was determined not to let Ruggieri push her to take that step. I knew he was her oldest friend, her confidant. That he wanted to usurp my place was understandable. How he wanted to do it was demonic.

"This is what I have made for you," I said to Catherine as I picked up a bottle of scent.

"Let me smell it," she said with a first hint of excitement in her voice.

"First let me say that they won't be appealing to you. The purpose of these perfumes is not to make you smile or think of a garden. They are created to inflame the Dauphin."

"Yes, yes," she said, greedy to smell the first one.

"In fact"—I was not finished explaining—"they might actually smell ugly to you."

"That's not possible. You've never created an ugly scent for me, René."

"But this isn't a scent for you, Your Highness. This is a potion. It's a tool."

She didn't want to hear any more, and reaching out she took the first of my three glass bottles, twisted out the stopper, tipped the bottle to her finger and wet it.

Having grown up in Florence, Catherine knew the art of perfume. How to apply it and how to appreciate it. She knew you never smell a scent directly from the bottle. You must put it on and let it interact with your skin, let the oils from the scent soak into your flesh and only then, after a few moments of letting the air modify it, can you sniff.

After waiting the prerequisite minute, she lifted her wrist to her nose.

Immediately, she recoiled. "It's foul!"

"I told you."

"What have you done?"

"Princess, you asked me to create an aphrodisiac, and that's what I've created."

"But it smells sour and wicked." She sniffed again. "Strange and unclean. What is in this?"

"A combination of things, Your Highness."

"Specifically?"

I had been dreading this question. My mistress was known for her intelligence. She was well schooled in Latin, Greek and French. She was a scholar of antiquities and mathematics. Politically astute, she understood the art of war and of politics. She had been raised Catholic and been a virgin when she married. Did she lust? Did she have passions? I imagined she did. I could see flashes of a warm-blooded woman in her eyes. But to explain to her what this perfume contained and what I had created was something I'd hoped to avoid.

"Tell me, René."

I listed all the ingredients but one. Hoping that I could avoid the one that was sure to upset her.

"Civet. Ambergris. Musk. Heliotrope. Bergamot."

"But that can't be all. I know those scents. I have other perfumes, René. You have used all those ingredients before. This . . ." She lifted her wrist to her hand again. "There is something else in this one."

I nodded.

"Tell me."

Ruggieri had stopped building the talisman and had turned to Catherine as if he might need to protect her from whatever I was going to say.

"There is an essence that should arouse the prince, for it will be familiar to him."

She was angered. "René, you are holding back. What is this?"

"The vapors I was able to remove from Diane de Poitiers's underclothing. It is the scent of her skin . . . her essences and her oils, Princess."

Catherine did not speak. Her dark eyes did not reveal anything she was thinking. Beside her Ruggieri too was silent, but I could guess what he was thinking—that this might be his chance to discredit and finally get rid of me and have her to himself.

"How did you get such a thing?" she asked without giving away what she was feeling. Was she angry? Horrified? Insulted? Had I, in my eagerness to help her, made a fatal mistake that would get me thrown out of court?

"I bribed one of Diane's ladies to give me several weeks' worth of underclothes. Once I had enough, I pressed half as if they were flowers. The others I boiled and captured the steam they gave off."

"And you added those two essences to your flowers, herbs and oils."

"I did."

"And you think that her stink on my skin will inflame my husband and make his passion grow?"

"I do."

"This is outrageous!" Ruggieri shouted. "How dare you insult Her Highness by suggesting she put on the cloak of a woman who is nothing but a consort?"

Ruggieri was an ungainly man with a large nose, a high forehead and small, startlingly green eyes that seemed to see through things. His voice was gruff, but his manner was one of superiority. His attitude angered me that day more than usual. I had not expected him there. It was my time with Catherine, and I did not appreciate his presence. Even more so I was horrified that he was seducing her into his world of black magic and heretical thinking. He was putting her in danger—didn't he see that?

"How dare *I?* How dare *you* bring your black magic here and put our princess in danger!" I shouted. "Are you trying to help her? What of the potential ramifications of your actions? If Henry or the king finds out she is wearing the blood of an infant in a vial on her neck—"

"The blood of what?"

Catherine turned to Ruggieri. For a moment the perfume was forgotten.

"The ways of magic are complicated, my lady," he said.

Her voice was low. "Are you telling me that you . . . Ruggieri, how did you get the blood of an infant?"

His face was hard. His eyes glittered at me with hatred. I had brought truth into the room, and he didn't appreciate it.

"I demand you tell me now," she said when Ruggieri still hadn't responded. Her words flew out with such force, the votives on the table flickered.

"I found a whore," he said. Then stopped. Even *he* did not know how to tell a princess this tale.

"Tell me!" She'd blown one of the candles out with that last shout.

"She had four brats already and the poor woman was in desperate need of money for food."

"You bought a baby and killed it for this—to make this amulet for me—you murdered an innocent child?" She slipped back into her chair, overcome with the idea of what her astrologer had done.

He rose, knelt beside her, took her hand. She wrested it away.

"Your life here demands it. It is in the stars that you will be queen. It is your destiny, and it is mine to help you achieve it. I would kill a dozen infants if it would bring you the glory and the power you deserve."

Catherine lowered her head into her hands. I could not see if she was crying or not. Her back was still. Her countenance hidden. I was nauseated by the idea of what Ruggieri had done. When she lifted her head, I could see that there were indeed tears in her eyes. As she spoke she looked from Ruggieri to me.

"That I have been reduced to this . . ." She

pointed to the vials of blood and then the bottles of scent. "I pray that what one of you have done achieves its goal . . . I do not wish to dwell on what will happen to us, to all of us, if it doesn't."

Chapter 18

THE PRESENT

"I brought Melinoe," Serge said. "To show her."

Jac heard the words and used them to pull herself out of where she'd been—lost in another reality, watching a story unfold like a movie playing on a private screen in her own mind.

"I can't believe what you've found. How amazing," Melinoe said.

The woman's voice dragged Jac the rest of the way back through the time spill, and she returned from the memory lurch.

"Jac, this is quite miraculous." Melinoe was inspecting the shelf of essences. "How did you know it was here? Serge said you just reached through the bottles. What made you do that?" she asked.

"I smelled something different," Jac said. She was speaking slowly, trying to remember exactly what had happened. "It wasn't a scent associated with anything you'd expect to find in a wine cellar. From there . . ." She hesitated . . . She didn't want to tell them she'd actually seen an illusion from another time showing her the way. She lied. "From there it was just a good guess. I've gone on so many digs, searched through so many ancient places . . . It's not unusual for there to be hidden doors and staircases or secret rooms and hiding places."

Melinoe held up an amber bottle. "Do you think what's in these bottles is still viable?"

"I haven't inspected them. But since there's no light source in here, they might be better preserved than normal. Archaeologists have found far more ancient perfumes in digs in Egypt that have retained their scent and not been corrupted."

"Do you think it's wise for me to open one and smell it?" she asked.

"It might not be," Serge said before Jac could answer.

"Let me look." Jac took the bottle from Melinoe. It was labeled *Melisse* in the same ornate handwriting as the notes in the book. "It's lemon balm," Jac said. "At home our laboratory has some oils that date back to the French Revolution and are still wonderful. But I've only smelled one scent that goes back earlier than that. It was only a figment of scent— but I could still identify some of its properties."

Carefully Jac uncorked it and held it up to her nose.

"It's faint but smells absolutely fine. Exactly the

way it should. When ancient perfumers prepared their ingredients, they didn't cut corners the way we do now. And René le Florentin was an excellent chemist."

She offered it to Melinoe.

"Amazing," she said after sniffing.

Serge took the bottle that his stepsister was holding and smelled it. "So this was made during the reign of Catherine de Medici?"

"If no one used this laboratory after René, then yes," Jac said. "And no one has a date for when he died—that's what you said the other day, right?"

"Right. We did the research, but there's so little we found. René was a figure in the shadows of history—important for what he created for his queen," Serge said, and then looked at Melinoe with an expression that Jac couldn't quite read.

Jac felt the electricity between them again, as palpable and confusing as it had been before. Jac didn't understand what it was she was seeing. There was nothing overtly telling about the way they responded to each other, but she was certain there were complicated emotions running like deep underground springs.

Melinoe reached for another bottle. "I want to smell more of them." She sounded like a child in a toy store.

"I think it would be better not to open any more of them until I can take an inventory and we read this notebook and know what René intended.

They will evaporate more quickly if we expose them to air, and there's very little oil left in most of the bottles," Jac said.

"Read what notebook?" Melinoe said.

Jac realized she hadn't shown her the book. "It appears to be René's records. Most perfumers kept copious notes. There may be clues here as to what René was working on. I can't read most of it because it's in Latin, but I believe there are formulas in here and lists of ingredients."

"Let me see," Melinoe said.

Jac opened the book to a list. She pointed and read. "He's used their Latin names, which are still the names we use for them. Several are very rare. Others can still be bought, but the modern equivalents would be very different than they were in the 1500s."

Melinoe and Serge bent over the book. Their shoulders were touching.

"What do you mean?" Melinoe asked. "Wouldn't a rose be a rose, to quote Gertrude Stein?"

"There were different strains of flowers then. The air and the water weren't polluted. There was no acid rain. On the other hand there were germs and bacteria we don't have now. So how things smelled and how ingredients interacted with one another would be unique to that time."

Jac pointed to a word on the list. "Here's ambergris. A lovely word for aged whale vomit that is a major ingredient in many wonderful perfumes. Everything the mammal ate affected it. Ancient ambergris would have totally different properties than what is washed up onshore today."

"So if you can figure out the formula for the elixir to mix with the breaths to get them to work, we will have to get ancient essences and ingredients," Melinoe said with resolve. "And if we can't get ingredients from the mid-1500s, then we need at least the oldest we can find."

"Yes, if we want to exactly re-create his experiment, we would need our ingredients to be as pure and authentic as possible. But I don't think it's likely we'll be able to find them," Jac said.

"We will find them."

Jac noted the resolve in the delicate-looking woman's voice.

Serge looked at his stepsister. "I thought we'd discussed this."

Jac didn't understand. She must have missed something.

As she fixed her dark eyes on him, Melinoe said, "You worry too much. I know what I am doing at all times."

"I worry too much *precisely* because you know what you are doing at all times."

Families have shortcuts and codes when they speak. She and Robbie had them. But this one was making Jac uncomfortable.

Robbie hadn't said anything about the psychological dynamics of these two stepsiblings. But then again Robbie hadn't planned on slipping into a coma as quickly as he had. He hadn't finished telling her a hundred things. A thousand things.

Thinking about her brother's death and the ashes she still hadn't decided what to do with made her wonder: "Do you know where René was buried?" Jac asked.

"Nothing was recorded. But I came across a mention in Catherine de Medici's daughter's diary that suggested it was here on the château grounds," Melinoe said.

"Is there a cemetery here?" Jac asked.

"There has to be," Serge said. "But we haven't found one yet."

Jac shivered. They were talking about another perfumer's death. Not Robbie's but a Renaissance perfumer's. Chills ran up her arms and her back. It couldn't be a coincidence, and Jac had discovered that for her, coincidences had a way of preceding portentous and often dangerous events.

Chapter 19

That night, Jac fell asleep easily, cosseted by the down pillows and comforter. Her dreams were full of the perfumer who had lived here so many centuries ago. In his secret laboratory, she saw him mixing up potions and recipes, stirring, shaking and sniffing. At one point he picked up his head and looked right at her, as if she were in the room with him, as if he could actually see her. And then he spoke to her.

All this I do for you. To see you again. To be with you again. Please God, it will work. Because without you I am lost to the world.

In her sleep, Jac felt the power of his words like a perfumed wind, blowing around her, embracing her. The most profound sense of longing overwhelmed her. Jac tried to go to him. Tried to move toward him. Wanted him to take her in his arms. Wanted to bury her face in his chest and have him stroke her hair. Wanted to feel his rough lips bruising hers. Oh, how she wanted him. But she was half a millennium away. And they were forever separated by time.

She woke up suddenly. Soaked with sweat.

The perfumer had seemed so familiar to her. Her feelings for him were the same as her feelings for Griffin. Was it possible that— *No.* She would not entertain the thought.

But she couldn't escape it, could she? Jac could almost hear Malachai asking her how she could even question what the dream revealed: that in a previous incarnation Griffin had most likely lived a life as the perfumer. Time was coming full circle again.

Suddenly, the still vivid images from the dream were replaced by images from past memory lurches. Her lover on the floor, dark ruby blood pooling beneath his body, his life force seeping out of him. He was dying because of her. Because he had loved her and not been able to let her go.

She had to stop the pictures bombarding her. There was no way out of the vortex of guilt and grief that would envelop her if she gave in to the memories.

Brushing her hair out of her eyes, she glanced at the digital bedside clock. In this medieval castle it was incongruous, but so was so much about this journey. It was only 2:35. Whenever she woke up in the middle of the night, she had trouble falling back asleep and was usually up for hours. Because of the dream and the panic that had ensued, she knew tonight would be worse.

Jac pulled on her robe and headed for the kitchen. A hot cup of tea laced with brandy was always a perfect antidote for late-night unease.

As she made her way down the hall toward the staircase, she heard the wind howling outside. A few more steps and she realized it wasn't the wind at all. It was a human cry. Alerted, worried, she moved in the direction of the sound. Someone was in pain.

She passed the staircase and continued on past one door . . . and then the next. The cries were more distinct now.

"You have me . . . you have all of me . . ." A man's muffled voice.

"I want more," the woman insisted.

"You have all of me."

"I need more."

Another cry. Then silence. Jac knew she should walk away.

"Make me feel more . . ." The woman was demanding, but it sounded as if she was also crying.

"I don't want to hurt you."

"I need to feel more." The woman emitted a cry of pain. Then: "Yes, please. More. I want more."

There was the sound of a slap. Flesh against flesh.

"Don't make me do this to you."

"Again, please again."

Flesh against flesh.

Another cry. "Yes, more."

"No more, Melinoe."

Her voice became strident, no longer a needy child but a demanding woman. "You want it too. You need it. More. Now. More."

Was that his hand slapping her skin? Or was he using an instrument? Where on her body was he hitting her? How hard?

"I can't do it anymore." Now he sounded tortured.

The moans were making the words hard to understand.

"You have to . . . Look how hard you are . . . how wet I am."

Smack. Smack.

"Yes, hurt me."

"I can't."

Jac had never eavesdropped on anyone having sex before. And as much as she knew she shouldn't be listening, she was riveted. These two souls were caught up in some elemental dance of psychological angst and desire. A ritualistic, fetishized version of lovemaking.

It sounded like they were whipped up in some kind of religious fervor. Like pagans worshipping at an altar. It sounded like torture. Like ancient passions bubbling up from deep in the earth, rising to the surface, exploding through these two damaged creatures. It sounded like a hell on earth and heaven at the same time. It sounded like exquisite pain and horrible beauty.

Jac knew she should leave, walk away and mind her own business. Serge and Melinoe were not related by blood. They had met when she was sixteen and he was seventeen. There wasn't anything wrong with them being lovers. But this way? Jac thought about the dark woman whose eyes always looked haunted, who moved with the grace of an angel across a room, whose haughty bearing spoke of a burden carried forever with determination. For noble Serge to be in her thrall like this, tied to her in some deep-blooded way, obeying her despite how strong he was, Melinoe must not be all human but part witch, part vampire, part Rasputin.

There was regret in the sounds coming from inside that bedroom now. And longing. Desperation, guilt and defiance. Did they enact this ritual over and over? How could they endure it?

She rested her head on the doorjamb. Felt literally weak with her own arousal. Confused by her own body betraying her, refusing to obey her determination to leave, to walk away. She was certain she would never forget these sounds; the sadness, the power, the ecstasy, it was like a perfume of awful desire, of illicit passion. An impossible possibility.

There was quiet now on the other side of the door. None of the rough ragged sounds of their lovemaking were audible. They'd finished. For a crazy second Jac even wondered if they had died. She wouldn't have been surprised to open the door and find them naked in each other's arms, expired. It was a strange thought—one she didn't understand—but she was obsessed suddenly with the idea that they were dead, had died in that last moment, that they would be happier freed from their terrible attraction, the unhealthy needs that bound them to each other.

She sighed without meaning to. Then, worried they might hear her and find her standing by the door, she hurried away, running back to her room. The tea forgotten.

Chapter 20

I had been creating fragrances, pomades and lotions for the royal family for nine years and was well known to the Dauphin. He often visited me in my laboratory, breaking my heart as he asked me to create perfumes for his mistress. I could not disobey. I had included some of the scents that Henry favored for his paramour, Diane de Poitiers, in the fragrance I'd created to help Catherine conceive.

To that end, I also made a second scent and used it in a cream—something of an experiment on my part. Something I hadn't explained to Catherine. If she did conceive, then I would tell her what I had done.

Getting an audience with the Dauphin could be a difficult task, but I'd sent word I'd created a fragrant gift for His Highness to give his mistress.

"What a surprise. I didn't order a new scent," Henry said when I was ushered into his bedroom. He was in the midst of being dressed by his courtiers, and there were clothes and shoes everywhere. The velvets and silks and laces were as opulent as his quarters. Everything here was spectacular. All that could be was gilded with gold and shimmered in the candlelight. I touched the back of a chair covered in thick velvet mohair, luxuriating in the sensation of the fabric on my flesh.

"No, sire, you didn't, but I was working on a new lotion for the skin and happened upon a formula that I felt sure you would want to give to Madame de Poitiers."

"I'm sure she'll be delighted you were thinking of her, Maître René. What are its properties?"

"I've used rose oil in a new formula that imparts a moisture and suppleness I haven't seen before," I said. Conveniently I left out the other ingredients I'd included, which would induce sleep when absorbed by the skin.

Despite the Dauphin being consumed with the affairs of state and the health of his father, he opened the jar and sniffed at it.

He looked older to me on this night. The growing, ever increasing conflicts between the Catholics and the Protestants were a constant anxiety for the Crown.

"It has a pleasant odor, thank you, Maître René. I'm sure Lady de Poitiers will appreciate you thinking of her." He smiled when he said her name.

I knew that the hours Henry spent with Diane de Poitiers were an escape. The cream I was giving him would hopefully make that time unfulfilling and leave him hungry for a woman. If my efforts were discovered, it could mean banishment from court. But if Catherine couldn't produce an heir, the marriage would be annulled and we'd both be banished anyway.

He closed the jar, signaling the end of the meeting. But giving him this gift wasn't all that was on my mind.

"May I speak, Your Highness?"

"Of course, René, what is it?"

"It is very delicate." I glanced at the men in the room with us. There were over a dozen, too many I didn't know.

Henry dismissed all but his valet of the bedchamber, with whom I was familiar. Perhaps it was dangerous to speak in front of him, but I had no choice. I would just bribe him later with gifts for his lady.

"Two days ago I took some lotions to the princess . . ."

As Henry allowed his man to tie his doublet he asked, "Why do you hesitate, René?"

"Before I continue, I must be sure you understand that what I am about to tell you I am relating only because I believe it is for the good of the Crown."

"All right then, I understand." He was annoyed at my coyness, and I resolved to speak without delay.

"When I went to visit the princess, that astrologer was there. The filthy Ruggieri with all sorts of talismans and amulets." I described what I had seen. "I even saw vials of blood."

"The devil you say! Whose blood?"

"That I don't know for sure. Ruggieri said it was the blood of an infant, but he might have said that for effect. It could have been the blood of any animal. But the purpose of my telling you this is that the princess is becoming more and more dependent on him, and it is a threat to your position. There are spies and enemies everywhere, as you know. What if the church were to hear black magic is being practiced in the court? Catherine would be blamed when it is not her fault. Like me, he hails from her hometown, and she's comfortable with him. But there are more important things now than her having Florentines around her."

Henry quizzed me on the details of what else I had seen and heard, then turned and walked to a chest of drawers. Opening one, he pulled out a small packet on a string.

"Does this look familiar to you? The princess gave it to me yesterday and begged me to wear it."

I took it from him.

Hanging from a red silken cord was a small leather pouch. It had been tanned and infused with a boring fragrance of basic lemon and myrrh.

Leather had to be scented after it was tanned, or

it stank. This was not the scented leather I sold in my shop. Thinking he was capable of all things, Ruggieri must have done this himself.

"Open it," Henry ordered.

I released the knot and pulled apart the folds.

Inside was a miniature glass bottle filled with clear liquid. Swimming inside were three heliotrope stones and a piece of black jasper. The top of the bottle was bound with some kind of hemp twisted with the iridescent threads from a peacock feather.

"Yes, these were the kind of things I saw."

"Catherine told me it was a good luck charm and begged me to wear it. I didn't pay much mind. A few stones and thread. She has her ways, and I do want to please her. But this sounds as if it's getting out of hand. I have heard rumors about the astrologer and his magic, but if you saw him performing it with the princess there, it is more serious than I thought."

"Yes. I saw him saying spells and teaching Her Highness how to say them as well."

The conversation could not have gone better had I written it myself. This is for you, Ruggieri, I was thinking. Not just for trying to oust me but for what you are doing to corrupt and endanger Catherine. This is for your dark ways and corrupt practices. For trying to sway the princess into believing you have powers and wisdom you do not have.

"His time at court must come to an end," Henry said. "You are right. If the Protestants were to hear that my wife was engaged in black magic and spread rumors to that effect, it could be ruinous for her and for me."

He held out his hand for the amulet, which I gladly gave him back.

"Thank you, René. You've proved yet again that you are a good friend to our family."

"I consider it my duty." I hesitated. "One other thing?"

"Yes?"

"Having the princess trust me allowed me to discover this travesty. If she were to begin to doubt my loyalty, then—"

He cut me off. "Have no fear. I would never tell her who spoke to me. As you said yourself, it is of greater benefit to me to have her faith in you unsullied."

I bowed. "Thank you. And you can tell Madame de Poitiers that the cream can be applied in both the morning and night generously. There's enough for a month in that jar."

It was easy to keep abreast of the gossip making its way through the court. Especially for me. I had learned early how small gifts to Catherine's ladies-in-waiting and the prince's men and even de Poitiers's ladies engendered confidences. Everyone who came to my shop had tales to tell. So I knew swiftly that there had been a huge row between the prince and princess on the day after my visit.

Lady Closier—one of Catherine's ladies and a member of her esteemed *escadron volant*, her flying squadron of ambassadors and spies—sat on the couch in my shop, and there she repeated most of the conversation to me as I plied her with wine. My fragrance emporium hung above the Seine, perched on the bridge as if it were a nest built by a bird. Unlike other stores, mine resembled a sitting room. I had chairs and settees. Glass vitrines filled with exquisite bottles created by fine jewelers. My laboratory, in the back, was an exact duplicate, in miniature of course, of the one at Santa Maria Novella where I had learned my trade. Sometimes I would be so caught up in working that I'd stop and listen for Serapino's footsteps.

"Their fight rang through the halls of the palace," Lady Closier whispered as she drank more of the robust red wine I'd offered. Customers engaged in conversation and plied with wine or chocolates always purchased more goods, so I always had plenty on hand.

"Henry demanded that Catherine tell Ruggieri to leave the court, or Henry himself would go to the church and report the astrologer as a heretic and sorcerer."

"And what did Catherine say?" I asked as I offered Closier a bonbon.

"She was furious and demanded to know who had told him about Ruggieri's spells."

"Whom did he name?" I held my breath.

"No one. He told her it was common knowledge that the astrologer was doing more than reading the stars and making entertaining suggestions about what the future may hold."

"How did she take that?"

"You know my lady is not afraid of her husband. Ever respectful, she is an independent and intelligent woman and never pretends otherwise. So she proceeded to argue with Henry, telling him that astrological predictions were not entertaining but rather important, and that banishing Ruggieri from court would hurt them all. Even be dangerous for the future of the kingdom."

"I can't imagine he took well to that," I said.

"Not at all. He was furious and told her that was nonsense. That he hadn't realized how far her reliance on Ruggieri had gone and she was confused about the man's abilities. She countered by reminding him that Ruggieri had foretold her future, saying she would be a queen years before she even married the prince.

"Then Henry said, 'Not a very difficult guess. You were the richest young woman in all of Europe. Certainly everyone knew a marriage would be made to put you on the throne or close to it.' "

"And what was the result of this bickering?" I

asked as I refilled her glass. Closier gave me one of the coy smiles that she was known for and, though we were quite alone, leaned closer as if to tell me a secret she didn't want anyone else to hear. Like all of Catherine's ladies, she was not without her charms, and I had slept with her. I knew how she smelled when she lay in my bed, satiated and spent. She was neither an inventive nor exciting lover, and after the conquest was over, I lost interest. That was usually the case with the women I bedded. The chase excited me, but then I grew bored. The ladies never seemed to mind when the liaisons ended as long as I gave them expensive bottles of perfumes and creams, promising them they were the very same the princess used. It often seemed they were more pleased with my gifts than they had been with my attentions. And my coterie of bright and beautiful chirping birds continued to return to the shop.

At that point I was unmarried but had two daughters and one son that I supported. I planned to take my son as my apprentice and give him my name as soon as he was old enough.

"My lady lost the battle," Closier said. "The prince, who rarely makes such demands on her, insisted that she send Ruggieri away or she would leave him no choice but to do it himself."

I turned away to fuss with a bottle of perfume I was filling for her lest she see the delight on my face.

"And did she agree then?"

"Yes."

"Is Ruggieri still at court?"

"No. My lady called him to her chambers and told him that for his own safety he needed to leave Paris. She was upset and wept as she bade him good-bye."

I wondered if Catherine would cry if I left the court. Lady Closier drank more of her wine.

"But I don't think that she's thinking that much about Ruggieri now," she added.

"Why is that?"

Outside a ship was going down the river, and shouts from the men on board filled the shop. I glanced out and saw the sails of the king's barge.

"The prince has been more attentive to Catherine than usual."

I sat down beside Lady Closier and touched her cheek with my finger. "Your skin looks lovely. You are using all the lotions I've given you in the morning and before you go to sleep?"

"Yes, yes, but don't you want to hear about the prince?"

I did, but I couldn't appear to be too interested. And besides, the idea of Ruggieri being gone had pleased me so much I felt a celebration was in order.

"I do, of course I do. But first . . ." I leaned over and kissed her. It was an easy way to test the waters and see if she would allow me to take pleasure with her.

My advance was met with a surprised resistance for a moment, and then her lips parted and welcomed me. It was late in the day, and I didn't concern myself with locking the door. I gently pushed her down on the chaise. I was pleased that she, along with the princess's other intimates, was following Catherine's regime and bathing once a week. Closier smelled of my perfumes mixed with the natural healthy oils of her own skin, and the scent aroused me.

It was not my artistry, but rather it was the art of perfumery that did it. Aromas bypass thoughts and go straight to one's emotions. Smelling Closier, I felt fulfilled, excited and desirous all at the same time. I wanted to bury my face in the flesh that was presenting the scent so gloriously.

A woman wearing my perfume was a gift to be enjoyed and reveled in.

I released my cock from my pantaloons and found her waiting for me, wet and wanting underneath her voluminous petticoats. Stroking her slowly, I felt her slickness build. If a woman is freshly bathed and you excite her, the salty scent can inflame the senses. Like ambergris, it isn't flowery or quiet. There are no blossoms it brings to mind. But it can drive a man mad. I lifted my fingers to my nose and inhaled. And then I burrowed under her skirts and buried my face between her legs. My lovers told me few men did this to them, and I was astounded. I found such excitement there in the dark, my head cosseted by the soft silks and laces that tickled my cheeks and forehead. In the quiet world between a woman's legs a man could forget the intrigues of the court and the quest for power and riches. The past disappeared; the future did not matter. The world existed in the woman's quivering flesh, the straining and throbbing between your own legs. Nothing else mattered but the want—the pure and demanding want. And to give yourself over to it was to indulge in the most perfect of moments.

Closier was writhing beneath my tongue, and I played with her a little bit longer, knowing that the more I waited, the greater would be my release. Finally she arched under me. Then came that odd tightening of her muscles, and I knew she was caught up in her own pleasure and enjoying "la petite mort," as the French call it. So apt a name for it too. For is it not a little death? A short time when your thoughts disappear and you become nothing but your own body.

I had heard men and women talk of romantic love and wondered what that must be like. I knew other kinds of love. For Catherine, my savior, the strong, willful, intelligent woman who I believed I would die to protect. For my creations. For Serapino, my beloved teacher, protector and family. But passionate love? No, that compartment of my heart had never opened. I satisfied myself with moments such as the one I was enjoying with Closier.

As I slowly entered her body, gliding in on her slickness, I felt the red hot-blooded warmth of her engulf me and surround me and throb to welcome me. It did not take long then. From her breathing I knew she had already exhausted herself, and I remembered she was not easy to please twice in one session.

I thrust into her deeply, again, and then again, and then let go with wonderful abandon, feeling elation and release.

As she cleaned up and I poured her a bit more wine, I asked her when the court was next leaving Paris. I was pretending to have forgotten that she'd been about to tell me something before our trysting began.

"The prince wants to go to Fontainebleau," she said and then remembered that she had gossip to share. "The most interesting development, René. The prince has been to visit Catherine every night for the last week and he has been more passionate than ever. I can tell from the look in her eyes."

"Really?" I asked, trying to sound only mildly interested.

"Yes, and Catherine is giving you the credit. She says it is your perfume, René. She has told me he is more aroused with her and that he does things to her that he never did before."

"The things I do to you?" I leaned forward and kissed her lightly on the cheek—in that moment so pleased by the news I needed to express myself.

She giggled and then continued. "There's more gossip too. Diane de Poitiers seems to have taken to her bed because of it. She sleeps and sleeps. The doctors have been called, but they can't find any malady."

"How upsetting," I said, feigning surprise and then curiosity. "She just sleeps?"

"They are saying that the prince must have turned away from her or that she's found out about his new passion for his wife and it's depressed her so much that she is looking for solace in dreams. Why are you smiling at this news, René? What is your secret? You have the most inscrutable eyes. I can't tell what you are thinking at all."

I didn't tell her, but at that moment I was thinking about Ruggieri and that I had bested him in this round of the dangerous game we were playing against each other.

Chapter 21

THE PRESENT
THURSDAY, MARCH 20
BARBIZON, FRANCE

He'd called her an hour ago—the last voice she'd expected to hear, the only voice she'd wanted to hear—and told her that he was at the inn in town and wanted to know if she could meet him. Jac had been expecting Griffin to send her the results in an email or via a package. Not to bring them to her in person.

When she asked why he was in France, he said he'd explain everything when he saw her.

And now they were in the lobby of the hotel, and she was smelling his wonderful lemon-and-honey-and-musk scent and wanted to cry. Why did she have to keep losing this man? *This* was who she was meant to be with. And yet he'd caused her more pain and longing, more lost lonely nights than anyone else in her life. She should hate him. But she couldn't. He was in her blood.

Jac's whole body vibrated like a violin string, reverberating from just this one brief embrace. Griffin let her go. She didn't want him to. She

232

wanted to stay within the familiar world created by his arms. Wanted to keep smelling his skin. No matter how much time passed, no matter how long it had been since she'd seen him last, as soon as they were together, she felt connected to him. No man had ever affected her on such a deep visceral level. Never had she met anyone who just glancing at across a room made blood rush to her face and heat her skin.

It was chemical. No, alchemical. Their connection was a combustion. Separate elements, when combined, caused a unique reaction. Just looking at his cheekbones, at the fine skin. His full lower lip. The thick hair shot through with gray. The hooded eyes. She always wanted to laugh at her first response to seeing him after any time had gone by—she actually felt weak. The word "swoon" had been created for this response, she thought, not for the first time. This man's unintentional physical power over her scared her.

"I thought that it would be better to explain all this in person," he said and smiled. "Would you like to have a glass of wine?"

"Yes, I would. I'm still in shock that you're here, in Barbizon."

"You need help, don't you?"

He pulled out a chair.

Jac was caught off guard. She had never doubted that once Griffin had loved her. She'd been sure of it. At least for a time. And she had never doubted that he was attracted to her still. The week they'd spent in Paris, searching for Robbie, had proved that to her. But she had no idea if she was important to him. Or how deep his affection still went. She didn't know if he thought about her the same way that she thought about him. He had been the single most important romantic relationship in her life. The one by which every other was measured.

"It's a crazy coincidence that you're here today," she said and watched his face. Did he remember they'd met on this very date when she was seventeen years old?

"There are no coincidences." He smiled.

"It's troublesome that both you and my brother got to know Malachai. I can't seem to escape him and his belief system."

"Well, I'd tie it back to Jung myself. I was already quite familiar with the theory before I met your good doctor."

"So if it's not a coincidence, then you chose today on purpose?"

"You ask questions you don't need to ask. You always have. You never have faith."

"What do you mean?" she asked.

"I'm here. Do you really need to ask why?" He pulled something out of his pocket. "But this should answer your concerns."

Jac looked down at the long thin package wrapped in silver paper with a silver satin ribbon.

With fingers that shook just a little, she untied it and found a velvet jeweler's box. Gingerly, she opened it.

Inside were two battered silver disks hanging on a silken cord. Each was shaped like a rose petal and studded with very small rubies that sparkled like drops of blood.

The smaller of the petals hung over the larger.

The first was engraved with the words: *One Day*.

The second with: *At A Time*.

"I had it made for you."

She turned to him and took a breath. She wanted to ask exactly what message he was trying to give her because she didn't want to misinterpret anything. Instead she simply said: "It's very beautiful." She hoped she didn't sound as moved as she was.

He lifted the amulet out of the box and slipped it over her neck.

She felt as if she were a warrior in a myth putting a mantle on. Preparing for battle. She told Griffin that.

"What battle, Jac? I hope not with me."

"Maybe with you." She laughed.

And he laughed with her. "Seriously," he said. "What battle?"

"I don't know actually. I've walked into something here at the château, and I'm not sure what it is or what to make of it."

Over a bottle of rosé, she told him about the house and the laboratory. About Serge and Melinoe and how Malachai seemed so keen that she should come that she'd almost not come.

"Robbie told me a fair amount about the breaths and the bell coverings," Griffin said, "but very little about the history or the people involved. We were so focused on the translations we didn't get to the rest."

Jac heard the wistfulness in his voice. "You miss him too, don't you?"

"Yes. But it's not as hard for anyone as it is for you. He was all the family you had, and now you're alone."

She nodded. Yes, alone. She thought about it every morning when she woke up. Every night before she went to sleep. Once they had been a family—brother, sister, mother, father, grand-parents—and now they were all gone. Only the people on the edges—cousins and aunts and uncles—were left. Yes, she was forging deeper relationships with them, but it wasn't the same.

"I'm alone, yes. But it's not as difficult as I would have imagined," she said, and then she told Griffin the secret that she hadn't told anyone:

"I'm not sure if he's really gone."

"Of course he isn't. You'll never really lose him."

"No. That's not what I mean. I actually feel him, Griffin. Some part of him hasn't left. It is as if

Robbie's hovering. Sometimes I can even hear him talking to me. He's waiting for something."

She could tell from the expression on his face that Griffin was worried about her now.

"It's very understandable that you'd feel he was still with you," he said slowly.

"I know what you think—at first I thought that too, that it was just my imagination creating a presence for me because I wasn't ready to lose him. So I could have him with me and not have to say good-bye. When I let the people from the mortuary take his body away, I remembered how he used to talk about our mother's death. That it was only a death of her body. Not her soul. Robbie believed in reincarnation so completely. He used to call the body an envelope for the soul."

The waiter came over and asked if they'd like to order lunch. The interruption brought her back to the reality around her with a start.

"You okay with just the wine for a while longer?" Griffin asked.

She nodded.

He told the waiter they needed more time. Once he was gone, Griffin pulled Jac closer to him and touched her cheek with his fingers. She felt the familiar roughness. His skin was callused from spending half his life on digs. She shut her eyes as a knife of longing cut through her. Jac didn't want to want him. But it seemed as if she were preprogrammed against her will to react to him.

"What are you really doing here? Why did you bring me a gift?" She knew her voice sounded angry. She didn't care. Half of her hated him for walking away from her all those years ago. For throwing out a life that they could have been sharing. Children that would have been theirs. And then a second knife went through her as she thought about the miscarriage she'd suffered eighteen months ago. A chance encounter with him after eleven years that had resulted in a pregnancy he'd never found out about. *She'd* been the one to push him away, on no uncertain terms, because they weren't good for each other. Not in any lifetime.

"I'm here because your brother asked me to help him solve a mystery and I agreed. Now you've taken up the same quest, and I know he'd want me to help you."

"So this is all about Robbie?"

"No, not all of it." He smiled. "And you know that." Griffin drank more of his wine. "Jac, I need to tell you what happened after I left you in Paris and went back to New York. I tried everything I could to put what happened in perspective. I told myself it was an event out of time. That because we were searching for Robbie, our emotions were strained. But those were just rationalizations. Our coming together after so long was . . . Jac . . . it was a miracle. I had forgotten what it was like to be with someone so completely. To not hold back."

She sipped her wine. Kept her eyes down. Played with the silver petals hanging around her neck. She wanted to hear this, and yet she didn't.

"Why didn't you fight harder in Paris for me to stay?" he asked.

"Let's not do this," Jac said. "I appreciate that you are here now. I love my gift. I will gladly accept your help in translating the bell jars. But I don't want to talk about the past. Or the future. I can't."

"And you can't tell me why?"

"There's nothing to tell. You'd said you weren't sure your marriage was over. I didn't want to fight your wife for you."

"Yes, I know that's the reason you gave me. But there was more, wasn't there?"

Jac didn't answer.

"Robbie told me about the reincarnation memories you were having in Paris and that you thought we'd been together in two different lives and in both I died because of you."

"Robbie told you that?"

Griffin nodded.

Jac wanted to curse her brother for breaking her confidence, but she knew why he'd done it—he was so certain she was wrong and that she and Griffin belonged together.

"I don't know that they were reincarnation memories. That's what Robbie and Malachai believed."

"But you believe they might be—enough so that you're afraid that you've been bad for me before and would be again?"

"It sounds ludicrous when I hear it out loud." And it did. Maybe even more so now that almost two years had passed since they'd been together in Paris.

"But it's why you pushed me to go. To save me from you?"

"What difference does it make now?" she asked.

"I went back to New York not knowing you'd sacrificed so much for me. I think that makes a difference."

"I can't see how."

Griffin leaned forward and kissed her. She tasted the wine on his lips. She smelled his cologne. She heard the barkeep popping a cork. Somewhere in the distance two men were talking. One second she was completely conscious of every sound and taste and smell, and then it all disappeared. Jac was aware only of the embrace. Of her life narrowing down to the pressure on her lips. Of the complete rightness of this kiss and at the same time the wonder of it.

She was remembering what she'd thought she'd forgotten. The way he held her when he kissed her, with his hands on either side of her face. The specific pressure of his lips moving on hers. The two-ness of them was woven into the fabric of who she was. This memory of him was so deep, she always had felt if she pulled the string of it and followed it, she'd wind up—where? The feeling of his palms on her cheeks, of his breath inside of her, of his hair brushing her face. It felt familiar in another way too. This was how the other women she'd been in the past had known him.

When he pulled back, she had to force her mind to make sense of where she was. Had to remind herself nothing had changed. She was still his poison.

"I'm not married anymore," he said as if he were reading her mind. "And the only thing that you can do to harm me is to push me away again."

She was shaking her head. She couldn't go through this again. She'd wanted this man her whole life, but she was so frightened by the old visions, she couldn't bring herself to act on her true feelings.

"I believe in ghosts too, Jac. I believe in the unknown. I've slept in the pyramids and am sure that there are things mankind used to know that we have lost. I believe in dimensions beyond this one. In secrets the universe has yet to give up. That there may be life in other galaxies. Not because of magic but because of deep science. But I can't accept that two people who feel the way we do for each other can be toxic for each other. I've studied reincarnation for years. I've read ancient Greek treatises on metempsychosis and what

Pythagoras wrote about the transmigration of the soul. I want to believe it—yet I remain on the fence. What I am convinced of, though, is this: even if there is reincarnation and we are absolutely reborn over and over in new bodies, our karma is not a *prison*. We are *not* doomed to repeat the past. We are invited to change our fate and repair past damages and write a new script. There is no logic to your scenario, Jac. What purpose would there be to coming back if we had no choice but to live a predetermined path? You can't believe that even if we were together before and hurt each other, that means we're destined to hurt each other again."

"But we have. You almost died because of me in Paris."

"I almost died because a criminal with a gun shot at you and I pushed you out of the way and was hurt. Jac, please." He put his hands on her shoulders and pulled her toward him so she was twisted around, facing him again. "You can't throw us away because of something you don't even believe yourself."

"I don't want to . . ."

"But?"

She shrugged. She tried to think. The wine, the physical closeness of him, the surreal circumstances of him being here . . . everything was suddenly very complicated.

"How about we try it my way?" Griffin said.

"Let me help you translate the formulas—if they even are formulas—and get to the end of what Robbie started. Then, when we're done, we'll figure out what's next. Okay? Can you just give us that much of a chance? A little more time before you doom us forever?"

She was looking at him, into his eyes, seeing the one face that was the only face she ever wanted to see. That he was here again was almost a miracle. While she was trying to figure it all out, he kissed her again.

She started to pull away, but he stopped her.

"I won't let you go. Not this time. Not until you give me a chance to prove how wrong you are. Besides, without me it's going to take you weeks, months, to find someone to do the translations. Especially because unless you agree, I'm not going to give you the work I've already done. I'm not going to tell you what I've already figured out. You might be able to let me go . . . but can you let the knowledge go?" he asked. And then, he smiled because he already knew the answer.

Chapter 22

MARCH 20, 1573
BARBIZON, FRANCE

It was exactly twenty-six years ago today, and I'd been at the Medici court for fourteen years.

"Come with me to Cloux. The king is so ill, René." Catherine arrived in my laboratory in the early morning. She looked as if she hadn't slept at all. "I've just had word that things have taken a turn for the worse." She tried to hold back her tears, but her eyes filled and overflowed.

Of all the people at the court, the king had been the first who was kind to her when she'd arrived from Italy, welcoming her and making her feel like a daughter. He'd also protected her through the barren years when many at court wanted the marriage annulled so a more fertile bride could be brought in. Francis stayed loyal, and she'd never forgotten.

By the time King Francis took to his deathbed, my princess had given birth to her first son and heir, Francis, and a daughter. Catherine gave my perfume credit for breaking the spell that had been cast upon her, and I was always careful to point out that it was not a spell that had needed to be

244

broken. She had just needed more time with Henry, I told her. And the sleeping potion in the cream I'd made for Henry to give to Diane de Poitiers had done the trick.

But spells? Magic? Not at all, I insisted, for the specter of Ruggieri was never far from my thoughts. I didn't want him back at court. There were enough rivals waiting in the wings, new perfumers who brought Catherine gifts all the time, trying to gain favor. I had my shop and my savings and a small hoard of precious gems, silver and gold, but every position at the court was precarious. I had been in France with Catherine for fourteen years and had seen how easy it was to fall out of favor. Not even for doing anything wrong. Sometimes simply because someone more interesting or novel had arrived.

"I want you to try to capture his breath," Catherine said softly. "If this process you're working on is really possible, I think we should have the king's breath, shouldn't we?"

We arrived at the king's summer residence at Cloux by nightfall and went right to the king's chamber. Surrounded by dour-looking men of the court, His Royal Highness appeared to be sleeping peacefully. I asked to speak to his doctor on the princess's behalf, and he told me about the elixirs they were giving the king. I had brought a Santa Maria Novella formula with me, but what they were giving Francis was almost identical.

I was able to reassure the princess that the king was not suffering. The mixture was made from poppy seeds, I told her. There was no finer drug for those in pain and distressed. But my mistress was still distraught.

"I am losing the only father I've ever known," she said to me as we sat vigil at his bedside.

In all the years since Serapino had taught me his process of capturing exhalations I had not been able to improve on his methods. It was difficult to guess which breath was to be a mortal's last, so it was necessary to catch one after the other when the end was near. That in itself was complicated, but usually you can hear the time when it comes. Breathing becomes labored, and a sound like a drum filled with seeds rattles in the chest.

Over the next seventy-two hours, Catherine and I remained by the king's side. Occasionally she fell asleep only to wake with a start, remembering where she was and why. She begged me to wake her if it seemed the end was close. But when it came, I didn't have to; she was holding his hand and whispering to him.

The doctors allowed me to capture breath after breath. Each time I filled all twenty-five bottles I had brought with me, one of the pages rinsed them out, and I refilled them all.

Three times we went through the filling process until at last the king took his final breath and died. I looked at the woman who sat beside me, trembling and weeping. In that moment, she had gone from being my princess to my queen.

Ruggieri, the astrologer, came to my mind. More than a decade had passed since that night, a month before her marriage, when homesick for Florence, Catherine had arranged for a dinner of some of us who had known her the longest—Ruggieri and I and some of her other confidants. There were thirty or so around the table in the cavernous dining room. Despite her wealth, she didn't treat us any differently because of our rank or station. She was but a fourteen-year-old girl. We were her friends who she could speak to in Italian. We were home to her.

It was that night, sitting next to her, whispering to her like a lover, that the ugly sorcerer told her he knew her future and asked her if she wanted to know what the years would bring. Of course, Catherine was eager. Ruggieri rolled out his charts inked on vellum, and Catherine stopped eating and drinking to examine them.

She put her hand on Ruggieri's hand and leaned closer to him. The sight of them conspiratorially whispering annoyed me. Her intelligent eyes scanned the star maps as he spoke. And then her pale cheeks flushed.

Getting up from my seat, I circled the table, stopping to talk to this person and that, and then made my way toward Catherine so it appeared I wasn't seeking her out—in case anyone noticed.

Standing slightly to the right of her chair, in the shadows of an alcove, I strained to hear the conversation, but the room was too full of noise and chatter. I had no choice then but to approach directly.

"You look like someone who's just been given a surprise," I said to her. And then looked at Ruggieri. "Have you cast a spell over her future, magician? What are you promising her?"

Even then he was proud and defiant and so sure of himself. "I haven't had to cast a spell—it's all written out. Even though she is marrying a second son, our duchessina is going to be the queen of France one day. It's in the stars."

And so the little man's prediction had come to pass. I knew my rival would soon be coming back to court because as queen, Catherine could demand it. More than ever I needed to prove my superiority over Ruggieri. And what would accomplish that better than solving Serapino's riddle of how to reanimate the breaths?

In the meantime, taking no chances, I would do to Ruggieri what he had done to me. He'd brought other perfumers to the court to try to diminish my position. I would bring other astrologers to try to diminish his.

Instead of going back to Paris with Catherine, I rode out in a different direction, to search out someone who might usurp Ruggieri's place: a Frenchman named Nostradamus.

Finding him, I convinced him to come to court and obtained a promise that he would arrive before the month was out. I returned to the Louvre, hopeful I had a plan to prevent my rival from gaining an unwieldy power, but when I arrived, I was distressed to find Ruggieri already in residence. The queen had not wasted a moment. Ruggieri was given his old quarters back and was seen coming and going from Catherine's rooms at all hours of the day and night. The years in exile had exaggerated his looks. More evil and dark than ever, he seemed not to care about his appearance or his cleanliness at all, and a stench followed him wherever he went. Catherine, who was so fastidious, seemed not to notice. Every day I was made ever more aware of the bond between them that seemed to defy logic.

The first time I visited her in her rooms after he'd arrived, I spied several bottles of revolting-looking liquids that reeked of his handiwork. Foul-smelling potions were always part of the spells he cast.

"You have to be careful, Your Highness," I told her upon sniffing one of the bottles. "There are elements of poisons in these. What has Ruggieri told you to do with them?"

"He's teaching me to read the waters. These are the liquids I put into the bowl. Do let me try to read yours."

I was stupefied. This was one of the most

intelligent women I had ever met! How could she think of engaging in this dangerous activity in the open? Reading the waters and trying to see the future through sorcery flew in the face of what the church professed.

"Surely the inquisition will not try a queen, yet I am worried nonetheless. What if the men of the church want to make an example to the world of their ultimate power?" I asked her.

She laughed as she assembled what she needed. A copper bowl from a shelf behind her table. A bottle of dark red-black viscous ink. A pure white feather pen with one black stripe at the top. A sheet of vellum. A silver plate. Six small votive candles and one taper.

First, using the pen and ink, she drew a blood-red pentagram on the sheet of paper. I wanted to ask her what the ink was made of, but I was too afraid. Besides, Ruggieri might not have told her the truth. If it was indeed human blood mixed with ink, the sorcerer would not have wanted her to know. But there was little doubt in my mind it was blood from a living creature and not dye from a plant that gave the ink its strange color.

Done drawing, Catherine placed the paper on the silver tray and then lit it on fire. Once the vellum had burned to ash, she used the ash to draw yet another pentagram, this one on the wooden tabletop. Next, Catherine placed the copper bowl in the center of the pentagram. After lighting the votives, she positioned each at a point of the pentagram. Finally, she spilled the contents of one bottle of liquid and then another into the bowl.

"Now we must wait for the water to settle and calm," she told me in a portentous whisper.

"And then?"

She held up her hand to quiet me as she studied the contents of the bowl. After a moment she seemed satisfied. "If I am to tell you your fortune, I need to study the water, looking for pictures of you. Just stay quiet for a moment longer, René. It takes great concentration."

I was flattered that she trusted me enough to perform this blaspheming in front of me. Like my old mentor, she sensed that even if what I was seeing was foreign and frightening, my loyalty was with her, not the church.

"Ah, there you are," Catherine said finally. "I see you in your laboratory, surrounded by all your tools and tinctures."

"Yes, my lady."

"You have a lot of secrets there, René, don't you?"

"From you? None."

"But I see you mixing mysterious dark potions. Much like Ruggieri's spells."

"You're mistaken. There are no black magic recipe books in my laboratory. There are only alchemical formulas I am working on to come up with a solution to use with the breaths. Perhaps that is what you're seeing?"

"No, these are different potions," Catherine said and then grew quiet again, watching the water, barely breathing lest she disturb its surface. "You know how to make many elixirs other than medicines, perfumes and lotions. You do, René. And you've used them." Suddenly she looked up. Away from the water and into my eyes. "You made something that you gave my husband for his mistress, and it changed their time together and I became pregnant. What was it you made? I see it here."

It wasn't possible that Catherine was divining this. No one but I had known the truth about the cream cut with powders that would seep into Diane's skin and put her to sleep.

Could Diane de Poitiers have figured out that the cream made her drowsy and told one of her ladies-in-waiting? Could other women of the court who each knew one side of the story have put all the different pieces together and shared it with Catherine? Was she teasing me about it now?

When I didn't respond, she insisted.

"What did you do, René? What were these creams you gave Diane de Poitiers?"

"Nothing, Your Highness. Simply creams to keep the skin supple, that's all."

"Why are you lying to me? Don't you under-stand that I will reward you for your ingenuity?

Never punish you . . ." She peered into the waters again and was lost in the glassy surface for several moments.

I watched her trying to make sense out of what she was seeing. Of what it meant.

What was going to become of her if Ruggieri's influence continued unabated? How far into this game could he push her?

"I know what you did, I can see it here. Come look." Her voice sounded deeper than usual and less animated. Almost as if she were in a stupor.

I leaned closer to the table, and as I did, I got a better whiff of the candles. These were not made in my shop. Not the perfumed candles infused with roses and lilies that Catherine preferred. These contained lavender, poppy seed and star anise. Had these candles been created by Ruggieri? Was he using herbs to drug Catherine and induce visions?

There was nothing in the water. Whatever Catherine thought she saw was in her own mind.

"You are mixing up the cream here . . ." She pointed. "And here you are giving it to my husband . . . and here his whore is administering it, and here see how she grows tired from it. How she stays in bed, sleeping so long in the morning. That was clever of you, René. Very clever. And very clever not to tell anyone. Your ability to keep your own council is important. You have so many secrets, don't you? Did you always? Even when you were a young boy? Secrets your mentor in the monastery taught you?"

"What is it you are asking, my lady?"

She looked up and into my eyes, held them for a moment and then wordlessly looked back.

"In Florence, when I went to the prison that day, they told me what you were accused of."

"I assumed they had."

"They said you had murdered the monk who had taught you everything you knew. That you had poisoned him."

"Yes, that is what they accused me of."

"Had you done that?"

"No, of course not. Serapino was ill and asked me to administer something to help ease his pain. But if the church had accepted my word, they would have had to accept that he took his own life, which would have meant he had not died a good Catholic, would not have been able to be buried in consecrated ground. It would have meant that God had failed him."

She nodded. "What men do in the name of God is atrocious. It's all around us, and the fight is heating up. In this battle of the Protestants versus the Catholics so many people will die."

She was right of course. The political climate was rife with the religious wars raging in England and France, and it worried all of us.

"In the water," Catherine whispered, "I can see bloodshed."

I nodded. "Yes, my lady."

"There are enemies of the Crown. And one in particular has begun to spread rumors that I am not on the side of the church. That I converse with the devil."

I had always feared the day Catherine would stand on the narrow ledge between witchcraft and devout Catholicism. I couldn't allow her the misstep that would push her to the side of the accused.

"You must give up these practices that Ruggieri has taught you."

She was about to say something and then stopped herself. "I need you to help me, Maître René. I need to send a message that my enemies will be able to read without any trouble."

"Of course," I responded with assurance. But I thought it strange that she was asking me to deliver a note for her. Unless of course she intended to have me deliver it along with a gift of fragrance.

"The nobleman in question brings his clothes to you to have them perfumed."

There were so many men who had me scent their garments I couldn't even guess who she might mean.

"I want you to create a poison and impregnate his clothes with it."

Revenge and nefarious activity was a Medici family trademark; nevertheless, I couldn't bear that my lady would engage in the black art of poisoning.

"I can't do that."

"It's not impossible. I've read that there are substances that could accomplish exactly that."

"Yes, there are. It's certainly possible. But it's murder of a most—"

"You would deny me now that *I* need *you?* Turn *your* back on *me?* I am alone here except for you and Ruggieri. Only we three share the same past and truly understand one another. I still remember coming to get you in the prison in Florence . . ." She shut her eyes as if the memory were too intense. "Oh, how that cell stank and how miserable you were. Do you remember when I finally got you out of there, when we stood on the street, how you kept breathing in gulps of air? Even the rotten air near the tanneries was better than the dungeon's stench."

She put her hand on mine. "Look in the water, René. Can't you see yourself? As you help me rise to power you become the most important perfumer France will ever know."

In that moment, the only thing I could see in the water was my own face reflected back at me. But there was a message in the way her fingers pressed into mine and the sound of her voice filled the chamber.

Catherine had never before asked me to repay her for what she had done for me. This was the first time since we'd left Florence that she had reminded me of my past, and now she was using it to tempt me with an alluring future. Her message was clear. Help her and my prominence would be guaranteed.

What if I said no? What would happen to me? I might be dismissed from the court, but I could survive that, could I not? I had my shop. Catherine had given me the deed to the land. I could sell it, and the price it would fetch plus the riches I had stored away would be enough. But where would I go? Back to Italy? I had been accused of murder there. Well then I could stay in Paris in my shop. But without Catherine's patronage I would be just another perfumer. Without Catherine I would lose my clients . . . I had no real friends outside of the court . . . no wife, no family . . . Catherine was my sun and my moon. I had lived in her orbit since I was fifteen years old. Without her I would be alone again . . . orphaned as I had been as a child.

Chapter 23

THE PRESENT

It was almost five PM. Griffin and Jac sat side by side in the small hidden laboratory behind the wine racks. He was poring over the notations in René's notebook. Jac had brought him back to the château after dinner to show him what she'd found and to introduce him to Melinoe and Serge. Melinoe been thrilled that the translator had arrived and welcomed Griffin, asking him what he'd already deciphered from the silver bells. Griffin said that he'd only begun to work on them, and they appeared to be incantations of some kind, but there was still so much he hadn't been able to figure out because of the combinations of ancient dead languages and arcane symbols.

Though she was clearly disappointed, she rallied and invited him to stay at the château to give him more time to continue his work in concert with Jac. But he declined, saying he was fine at the small hotel in town.

Jac was also disappointed that he hadn't agreed to move in, more than she would have imagined. Had she unconsciously been anticipating a midnight tryst? That didn't make sense. If that was the case, she could certainly go back with him to his hotel.

No. This was something else. Jac felt that it was imperative Griffin be here. In the château. That he *belonged* here. Seeing him sitting at René's worktable, hunched over the perfumer's papers, Jac had one of the strongest feelings of déjà vu she had ever experienced. And then, while she was watching him, she felt a physical push toward him, as though someone was actually pressing on her shoulders. She even turned around.

For a second she thought she saw Robbie behind her. His hands poised to push her again. Laughing as he lunged.

Despite trying to resist, she fell into Griffin.

He looked up.

"Sorry," she said, not wanting to explain. Not now.

Griffin brushed a lock of his salt-and-pepper hair out of his eyes with a familiar gesture. The moment was surreal. Being in the château, feeling the past so alive, sensing the perfumer who'd lived here almost five hundred years ago, and at the same time aware of Robbie's unreal presence and the reality of Griffin's as he sat here helping her. And helping do what? Search for a formula to bring the dead back to life. It was all too fantastic.

"These first ten pages are all ingredients," Griffin said. "I assume you got that far and know what they are?"

259

"I recognized some of them—spikenard, frankincense, myrrh, ambergris, civet, lemon—but not all of them. And not the formulas themselves. I'm sure it's written in Latin, but I'm hardly fluent."

"It's fifteenth- or sixteenth-century Latin. I'll do my best." He read for a few minutes. "He says that the most important thing is the quality of the ingredients," Griffin said, then read more. After a few seconds, he pulled out his phone.

"What are you doing?"

"I have an ancient Latin dictionary app."

"On a twenty-first-century cell phone. Of course."

He smiled. "But it doesn't matter since the phone doesn't seem to work down here." He went back to the notebook. "I think these are saffron, cinnamon and pepper, but I'll need to check when I can get online."

"Those are all easy enough to find," Jac said.

"Dragon's blood. Aloewood. Tutty," he continued, working from René's notes. "Have you ever heard of them?"

"Some of them. Aloewood is also called agarwood. And it's a very important perfume ingredient. Most of us refer to it as oud. It's actually a resinous heartwood that forms in evergreens from Asia when they become infected with a certain type of mold."

"Did you ever wonder who was the first person

who thought, Hmm, if I mix a tree fungus with an orange blossom oil, it might smell good?"

"All the time. Robbie and I used to make up scenarios and enact them. Like the moment someone decided to use whale vomit in a perfume."

"What kind of tree does aloewood come from?"

"It's called heartwood. It's light-colored and doesn't have much of an aroma. But once infected, the tree produces an aromatic resin as a response to the attack. It's very rare and was highly prized and important in many religious ceremonies going back to ancient times. It's even mentioned in the Sanskrit Vedas. Since the mid-1990s the trees have been listed as an endangered species, but some countries have created whole plantations of them."

"Off the top of your head . . . you just happen to know all that?"

"Robbie knew it . . . The past year working with him has been an amazing education . . ." Her voice drifted off.

"How about tutty and momie. Have you ever heard of them?"

Jac shook her head. "No, but there were a lot of ingredients used in the Renaissance that we don't use anymore. I have some books upstairs from my grandfather's library that Robbie was using to research this project. I'm not sure—but maybe we'll be able to find them there. Only one of the books is written in English. The other two are copies of Italian texts from the sixteenth century."

"And people wonder why studying a dead language like Latin is so important."

By the time Jac came back downstairs with the books, Griffin had translated more of the notes. "I'm certain this was René's workbook. Each of these lists varies only slightly from the others. As if he was refining one formula. At the end of the book here"—he showed her a page—"is a more formal recipe that features aloewood, tutty, momie, black henbane, honey, ambergris and musk pods."

"In Greek mythology henbane is called the plant of forgetfulness. It's a powerful hallucinogenic," Jac said. "Greek oracles burned it to help them go into trances. And a beer made from henbane was often left with the dead to help them pass over and was also drunk by mourners to ease their pain."

Griffin was riffling through one of the books. "This fits too. Listen." He read: " 'Henbane was part of every ancient alchemical laboratory. It's been found at Celtic Neolithic burial sites. According to the historian Albertus Magnus, sorcerers burned it and then searched for demons in its smoke. Mixtures of henbane and barley were found in ritual funerary drinking vessels, probably drunk by shamans to help the dead's passage to the next life. Zoroastrians reported that a man could drink it and spend a week in the afterlife.' "

"So its been associated with magic rituals going all the way back through history," Jac said.

"Now let's see what we can find out about the other ingredients."

For a half hour Griffin worked on the Latin text and Jac searched through the texts written in English. She loved the old and yellowed books. Loved the feel of the leather covers. Loved knowing that her grandfather had pored over them, and his father before him.

"Dragon's blood," Jac said. "Got it." And she read: "'A botanical extracted from Dracaena, *D. cinnabari*, it was used as a medicine, incense and a red dye.' According to this book it was important in medieval ritual magic and alchemy."

"So much of what was called alchemy is what we would refer to today as science rather than magic."

They both went back to reading. Fifteen minutes passed in silence. Here, deep underground, the only light from an electric lantern, Jac felt as if she were in the netherworld of her beloved Greek myths. She looked up to tell Griffin—but stopped, struck by a vision of sorts.

Jac sensed great sadness in the room. The emotion seemed to be perfuming the air. Hovering over Griffin like a cloud. She was looking at him but was seeing the ancient perfumer. His head bowed low. His shoulders slumped in misery. Working on his notes. Bereft.

"Here's something else," Griffin said.

The scene wavered, and Jac was seeing Griffin again. René was gone.

"I found a mention of tutty," Griffin continued. "It's in this copy of a fourteenth-century book, Francesco Pegolotti's *La Pratica Della Mercatura*. Translated it means *The Merchant's Handbook*. Tutty, Pegolotti wrote, was the charred scrapings from inside chimneys. It was imported from Alexandria and described as a very expensive nonperishable fragrance."

"The wood burned then would have different properties from wood burned now, as would the chimneys themselves. We can try, though."

They both returned to their reading. After a few minutes Melinoe interrupted them. "Would you like to come up for dinner?"

Jac hadn't realized how much time had passed. She looked at Griffin. "I'd just as soon keep going—you? I'd be happy with a sandwich later."

"We can do better than sandwiches. Just come up when you are done. Are you getting any-where?"

"I think so," Jac said.

"How soon until you can mix something up?" she asked.

"Oh, we're nowhere near that close," Jac said. "We've only just identified what we think is René's final formula and are working on his lists of ingredients. The problem is this was written over four centuries ago. I'm not familiar with some of what he used or even if it's available anymore." Jac felt a wave of frustration. What if she had the formula but never could find the right ingredients? Or what if she did but they never figured out what to do with the mixture?

As if reading her mind, Griffin asked both women, "Do you know what's supposed to happen with this substance? How it is used to reanimate the breath?"

"No," Jac said. Melinoe shook her head.

"Robbie told me he thought that the potion would be mixed with the breath and then if a newborn inhaled it, the deceased's breath would take root . . . The baby would host the old soul. Integrate. You'd live on in this new life," Griffin said.

"Yes, that's what Robbie and I constructed from what Thomas Edison and Henry Ford believed. They were fanatical about the idea of reanimating a dying breath," Melinoe said. "But surely it has to be in René's notes."

"It's written in fifteenth-century Latin, so it's going slowly and we're working it in sections."

"Can't you look ahead? Is there at least some mention of how to make whatever it is—a tincture, a formula?" Melinoe asked impatiently. "Are the incantations on the silver coverings a spell that's said when you use the elixir?"

"We just don't know anything yet," Griffin said

as he carefully turned the pages of the book, scanning each one. "Wait . . ." He looked at Jac. "You didn't even skim through it when you found it, did you?"

"It's in Latin," she said, not understanding why he was repeating Melinoe's question. "There was no point."

"Well, this part isn't in Latin. It's in French." He handed it to Jac, who read it for a few moments in silence.

"It's a formula for a perfume called Soul Water . . ." She read it out loud haltingly, translating into English as she went.

Take of good brandy, a half of a gallon; of the best virgin honey and coriander seeds, each a half of a pound; cloves and henbane, an ounce and a half; nutmegs, aloewood and dragon's blood, an ounce; tutty and momie, of each an ounce; benilloes, number four; the yellow rind of three large lemons. Bruise the cloves, nutmegs; cut the benilloes into small pieces; put all into a cucurbit and pour the brandy on to them. After they have digested twenty-four hours, distill off the spirit in balneo-mariae.

To a gallon of this water, add damask rose and orange flower water, of each a pint and a half; of China musk and ambergris, of each five grains; first grind the musk and ambergris with some of the water, and afterward put all into a large matrass, shake them well together, and let them circulate three days and nights in a gentle heat. Then, letting the water cool, filter and keep it for use in a bottle well stopped.

"A cucurbit? A balneo-mariae? Benilloes? What are these things?" Melinoe asked.

"The first is a still, the second is a double boiler. A matrass is a vessel for digesting and distilling. Benilloes are vanilla beans."

"And things like dragon's blood and tutty? Do you know what all those ingredients are?" Melinoe asked. She had come closer to Jac and stood behind her. She was wearing an expensive perfume that day, which Jac recognized as Golconda by JAR. Carnation and cinnamon. An unusual scent— one that, at over eight hundred dollars a bottle, very few women in the world wore. It suited her.

"No. I've never heard of quite a few of them. We're working on that challenge now."

"Aren't they here?" Melinoe asked as she pointed to the shelves.

"No," Jac said. "That's one of the mysteries we've encountered so far. The supplies here are rather pedestrian. The more exotic ones are almost too conspicuously absent."

"Why do you think?" Melinoe asked.

"Maybe René destroyed them . . . Maybe the experiments went wrong and he didn't want anyone to try and re-create them," Jac said. And then shivered. She didn't know why, but the thought frightened her.

"But you'll be able to find what's not here once you can figure out what it is?"

"Even if we do figure it out, the problem will be whether or not the mixture will be the same if we use modern-day equivalents," Jac explained.

"Yes, you mentioned that before," Melinoe said.

"Why wouldn't it be the same?" Griffin asked.

"Each item grew or was extracted from plants or herbs or woods under circumstances we can't re-create. Ancient ambergris, for instance. The whales in the sixteenth century had a different diet. The environment has so radically changed that the way the ingredients' odors mix today will result in an altogether alternate fragrance. If it even was a fragrance. That's just a guess. We don't know for sure how this was intended to mix with the breath—and then how to use it? Drink it? Apply it to the skin? We're still really in the dark."

Melinoe shook her head. *Like a petulant child,* Jac thought. "No. We are not. We can't be. We've come this far, and all this effort will not go to waste. Your brother's lifetime will not go to waste."

Jac winced. What Melinoe was saying was too personal to hear coming from a stranger.

"What if there are samples of these ingredients somewhere?" Melinoe looked at Jac. "Are there museums that would keep ingredients?"

"There are two fragrance museums, one in Grasse and one near Versailles, but I don't think they have ancient ingredients. And if they do, I doubt they'll relinquish what they have."

"Money," Melinoe said, "has amazing properties too. Institutions and collectors often want items they don't have and are willing to deaccession one in order to purchase another. You don't need great quantities of any single item, do you?"

"No, but even an ounce of ancient ambergris could be worth hundreds of thousands of dollars if you actually could find it."

Melinoe shrugged as if the amount were as insignificant as the dust on the shelves. "You leave the acquisitions to me. Just figure out what we need and make a list." She walked toward the door and then stopped.

The low light exaggerated the wing-shaped white streaks of hair on either side of her forehead. She was wearing all black. A tight-fitting sweater. A long pencil skirt made of black lace. High-heeled black boots with stiletto heels. Today her fingers were stacked with diamond and emerald rings, and she had a pair of pear-shaped emeralds hanging from her earlobes. She emanated energy and resolve. A diminutive lightning bolt.

Jac was certain that Melinoe meant every word

she said. If the ingredients existed, she would find them and pay for them. But first they had to know what they were searching for.

Once Melinoe left, Jac and Griffin returned to their research, and it was more than forty-five minutes before either of them found a mention of what they were looking for—the most obscure ingredient on the perfumer's list.

"You aren't going to believe this," Griffin said in a voice that belied his excitement.

"What?"

"Wait—let me just cross-reference it."

"Don't make me wait."

He ignored her as he flipped back to a page in another book. Jac glimpsed an illustration of an Egyptian mummy.

"You mean 'momie' as in 'mummy'? Really?"

"Yes. This is amazing, Jac. First from Pegolotti. He lists momie as a medicinal spice collected from the tombs of the dead. Collected from embalmed but not totally dried-out corpses. According to him, it was imported from Egypt and the Eastern regions. And here is another mention in the *Livre des Simples Médecines*, written in the fifteenth century . . ."

> Momie is a spice or confection found in the tombs of the people who have been embalmed, as they used to do in ancient times, and as the pagans near Babylon still

do. This momie is found near the brain and the spine. You should choose that which is shining, black, strong-smelling, and firm. On the other hand, the white kind, which is rather opaque, does not stick, is not firm and easily crumbles to powder, must be refused.

Momie has binding qualities. If a compress is made of it and the juice of shepherd's purse herb, it stops excessive nasal bleeding. Furthermore, to treat spitting of blood through the mouth because of a wound or a malady of the respiratory organs, make some pills with momie, mastic powder, and water in which gum Arabic has been dissolved and let the patient keep these pills under the tongue until they have melted, then let him swallow them.

Jac shivered. "An ingredient taken from the spines and brains of mummies . . ." she whispered, almost afraid to say it out loud. Where and how would they ever collect such a thing?

Chapter 24

MARCH 20, 1573
BARBIZON, FRANCE

In Paris the members of Catherine's flying squadron flit about the court and its environs like butterflies. When she was princess, there were only a handful of them; now there are dozens. These women are not at all the salacious whores that the enemies of the court like to suggest. I have known many of them to be the most intelligent and clever women in Paris, culled and cultivated by Catherine. She gathers them around her for their stimulating conversations, educates them in certain arts, dresses them, houses them and otherwise cares for them—not only out of the goodness of her heart but also to engender their loyalty to her.

The queen needs her supporters and she needs to trust them.

It's not unusual for some of these women to visit my shop to buy a fragrance or pick up supplies for Her Majesty. Sometimes they bring straightforward requests; sometimes they carry notes that ask for more clandestine concoctions.

The woman who entered my store that morning

on May 16, 1569, was masked, which was not usual. But that mask couldn't hide her scent, deeply redolent of a garden at dusk. And the mask didn't conceal her luxuriant hair, the warmest brown of cherrywood, twisted into a spiral except for the few escaped tendrils that curled fetchingly and framed her long neck. Her pale-green satin gown accentuated a narrow waist. The bodice was cut very low, as was the style, especially for ladies of the court, and her honey-colored flesh was abundant above the tight bustline.

It was a curious thing about Catherine's court: despite the suggestive and revealing clothes, her ladies were highly chaperoned and expected to be chaste unless Catherine asked otherwise of them. I had befriended many members of the squadron, and they talked freely with me when they came to the shop. Over wine, I was privy to their stories of how they danced with and seduced noblemen in order to gain secrets for their queen and how they were rewarded by her. It was an enviable life compared to some of the alternatives, but I knew how these women feared what would happen to them when they grew old and wrinkled. When the bloom was off their cheeks and their breasts sagged, would Catherine still care for them? How would they fare without families to tend to them in their dotage?

"Maître René, I have a note from the queen," my

visitor said as she reached into the pocket of her frock and pulled out a letter for me.

The queen was at Fontenay-sous-Bois, where the court had moved for several weeks, and it was not unusual for one of her ladies to return to Paris if there were things the queen needed.

> Dear René,
> The bearer of this note is Isabeau Allard . . .

I looked up at the woman. "Isabeau Allard?"

She nodded.

"You were married to the comte Allard?"

Again she nodded.

Allard had been a customer of mine for several years prior to his death. He was a young man killed in a battle two years before. I wasn't sure if I should mention this to the woman who stood in front of me, but Allard had been a favorite of mine. He always took his time in my shop and praised my goods generously.

"I knew your husband," I told Isabeau. "He was a fine gentleman."

She nodded, and for one very small moment the slits in the mask went dark as she shut her eyes. When she opened them again, they were clear but held a trace of sadness.

"It's kind of you to tell me, Maître René."

"Were you married long?"

"Only little more than two years."

"I'm sorry."

"I was luckier than many. To marry someone who you actually enjoy was a blessing. My father chose well."

I returned to the letter and read the rest of it.

Dear René,

The bearer of this note is Isabeau Allard. I have need of your lotion, the one with the apple base. Two bottles should suffice. As well I would like a bottle of my fragrance, and find something for Isabeau that suits her, as she will be part of the dinner party we are holding for an important nobleman whom I want her to impress. I will also need scent for two other of my ladies who will be at the dinner. All different scents that complement one another and do not compete.

And it was signed in familiar slanting handwriting I knew as well as my own.

Catherine

"It's clear?" Isabeau asked. "You understand? Catherine said you would."

I looked up—she had removed her mask. She was very lovely, with a high forehead, strong cheekbones and full lips. It wasn't just beauty; there was something impish and mischievous about her that caught me off guard and, I would have to say, made me curious about her right away.

"Yes, very."

"The queen wanted me to tell you that I read the note and know what's in it and what it refers to. In case you had any questions."

"That was wise. This is a dangerous business."

"But a necessary one," she said with a meaningful lilt to her voice. "There are so many intrigues at court."

"As your husband must have shared with you."

"It's why what I do for the queen is so important to me. I can't put on armor and go fight for my husband's honor the way his brother did, but I can fight this way."

As she spoke she squared her shoulders and in fact took on the stance of a soldier. Allard, I thought, had been a lucky man.

"It will take me a few minutes to prepare the apple lotion," I said. "Would you like wine while you wait? Or drinking chocolate?"

"Chocolate, please."

As I set to preparing her drink, I engaged her in small talk. She had a lilting, almost musical voice, and it was pleasing to listen to. "Have you been traveling all day?"

"Yes, I came straight here."

I glanced back. She didn't look as if she had been traveling for five hours. But even more curious she didn't smell as if she had been traveling. There was no scent of horses or sweat about her. Had I been asked, I would have guessed she'd bathed within the last two hours.

When I brought her the cup of chocolate, I leaned closer than warranted and sniffed.

"Are you wearing a fragrance?" I asked.

It was the custom to apply fragrances liberally, and indeed many women were too liberal with them. "Just lemon rose water. My husband used to buy it for me. From your shop I believe?"

I remembered. "Ah yes, he did." It was curious that I'd been selling Allard my fragrant water for this woman to wear to please him. But she smelled of a much more complicated scent than the simple citrus water.

"I still have the last bottle that he gave me, though there's not much left. That's why I was volunteered to come into Paris today. In addition to the perfume the queen wants me to wear to the party, I wanted to ask if I could buy more of your lemon rose water."

"Of course. But first I have a favor to ask you."

"What is it?"

"Tell me what you are mixing with my water."

"Nothing. I use it from the very same bottle that you sold my husband."

"May I approach so I can smell it on your skin?"

Isabeau looked surprised but smiled and agreed.

I stepped closer and leaned forward. Sniffing her neck. The fragrance was immediately intoxicating and like nothing I had ever smelled before. Her skin did something to my scents that was new to me.

Now, recalling that moment, I can still feel my shock.

"What is it, Maître René?"

"Rose essence has a certain aroma . . . It's one of the most powerful and lovely of all the scents a perfumer can use, but it's the scent of a rose past its bloom. The day after it is at its most perfect, if you will. It has to be, for the rose has been plucked and is on its way to dying . . . but something about the scent on you . . ."

I watched her as she listened to me. Up close her sparkling blue eyes had the depth of pools of water. As if, I thought, a man might literally be able to swim in her eyes.

Inhaling her scent and staring into her fathomless eyes . . . Something was happening to me. I was coming awake after a long sleep. Becoming aware after being ignorant.

"What is it about the fragrance?" she asked, breaking the spell.

"Yes, yes, on you the scent smells different. I smell something impossible—I can smell the roses blooming. I don't know how or why. That's the reason I asked if you had mixed my water with anything. Perhaps you have been walking in a garden today? Did you pick any flowers?"

"No, I've spent the day in the coach. There were strong winds, but I didn't get out and I haven't been around flowers."

I shook my head. It was so curious, but there was work to do so I dragged myself away from the wondrous aroma of blooming roses, left her in the anteroom and went into my laboratory to mix up the poisons that the queen had requested.

It had been years since that first time, while she was reading the bowl of water, that Catherine had asked me to assist in her nefarious deeds. I'd now helped my lady dispose of many of her enemies with poisons. But each time, I still tried to build up a wall around each request. I never asked the names of the men or the few women who she had wanted to rid the world of. The first time she offered that information I refused it.

"I thought you were harder than that, René," she said when I stopped her. "So do you have a soft heart after all?"

She laughed and I with her, but I couldn't answer. It wasn't so much a soft heart as a guilty soul. If I knew their names, I would have to think about their families. I might one day be forced to meet one of their wives in my shop or at court and have to look into her eyes, knowing I had been responsible for her husband's death.

But my queen didn't care that I didn't want to

know who she planned on killing with my poisons. She needed an ally, a partner, and so in the end, each time, I had no choice but to listen to the names of the men and women who together we did away with.

As I mixed up these new elixirs, I tried not to think of Allard, but I couldn't think of anything else. The knight had been one of Henry's closest allies, but the queen had suspected him of being a spy. And so she did what she often did to spies. Unfortunately, after the man's death, she discovered she'd been wrong about him and out of guilt had brought Allard's wife to court.

Catherine had mourned her mistake and vowed to change her tactics. In fact for a full year after the "Allard Incident," as she referred to it, she asked me for nothing but soaps and lotions, candles, scented gloves, pomades and perfumes.

But then the day came when she once again took up her old ways. "As much as I don't want to, René, I have to protect France. I have to protect the Crown. And this is the only war I can wage and win."

And so she had gone back to choosing who should live and who should die, and I went back to aiding her when she needed me to.

Carefully, while Isabeau sipped the chocolate, I prepared the lotion Catherine had asked for, mixing ground apple seeds and almonds. As I always did when working on this formula of

Brother Serapino's, I thought again how his lessons had been so very instrumental to me in serving my queen. A blessing? Or a curse? That afternoon I still didn't know. But today I do. Sadly, today I do.

I made two bottles of the lotion Catherine had requested.

With care I secured the stoppers, wrapped the bottles in cotton and slipped each into a leather pouch stamped with my mark. Then, items in hand, I returned to Isabeau. She was sitting on the couch, delicate china cup in hand. Smiling, she greeted me.

"That didn't take long. This chocolate is so delicious. What makes it so much better than what we have at the court?"

"I add vanilla that comes from an orchid plant grown and cultivated by the Aztecs. The fruit ripens almost a year after the flower blooms. Since it's imported, it's quite expensive. Too dear for the castle to use in cooking for so many."

"Do the chefs use them for Her Highness?"

"I wouldn't be surprised."

"Could I see what they look like?"

I pulled out a drawer and withdrew one of the long skinny beans, and Isabeau ran her finger down its dark-brown wrinkled bark. Then she lifted it to her nose, inhaled and after a moment sighed. "What a wonderful aroma. Do you grind this up? What else do you use it for?"

"Chefs use it in custards." I took a knife and slit the pod open, scraped off some of the sap and offered her the knife. "In addition to chocolate, I also use it as an ingredient in some of my perfumes. It mixes especially well with roses."

Her curiosity was appealing. I watched her sniff the brown seeds and then rub them between her fingers and taste them.

"They need to be mixed with sugars," I said, laughing at her wrinkled nose.

She finished her drink and put the cup down.

"So now that I've made the apple lotion"—I gestured to the two pouches down on the table— "let's prepare a scent for you."

"Something to make me impossible to resist," she teased.

"That's already been taken care of by your maker."

Charmingly, she blushed. "Wonderful enough to ensure that the duc de Vendôme not only has a delightful time but finds himself compelled to answer all my questions so the queen can use them to her political advantage."

"Spying is a dangerous game." I was suddenly angry at my patron but not sure why.

"Not for us, Maître René. Catherine has schooled us in the ways we can endear ourselves to the men she entertains. We don't always have to compromise our virtue."

"Always?"

She smiled coyly. For a moment I found Isabeau almost repulsive. I was seized with an urge to grab her and shake her and chastise her for what she was doing. It was wrong. It went against nature. She was sullying her soul. And then the moment passed, and I wondered at my odd reaction.

"Don't you find it unpleasant work?"

"It can be . . ." She nodded. "But what work is not sometimes unpleasant? Who has a life of all pleasure and no pain?"

I saw the evidence of what she'd suffered in the way she shrugged her shoulders and in the tone of her voice, and for a moment felt a new pang of guilt knowing that I had inadvertently been partly responsible for it. Although I knew that was foolish. If I had not made the poison the queen used, someone else would have. If I had refused, there would have been another to step into my place and provide what she wanted. Back then, that was how I justified my deeds. And how I thought I would be able to go on justifying them for all of my days. But I'd only just met Isabeau.

"I think I will need to try some essences on your skin and see how they react—would you be willing?"

"If you think that it's necessary."

"I do, especially because the lemon rose water smells so different on you than it does on anyone else. I want to test what I prepare for you."

It was late afternoon. The shadows in the shop

lengthened. The cacophony of smells became intoxicating. And I became absorbed by the phenomenon that occurred with every essence I tried on her skin.

Isabeau's chemistry accentuated and changed each one. What I smelled on her was not what was in the bottle but instead the aroma of that particular flower in bloom. Before it was picked! Before the effleurage process had begun.

I had never heard of such a thing; never before had it occurred.

"I don't understand," I said as I stroked jasmine absolute on her wrist, waited a few moments and then lowered my nose to her hand. The aroma was of a fresh sprig of the white flowers, ripe and ready to be plucked. This was not an oil-based residue of pressed petals—it was blooming flowers.

She lifted her wrist to her nose and smelled.

"Have you ever noticed this before?"

"I was not aware of it, Maître."

I tried essence of lavender next, putting a drop of the tincture on my forefinger and then stroking it against a clean spot higher up on her arm.

"Again," I said to her. "It's happened again."

She lifted her arm to her face.

"Can you smell it?" I asked.

"Fresh lavender from a garden. Is it not the quality of your ingredients?"

"They are the same ingredients I used yesterday and the day before."

Next I lifted the bottle of lily of the valley and repeated the process to the same end.

"There is no more room on your arms," I said to her finally after I'd tested another four scents.

With a provocative gesture, she lifted her chin, offering me her neck.

I wet my finger with the scent of violet, then slowly dabbed her skin. Leaning in, I breathed deeply.

"You are becoming a garden." I smiled as I next applied orange blossom to the other side of her neck. My finger lingered even longer as it made its way down the elegant column.

She didn't pull back. Nor did she comment, but she did close her eyes. With pleasure, it appeared.

I leaned in to smell the orange blossom and was overwhelmed with desire.

"I still have heliotrope to try, but the skin on your neck is all scented."

Without saying a word she pushed out her chest, inviting me to anoint the tops of her breasts and cleavage.

I tipped the bottle over, wet my forefinger and traced the swell of her breasts with the oil. Her breath quickened. I leaned down toward her glistening skin and inhaled. Fresh heliotrope, smelling of pepper and licorice and sweetness, mingled with all the other flowers that were blooming on her skin, and then, without forethought, I pressed my lips to her flesh.

She moaned and thrust herself toward me.

I grabbed her around the waist and pulled her closer, bruising her neck with kisses as I undid the twist of her hair. The thick dark ropes fell around my face like a velvet curtain, and I was enclosed within her.

Isabeau tasted sweet. I can no more explain this than I can explain how perfume turned to living flowers on her skin. But as I pressed my lips to this spot behind her ear and that spot in the hollow on her neck, and then when I finally lifted her face and kissed her mouth, I tasted liqueur. All I could think of was that she was a creature made by bees from nectar collected from flowers and turned into honey.

My kiss was returned with a surprising joy and playfulness that inflamed me all the more. There are women who want sex to reassure themselves they are desirable. Others who use conquest as currency and allowed me to take them to ensure their ability to obtain the special scents that supposedly only the queen wore. I had a shelf of those—none of them truly worn by Catherine, of course—that I would sell for either favors or exorbitant sums as long as the wearer promised she would never tell anyone she was wearing one of the queen's originals. But often they bragged about their exclusive scents, and word got back to Catherine, who teased me about how I was becoming rich off her.

Isabeau was not reacting like a woman who wanted anything from me. She seemed to revel in my touch and enjoy my lips and my tongue in a way that was unfamiliar to me. Few women I'd known got this much pleasure from the act.

And then, in the evening shadows, as small waves from the river slapped against the foundation of my shop, Isabeau took my face in her two hands and kissed me, pushing my lips apart with her tongue and exploring my mouth.

Her gown was a complicated affair made even more so by her undergarments, but she undressed as if putting on a show. Doing a small dance, twirling this way and that as she disrobed.

"Is this what Catherine has taught you to do?" I asked as she slipped out of the first layer of silk.

She searched my face, wondering how to answer.

"The truth, Isabeau. I am most intrigued by the truth."

"Yes, then."

"Does she have you do this for many men?"

"Not for many."

"How many have there been?"

"Why do you want to know?"

"I don't know except I want to know you. *All* of you. I need to understand what about you makes the perfume blossom. What secrets you have. So tell me how many have there been?"

"There have been five men."

"And you spied on all of them?"

"Yes."

"And did you bed each?"

"Four of them."

"For how long?"

She hesitated. I went to her and took over the job of undressing her, unlacing her corset, smelling roses and lemons, smelling my scent on her clothes. My own skin was burning, my desire making it more and more difficult for me to proceed slowly. I was overcome with the need to rip off her clothes and take her quickly, but something warned me that I would be forgoing great pleasure if I rushed.

"It's all right. I won't be shocked," I reassured her.

"I was with the first for almost a year. Only a few months each with the others."

"And were you a good spy?"

She threw back her head proudly, defiantly. "I was."

Her bravery incited me. I finished unlacing the corset, releasing her full breasts and with them a new infusion of the rose scent.

Reaching over to the table, I pulled the bottle of lily essence forward, uncorked it, wet my fingers and then very gently painted circles around her dark nipples, making her skin glisten with the oil.

"Did any of them do this to you?" I asked.

"No," she whispered.

I could barely hear her voice.

As if she were a fragile glass bottle, I unwrapped the rest of her body oh so carefully until she was standing before me, in the twilight, completely naked. And then I anointed every inch of her skin with oils of flowers until she glistened.

"My garden," I whispered to myself as much as to her.

Her eyes were heavy lidded, her lips moist and parted, her cheeks flushed.

"Has any man ever made you want *him?*" I asked.

"No," she moaned.

"No one has ever pleased you without pleasing himself?"

She shook her head.

I got down on my knees and pushed her legs apart slightly and then buried my face between her thighs. Here was the only part of her body I had not anointed, but it glistened on its own. And here was the only part of her body that did not smell of my flowers but of her own sweet honeyed essence. The odor was neither sour nor stale— Isabeau's essence was a perfumed liqueur, and as I licked her I became drunk.

Everything about that late afternoon is emblazoned on my mind. I can remember how the candles sent red highlights dancing through her hair and how her throaty laugh of pleasure sounded like nothing I had ever heard. I thought I had pleased women before. Thought I had understood passion. But this was a thing of itself. I had never known a woman who enjoyed sex the way Isabeau did. Who luxuriated in our coming together the way I had seen others luxuriate in ermine cloaks and jewels. She gorged on it the way I had seen men gorge on food. She drank it in the way I had seen partygoers imbibe. She was joy and felt joy and made me feel it too. And with that joy, for the first time that I could remember, I felt a lightness about the world. I ceased to worry, to be anxious.

When she put her hands on either side of my head, her fingers weaving through my hair, and held me, I felt a pressure inside that I could not control. *So this was being wanted,* I thought. Every moment of my lonely life came pouring out of me, and I wept. With my head between her thighs, sucking on her nether parts, listening to her rapture, tears poured out of my eyes. That I had lived so long and not known this! That I was only finding it now—with someone who was above my station and as impossible a partner as the queen herself would be. A cruel joke.

And then Isabeau pulled me up with her beautiful little hands and kissed my mouth that was wet with her own juices. Together we fell back against the couch, and as I slid inside of her, my very life exploded.

Chapter 25

THE PRESENT

Griffin was still bent over the same book, trying to decode more of what he'd found in Florentin's papers. Jac was sitting in the same position she'd been in—how long ago? One minute? Two? Five? However long the episode had lasted, Jac was almost certain she'd accessed someone else's memory bank.

She'd left her own consciousness and disappeared for what had seemed like days. Jac had memory-lurched into René le Florentin's life almost five hundred years ago.

She'd thought his thoughts and felt his love and his frustrations. And this wasn't the first time she'd done it since she'd come to the château. There was no denying it now.

Jac fingered the red silk tied around her left wrist—the connection to the present that kept her tethered to her own time and place during lurches. She rolled the thread against her skin now and tried to focus on what she'd seen and learned. This episode hadn't been as frightening as some in the past had been. Was it because of the bracelet?

"Jac?" Griffin sounded worried. "Are you all right?"

"I'm fine."

"We should stop. It's almost nine o'clock, and I think we've found out as much as there is to know about these ingredients without going inside of le Florentin's head."

She didn't say anything. Just looked at him. But he guessed.

"Is that what just happened?" he asked.

"I think so. Or my overactive imagination acting up."

"Resistance is futile," he said, laughing as he quoted the Borg line from the *Star Trek* episodes they used to watch when they were together. "Were you seeing another of your past lives?"

Jac hadn't yet told Griffin about Malachai's theory that she was a memory tool, able to tap into other people's past lives. But she told him now. He listened and halfway through, when he heard her voice crack, he took her hand and held it until she finished.

"So you think that I'm the perfumer? And you're the woman he was in love with? Isabeau? And you are remembering his life?"

"I'm afraid to think it," she whispered as she nodded.

Griffin put his arm around her. "Let's get out of here, go into town and have a late supper. We've done enough for one day."

Jac went up to her room and got her handbag. She didn't see Melinoe or Serge and didn't look for them. She just wanted to leave the house and clear her head.

They ate at a lovely local restaurant, Le Relais de Barbizon, and afterward took a walk through the village, pausing to examine the well-preserved stone buildings.

"This is a little confusing for me," Jac said. "Even though we're not at the château, the sense that I'm still in the past hasn't quite dissipated."

"Maybe it's because the town itself is so steeped in previous centuries. René le Florentin walked these same cobblestone streets. Passed many of these buildings."

They walked back to the Hôtel les Pléiades, where they sat side by side on a banquette in the darkened bar and drank cognac that the barkeep had poured from an old crystal bottle.

For a while they didn't talk. The fire was crackling, and there was no one else around. The companionable silence was soothing. After a while, Griffin reached out and brushed a lock of Jac's hair off her forehead.

"I always miss you when I'm not with you. And when I'm with you, I always feel we belong together."

Jac heard the words and wanted to respond, but she was still plagued with fear. If her hallucinations were past-life memories, she was his poison. And if the fugue states were not past-life memories, what were they? An aberration? Insanity?

It was the conundrum of her life. One way, she was the incarnation of Griffin's destruction—and the destruction of all the men he'd been. The other way she was delusional or victim of some kind of brain anomaly.

Leaning forward, Griffin kissed her. For a moment her confusing thoughts fought against the embrace. She needed to figure this out once and for all. And then it didn't matter. There was so little she could count on. At least there was this warmth searing through her. This actual want. This unquestionable urge to be with this man.

The kiss was tender and determined at the same time, it tasted of cognac and desire, and when it ended, they separated and were silent, overwhelmed by its power, by its pull.

Jac reached for her drink and took a sip. Was Griffin her fate? she wondered yet again. And then she heard her brother's voice answer:

You are fate. Once you were Moira. The woman you dream about. That's why you can remember other lives.

No, she almost said out loud. Greek gods and goddesses are myths. Jac had spent her whole adult life finding the seeds of those myths to prove that man had created these stories in order to explain away what they otherwise couldn't understand or process.

She looked at Griffin. He clearly hadn't heard anything. Of course not. Robbie's voice had been in her head.

"It's been such a long and strange day," she said. "I'm going to ask the waiter to call me a taxi. I should go back to the château."

"No, you shouldn't," he said hoarsely and took her hand. "You should come upstairs with me."

Griffin's room was on the second floor. A large corner room decorated with tapestries and heavy damask curtains in gold and blue. There was a fireplace already lit, a couch, desk, chairs—Jac saw it all in a blur as they fell onto the bed.

Slowly, carefully, Griffin undressed her. In the golden light, his expression showed the same determination that she'd felt in his kiss. He wasn't rough, but there was a force to his actions. As if he were anticipating that she might protest.

And she did think about protesting, but her body fought her mind. She knew where they were headed was dangerous. Once they made love, once he held her naked in his arms and slipped inside of her—she would never be able to walk away from him again.

"Jac . . ." he whispered as he traced the outline of her lips with his finger. "Stop thinking. This is right."

He kissed her. For a moment she held back, and then she pushed her lips hard against his. She wanted to stop thinking. To just be here with this man, who for better or worse she never had been able to break away from. It seemed she never really breathed deeply except when she was with him. Never really felt everything fully unless she was feeling him. Jac didn't need a man to complete her. But he was the only man who she completely connected with.

He pulled back. For a moment he just hovered above her. Looking down. Not moving. She didn't move either. Didn't say a word. Just watched him watching her.

He smiled. Then stood up, unbuttoned his shirt and shrugged it off. Stepped out of his jeans and underwear. The fire outlined his body, and she sucked in her breath. Her first sight of him naked always astounded her. There was a Greek sculpture she often visited in the Metropolitan Museum that reminded her of Griffin. Long and lanky and graceful, it was a perfect expression of sexuality. But it was cold marble. Griffin was warm flesh.

He came to her on the bed and undressed her, and when she lay there, as naked as he was, she reached out and touched his mouth, traced the line of his neck. His Adam's apple. His collarbone. She stared at him. Griffin was everything she thought of when she thought about sex, about release, about desire. All her life, no matter who she had been with, it was this man she was staring at now who she wanted, who she never had to tell what to do to her or how to move or how to touch her. It was this man who understood how to hold her and move her and move in her and what to whisper to her and how to bite gently in the space where her shoulder met her neck and how to put his hand under her and touch her while he went inside of her, who looked at her with an expression that turned her into liquid. They generated heat. They built fire. They created alchemical gold.

Above her, Griffin's eyes closed. And then René's opened.

Rather than being frightened, she was heady with the experience. Two men. Both different. Both the same. Her insides were on fire. Her heart was opening. Breaking. Healing. They had been apart. They were together. Joined. In the past, in the present, in the future.

The feeling was so overpowering there were moments when Jac was sure she wasn't herself any longer but the French lady who was the perfumer's lover, and as René, Griffin was rougher. Taking her not as an act of tenderness but as something desperate. As if this was the last time they would ever make love. The last time they would ever be together. Isabeau felt it, and Jac suffered her fears.

René thrust up inside her, more deeply, and she clenched around him. She smelled lust and honey, woods and desire. Smelled magic. The magic of what he was doing to her.

Then Griffin was back.

She was on her stomach now, and his hands were under her, teasing her as he slipped in and out, and she was lost to the rhythm of the ride. Lost to the time and the place. Swirling on herself, down and in on herself, feeling the tension building, tighter and tighter, growing in intensity, blocking out all reason and sending her into a vortex of emotional and physical response that she hadn't felt in so long, so long, so long . . .

"René." One word from her lips. Soft. A whisper. Jac orgasmed, or Isabeau did. Who was she? It didn't matter. Who was he? He was her all. And he always had been. This man who had been so many men to the many women she had been. This man—her fate. Toth, an Egyptian perfumer, and René le Florentin and Giles L'Etoile, another perfumer in revolutionary France. All these men. These lips and hearts and cocks and fingers and legs and eyes. All one. All the same.

"Griffin." Another word from her lips as she became lost in the waves as they washed over her and she emerged in the luxurious ebbing. She was shaking. Sinking deeper into exultation. Her womb was vibrating. He was playing her like a musical instrument, and every movement he made set off another trill of quivering and trembling.

"Jac . . . Jac . . ." He wasn't just saying her name; he was taking her and giving her and being with her as profoundly as he ever had.

She had lost all ability to speak, to say his name, to say any name, to know her own name or place. She only knew that she was alive with him, through all time, and this was a celebration that they had found each other like this over and over and over again and would always and then . . . she burst.

Colors. Lights. Smells. Shuddering. Tremors. Alive with him . . . alive . . . and then even somehow more alive.

Chapter 26

THE PRESENT
SATURDAY, MARCH 22
UPPSALA, SWEDEN

Two days later, in Sweden, Melinoe, Jac and Serge began their search for samples of the ingredients in René le Florentin's formula. A black limousine with tinted windows picked them up from the small airport in Berthåga. While they drove to Uppsala, Melinoe regaled Jac and Serge with stories about the wunderkammerns of the Middle Ages, the most famous of which they were on their way to visit.

"The Augsburg Cabinet of Curiosities was a gift to King Gustav II from the German city of the same name. In 1632 it held over five hundred precious objects both artistic and natural. It was the age of exploration and the beginning of the scientific revolution. Trade routes were open and merchants were bringing strange and wonderful things back to Europe.

"I've always been fascinated with these cabinets. They really were the precursors to our museums. Man has forever thirsted for knowledge and needed to examine the world in order to understand it. Dissect it in order to comprehend it. These cabinets are the era's depositories of knowledge. Some cabinets were devoted to science, some to nature, others to the arts," Melinoe said. "I read Peter the Great's was filled with teeth that he had pulled. He thought he was a dentist."

"I've seen the one in the Getty," Jac said. "It's really a work of art, but its contents were gone. Is the Augsburg cabinet more complete?"

"It holds about twenty-five percent of what it once had. Few cabinets weathered the tides of time very well. And when you think about the oddities that were collected along with the precious stones and artwork, it's not surprising so many are gone. But imagine—once it held a mermaid's hand, salt made from tears, a hatband of snake bones, a two-headed cat, a decanter of everlasting sadness, virgin's milk, and the horn of a bull seal."

"The milk would have certainly spoiled by now." Serge smiled.

The fifteen-minute drive passed through fields and forests: lush countryside with long stretches of rolling hills dotted with picturesque houses and picket fences.

Jac thought of Griffin, whose plane was flying over the Atlantic. He had left for America that morning to be with his daughter for her birthday. Before he left, he'd finished translating Florentin's papers, as they'd come to calling them, and started on the bells. But the silver containers were proving a more complicated task since so many of the symbols remained a complete mystery. He said he'd be coming back within the week to keep working on them. She wanted to believe him, but at the same time she was afraid to. The two nights they had spent together had shaken her. What tragedy was yet to come?

"Here we are," Melinoe said, interrupting Jac's thoughts. "The museum is just up ahead."

Jac looked out the window at the Gustavianum, a stone two-story building facing a cathedral, nestled in the fifteenth-century university town.

"The museum houses one of the last astronomical theaters, lit by the natural light from the cupola." Melinoe pointed up.

The copper cupola, now green, sat on top of the graceful rectangular building like a well-designed onion.

"It is one of the city's landmarks and has a disturbing history since autopsies and vivisections were performed here in the 1600s, before they were commonplace and acceptable."

It was not the first time Jac noted the woman's fascination with the gruesome. What was it about disturbing events that ignited Melinoe's interest?

"Have you been here before?" Jac asked.

Melinoe nodded. "With my father when I was a girl. We came to see the very object we will be visiting today." Her voice hitched when she referred to her father. She looked over at Serge, who gave her a sympathetic glance.

The driver opened the door. As Serge got out and offered Melinoe his arm, Jac thought that Melinoe was very much like one of the objects she collected. Rare and unusual. Created, it seemed, out of base materials but greater than the sum of her parts. Intense, intrepid, determined—and sexual in an almost predatory way. She'd seen how Melinoe touched Griffin's arm when she talked to him. Leaned into him. Serge had kept his eye on her when she did that, clearly not happy about it. And now he was watching her like that again as Melinoe spoke in the same seductive way to the gentleman who had come out to greet them.

Melinoe introduced Dr. Aldrick Ebsen, who then took them up to the room where the cabinet was on display.

"Philipp Hainhofer was the architect of this

amazing gem," Ebsen said. He spoke in English with a strong Swedish accent. He was in his early sixties, with a thick head of white hair and sparkling brown eyes that he didn't take off of Melinoe. The museum director was falling for her charm.

"Hainhofer himself called this cabinet the eighth wonder of the world, and in the first third of the seventeenth century it was probably true," he explained.

They were ascending an old stone staircase with a simple handrail leading up to the second story, and the curator continued to regale them as they climbed.

"It was a time capsule of its day, wasn't it?" Melinoe said. "A symbol of the art, culture and science of its era. And it says much about the class system. Today museums are open to everyone, but then only royalty and the aristocracy had the time or the finances to indulge in studying the natural world."

"Exactly. In examining the cabinet's contents, you can literally travel back to the Middle Ages and see what enticed and enchanted the learned men of that time."

Since she'd come to stay at La Belle Fleur, Jac had gone back to the Middle Ages a different way—taken a much more upsetting route. She was sure she'd prefer examining a cabinet.

They walked into a large light-gray room that

glittered with dozens of different size cases holding antique globes, shining brass telescopes, rare books, silver and mapmaking instruments.

In the center, enclosed in a large glass cylinder, was the item they had come to see. The ebony, warm golden woods, semiprecious stones and gilt trim glowed. Over eight feet tall and half as wide, it was an imposing piece that seemed to soak up all the light in the room and outshine all the other treasures.

Jac's eyes were drawn to the top of the cabinet. A dark-brown textured cup was encased in gilded silver and decorated with iridescent mother-of-pearl, twisting coral branches and crystal, all held up by an exquisitely sculpted silvered sculpture of Neptune, god of the sea, with his trident.

"That is a Seychelles nut," Ebsen said, noticing Jac's fascination with the crowning arrangement. And then he turned back to Melinoe.

"I've closed off this room so that you can view the cabinet in private. If you will allow me . . ." He gestured to the center of the room. Melinoe followed him, Jac went next, and Serge held back. He was acting strangely. Jac wondered if he was jealous of how Melinoe was treating the curator. Surely he'd seen his stepsister act out before. So what was bothering him?

"Your request was quite unusual," Ebsen said. "We haven't returned all the items to the cabinet since we took them out and put them on display."

"And I do appreciate you doing it for me now. I just really wanted to be able to experience this marvel the way its maker intended," Melinoe said.

Ebsen opened the glass case. The door swung out, and he was able to slide the cabinet forward so they all could stand around.

"It really is an architectural marvel," Ebsen said as he rotated it. "This upper section of drawers and compartments rests on a ball-bearing device so those who came to view the cabinet could sit and watch it move. Down here . . ." He pulled out a drawer, which turned into a small stepladder. "This enabled visitors to reach the uppermost parts to view them. And here . . ." He pulled a fold-out table from the undersection. "A viewing table complete with a cushion. A luxurious respite for your arms if examining the masterpiece exhausted you."

The marvel that was the cabinet was difficult to take in. There was so much to look at and examine at once. The insides of the doors were inlaid with semiprecious stones: agate, jasper, lapis lazuli, bronze reliefs, paintings, gold, more silver, all meticulously designed.

Jac was riveted to a glowing bowl filled with perfectly replicated ceramic fruit, all made of jewels.

Opening yet another door, Ebsen showed them what he called a virginal and explained it was a keyboard with a mechanism, which could be set to a clock to play automatically at a certain time, and a diorama with small wax-and-fabric men set up in a scene. There were several automatons—scenes from history and mythology—that especially interested Jac. One box displayed Apollo and Cyparissus, showing the latter's transformation into a cypress tree that rotated, one side showing the grotesque boy, the other the fully formed tree.

"There are mathematical instruments and relics here. And what surprises many is that there are also games. It's important to remember that this was a pastime and not just a treasure."

Ebsen pulled out a board, which opened to reveal two halves.

"This is the game of Goose, where the player advanced based on a throw of the dice." He withdrew another board game. "And this is roulette."

It was numbered from I to XII, with markers in between. Fruits and scrollwork decorated each corner.

"We have four decks of playing cards." He withdrew one to show them.

Jac thought of Malachai and how much he would have enjoyed seeing those late fifteenth-century cards. He collected them and had more than forty antique decks, but none this old.

"At the time memento mori was quite popular." He showed them a seemingly ordinary portrait that upon closer inspection revealed a grinning skull. "Quite a curious preoccupation of the era. Art to remind you that you must die. Perhaps they believed that collecting itself staved off death."

"Yes," Melinoe said, her voice laced with determination and sadness. "Amassing beauty that outlives you keeps you immortal," she said.

"Do you know what items are missing from the cabinet?" Serge asked.

"Not all of them, no. But we do have several receipts for things that were removed. King Gustav's widow took out a sculpted wax image, an ivory perspective, a step counter, a book of birds, a small ring and two opals."

At the mention of the stones, Melinoe's eyes narrowed.

"That's what I'd really like to focus on. The natural objects that are in the cabinet."

"Ah yes, so you said on the phone. Let's all have a seat back here. It will be easier to examine the items."

He showed them to a small wooden table with four folding chairs that clearly had been placed there for their visit alone.

The three of them took their seats. Ebsen opened a green felt coverlet and placed it over the tabletop.

One by one he brought over precious stones, pearls, shells, nuts and small unrecognizable rocks and told them as much as he knew about each. He pointed to an uneven gray-black rock the size of a child's fist. "Ambergris," he said. "Do you know what it is?"

Jac started to speak but under the table felt Melinoe's hand touch her lightly on the upper thigh.

"No, I don't think I do," Melinoe said.

Ebsen explained: "This substance consists of mostly cholesterol secreted by the intestinal tract of the sperm whale. It's usually found floating in the sea or washed up onshore. It has a foul odor at first but, after aging, is one of the most precious ingredients in fine perfumes—and has been since the sixteenth century. It's outlawed from being traded now in many countries, I believe."

Jac stared at the large lump of hardened wax. She'd worked with ambergris but never seen this large a chunk of it. A piece this size was worth hundreds of thousands of dollars. There was no finer ingredient to fix a scent and add richness and roundness to a perfume. In America, where it was banned, niche perfumers who didn't sell their creations in bulk bought it on the black market and used it anyway. A piece this old would have its own wondrous odors. The longer ambergris aged, the more unique its properties. Jac's hand itched to reach out and touch it, but it was Melinoe who picked it up and felt its heft.

"Is it all right if I hold it?" she asked Ebsen, too late for him to object.

"I think it will be all right." He smiled.

Serge chose that moment to stand. "Can you show me how the drawers that held these objects were made? I'm an architect, and while the inventory is fascinating, the construction is even more so."

Ebsen nodded, and the two men walked back to the cabinet.

Melinoe looked at Jac. "The ambergris appears right to you?"

"Absolutely, it—"

Melinoe interrupted her. "Perfect. Let's see what Ebsen is showing Serge."

Jac stood up, and so did Melinoe. As she did, her handbag fell and spilled its contents; she bent to pick them up.

"I'll be there in a moment," Melinoe said.

Jac joined Serge and the curator who, with delight, was in the process of pointing out and explaining the different joints and closures, hinges and other aspects of the cabinet that they hadn't yet discussed. After a few seconds Melinoe joined them.

"Well, this has been an amazing treat," Melinoe said when Ebsen finished. "And now we have another appointment. I can't thank you enough, Dr. Ebsen." She took the curator's hand and held it in her own for longer than seemed normal. The pale man blushed and became flustered and told her that the pleasure had been all his.

"The pleasure," Melinoe said as she smiled at him intimately, "is truly all mine."

Chapter 27

Upon returning to the château in Barbizon, Melinoe invited Jac to meet them in the library for drinks to discuss their journey.

Jac was impatient to learn the purpose of the trip they'd just taken. She still didn't know why they'd flown to Sweden and back just to examine an ancient piece of ambergris. She had thought Melinoe was going to try to buy the ancient material housed in the Gustavianum Museum— but she hadn't even broached the subject.

Masculine brown leather armchairs were arranged around a glass slab coffee table that rested on stacks of books. The walls were covered, floor to ceiling, with dark mahogany shelving and molding. The ceiling was a dark blue and painted like a night sky, with tiny pin lights illuminating the constellations.

Once they were seated and everyone had one of the martinis that Serge made, Melinoe nodded to her stepbrother, who spread out a sheaf of papers on the coffee table.

"So far we have been able to obtain the following ingredients." He read out loud those that had been fairly easy to find. "Although they aren't old, they are pure, and depending on what you think"—he looked at Jac and waited for her to comment.

"Every scent will be affected by the time from which the ingredients came," Jac said. "So it's more an issue of which are stable over a long period. Five-hundred-year-old lemons, nutmeg, vanilla beans or cloves or their essences wouldn't be viable anyway. The ambergris would—"

"The ambergris isn't an issue anymore," Melinoe said and smiled. For a moment it reminded Jac of Malachai's smile. Enigmatic. Secretive. But Melinoe's was more suggestive.

"Why?" Jac asked. "Do you think that you have a chance of buying it from Dr. Ebsen?"

With a flourish and a flash of her diamond rings and bracelets, Melinoe placed a chunk of a gray-black waxy substance on the table.

Jac recognized it immediately.

"But that's from the cabinet we saw today," she said. "How did you get it? I didn't hear you and Ebsen negotiate for it."

Melinoe looked at Jac as if she were a young child, not yet used to the ways of the world.

"We switched the ambergris for a more recent piece that Serge bought on the black market," Melinoe said.

"Switched?" Jac was astonished. "When?"

"When Dr. Ebsen showed me the mechanics of the cabinet," Serge said.

"You stole it. I don't understand . . . How could

you do that? What will happen when they find out?"

"We made sure the two pieces were almost identically shaped—we had a photo of the ambergris in the cabinet, and we chiseled the new one till it resembled the old," Melinoe said without a hint of remorse or worry. "It makes no difference to the people in the museum which hunk of whale vomit they have. They aren't going to make a perfume with it. To them it's just a dusty relic. To us . . . it is an internal component of the miracle we are going to perform." As she spoke, Melinoe caressed the ambergris, and her face took on an almost beatific expression.

Jac had seen a gorgeous statue by Bernini in a church in Rome, *The Ecstasy of St. Teresa*. On the saint's face was an otherworldly look of intense orgiastic pleasure. Melinoe had that same expression on her face now.

Jac had more questions, concerns and outrage, but Serge didn't give her a chance to express any of them.

"We've found some tutty," Serge continued. "There is a perfumer in Grasse who has been collecting archaic ingredients for years. He was willing to sell us half of his bottle. He says it has a particularly ashy scent and that he'd tried to use it in a few fragrances, but it's never added anything that was to his liking. He's sending it to us—we should have it in a few days. The only problem is it's only a hundred years old. Not quite old enough, but it might have to do."

Jac was still trying to process the fact that Melinoe and Serge had stolen ambergris right out from under the nose of the Gustavianum curator. It had to be a felony. They could be arrested. She would be an accessory.

"I'm concerned about the ramifications of stealing the ambergris. I'm not comfortable working with it knowing—" Jac started, but Melinoe interrupted her.

"Darling girl, you need to relax a bit. This isn't the crime of the century. We simply exchanged one lump for another. Same item. Same value. I paid over sixty thousand euros for what I left in Uppsala."

Jac looked from Melinoe to Serge, who appeared as unconcerned as his stepsister. These people were worth more money than some small nations. In so many ways they believed rules did not apply to them. How many of the antiques Melinoe owned had suspicious sales histories? Jac hadn't thought about that before, but now she looked around, wanting to know. More importantly, how could she stay here and continue to work on this project knowing what she did?

As soon as she'd completed the thought, she felt Robbie behind her. Actually sensed his hands on her shoulders. Robbie wasn't really gone; he was with her right there in that room. And was waiting for her . . . expecting her to find a solution so his soul could return and they could be together again. But how? she wished she could ask him. Reborn in an infant? Transferred into a comatose patient about to be revived? Or added to her own? It didn't matter. Jac knew, despite all her misgivings, she couldn't leave here until she knew that it was possible to reanimate a breath . . . or that it was impossible.

"How soon can we take the next trip?" Melinoe was asking Serge.

"I'm waiting for a phone call."

Jac was almost afraid to ask. "The next trip?"

Serge nodded. "There is an eccentric collector who lives in England. In Bath. He's a self-professed alchemist who has spent a small fortune assembling an authentic sixteenth-century laboratory. A working laboratory he has been using to discover the methodology to turn lead into gold . . . which he believes will lead to the secret to immortality."

"And he has momie?" Jac asked.

"And more tutty if we don't get enough from Grasse. And some ancient dragon's blood," Serge said. "And musk pods that are more than four hundred years old."

"He has everything we need," Melinoe said.

Up in her room, Jac looked out the windows at the deepening dusk. Melinoe had said dinner was going be served in half an hour, but Jac didn't want to eat with Serge and Melinoe. She needed some time by herself. She could go down later and get something to bring up. What she wanted to do was call Griffin.

When he didn't answer, Jac left a message and, while she waited for him to call back, opened the book she'd been reading about Catherine de Medici and her reign in France. Every reference to René le Florentin was chilling. She felt as if she were reading about someone she knew. Of particular interest was the description of a room at the Château de Blois where two hundred and thirty-seven cabinets were concealed behind wood paneling. The author noted that it was the queen's private chamber of horrors, her own apothecary where she kept not only papers and jewels but also her perfumes and possibly poisons.

Jac found herself nodding. She could picture the room so clearly. There were poisons in those cabinets.

But how did she know?

The author was painting Catherine, a descendant of the villainous and unscrupulous de Medici family, as a ruthless matriarch. A woman who was wife to one king and mother to three more, who believed her job was to protect her adopted country, France, at all costs, no matter what it took and no matter who stood in her way.

But Jac sensed another woman behind the

legend. One who loved a man who kept a mistress. Who was ignored by her husband for years of their marriage. Who made do with the crumbs of emotion he doled out to her. A woman who threw her heart into her children and fought to keep peace in France using whatever tools and weapons she had. Who, when she did the wrong thing, believed with all her soul it was for the right reason.

As Jac read, she could envision the castles and the countryside, the courtiers and processions. She could even smell the scenes. The fresh air in the countryside and the stench on the streets. The always present scent of paraffin, of perfumes, of the unwashed, of the unclean. She could smell the fragrances that René le Florentin made for his queen so well that Jac thought that if she was put into a laboratory right then, she could re-create them on the spot.

Her phone rang. Jac answered and started in right away to tell Griffin about what had happened, but he stopped her.

"I need to call you back. Just five minutes. In the meantime can you go outside? There's something I want you to look at for me at the ruin near the vineyard Serge showed us."

"Why would . . ."

"Jac, can you? Please?"

She heard the insistence in his voice, and so, without understanding why he was asking her to do something so strange, she did as he requested.

Outside she made her way toward the folly. The structure was a stone edifice without a roof. Most of a marble floor, a dozen columns, partial walls, the remnants of a marble basin—all overgrown with ivy.

No one had been sure, Serge said, if it was a real structure or if it had been built in the eighteenth century when it was in vogue to erect faux antiques on one's property, romantic trysting places built to resemble old ruins.

As Jac stood in its shadow, twilight descended around her.

Her cell rang.

"I'm here," she told Griffin. "I think that . . ." She paused.

She was looking into a charming structure but seeing something quite different. For a moment it was a complete building. A medieval chapel with a stained glass window and an altar and pews and . . . and then the mirage disappeared and the ruin was back.

"Jac?"

"Yes."

"Are you there? Are you all right?"

"It's just the light playing tricks on me."

"What kind of tricks?"

"For a moment I thought I could see what this once was. A chapel that belonged to the house. It had a baptismal font and an altar and an opening in the floor that led to a crypt."

"You just saw all that?" He sounded worried.

"No. The way the sunlight was hitting the ruins, I could see the layout and was just guessing about the rest." Over the years, Jac had become adept at telling quick lies to hide the truth of her hallucinations when they proved too difficult to explain. Now she was falling back into the old pattern.

"Why did you want me to come here?" she asked Griffin.

"I needed you to call me from out of the house. I didn't want anyone listening to our conversation."

"That sounds ominous."

"It might be. I've done some research on Melinoe. She has a reputation as a ruthless collector. Over the years she's resorted to some questionable practices in getting what she wants."

"Illegal practices?"

"Not exactly, no. But not reputable either. You can't trust her, Jac. And I'm not sure her stepbrother is any better. There are so many rumors swirling about them. Their odd relationship with each other is just the beginning. I think you should give this up and go back to Paris."

Instead of this reinforcing her fears, it had the opposite effect. It made her more determined not to give up. If anyone could finance and make it possible to discover René's secrets, it would be

Melinoe. Robbie had thought so. Robbie had been so sure of it he'd had his last breath captured.

"I need to see this through."

"But it could be dangerous."

Jac had been going to tell him about the ambergris switch, but now she refrained. It would only give him more reason to insist she return to Paris.

"I don't need to trust them, Griffin. I just need to create the formula and find out if it's real—or just another fantasy."

"And you have to do that with them?"

"We have almost all the ingredients. They've found them and paid for them. I couldn't have done all that. What we don't have, we're going to pick up tomorrow."

"I'm coming back then."

Jac felt a moment of sheer happiness that he was returning. That he wanted to be with her. But it only lasted for a moment. She didn't want to pull him into this quest. She imagined the face of the tragic perfumer who had lived in the château so long ago.

"Come back to do what? To protect me?" She feigned injury. "I'm not a little girl, Griffin. I've managed on my own for a long time; I don't need you to swoop in and save me."

Chapter 28

Jac closed her phone. Pushing Griffin away was the last thing she wanted to do, even though she knew she had to. Overwhelmed with sadness, she sat down on the stone steps of the folly. Was she making a mistake? There was no one to ask.

A text came through.

> It won't work . . . I know what you're doing. I'm coming back the day after tomorrow. It's the soonest I can manage. Be careful till I get there.

The reassurance that he was returning was almost strong enough to wipe out the fear that he was returning.

Suddenly in the distance she could see someone approaching. Even from this far away she could tell it was too large to be Melinoe. It was Serge.

"Jac?"

She slipped the phone into her pocket, not wanting to alert him that she'd come outside to take a call.

"What are you doing out here so late?" he asked.

"I was restless."

"You're upset about what happened today, aren't you?" he asked.

Was this why he'd come looking for her? Were he and Melinoe worried that she was going to walk away now—or, worse, go to the police?

"Yes." She nodded. "Upset and worried."

"Don't be. It was harmless. We left something of equal value."

"But Melinoe—"

"You can't blame Melinoe," he interrupted. "She's spent so many years working on this . . . buying the breaths . . . the château . . . She is obsessed."

Jac was worried that she was beginning to share the same obsession. Hadn't she just ignored Griffin's warnings? Her own desire to re-create the formula for the dying breaths was so strong . . . she was now under the same spell Melinoe was. Jac felt a sudden wave of compassion for the enigmatic and curious woman.

"How can you just accept what happened today?" Jac asked. "It was wrong."

She'd liked Serge from the moment she'd met him. There was something solid and reliable about him. Something that suggested he would be a ballast in a storm. Was that what Melinoe saw in him too?

"When you truly understand someone's psyche, it's far easier to excuse their excesses or their faults," he said.

They were walking around the folly now, having fallen into a stroll without articulating that was what they were going to do.

"And you understand her psyche?"

"I'm part of it. She and I share a history. We lost everything together on the same day. We were all we each had. We've tried to live separate lives, but something connects us."

"Grief," Jac said. She and Robbie shared a similar pain. "I felt that kind of bond with my brother too." Except for one part of it, she thought.

Serge nodded in understanding. "He was a special person and you were lucky to have him."

Jac heard something in Serge's voice. Jealousy?

"Sometimes I wish that Melinoe and I were able to stay close, the way you two did, but still have our own lives, our own selves."

"Why can't you?"

Jac was certain Melinoe would be furious if she knew they were talking about her behind her back. The fact that Serge was exhibiting nervousness now, looking to the right and left before he answered, proved it.

"She saved my life . . ." Serge said. "I was stabbed. Lying there dying. Melinoe called the ambulances, stayed with me in the hospital, nursed me back to life. All that despite what my life cost her. She loved me that much." He paused. "I owe her everything," he said simply, without emotion.

"And she *demands* everything." Jac should have not said such a thing. It wasn't her place. It wasn't her business. But it had slipped out.

Jac watched his face and the play of passion and pain she saw there. She knew their relationship was far too complicated for her to understand.

"You shouldn't judge her," Serge said.

Jac thought about what Griffin had said about Melinoe. About how Malachai had spoken of her. She'd enchanted him and then damaged him. Malachai! A pillar of emotional reserve and cool calm. How powerful Melinoe must really be.

Maybe Serge was wrong; maybe she *should* judge this woman who she had agreed to help, a collector so obsessed with their goal that she had stolen something from a museum, who used people with a finesse they were oblivious to. Made them love her despite her power over them. Maybe she should judge Melinoe even more harshly. But if she did, it would mean she'd have to give up their shared goal. Because it was her goal now too. And she couldn't imagine giving up.

Chapter 29

MARCH 22, 1573
BARBIZON, FRANCE

I climbed the stone steps from my laboratory in the Louvre and entered the queen's chamber. Again, she was with the man I dreaded seeing, Cosimo Ruggieri. In front of them, on the table, was a small waxen figure of a man with hair the color of fire and dressed in formal attire.

Catherine looked up. "I have a problem, René, and I need you to help me."

I bowed. "As is my duty and privilege."

"One of my ladies has found out some important information. While we were in Fontainebleau, she discovered that one of the leading members of the Protestant opposition is planning an uprising, and I need to prevent that from happening."

"Of course."

"But everyone is now wary of us."

"And so you have resorted to black magic once again?" I asked.

"I didn't invite you here to be impertinent," Catherine snapped at me.

"No, you didn't. I apologize." I glanced over at Ruggieri, who was smiling slyly at her rebuke.

"What can I do for you, Your Majesty?" I asked.

"Once before I asked both of you to work on the same problem together and the results were superb. Again I am asking both of you to help me."

I looked at the doll. I knew what it was for. This was obviously Ruggieri's solution. Mon Dieu, but he was flirting with disaster and putting the queen in a precarious position if it were to be discovered.

There was much talk about the totems that were fashioned with bits and pieces of a person's hair, fingernails and some cloth taken from one of their items of clothing. Pins were then stuck in the little doll in the places where you intended the victim to feel pain.

It was said that Ruggieri had killed people with this method. I couldn't imagine it was possible, but that wasn't what worried me. I was solely focused on the problems my mistress was inviting by including the magician in this effort. The conflicts between the Protestants and Catholics were at the heart of all her efforts, and yet she was risking her own credibility with both sides by engaging in Ruggieri's nonsense.

"We are working on the problem one way. I'd like you to work on it from another so there's no chance of failure. I would like you to create a gift for a certain gentleman. Something I can have a lady in my squadron give to him that will not be suspect. But something that will cause his demise and send a message to the Protestants that they do not have the blessing of God on their side."

"Your Majesty, we don't need a perfumer to create such a thing. I can—"

Now it was Ruggieri's turn to receive Catherine's icy stare and my turn to smile. Except I couldn't. Something the queen had said made me worried.

"Which lady, Your Highness, has discovered this?"

"Isabeau Allard," she said. "Why do you ask?"

Ruggieri was watching me carefully. How I answered was crucial. Ruggieri would seize on any perceived weakness.

"You sent her to me and asked me to create a perfume for her to aid her in seducing someone at court. I was wondering if this was the fruit of that labor?"

"Indeed it was. Isabeau has managed to insinuate herself into the man's life, making herself quite indispensible and all the while delivering important information to me. Isabeau has become invaluable."

"I'm glad," I said, "that it was a success."

I was sick to my stomach. I had not heard from Isabeau Allard since that first day she'd visited my shop. Every night I went to sleep thinking about her, trying to conjure up the scent that emanated from deep inside her. Every morning I spent hours at the perfume organ, trying to re-create it. She haunted me. The sound of her pleasure and feel of her hands on my body came to me in my dreams. I was like a lovesick youth. I lost my appetite and need for sleep. I wanted to see her again, feel her, taste her . . . to smell her! But I could not approach her. Isabeau was in the queen's retinue and out of my orbit.

Daily, I had invented errands that allowed me to walk through the castle in the hopes I would run into her, but so far I'd failed. It had been three weeks of torture. Now, at last, I had learned why.

"Has she gone back to the Protestant's court then?"

"Why are you asking me about this, René?" Catherine questioned. She was scrutinizing me.

"Only because I was thinking that if Lady Allard was going back, she might need more perfume. I don't remember exactly which formula I gave her, though. Perhaps if she came to my laboratory I could make some more."

"I cannot allow her to go with him back to his court—that would be folly on my part. She's my bait to keep him where I can see him."

I wanted to hear more and, at the same time, listen to none of this. I had lain awake at night trying to imagine Isabeau with the Protestant duke. I had wondered just how far she would go for her queen and how she felt about it and how she survived it. Pictured him touching her . . . worse, her touching him back. The imagery made me ill.

I glanced over and saw that Ruggieri was staring at me again. Busying myself with the bottle of scent I had brought up for Her Majesty, I wiped at the gold cap to get rid of smudges.

"Well," the queen said, "Isabeau Allard needs more than a perfume now. I want you to concoct something much more lethal."

"Yes," I said, feeling a sudden burst of happiness. Catherine wanted to dispose of the duke. Isabeau would be freed of him. "There are all manner of ways we can do that with formulas any of your servants can put in his food or drink. You don't need to ask one of your ladies to do it." I didn't want Isabeau to have a murder on her conscience. It was one thing to seduce a lord to get information but quite another to kill a man.

"Of course, we could, but she tells me he is already suspicious and he has a tester. It must be something she can give him—he is so besotted with her, he trusts her, René."

"I need to think about this puzzle and consult my notebooks."

"The duke is planning to return in a week's time. I'd like it to be ready by then."

"Yes, Your Majesty."

I stood, assuming I had been dismissed. "Wait, René, I want to show you something." She withdrew a silver box from her pocket. It was the size of an egg and encrusted with pearls and emeralds that shaped a fleur-de-lis. It had a small latch made of rubies, which she opened and then held the box out to me.

"What do you think of this?"

As I took it, I saw Ruggieri's lips slide into another of his sly smiles.

"Smell it, René. Tell me your opinion."

The egg was filled with a waxy substance that was uneven and mottled with specks of the ingredients that had gone to scent it. Bits of petals, I realized. The effect was quite pretty and reminded me of the soap I'd made as a boy in Florence. I leaned down and sniffed at the pomade. It was a simple scent, unsophisticated and common.

"Other than the design, which is something we perfected at Santa Maria Novella, I'm not impressed with the scent, I'm sorry. Was it a gift?"

She nodded. "Ruggieri found a young perfumer who he thought I might be interested in bringing to the court. This is his work."

I turned to my nemesis. "You're looking to bring more perfumers to the court, Ruggieri?"

"This man, Oliverotti Ferante, does work for a noble family in Tuscany. While I was exiled there, I made his acquaintance and thought his style fresh and exciting."

I wasn't surprised Ruggieri was scheming to get rid of me. Was Catherine aware of what he was attempting? She was too shrewd not to. Was she showing me the egg as a warning? Reminding me that if I didn't agree to her nefarious requests, I could be replaced?

Focusing my ire on Ruggieri, I turned to him. It wouldn't do to show my consternation with the queen herself. "I think you should stick to your charts, Astrologer. This is nothing but a simple jasmine-and-lemon scent. It takes the imagination of a five-year-old. And the quality of the wax is substandard. It's not even a clean pour."

I handed the egg back to Catherine.

"Have no fear, Maître René, you are the perfumer to the court." Catherine smiled. "But your jealousy is refreshing. After all these years I've come to think of you as a stoic."

"No, my lady, I have feelings."

"Even if you have never shown them to me," she said a little sadly.

"Why would I? You are my queen. You have the burdens of the court on your shoulders; you don't need mine also."

"But we have been together so long. You and I and Ruggieri. We are a family of sorts." She looked from me to the astrologer and then laughed. "There should be no rivalry between you two, but I suppose it's inevitable."

"There is no rivalry," Ruggieri said. "That would be like the moon being in competition with a mere star."

"So now you are the moon?" I asked him.

"Are you suggesting that mixing up scents and

soaps can compete with the art of astronomy and astrology and being able to see the future and foretell what is to come?"

I knew that Catherine was enjoying this and had pitted us against each other on purpose. It would be so easy to have these meetings with us separately, but she chose to inflict us upon each other. What pleasure did it give her? Or did she just think that this was the way to make each of us work that much harder to accomplish what she asked of us?

With a sense of dread I took my leave and returned the way I'd come, via the stone staircase, down to my laboratory. As I ruminated on what I'd learned about Isabeau and the success of her seduction, I took out my notebook and began to peruse its pages. There was something in Serapino's notes about a poultice and the danger of overmixing one ingredient because when it touched the skin—

My door opened. The one to the queen's private room. The door I had just closed. In all the years since I had been in the court, I had opened this door to go up to see her, but the queen had never come to see me.

I stood and watched as she— But it was not the queen but Ruggieri who entered.

"What do you want?"

"To extend an olive branch."

I didn't trust him. "Is that so?"

"I think Our Highness is pitting us one against the other. Perhaps it would be in both our interests if we can make peace with each other."

There was no way to know what his motive was, but I doubted that anything he said was genuine. He was a man who put on the robes of a priest and said a Black Mass. A magician. A heretic.

"I want to help you, René."

"I'm very capable of working on my own, but thank you."

"No, not with the poison the queen asked you for. I know you can create that. It's just a formula and a bit of cleverness. No need for magic with that."

"What then?"

Ruggieri walked around to where I was standing and looked down at my open notebook. He was examining the drawings of alembics with notations beside them when I flipped the book shut.

"If we joined forces, we could work on your experiments with your collection of dying breaths. Catherine told me you haven't yet been able to figure out how to reanimate them, and I sense she's getting impatient, funding all these experiments without seeing any results."

Catherine had been talking about me and my experiments with this madman? A charlatan who didn't understand science at all and had no respect for reason? Why had my queen confided in him?

And then I realized it didn't matter why. All that was important was that the bond between them was so strong. I supposed it stood to reason. After all, Ruggieri was the one person in the world who had been able to help Catherine cope with her own strange abilities to see the future. For that, he had earned a place in her heart that no one could usurp.

"Are the formulas for reanimating the breaths in that book?" Ruggieri pointed to the notebook I'd prevented him from looking at. "They might have much in common with my own ideas for bringing the dead back to life."

"I have no intention of working with you, Ruggieri. My experiments are nothing like yours. Play with the devil if you want, but don't equate your work with mine. I'm a man of science, not spells."

"You are making a mistake. I've seen in the bowl of waters what will happen to you if you don't work with me, René. You can't succeed on your own. You will lose her and in losing her wind up a bitter old man."

Lose her? Who did he mean? Certainly not the queen. But how did he know about Isabeau? There could be only one way. I did not believe in his sorcery. I must have given myself away by asking the queen too many questions. My desire must have been visible on my face.

"You mean that's what you want to happen.

That's what you dream in hopes that you will make it so," I spat out at him.

"Together we would be so much stronger. So much more powerful if we are working on the same side. There's nothing that you could want that you would not have," Ruggieri said.

"All I want is for you to take your leave now. And not the way you came." I pointed to the main door to the laboratory. "You are not welcome here, Ruggieri. Go spew your blasphemous garbage elsewhere."

I walked to the door, opened it and held it for him.

He walked past me and then stood on the threshold for a moment.

"There will be a day, René Bianco, when you will realize the limitations of your talents and wish for magic to save you, but it will be too late."

I laughed. "It's so easy for you to make pronouncements, isn't it? To suggest the coming doom and the dire days ahead. What is anyone to do with these utterances other than to fear them? It may work with Catherine and with the ladies of the court who line up for you to tell them their fortunes in love and family matters, but you leave me unimpressed. The world is made of matter and minerals, and that is what I deal in, not dreams. Not nightmares."

"Or so you want to believe," he said, then turned and finally left.

I listened to the echo of his footsteps as he walked down the darkened hallway. One of the torches had gone out, and no one had relit it. A cold wind blew through the passage into my laboratory.

That was odd. My rooms were deep inside the first level underneath the castle, far from any exits. But the wind was real. And strong. And it had carried with it the noxious odor of burnt wood and sulfur.

I shut the door on the man and the smell and pulled a square of linen from my pocket. I always kept a handkerchief soaked in lavender and orange blossom to bury my nose in when I smelled something unpleasant, but not even that helped with this. It was as if the burning scent was inside me, and the more deeply I inhaled the more intensely I smelled the nasty fire.

The linen was well woven and fine, and I was aware of its texture as I folded it up and put it back in my pocket. Linen impregnated with a scent . . . It made me think . . . what if I could impregnate linen with a poultice that I overmixed . . . went against the warning in Serapino's notes . . . What if I fashioned the linen into an undergarment . . . a gift for Isabeau's nobleman to wear next to his skin . . . fragrance and lime and arsenic? I knew what the symptoms would be.

And so I planned my next murder. One I am

ashamed to say I enjoyed with a little too much relish because if I helped Catherine dispose of the Protestant, then Isabeau would be free of him. And then I might entreat her to come to me.

Chapter 30

THE PRESENT
SUNDAY, MARCH 23
BETWS-Y-COED, WALES

The plane ride across the channel to Wales had been uneventful. But a storm ruined the limo ride through the countryside. The glimpses of the long stretches of unspoiled rough landscape, sloping mountains and forests around them were blurred by sheets of rain.

The weather was still bad when they reached Betws-y-Coed and pulled up in front of a seventeenth-century castle, but the chauffeur had a big umbrella and escorted each of them, one at a time, from the car to the door, so no one got soaked.

Serge lifted the brass knocker and let it drop twice. And then a third time.

The door was opened by a small man who was in his late seventies.

"I'm sorry, I forgot it was up to me to get the

door. My man has had to take his wife to the hospital—she'd got a bit of pneumonia—and the cook is half deaf—but come in, come in. I'm Chester Bruge."

They stood in the front hall, shaking off the rain. "Don't worry, the house can handle the weather and the water. It's survived much worse. Let me warm you up."

He brought them into a well-appointed drawing room where a fire welcomed them.

"It's four, but not too early for a nip of Macallan to chase the chill, don't you agree?" Chester said as he generously poured the expensive scotch into heavy cut crystal glasses.

Allowing only a bit of small talk about the plane ride and the storm, Melinoe got to the subject at hand. "How long have you been putting together your alchemical collection?"

From what Melinoe had explained, Jac knew that Bruge's collection was thought to be one of the most complete in all the world, some said more extensive than anything in any museum.

"Over fifty-five years," Bruge told her. "I studied medieval history at Cambridge. One of my professors was a preeminent scholar of alchemy. I took one class about John Dee and the School of Night and was smitten. The more I learned, the more curious I became about magic. I very much believe in magic and that it was the forerunner of modern-day science." He smiled.

Bruge was a short, spry man with sparkling green eyes and a bald head shaped very much like an egg. And when he smiled, which he did often, his cheeks dimpled. Jac thought he looked something like what an elf might—except that he was wearing what appeared to be a very expensive navy jacket, white shirt, navy foulard pocket square, gabardine pants and highly polished oxfords.

"Do you work in the laboratory you've created?" Melinoe asked. Her voice seemed higher pitched and more innocent than normal to Jac. As if Melinoe were acting the part of a slightly less sophisticated, more naive waif. The pretense didn't sit well with Jac. Serge didn't seem to be paying attention to the subtle subterfuge. But Bruge appeared to be enjoying it.

"Of course I do. My goal was never just to build the laboratory and stock it, but rather to find the holy grail myself. I became a chemist and a botanist in order to work with the materials and understand them better."

"And have you achieved your goal?" Melinoe asked.

He shook his head. Jac was reminded of Malachai, who had devoted his life to the study of reincarnation but, like Bruge, not found what he was looking for. The more elusive the goal, Jac thought, the more obsessed Malachai had become. She didn't blame him for hating this woman who had outsmarted him and bought the collection of breaths out from under him, potentially robbing him of a world-shattering discovery. Malachai had, over the years, held several astonishing discoveries in his grasp—for at least a few moments—but had never managed to reach the end game with any of them.

After a few more minutes of conversation about how Bruge had amassed the items needed to re-create an authentic alchemical laboratory from the Middle Ages, he suggested he show them his "little treasure," as he called it.

From the drawing room, he led them back out to the front hall.

"It's a short walk. There are enough umbrellas here." He gestured to a Meissen stand. Each of them took one of the black-and-white umbrellas and followed Bruge outside.

In the rain, which had been reduced to more of a mist, they crossed a formal garden with late-blooming large ruby roses, their heads hanging as if they'd been beaten into submission by the pelting water.

A steep, twisting stone path led them into woods filled with ancient oaks and yews. They hugged a swollen stream that flowed around boulders. Fans of verdant green ferns grew abundantly in the wet soil.

The sound of waterfalls and birdsong were musical accompaniment to what was becoming a trek. Melinoe's high heels weren't up to the task. Bruge had offered boots, but she'd refused. Jac was surprised that somehow Melinoe was managing without stumbling or falling behind.

The path led to a pond fed by a waterfall that flowed over moss-covered rocks. Jac took in the scents of the ripe rich earth and the iron in the water and felt a sense of peace. Here tall hollies and towering pines stood like sentries. The evergreen minty aroma was fresh and powerful.

This ancient site had probably looked and smelled like this for hundreds of years. The cascade only dropped about six feet, and the gentle movement was mesmerizing. Large and feathery willow trees lining the shore almost hid the small ancient stone hut nestled a few feet back. The mystical shed did indeed look as if it had been here since the Middle Ages.

Inside it was just one small room, and the space felt crowded with all four of them inside. The walls were plastered, the ceiling was beamed and hung low, and there was an open hearth, two small mullioned windows, and a wooden floor with wide planks. Everywhere were papers, ceramic jugs, a variety of old uneven glass flasks and shelves of dark bottles. On a simple wooden table, on top of a stack of books, sat a human skull beside an hourglass.

"This was the alchemist's laboratory. It wasn't in this state when I bought the castle, but I stayed true to its bones when I had it renovated." Bruge lovingly ran his hand over the rough-hewn table. "We didn't alter anything. Just refurbished it."

Jac could easily see that the hut was in use. The beakers and alembics contained liquids and solids. She noticed accoutrements for measuring and heating. So much of it reminded Jac of the similarities between the arts of alchemy and perfume. Each took elements from nature in order to create an elixir for a kind of immortality. For didn't perfume keep the smells of flowers and trees and woods and minerals alive for decades—sometimes even hundreds of years?

On the walls of the little shed, Bruge had hung framed engravings from the seventeenth and eighteenth centuries. Now, as he showed them off, he explained their significance.

"All these woodcuts were in Basil Valentine's *Azoth*. These are portraits of John Dee and Nicolas Flamel." He pointed to a very complex print. "This is the alchemical tree standing under the influences of the heavens, letters of the alphabet, signs of the zodiac and states of matter. This is the beast of Babylon. These are symbols of the Hand of Philosophy—the salamander, the star, the key. Here is the symbol for copper, here for iron, for lead, silver, tin and gold," he said, pointing to the highly designed emblems. "These, though, are my prizes." He pointed to a series of six framed prints on the opposite wall. "These are from Heinrich

Khunrath's occult work *Ampitheatrum Sapientiae Aeternae*. Translated to mean *The Amphitheater of Eternal Knowledge*. These were drawn in 1595. There are only three copies of that first edition. These are from a later seventeenth-century reprinting. Look at how complex they are. Scholars I have discussed them with believe Khunrath created them as a kind of meditation tool to encourage a focus on the nature of the universe and on the links between the earthly and the divine, the corporeal and the spiritual."

Jac studied the dense circular prints that included Latin inscriptions, flames, and human figures—one a hermaphrodite—angles, globes, chemical charts, animals and birds, including a giant peacock that Jac knew was the symbol for reincarnation.

The prints looked familiar to her, and as she listened to their host continue, she tried to figure out why.

"One scholar"—Bruge closed his eyes as he spoke, as if this way he might concentrate more intently on what he was saying—"Urszula Szulakowska says Khunrath's images are 'intended to excite the imagination of the viewer so that a mystic alchemy can take place through the act of visual contemplation.' She believes the images work much like a mirror, and that the celestial spheres reflect the human mind, which allows for an 'awakening' of the 'empathetic faculty of the human spirit' to unite, via imagination, with the heavenly realms. She calls Khunrath's images 'the alchemical quintessence, the spiritualized matter of the philosopher's stone.' "

Finished quoting, Bruge opened his eyes and smiled at his guests. "Forgive me. I'm very passionate about the subject. This project has been a labor of love for my entire life. Now that you are here, do you have any questions?"

Suddenly Jac knew why the prints looked familiar. So many of these visuals were on the silver bells that protected the bottles of dying breaths. She looked at Melinoe and Serge, but neither of them seemed to have noticed. She'd have to tell Griffin. Perhaps the prints could help them understand the cryptic engravings . . . Maybe they included instructions on how to proceed with the experiment once they had the elixir. She was about to ask Bruge what some of the symbols on certain prints meant when Melinoe began talking.

"The items we talked about over the phone?" Melinoe said. "Are they here?"

"Yes." Bruge nodded. He gestured to the hundreds of bottles on the shelves. "Right here."

"On the phone you said you'd allow our expert to smell them to see if there is any way she might be able to re-create the scent?"

"Certainly," he said. "You said you were interested in tutty . . ."

As Bruge turned his back on them to search

the shelf, Melinoe looked at Serge. Jac tried to interpret the glance but wasn't sure what Melinoe was trying to communicate. Serge, however, seemed to rise to another level of alertness.

As Bruge searched for the tutty, the shadowy room was working some kind of magic on Jac. The combined scents reminded her of the smells inside the memory lurches she'd experienced in Barbizon. During those fugue states, when she was remembering the life of the perfumer René le Florentin, these were the smells that hung in the air of his own shop on the banks of the Seine in Paris.

"Here is the tutty," Bruge said.

Jac took the proffered bottle gingerly from the alchemist's fingers and held it up to the light. Inside was a dark, solid substance.

"May I?" Jac asked as she fingered the cork.

"Yes, yes, go right ahead."

The cork eased out without much effort, and Jac leaned down to sniff. Despite the years since this had been harvested, Jac could still smell burning wood, ash and ancient decaying pine. The odor conjured up memories that were not hers. She closed her eyes and saw René haggling over prices with a Frenchman who had traveled around the world. Saw René smelling the goods from China and Egypt. Handing over coins of gold in exchange for silk pouches of spices and thick glass jars of tars and resins.

"Can I smell it?" Melinoe asked.

Jac handed it to her and watched as Melinoe inhaled the scent and then frowned. "It doesn't have any odor."

"It does. Try to concentrate, give it a few seconds," Jac said.

"Don't be disappointed if you can't smell it," Bruge added. "It can take training to be able to detect the subtleties of an inert material like that."

"Are you sure you smell something? Are you sure it's active?" Melinoe asked Jac.

"Yes. Enough so that I should be able to work at re-creating something like it."

"But not exactly the same thing?" Melinoe asked.

"Very close. But it won't be made of the same materials. My copy will have synthetics in it. If the formula requires—"

"Don't worry about that now." Melinoe gave Jac a sharp look as she interrupted her.

Jac remembered Melinoe's admonitions not to discuss any of the details of their experiment or goals.

Melinoe handed the bottle to Serge and then turned to Bruge. "Would you be willing to give us a sample so we might be able to re-create it more accurately?"

He shook his head. "As far as I know there is no other tutty from the Middle Ages available anywhere. Even taking a small bit of it would diminish my supply, and my ingredients are more precious than gold."

Serge handed the bottle back to Bruge, who corked it and replaced it on the worktable.

Melinoe pursed her lips together as if she were not allowing herself to say what she was thinking, and instead smiled as she put her hand on Bruge's arm.

"Might we smell your specimen of momie?"

Bruge searched the shelves and then seized on a small skull that fitted in the palm of his hand. It was made of a dark-green crystal streaked with amethyst.

"The container itself is a treasure," he explained as he held the skull out so the thin rays of light streaming through the window illuminated the crystal. "It's made of fluorite, which teaches us to be interdimensional and leads to spiritual awakening. The rock's magical abilities are said to advance the mind from one mental reality to the next and at the same time help us to increase and assimilate our life force."

"How old is it?" Melinoe asked.

"The container has been dated to the mid-1500s. And the experts I've talked to think its contents date to approximately the same time. Most of the ingredients you asked about do. I found this amazing cache when the Arno flooded in 1966. The stonework in the basement of an apothecary shop in Florence was loosened, and a section of a nineteenth-century wall disintegrated, revealing an ancient closet full of supplies. I paid handsomely to purchase the entire group. And everything— every chemical, element and compound—was intact. I'm not sure what the original constitution of many of them had been—for instance, was tutty once a liquid? A putty? Or hardened the way it is now? At least we know this—" Bruge opened the top of the skull's head, revealing a black, hardened substance. "According to some ancient texts, momie was once viscous."

"I've read a bit about it in a fifteenth-century book, *Livre des Simples Médecines*," Jac said. "It's such a strange ingredient. Have you used it for any of your experiments?"

"No, I haven't yet come across any that call for it. Do you have a specific use for it? For the tutty?" he asked.

Before Jac could answer, Melinoe interrupted.

"We're investigating creating a line of historical fragrances based on different time periods. This one would be a medieval fragrance."

Jac wasn't surprised that Melinoe wasn't telling Bruge the truth, but something about the way she told the lie so easily and with such aplomb shook her a bit.

"Would you like to smell it?" Bruge offered Jac the bottom half of the skull.

She bent her head down. Someone had gone into a tomb . . . exposed embalmed corpses and then harvested this from the brain and the spine. Like tree resins, momie was corpse resin. She shivered and sniffed the shining black solid. Once it might have been aromatic, but it seemed scentless. Jac concentrated. Inhaled. Ah, there was a hint of something . . . She inhaled again. This time she was able to begin picking out odors. Anise, cumin, cinnamon, sweet marjoram. The ancients wrote sophisticated pharmacopoeias that listed medicinal spices in their formulas for both magic and religious rituals. Jac had read some of them and knew that embalming fluid was perfumed in order to please the gods, offering the dead a smooth passage to the next world. Medicinally, the intense spice mixture was also powerful enough to prevent putrefaction.

"Can I smell?" Melinoe asked.

Carefully, Jac handed over the skull.

She watched Melinoe dip her head and sniff. A look of frustration crossed her face.

"It's very faint," Jac said.

Melinoe tried again, then looked at Bruge. "Is there any way to stir it up—or add water to it? I want to smell it."

"Yes, it can be softened with honey," he said. "I found a recipe for that. Honey was the most popular way ancients preserved food and meats since it has very powerful bactericidal and fungicidal properties. It was said that when Alexander the Great died his body was encased in honey for the transfer to Alexandria, where he was to be buried. Some scientists believe honey is a greater food preservative than most spices."

"Have you done that? Have you added honey to this? Diluted it?" Melinoe asked in an agitated voice. There were spots of color in her pale cheeks, and her cool silvery eyes flashed like lightning.

Jac could smell Melinoe's intensity, and it frightened her. And it seemed to disturb Bruge, who backed up a little.

"No, madam. I haven't." He sounded miffed. "As I said, to date I've never found a formula that called for that ingredient so I haven't had to manipulate it."

"How do we even know this is what it's purported to be? It might just be tar," Melinoe said.

Now Bruge responded with outrage. "Why would I want to fool anyone like that? These items are in my personal collection, which I neither sell nor show for profit."

Serge stepped in to repair the damage Melinoe had done. "I think you misunderstood. My stepsister wasn't suggesting you were trying to fool anyone. She was asking how anyone would know, after so many centuries, what this originally was."

"Because I had every one of these items tested in my laboratory in Geneva, where our cosmetics are made. If these weren't the original alchemical substances, they wouldn't be here."

"I do apologize," Melinoe said. "I've just been looking for the right ingredients for so long without any success. And now to find them. It's overwhelming . . ."

Bruge nodded. "I understand passion, my lady. I do. I've had my share of frustrations over amassing these elements and items." He looked from Melinoe to Serge to Jac. "Is there anything else I can show you?"

"Yes, do you have any aloewood?" Jac asked.

"I do. Let me get it . . . but first . . ."

Bruge walked over to a shelf and pulled off a book. Then he turned to Melinoe, who was standing by Serge. "I think you might find this of particular interest." He put the volume on a table and pulled the lit candelabra closer. "Come look." He opened the book, and Jac saw a flash of color. "Since you collect incunabula as well and are interested in this time period, you might enjoy these alchemical maps from the late fifteenth century," Bruge said.

"How can you keep all this here?" Melinoe asked, looking around the drafty hut.

"There's no value to any of these things if I can't use them in my quest. I work here, my dear lady; it is my own laboratory. One day it will all be donated to a museum, and if one or two of these pieces are a bit worse for wear—so be it. They were made to be used. Don't you use what you collect?"

"I do, yes, but"—she touched the book—"I have a temperature-controlled library for the books and papers."

"I'm sure it's state-of-the-art. But so cold and inhuman. The monks who toiled away at these pages worked by candlelight in drafty rooms. I am only keeping them in their natural environment."

Jac could see that Melinoe wanted to argue with him but was holding back. Melinoe and Bruge had such opposite methods when it came to their practices. She seemed to collect in order to live, and he seemed to live in order to collect. Jac was sure that he got more pleasure from his way than she did. For all her extravagance and exotica, Jac had never seen any pure enjoyment on Melinoe's face except when she was showing her collections.

"Now, dear"—Bruge took Jac by the elbow—"the aloewood is over here." She sensed that he was proud of himself for having given Serge and Melinoe something to do so he and Jac could pay attention to the scents and elements without any more interruptions.

Taking an amethyst bottle off the shelf, he handed it to Jac. She uncorked it and sniffed. This resin was rich and scented of timber. The aloewood was the most potent of the three items she'd smelled so far.

An up-to-date version of this would suffice if it had to. But how was she going to re-create the tutty or momie? She'd memorized their aromas, but she wasn't the scientist her brother had been. He always said she had "the nose" to identify and isolate notes like no one else he'd ever met. And that she had an innate artistry to create a higher level of masterpiece than he could. But when it came to understanding the chemical agents and how to re-create versions of scents from nature, Robbie was superior to her.

Now, in order to try to give his soul new wings, she needed his expertise, and she didn't have it. She felt the sting of tears.

Bruge was looking at her empathetically. "What is it, dear?"

His kindness, her stress—the combination was lethal. She didn't want to break down here in front of him—or the others. She shook her head—"I'm fine"—but her voice wavered.

"Are you sure?" he asked.

Jac nodded. "Yes." She cleared her throat. "All these smells, certain combinations cause a slight allergic reaction. I'm overly sensitive."

Bruge was watching her. She was certain he didn't believe her lie.

And then, behind her, she felt that odd little push she'd felt twice before. It gently shoved her closer to the table and the old mercury mirror hanging above it. In its smoky surface, Jac saw her own reflection, and behind her a sudden flurry of—what was it? How could she explain it? Atmosphere? Cloud? Fog? A quick blur—a whirlwind of mist. It had substance and temperature, and she felt it as a warm vapor that settled on her shoulders as it surrounded her. A quick embrace. This miasma was a message from Robbie to remind her he was still with her. To stay strong and focused.

And then it was gone.

Jac looked at Bruge.

He had seen it too. Jac could tell from the way he was smiling at her. Neither Melinoe nor Serge had noticed anything. But the elderly man was aware of it all.

He took her hand. "You are very lucky, my dear. To have such a guardian angel. Don't doubt him."

Jac nodded. Didn't trust herself to speak—not for fear that she'd break down but rather because anything she said would give Melinoe or Serge information she didn't want them to have. She glanced around. The two of them were talking to each other, not paying attention.

"You don't seem surprised by what you saw?" Jac said to Bruge in a low voice.

"I have been seeing visions—like the one of your brother—for decades."

"You even knew who it was?"

Bruge smiled enigmatically. "There are more questions in the world than there are answers. A wise man once said you have to live the questions and then one day you might live your way into the answers. It's how I've conducted my life. Magic is real, my dear. Just watch a tree grow. Or a bird fly. Science and the occult are twins. Every dark has its light. Every right its wrong. Every time its season. Now, have you gotten enough of those smells to do what you need to?"

She nodded. "I'm not sure."

"Well, if it would help, please, just come back. I'd love to host you and show you more."

"I should be all right. I have a kind of photographic sense of smell. My problem won't be knowing if I've re-created them; it will be knowing what synthetics exist that might enable me to re-create these scents."

Melinoe closed the book she and Serge had been examining. "Mr. Bruge, what would I have to offer you to sell us just a small portion of your supply of tutty and momie?"

"I don't believe that there's anything that exists you could offer me. There are no known fifteenth-century examples anywhere. They are irreplaceable and essential to my experiments."

"I have unlimited funds," Melinoe said.

"That you would spend on a perfume?" Bruge was now looking at her suspiciously.

"Yes," she said defiantly.

That was the wrong tack to take with him, Jac thought.

"I'm sorry, madame. The thing is I have unlimited funds too."

"Surely there is something you want that you don't have."

"Of course. But nothing you can give me."

"Don't be so certain. What is it you want?"

Bruge looked at Jac, smiled, then looked back at Melinoe. "Youth. Immortality. Freedom from this tired body."

"Ah, but perhaps I could offer you that."

For a moment no one said anything. And then Bruge spoke. "It's getting dark out, and the rain has picked up again. I think we should go back to the house now. Where the brandy is waiting. And you can tell me how you are going to trade my store of elements for a miracle."

Chapter 31

Jac was not sure exactly what happened on the walk back to the castle. The terrain was rocky and slippery. The path steep. It had begun to rain again, and each of them was manipulating an umbrella. There was no amiable talk since the silk shades enclosed each of them in their own cocoon-like space.

Bruge led the way. Serge followed. Then Melinoe. Jac at the rear. The sound of the rain beat a steady, loud pattern on the umbrellas, so at first she wasn't even sure she heard anything out of the ordinary. Trees limbs were bending in the wind; leaves and bits of debris were blowing.

Then a sudden movement alerted her. Jac glanced over in time to see a gust pull Bruge's umbrella away from him just as a tree branch fell, hitting him.

He let out a shout—a mixture of pain and surprise—as he dropped to the muddy ground.

Serge was beside him in seconds. As Jac approached, Melinoe pulled her back. Her hand trembled where she touched Jac's arm. "Let Serge see to him. He has first aid experience," she said. "We should call for an ambulance. Hold the umbrella over me," Melinoe said as she fumbled to get her cell phone out of her bag. She punched in the emergency number. Listened. "Damn," she said. "There's no signal. I'll stay here in case Serge needs help. You can get back to the house faster than I can in these shoes. Call from there—the landlines must be working. Call for help and then ask our driver to bring the car down as close as he can get and then to come with you back here."

In the downpour, Jac ran as fast as she could, slipping and falling several times on the narrow, rocky path. Finally she reached the gardens and then the house. The phone was working, and she called for help.

Then she did as Melinoe asked and got the limousine driver to get them as close as he could to the woods. After that they took off by foot. Finally they reached the spot where Jac had left everyone.

Melinoe was holding an umbrella over herself and Serge, who was holding his over the collector's inert body.

"How is he?" Jac asked.

Serge looked up, his expression saying everything.

"No!" Jac looked down at Bruge. It was inconceivable to Jac that he was gone. This man had just asked Melinoe for more time, for immortality, for youth. How could he have died in the minutes it took her to get back to the house and call for help?

The next four hours stretched on interminably. The ambulance and medics came and took Bruge's body. Police arrived and questioned all three of them, taking long statements about what had happened. Finally, at nine that night, the police said they were free to go.

The chauffeur drove them back to the airport, but the storm prevented the plane from taking off for another two hours.

Finally, at eleven o'clock, they were airborne. Exhausted and saddened, Jac sat looking out of the window, watching the night sky. She couldn't stop thinking of how Chester Bruge had been talking about wanting more time just moments before all the time he was ever going to have was extinguished.

The irony of it disturbed Jac. The coincidence of it seemed impossible.

Once again she heard the familiar refrain of Malachai's voice telling her there were no coincidences. It was what he always said to convince her that past-life memories were real. But this coincidence had nothing to do with regressions and ancient karma. Something else had happened in the rain. Jac just wasn't sure what.

She slept fitfully that night and was glad when morning came and she could finally get out of bed. The sun was shining brightly as she made her way down to the dining room at seven thirty. Serge was already there.

He had eggs on his plate but was just pushing them around. She was surprised she was hungry enough to eat.

"It's odd, isn't it?" she asked him. "To be so moved by his death. We didn't even know him and yet we're mourning him."

"It was a terrible thing." Serge's face was pale. He looked like he hadn't slept at all. His hand shook as he poured himself a second cup of coffee.

"For you most of all," Jac said.

His head jerked up. "Why me most of all?"

"You were the one who tried to save him," she

said and watched him visibly relax. "Serge, you can't blame yourself for his death."

His eyes, Jac thought, looked haunted.

"I can. It *was* my fault," he whispered in a tortured voice.

"You did absolutely everything you could," Melinoe said as she walked into the room.

This morning she was wearing a deep-ruby velvet tunic with black leggings, and her fingers and wrists were covered with sparkling stones of the same color. Her lipstick matched too. The teardrops that hung from her ears were also blood red. Despite the perfect clothes and jewels, she looked exhausted and somewhat distraught. She put her hands on Serge's shoulder.

"Nothing was your fault," Melinoe said, her fingers digging into his skin.

She must be hurting him, Jac thought.

Serge twisted around in his seat to look at his stepsister, and Jac saw the most painful expression of need on his face. He was waiting for Melinoe to absolve him. For her to take away his grief. But could anyone ever do that for someone else? Would anyone ever be able to do that for her?

Chapter 32

MARCH 24, 1573
BARBIZON, FRANCE

The note was delivered by a page, and there was nothing unusual about its appearance or delivery to alert me that it was portentous. The seal was dark red and appeared, with a cursory glance, to belong to the queen, so at first I was confused by the unsigned message.

> I am going to evening matins at Sainte-Chapelle. If it is possible for you to meet me there, we might have some time afterward.

As I was noting that it was not the queen's hand, a particular scent wafted up toward me. No signature had been required after all. I recognized the perfume and knew without a doubt and with a quickened heart who had sent the letter.

Of all the churches in Paris, I preferred Sainte-Chapelle. Smaller than Notre Dame, it is one of the most beautiful and intimate, and if you want to talk to God, it's best to do it where you don't have to shout to have yourself heard. Yes, I am a cynic when it comes to religion. Having been raised by monks, I am all too aware of how the rules of the church benefit the church and not the common man. But we fragile humans need to believe in something. Need to have someone give us answers and rationales for the terrible things that happen at random and without recourse. Saying the almighty has his reasons, even if they are not visible to us at the time, enables many poor souls to accept the suffering of their lives here on earth. And that is, in the end, if not a good thing, at least a reassuring one.

If you had asked me what I believed in as I prepared to leave for Sainte-Chapelle, I am not sure what I would have said. The marvelous events assigned to the saints were just as fantastical and absurd to me as Ruggieri's magic. But that night in the small church, a miracle did occur. I am sure of it. And if there is a God, I thank him for it.

When I arrived, the church was awash in glowing colors as the setting sun illuminated the west wall of stained glass windows. A marvel of architecture and design, the apse is almost all windows on three sides so that at every time of day you feel as if you are enclosed inside a jewel box. No queen or king ever had such riches. Rubies and sapphires and citrines and emeralds at your feet, on your hands, your face, painted across the lighter-colored garments of the parishioners.

I took a seat and tried to find Isabeau in the congregation without being obvious. She would be with other ladies-in-waiting, and I didn't want to arouse suspicion among them. When I didn't see her, I planned to tarry afterward, assuming her plan was to break away and find me.

Soon after I was seated, the chants began. The monk's songs, the heady incense, the intensity of the colors, all began to work on me. I felt as if I were slipping deeper inside my mind, leaving my surroundings and entering a profound state of peace. So preoccupied with Ruggieri and the jobs Catherine had been giving me of late, I had been unable to settle my mind for quite a while. But that evening I was lulled into a state of calm by my surroundings. I didn't fall asleep, I'm sure of it. But I was in a half dream state, floating on the scents and the sounds.

As the Mass continued, I held my rosary and automatically moved my fingers on the beads as I had been taught so long ago. All habit. I was no more praying than I was sleeping. But the movements of my fingers were as mesmerizing as the sounds and the smells.

It was in this state that the work I had been doing since I'd left Florence came to mind. The souls of so many people were trapped in bottles and locked up in a cellar room in my store. By this point in my life, I had collected over twenty dying breaths. From Serapino's to King Henry's and

Catherine's sons' as well as those of others not as famous. Despite all my work and labor with Serapino's unfinished formula, the solution still eluded me all these years later.

I'm no longer quite sure how my thoughts progressed the way they did or where my inspiration came from. I recall there were massive amounts of roses in the church. It being summer, they were in bloom in all the gardens of Paris. The nuns had picked huge bouquets and placed them not just on the altar but in front of the statues as well.

The scent of roses has always been a talisman for me. My mother smelled of roses—it was one of the few memories of her that I had. The very first fragrance I'd created for Catherine had a rose base. Isabeau's husband had bought her a rose-infused water from me.

The roses that filled Sainte-Chapelle that evening were deep blood red and fully opened. The very next day they would begin to die, but during that Mass they were at the apex of their beauty, offering up their most exquisite scent.

I suppose it was because I was thinking about the roses that the sonorous hum of the priest's voice intoning the Latin liturgy reminded me of buzzing bees. That, coupled with my previous ruminations about Serapino and the dying breaths, jolted my memory, and I suddenly remembered something long forgotten. My mentor had talked about bees just before he died.

At the time I had been so scared. Serapino was expiring before my eyes—and I was trying to capture his breath so I could keep him with me forever. His last words had seemed incoherent mumblings brought on by the potions I'd administered.

There in the Sainte-Chapelle in Paris, in the jewel-toned light, inhaling the myrrh and frankincense and the roses and listening to the chants I'd heard since I was a babe, I wondered . . . What if the last thing that Serapino had uttered had meant something? Could he have been giving me a message? Were bees or their nectar part of the formula for the elixir that might animate the breaths?

I spent the entire Mass lost in my ruminations. In fact so deep was my meditation I didn't realize the service was even over until I felt a coolness on my skin, opened my eyes and saw the church was empty.

The scent of extinguished candles and paraffin now mixed in with the perfume of lingering incense and flowers. Rising, I walked toward the back of the church.

The sun had dropped lower in the sky, and the great rose window on the south wall was barely illuminated. With almost no light in the chapel, I couldn't be sure if anyone lingered in the shadows.

"Isabeau?" I whispered.

There was no response.

I walked the perimeter of the apse, peering into the shadows.

My heart fell. Isabeau was not there. Had something happened to prevent her from coming? Hesitant to give up, I walked from the rear of the church back to the altar and then down the opposite side. I had just accepted that she wasn't there when, as I passed the confessionals, I heard my name whispered.

I stopped. Turned. The heavily carved wooden door opened just enough for me to glimpse inside and see Isabeau.

Quickly, I entered the small space.

In Santa Maria Novella, I had been dutiful, confessing my sins weekly and doing my penance. But it had been almost forty years since those days when I acknowledged my petty jealousies and desires to my confessor. And since then, my list of sins had grown long. No one but Isabeau could have enticed me into a confessional that night.

The interior of the confessional at Sainte-Chapelle might have been as elaborate as the one at Santa Maria Novella, but I don't know. I can remember the walls were painted the same royal blue with gold fleurs-de-lis as the rest of the church, but I only saw them as backdrop for Isabeau.

As soon as I shut the door behind me, she pulled me to her and pressed her lips on mine. Oh, the sensations! And the smell! I had wondered if I'd imagined her scent all those weeks. Could she really have smelled the way I remembered? Had I been drunk? Could any woman really smell of a blooming garden?

But she did, and it was even more intoxicating now in the small space. Without room for us to lie down, we knelt upon the prie-dieu, facing each other, embracing as if we might never see each other again.

Neither of us was thinking that anyone would come back to the confessional now that the Mass was over. We felt safe in our blasphemy.

Isabeau's fingers worked the buttons on my doublet and then my shirt, and within minutes she was touching my bare flesh and I was shaking with desire.

My being was centered on the rising pressure in my groin. Everything pushing, pulsing. At once I yearned to relieve and also to prolong its exquisite pain.

I buried my face in Isabeau's neck. Smelled her hair . . . her skin. There was no longer a world outside of this cramped enclosure.

I had so many questions I wanted to ask her. Was she all right? What had she endured with the duke? How were her actions resting with her? Was she afraid? Was Catherine demanding too much?

But I didn't speak any of them. I couldn't. My mouth was too busy making a trail of bruising kisses from her lips down her neck, down across her chest, until I found the swell of her breasts and then one of her erect nipples waiting for me.

With both hands I lifted her skirts and found her naked flesh beneath all the layers of silks and lace. How hot her skin was. Burning. Fevered. And the place between her legs was so wet with juices that they dripped down her thighs. I moaned at this tactile proof that her desire matched mine and forced myself to not dwell on what she had been doing in the weeks since I had seen her. But I could not resist the torture of asking.

"Do you come to the duke like this? All wet and wanting?" The whisper escaped my lips.

"How can you ask?"

"How can I not? Are you ripe like this for every man?"

She laughed. It came from deep in her throat, and the sound almost brought me to climax.

"I don't open my legs for him, René. I never have for any of them. There are other ways to take care of men. I may be a widow and so not a virgin, but I am one of the queen's ladies. It is a privilege for these men to be with me. An honor that the queen bestows on them. They accept what I offer, the way I offer it."

Her hand had worked its way to my pants, and she had released my cock and was stroking it with her long, lithe fingers. I knew then that the men she seduced probably never even realized they were not getting the prize.

"Be careful," I whispered. "You are too good at what you do."

"Yes, that I am," she said and squeezed me in a certain way that stopped my feeling of imminent release.

Beneath my hand she was writhing. Her thrusting, an invitation I found impossible to resist.

Sensing how close I was, and she was, I maneuvered so I could enter her.

As much as both of us yearned to let go, we also knew it might be a long time before we saw each other again and so we lingered, went slowly, savored every stroke, every clench.

Kneeling on a velvet cushion embroidered with the king's fleur-de-lis, we consummated our mutual confession. I no more took her than she took me. Never before had I been with someone so expert, and while I resented it, I also found it exciting that this woman who knew so much was choosing to be with me.

Deep inside the church, deep inside the confessional, deep inside of Isabeau, no sound penetrated our hideaway. It wasn't until we had both exhausted ourselves and slumped to the floor that I heard the dull roar.

Recovered, my breathing returning to normal, I pushed the confessional door open and leaned out and listened; the sound was much louder.

"What is that?" Isabeau asked.

It wasn't a roar now that it was clearer, but instead screaming and shouting rising up to meet us.

I stood. Quickly I redressed, fastening my clothes with racing fingers. Isabeau did the same. Once we were properly attired, we made our way down the nave and out onto the stone terrace that overlooked the inner courtyard. There before us was a scene out of hell similar to the one carved into that first confessional I'd visited at Santa Maria Novella.

"Get down," I said, and as I dropped to the stone floor, I pulled her with me. The spaces between the stone columns were more than wide enough for us to see the melee and madness going on below.

"Is it the heretics?" she asked.

I nodded. "Yes, the Huguenots." These were the men who had broken away from our church and its rituals and sacraments. Who stole into our churches to defile our statues and saints. Who claimed Catholics were obsessed with dying and the dead. That our pilgrimages did nothing to help people find redemption. Who wanted a simpler religion based on faith in God as the righteous path. The Protestants, one in every twenty Frenchmen by then, wanted freedom to worship and have churches of their own.

Their heresy was not only a threat to our souls;

many Catholics believed it was the very reason that plague, famine and disease were visited upon us. God was angry, the Catholics said. And only when all men and women once again worshipped and prayed the right way would God grant peace.

But the battle was not all about God. Is it ever? It was about power, rivalry and wealth. A struggle between the Crown and a faction of the nobility: Louis de Bourbon, Gaspard de Coligny and Henry of Navarre on one side; the House of Guise on the other. And my queen trying to juggle them all and keep the peace.

To date there had been two civil wars, and recently there had been several uprisings instigated by the Huguenots. And from my perch on the terrace, it appeared this skirmish below was their doing. They had lain in wait till the service was over and attacked as the congregation exited the church.

There were bloodied and broken bodies everywhere. The clash of sword fights rang out as individual battles erupted. Knights and ladies who moments before had been praying now lay on the cobblestones, many of them past help.

While Isabeau and I had made love, men and women had been ambushed. By staying in the church, we had been protected. Our coming together had been a miracle and had saved our lives for a fate that was yet to be determined. One that might be far better . . . or far worse.

Chapter 33

THE PRESENT
MONDAY, MARCH 24
BARBIZON, FRANCE

Griffin called Jac from New York later that morning.

"I'm taking a six PM flight. I'll be in Paris by morning. I have a meeting in the afternoon, and then I'll take a car to Barbizon. I should be there by early evening."

"It will be good to see you."

"You sound tired," he said.

"It's nothing." She had almost told him what had happened during the trip to Wales. It wouldn't be fair for him to be stuck on a plane with nothing to do but think about the situation and stress over it.

"You sure?" he asked.

"I don't remember you being such a worrier when we were in college."

"I was at that age when you think you are immortal and nothing can ever happen to you."

"Well, we know that isn't true anymore," Jac said.

"Oh yes, that we do know," he responded, his voice dropping into a deeper register as if he was reflecting on his own tragedies. *Of course he had them,* Jac thought. His ruined marriage. His parents' deaths. And his own mangled career as a scholar that had been destroyed when he'd been accused of plagiarism by his own father-in-law. Even when Griffin was able to prove that the printer of his book had left out the two critical pages of footnotes, it was too late. His reputation had been tarnished. Four years later he was still rebuilding, repairing, fighting to regain some measure of the success he'd had before.

"How was New York?" she asked.

Griffin had gone to see his daughter, but that meant he would also have seen his wife. They were separated but not yet divorced. Jac hadn't been able to stop herself from worrying that being back with them both, he'd have second thoughts about the breakup of his family. Even though he'd told her there was no possibility of a reconciliation. They'd tried to do that before and had failed.

"It was wonderful to see Elsie," he said.

"How was her birthday party?"

"Terrific."

"And Therese?" Jac was mad at herself that she'd asked.

"Fine. She was fine. I can hear the uncertainty in your voice, though. We're not getting back together, she and I. Trust me," Griffin said, making her smile.

She almost said she was sorry, but she really wasn't, and he'd know that. "I do," she said instead.

After getting off the phone, Jac walked out of her bedroom and ran smack into Melinoe, who was strolling down the hallway.

"I was just coming to talk to you," she said.

"You were?"

For some reason Jac wondered if Melinoe had been lingering outside the room and listening to her calls.

"If you have a few minutes, would you join me in the library?"

"Of course," Jac said and walked with her hostess down the formal staircase and across the marble-floored foyer.

Unlike the rest of the château, where the artwork, collectibles and objets d'art demanded your attention and were distracting, the library, which was Serge's domain, was calmer.

Serge was already in there, sitting on the leather couch. Laid out in front of him were three amber bottles and a green crystal skull.

Jac recognized them instantly. The ingredients that Chester Bruge had shown them only twenty-four hours ago.

She sat down in one of the chairs opposite Serge. Melinoe sat beside her brother.

For Jac, seeing the items out of context here at the château was disconcerting and frightening.

"How did you get them?" Jac blurted out.

"We borrowed them," Melinoe said before Serge could answer.

"But when?"

"Yesterday," Serge said. He was looking down, staring at the bottles with a sorrowful expression.

A lot of time had passed between the moment when Bruge fell and Serge went rushing to the elderly man to help him and the moment when Jac returned to the path with the limo driver. What had happened during those thirty minutes?

"These ingredients are useless to everyone but us. We couldn't just leave them there in the shed once we knew what had happened to Bruge," Melinoe said as if it were the only logical conclusion.

"You went back inside after he collapsed?" Jac asked.

"I was going to try to convince Bruge to let us have portions of each one in exchange for telling him what we were working on and offering to include him in the project. I'm certain he would have agreed," Melinoe said.

"But we will never know," Jac said.

"No." Melinoe's face betrayed no emotion except for the hint of stubbornness and the defiance in her eyes that was always there.

Jac had never seen the woman soften. Not even what Jac had heard on the other side of Melinoe's bedroom door had been tender.

"I would think you would be excited," Melinoe said to Jac. "Now, you can create the perfumer's potion using all authentic materials."

Jac was staring at the fluorite skull. Remembering how proud of it Bruge had been when he showed it to her. And now it was here. Stolen, as the kindly man lay dying.

"You will begin tomorrow, won't you?" Melinoe half asked, half ordered.

Jac wanted to, but using pilfered ingredients was an impossible way to begin formulating the elixir. Except what choice did she have? She needed to know if this goal was achievable as much as Melinoe did. They were sisters in this quest—for different reasons, but each as desperate as the other to prove that the impossible was possible.

"You are worried about how we got these, aren't you?" Serge asked Jac.

Melinoe put her hand on her brother's arm. "Serge, it's pointless to have this conversation," she said. "We had a goal. We achieved it. The circumstances were unfortunate, but now we need to move on. We always do, don't we?"

"We always have, but these circumstances *are* different," he said.

Melinoe's fingers caressed her brother's forearm, as if trying to calm him. "Not so different. You've handled far worse. You know you have. You are the strongest man I know. This is not like you."

Jac wasn't sure she understood the subtext running under their conversation, but she knew there was more to it than Melinoe helping herself to the ingredients while Serge tried to assist Bruge.

Had they been involved in a similar situation before? Was Melinoe referring to the awful murder-suicide of their parents? Had witnessing death brought back the horror of that long-ago tragedy?

Whatever Melinoe was saying, it was having an effect on Serge.

He squared his shoulders, looked at Jac and said: "Let's concentrate on moving forward. How long do you think it will take you to make up a formula?"

"From the description, a couple of days. The problem is what to do with it once we have it."

"Has Griffin been able to translate the engravings?" Melinoe asked in a tone that assumed Jac had heard from him.

"Not yet, no. He's searching for a key to unlock the cryptic language. I might have found something to help him, though. I noticed similarities between some drawings on Bruge's wall and the engravings on the bells . . . I was hoping that Griffin might get a look at some of his books . . ." She trailed off.

"There are other versions and copies of those books. I'll get them so they're waiting for him."

It sounded as if Melinoe knew when Griffin was coming back. But how could she unless she was listening in on Jac's conversations? Had she been lurking outside her bedroom after all?

Jac was trying to figure out a way to trick Melinoe into revealing what she knew when Serge asked, "Jac, do you know when he is coming back?"

"Yes, tomorrow, I think. Or maybe the day after."

Melinoe paused.

"Jac, I think it's time to tell you that your brother did have an idea of what to do with the breaths," she said conspiratorially. "Robbie was going to pierce the cork in the bottle with a syringe and feed in the potion. He wouldn't corrupt the breath that way. Then the mixture could be inhaled." She paused again. "Serge, we might need to get some medical supplies. You can take care of that too, can't you?"

"Yes, of course."

Melinoe was still caressing her stepbrother's arm. As if he were a wild cat, Jac thought, and Melinoe was his eccentric and slightly mad owner, soothing him, hypnotizing him with her touch.

And he'd responded. Jac could see it in his face.

Jac stood up. The atmosphere here was suffocating. Melinoe's passion and her desires weighted down the very air as if she were wearing an overbearing perfume that she applied too often and too heavily. For a moment Jac thought about leaving La Belle Fleur. Except there was no alternative but to stay if she wanted to re-create the formula. And she did. As much as Melinoe. Maybe more because now that Griffin was back in her life again, Jac was desperate to know what had happened to René le Florentin and how the ancient perfumer's existence and hers were connected.

"I think I'll go to the laboratory and go over the list one more time tonight and then get an early start. Let me take these . . ." She pointed to the containers on the desk.

"Serge, help her," Melinoe said.

"No," Jac said even though Melinoe was right. She really shouldn't try to carry them all herself. But Jac didn't want anyone to go with her. When she was there, alone, the small room offered itself to her differently. The communication with the spirit who had used it before her was more direct. The perfumer whose life she was piecing together revealed more of himself to her when they were alone.

"Here's the box I packed them in to bring them here. You can use this to take them downstairs," Serge said.

Very carefully Jac carried the box out of the library and headed in the cellar's direction. With each step her excitement grew.

Jac knew that this time there was no hypnotic drug she was inhaling. Her visions weren't induced by any specific material. It was more that the laboratory itself was the portal. She'd had other memory lurches outside of the cell-like room—when Serge had showed her the folly and in her own bedroom. But it was in the underground cellar that her path to René le Florentin was strongest and where she could channel him the easiest. And where she felt the closest to him.

She was confused by how feelings for him overwhelmed her. Deep abiding love. Passion. So visceral that when she came out of the trance she wanted nothing more than to put her hands in between her legs and bring herself to orgasm to relieve the longing.

Jac climbed down the stairs, cradling the box, holding tight to the handrail. The darkness waited for her . . . *He* waited for her.

Two years ago Jac was still fighting the possibility that she could access her own past lives, much less anyone else's. But a few months ago she'd stopped arguing with Malachai and her brother, who both believed she was a memory tool—that rare person who could access not only her own past lives but other people's. Taking the time between seasons of her cable TV show to work with Robbie building fragrances in Paris had opened Jac's mind to the idea that she didn't have to understand in order to acknowledge other realms and constructs. She'd listened to her brother talk about Buddhism, reincarnation and karma, and being in the moment with a more relaxed mind. She'd almost reached a place where she believed that if this was her ability, she could deal with it. Even if she didn't like it and still wished she could shut it down.

When she'd told Robbie that, he said he was certain she'd be able to control it once she fully accepted it, but that there was still something in the past she needed to know. And once she did, she'd be able to make her own decisions about opening herself up to this other dimension.

Jac turned on the light in the cellar and made her way to René le Florentin's laboratory. There was no electricity in this room. Since it had remained hidden for so many centuries, it had never been wired. Jac was glad of that. She put down the box, lit the candelabra that René had used, then closed the door and ensconced herself inside René's world.

She unpacked the box, placing each new bottle on the shelf amid the others. Sitting in his chair, at his desk, Jac stared at the worn wooden table where he had mixed his elixirs and worked on his brews.

There was no reason to wait till tomorrow, was there? The night was quiet around her. No one cared that she was down here. She had everything she needed to begin.

Each beaker had been one René had used in building this same formula. Each glass was as cool in her hand as it had been in his. Each pipette and measuring device was one he had touched. Every action she took was mimicking his. After a gap of almost five hundred years.

Take of good brandy, a half of a gallon . . .

Jac poured René's brandy. The amber liquor gleamed as the river of it flowed from bottle to beaker.

. . . of the best virgin honey and coriander seeds, each a half of a pound . . .

The honey was new. It came from Provence and was scented with lavender just as it would have been in René's time. As she poured the thick syrup, she remembered something Robbie had once told her: in Hinduism honey was one of the five elixirs of immortality. She felt her brother with her as she watched the slow journey of the glistening gold. He hadn't gotten this far—hadn't found the formula with all the ingredients—but he had believed.

This I do for you, she thought. Beside her, she could almost see him nodding.

Jac shook her head; this wasn't the time to focus on the impossibility of what she was experiencing. Circling around her were the mysteries of the ages that the most learned of men and women had tried to understand. She knew sometimes the only answer to explain the unexplainable was that there was no answer.

Hard to accept for someone who preferred reason to fantasy.

Glancing down at René's formula, Jac counted out the noted amounts of coriander seeds. Then added the cloves, henbane, nutmeg, aloewood and dragon's blood. The scent of the concoction was more food than fragrance.

Now it was time to use the ancient essences that Melinoe and Serge had procured. For a moment Jac hesitated. What *had* happened in the woods in Wales?

There are no coincidences, Malachai always said in reference to reincarnation memories. But it meant more than that. Here in the dimly lit laboratory that had been built by René le Florentin to aid him in his search for a way to bring back the dead, Jac thought about the man who had collected these ancient ingredients. She'd seen when the branch struck Bruge, but not hard enough to kill him. It had been a serious blow to the head; she knew that because when she had gone back she'd seen the pool of blood. Serge had said the branch caused his fall, and when he hit the ground, it was the rock he fell on that bashed in his skull. And then in those moments after Bruge had fallen, while he lay dying, while they waited for the ambulance, Melinoe had gone back and stolen the last necessary ingredients.

Certainly she was wily and intelligent and seemed more than capable of acting that quickly. But there was another possibility that Jac hadn't wanted to consider before. Didn't really want to consider now.

Instead she opened the bottle of tutty, inserted a knife and began to scrape at the hardened ash. Tipping the bottle over, she spilled a half dozen curls of the substance into a small glass dish. She needed an ounce. Then she went back to scraping.

While she worked, her mind went over and over the accident in the forest. Surely Bruge was owed at least this. He was a man she'd only known for an hour, but he deserved homage. If his rare collection helped her re-create this elixir, he would have helped give her the greatest gift of her life.

After she had amassed a small mound of the dark chimney residue, she added a few drops of the brandy mixture and watched it liquefy.

Satisfied, she poured it in with the other ingredients.

Now it was time for the last component. Jac reached for the skull casket. Opening it, she looked down at the momie. What had made someone think to examine the embalmed corpses and take the sap from the area between the brain and the spine and use it as a scent? Perfumers—even ancient ones—didn't use human elements. But magicians did. So what did that say about René?

She was slightly nauseated as she scraped a clean knife over the residue. Unlike the tutty, it was too hard to even scratch. Over hundreds of years it had turned into a solid. And a few drops of brandy did nothing to soften it.

Stumped, she sat and stared at the black brittle.

What to do to get it out?

The purest method would be to heat the skull, but then she'd risk releasing elements from the fluorite into the substance and contaminating it.

She had no choice.

Using the same balneo-mariae that René had used, Jac heated the water in the lower section and then placed the skull inside of it. She watched the surface of the dark material, and within a few minutes could see it begin to glisten. Using ancient tongs she lifted the skull out of the water and put it down on the table. Then, using a clean knife, she dug into the substance. Finally it was malleable. Sticky. Viscous.

Once again, Jac felt nauseated. She wondered what René had thought of using such an element. A man who distilled roses and orange blossoms. Who reveled in the scent of lilies and surrounded himself with the most glorious scents from nature.

What kind of desperation had made him spend the last years of his life so obsessed with bringing back the dead that he would resort to using the death blood of corpses?

It was while she was mixing the momie into the honey-laced brandy that she remembered something about the time she'd spent in Bruge's alchemical laboratory. Serge and Melinoe had been looking at a book and talking only to each other. Was that when they'd been planning what happened next? Was the accident in the woods premeditated? But they couldn't have accounted for the branch falling. Had they been planning on killing him some other way in order to steal the ingredients? Was Melinoe capable of something so egregious? Was Serge that much her puppet that he would have agreed to do that for her?

He was an intelligent man with one fatal flaw. His passion for his stepsister defied logic, but then again, passion always did. Great leaders have lost kingdoms over lovers. Was Serge capable of killing someone to please Melinoe?

Of course he was.

She was more than his stepsister. Melinoe had saved his life. She was his lover and his family in one.

So was that what had happened, or was Jac's imagination running wild?

Serge could not have killed Bruge. Jac had watched him try to save the man's life.

But it was time to concentrate on the elixir. Jac returned to René's notes. She reread everything she'd done up to this point. The words swirled on the page. She was tired, but she wanted to finish. She wished Griffin were here. Maybe he'd be able to help her figure out what she'd seen in the rain, in the woods.

Griffin. . . . The man she'd spent her lifetime missing had returned to her, but the dilemma that had confused her for the last two years still had to be resolved. Was she hallucinating or remembering past lives?

Even if they were reincarnation memories, Griffin said she didn't have to accept the inevitability of them repeating themselves. If you believed in karmic responsibility, you could rectify your past mistakes and change the future.

She was drifting off. Not concentrating. Jac wished she had some coffee but didn't want to leave the laboratory while she was this close to finishing. She dipped a clean spoon into the pot of honey and ate it. The sweetness would give her a burst of energy. Even if she'd crash harder on the other side.

Jac counted out the vanilla beans the recipe called for, and then read on.

> . . . benilloes, number four; the yellow rind
> of three large lemons. Bruise the cloves,
> nutmegs; cut the benilloes into small

pieces; put all into a cucurbit and pour the brandy on to them. After they have digested twenty-four hours, distill off the spirit in balneo-mariae.

She had forgotten to get the lemons. She was going to have to go back to the kitchen after all. But first she poured the brandy mixture on the other ingredients. Watched the swirl of colors. Breathed in the scents as they mixed together. The fragrance was so provocative. Like nothing she had ever smelled. It was the odd tutty and momie. She could only begin to imagine what the elixir would smell like after it was distilled and she added the final items.

The aroma had filled the small laboratory. René must have sat right here and inhaled the very same scent.

Jac needed to get the lemons . . . but she was slipping . . . the air was waving. She was letting go of the present and entering into the past. *His* past. She smelled not only the scent she was building but also another. An ancient one that René had created for himself and wore religiously. Oak moss, pine, musk. Sensual waves of scent enveloped her like a man's arms. Like Griffin's arms. No, not Griffin's. René's.

She closed her eyes. Her fingers gripped the edge of the desk as if part of her was resisting leaving, as if part of her knew that it was unsafe to go into that long-ago darkness because what she might find there might be dangerous. But she had to go. To see him. The mysterious, cautious, mercurial and determined René le Florentin. To learn from him. To feel the power of his passion for the woman he was in love with . . . passion for her.

Chapter 34

MARCH 24, 1573
BARBIZON, FRANCE

"Is that a new perfume, René?"

Catherine was back in Paris. She'd been meeting with Protestants in Navarre, and she looked exhausted. We were no longer young, she and I, and the toll of the political burdens she carried was aging her.

"Yes, Your Highness. Not as floral as what you've been wearing. I've been experimenting with woods and spices from the Far East."

I handed her an elaborately carved box that I had purchased in anticipation of giving her this gift. Her eyes lit up as she took it. Despite my ulterior motive, I cared about Catherine and was glad I was able to please her.

The queen opened the box, and smiled when she

saw the small vial encrusted with pink-tinged pearls nestled in velvet.

"How very lovely—" She'd found the chain tucked behind the bottle. "What is this?"

"A scent bottle to wear like a piece of jewelry." I'd gone to the court jeweler with the idea, and he'd created the bottle to my specifications. Isabeau and I had talked of how best to ask the queen to release Isabeau to marry me, and the gift had been her idea. I'd thought it inspired. Now I was sure it had been.

"How clever you are, René. The women of the court will all besiege you now for their versions." Catherine unscrewed the top—one large pink pearl. Attached was a small wand studded with minuscule rubies that gleamed with the oil it brought up. At the very tip was a teardrop-shaped diamond, wet with my newest scent.

"You and the jeweler Charpitier have outdone yourself," she exclaimed with delight.

"He has for sure, Your Majesty, but you haven't even smelled the perfume. Allow me."

I took the wand from her and drew it across her wrist. How different this gesture was than when I applied perfume to Isabeau's skin. That was a seduction; this was a privilege.

Catherine lifted her hand to her face and sniffed. Once, and then again. "How curious this is, René. I've never smelled anything like it. It's very exotic, very foreign, yes?"

"Exactly. I was thinking of ancient Egyptian queens and Indian maharajas when I was mixing it. Picturing deserts and oases."

"Thank you, it's a very charming presentation." She recapped the bottle, lifted it and hung it around her neck. The glow from the pearls helped soften her haggard complexion.

"I'm glad it pleases you," I said.

She studied me for a moment and then asked, "What is troubling you then?"

Catherine knew me too well.

"I wanted to ask a favor of you."

"Of course. You know I will do anything I can for you."

"I'd like you to release one of your ladies-in-waiting and allow me to take her as my bride."

Catherine's eyes grew wide. She tilted her head to one side and stared at me as if she had never really seen me before.

"I thought you were a satisfied bachelor. Over the years it's been said that you tire of your women quickly and prefer variety to companionship."

"Over the years I have."

"It occurs to me once again that there is much I don't know about you. It's not that I don't care for you, René; it's just the reality of being in this position."

"I know that."

"But it's not right. There are so many things I should know . . . What is your favorite food? Do you like to read? What music do you prefer? Do you miss Florence even now as much as I do?"

"You shouldn't trouble yourself with such questions, Your Highness. I have never expected you to waste time on trivialities about whether or not the Seine had replaced the Arno in my dreams. I am only talking about my personal life now because I need you to release the woman I wish to wed."

"Who is it?"

"Isabeau Allard."

"Oh, René," she said after a moment. Her voice was tinged with regret, and her eyes gazed on me with sadness. Then she got up and walked over to the window that faced the river. There was a strong breeze blowing in, and it carried the scent of the new fragrance that I'd made toward me.

Now whenever I open a bottle of cinnamon, I feel a rush of anger. A scent memory connected forever to that terrible moment when I realized she was not going to grant my request.

"I wish that it were that easy, but she is one of the most important women I have in my court. A better spy than any man who's ever tried to glean information from the enemy. To release her would be to destroy more than a year of hard work. I rely on her, René. No, more than I, the *country* relies on her."

I could see that my queen was indeed torn. But Catherine, the woman who said *The Prince* by

Machiavelli was her favorite book, never let her personal feelings interfere when it came to ruling.

"If you had asked for the hand of any other woman, not one as entrenched in the political intrigue that is so critical to France's well-being, I would have not only granted it but given you a lavish wedding as my gift . . ." She shook her head. "But I cannot release Isabeau now. In fact, I am afraid I am going to make this even more difficult because I have to send her away again. And I implore you to let her go without making her departure any more painful than it will already be. She has work to do, and I need her mind sharp and her heart unburdened."

I wanted to grab Catherine by her shoulders and shake her, get down on my knees and beg her. I wanted to do whatever I could to change her mind even though it was impossible. No one ever came between Catherine and her plans for France. And if she believed Isabeau was essential to those plans, I knew there was little I could do.

She reached for the necklace, and I saw that I had made a mistake in bringing a gift. "So what was this, René? A bribe?"

"Not at all. It is a gift in honor of your return. And you wound me to suggest anything else. You know where my loyalty lies. I am your liege. We have traveled a long road together, my queen."

She looked off into the distance. Was she, like I

was, remembering the awful dungeon where she had come to rescue me?

"Back there in Florence, did you poison your monk, René?"

All these years and she had never asked me before.

"Not in the way you mean, no. He was in agony and asked me to administer the poison, and I could not deny him release for all that suffering."

I was picturing Serapino's deathbed and the pain that lined his face.

"So when you poisoned for me, it was your first time?"

I nodded.

"I have asked a lot of you, haven't I?"

"You asked nothing of me. You saved my life."

She walked to me and took both my hands in hers. Her skin was dry and cool. The skin of a woman who had turned herself into a queen, who focused on the affairs of her country and ignored her own heart. Since Henry had died, a part of her had died too. I wished for her what I had found. Another human soul to lay with her and bring that buried part of her back to life.

"There are so many other women in court—find someone else and I will give you a fine wedding and fill your house in Barbizon with gifts," she said.

I smiled at her. "I can't do that, Your Majesty."

Had she really forgotten how the human heart

worked? Or was she just trying to convince herself that my request could be so easily fulfilled?

"Why Isabeau? What is it about her?"

"Except for Your Majesty, who is on another level, when other women wear my perfume it complements them by making them smell more lovely. Isabeau is the only woman who complements my perfumes by making them smell more beautiful."

I did not do as Catherine asked. I got a message to Isabeau straightaway and asked her to meet me in the Tuileries.

"I will refuse to work for her anymore. I will take my own release," Isabeau said after I'd explained.

"So that we can run away and be fugitives?" I asked. "We don't want to live like that."

"I don't care how we live. I want to be with you. To belong to you. To spend every night by your side, not sleeping by myself in the palace, dreaming of being in your bed."

"Please don't speak so loudly. Don't look as if you are so distraught."

"I know she has spies everywhere. I can't forget that. I am one."

"And she values you. She is not going to let you go."

We walked on, not speaking. The complicated future that we faced was as rock-strewn as the path we were on. The days and nights of furtive meetings and long absences stretched out before us, bend after bend.

"So what are you suggesting?" she asked.

"That we wait for your current assignment to be concluded and then, when you have fulfilled her needs . . ."

"No! I can make the duke tire of me and then—"

"She's too smart, Isabeau, you know that. If Catherine suspected that you had manipulated him and became angry at you, our fate might be even more miserable. What if she decided to punish you?"

"So I am to be her prisoner?"

"No. You aren't a prisoner."

"But if I leave, I leave in disgrace. With nothing. Can you give up your position?"

"Yes, yes, of course."

"So we can go to Florence. You can take me home with you."

Home? Paris was home. Barbizon was home. The magistrates in Florence had been clear with Catherine that if I returned, I would return as a prisoner. In their eyes I had murdered a man, and they didn't want me on their soil. But that had been decades ago. Would it still matter? Would anyone remember?

"I need to tell you about Florence. And why I left," I said.

As we walked down the sandy allée lined with chestnut trees, under the dappled shade they offered, I told Isabeau the story of my childhood. How I was orphaned and taken in by the monks of Santa Maria Novella. How Serapino had made me his apprentice and taught me everything he knew. I told her about his dying breath theory and his experiments and how he'd taken ill and what he had asked me to do for him. I explained how I never questioned what I owed him or worried about the ramifications. And finally, I recounted the details of my trial and sentence—which to that day I had never spoken of to a living soul—and how Catherine had come and plucked me out of the jaws of danger.

"So I can't go back. We would have to find someplace new."

"Can you leave your store?"

"It's just a building made of wood and stone," I said, but she must have heard some hesitation in my voice. "And, yes, endless bottles of priceless essences and spices and herbs and hundreds of wonderful scents that clients come from far away to purchase. But I have my notes, and I can re-create everything."

"What if Catherine heard of your plans to defect and destroyed your shop and your notes before we were able to depart?"

"Catherine is determined but not cruel." Even as I said it, I knew I didn't believe it. She was ruthless, and I had no doubt that despite her loyalty to me all these years, like everyone else, I was dispensable. If it suited her, she would turn on me.

"I can't let you give up everything you have worked for," she said.

"It's not your choice, Isabeau."

"But it is. It's my choice. And I choose to stay at court and do what Catherine wants until we figure out another way."

It was because of me she was saying we should stay. I'd intimated I was loath to leave. *I* was the coward, and yet she shouldered the blame. I was about to speak, to protest, but she reached for my hand and lifted it to her lips and pressed her mouth against my palm. She kissed me and then quickly dropped my hand and ran back to the palace.

I sat on a stone bench in Catherine's great and grand gardens, under the shade of the trees, and rested my head in my hands, thinking through what Isabeau had said and not said. I had feared she'd find me suddenly monstrous after hearing how I'd helped Serapino to die. Instead she'd been understanding.

Catherine had forbid me to see Isabeau anymore. But how could I give her up? I closed my eyes. Suddenly, all around me, a garden blossomed. Roses and camellias and gardenias. Except it was not yet the season for such flowers. We had weeks to go.

I opened my eyes, expecting some extraordinary event to have occurred and that there would be blossoms and beds of riotous color surrounding me. But I saw nothing but the same trees and grasses of a few moments ago.

And then I realized—it was my hand, where Isabeau had kissed me. She'd left her breath, and in her breath was the garden.

Chapter 35

THE PRESENT
MONDAY, MARCH 24
BARBIZON, FRANCE

Jac woke up in the laboratory, feeling drugged and groggy. Looking at her mother's wristwatch, she calculated that she'd been sleeping there, at René's work space, for over three hours. The dream—but it wasn't a dream—wasn't blurred and ephemeral. The memories were as fresh as if she'd lived them the day before. As she relived what she'd experienced, sadness overwhelmed her, and she sat there and wept.

After a few minutes Jac roused herself. The solution needed to macerate for twenty-four hours, and it had already begun without one important ingredient. She needed the lemons.

Serge was in the kitchen. He was wearing maroon silk pajamas and a silk robe, with distinctive paisley velvet slippers from a store Jac knew on the Right Bank in Paris. Despite all the accoutrements he looked tired. His skin looked gray.

"Good evening," he said.

"Hi. Can't sleep?"

He nodded. "The last twenty-four hours have left me shaken."

"Me too."

"Would you like a cup of chocolate? I made enough for an army."

"Yes, that would be great," she said.

As he stood, he seemed to take note of her clothes. "At least I tried to go to sleep," he said.

"I've been downstairs all night. I started mixing the formula. I didn't think I was going to but . . ."

His eyebrows lifted. "Really? How far did you get?"

"I've done everything but add the lemons."

"And after the lemons—what next?"

"We wait twenty-four hours before the next step."

"What does it smell like so far?"

"A very aromatic liqueur. The brandy is over-whelming everything else." She thought about René and his personal oak moss and musk scent.

"I'm relieved that you have everything you need . . ."

"Except the lemons." She smiled. "By far the easiest ingredient."

He smiled back at her, but it was halfhearted. Serge turned off the burner and poured out the dark shiny chocolate. After putting a steaming cup in front of her, he returned to his seat.

"You did everything you could to save that man's life," Jac said.

Serge picked up a spoon and stirred the liquid in his cup, but he remained quiet.

"I watched you. You gave him your own breath." Jac lifted the cup and took a sip. "This is delicious. My grandmother used to make it just like this with real melted chocolate, not powdered cocoa."

"It takes more time to melt the chocolate, but it's an effort that more than pays off." He took a sip but then shook his head as if the taste had been so good he felt guilty.

Or was that Jac's imagination?

"It's very difficult to watch someone die," Jac said.

"Yes. It is. And I've seen too many people lose their battle . . ."

She interrupted. "Serge, how could Melinoe have gone back and taken the ingredients from Bruge's laboratory? In that moment—with all that was going on—how could she have been so merciless?"

"She's not someone who is easy to understand."

"No one is easy to understand . . . but how can you watch someone dying and think to use that moment to steal something from them?"

"I'm sorry."

"What are you apologizing for?"

Serge turned away. Looked at the stove. At the sink. Anywhere but at Jac's eyes.

"It didn't happen exactly the way you think it did . . ." he whispered.

Jac had to lean in to hear him.

"What didn't?"

"Bruge's accident . . . it *was* an accident . . . but . . ."

"But what?" Jac was certain that Serge, despite his one weakness for Melinoe, was not a cold-blooded killer.

His face was collapsing. His features softening into misery. His eyes filled with tears that remained unshed. His voice was barely even a whisper now. "Melinoe had wanted me to create some kind of accident so he'd be hurt and then to help him . . . save him . . . so that he'd feel so grateful that he'd sell her the ingredients."

"Did you somehow make that branch fall?"

"No, it just happened. The branch broke off and knocked him down."

"And then?"

Serge was quiet. Had Bruge really cracked his head on the stone, or had Melinoe bashed his head in with the rock?

Jac didn't bother to ask. Even if Serge knew, which she doubted, she was certain he'd never turn his stepsister in.

"When Melinoe realized that Bruge had been mortally wounded, she took advantage of that fact to go back and take what she wanted?" Jac asked.

Again, Serge didn't respond. But someone else did.

"No!"

In reaction to the single word, Serge closed his eyes.

Jac turned. Melinoe stood in the doorway. Her hair was wild with Medusa-like curls. Her eyes blazed with anger. The skin around her mouth was white with rage. She was wearing a long silk black robe edged with silver lace. Her large diamond earrings sparkled in the dim light. She looked like one of the furies.

"Discuss our business with a stranger? Serge, how could you?"

Even though she'd voiced it as a question, Jac knew it was an accusation. There would be consequences for Serge for having broken a confidence. And for her too, she feared. For she'd been the one to hear his confession, and that might have been the greater sin.

Chapter 36

MARCH 25, 1573
BARBIZON, FRANCE

The following week there was a crisis at court.

For months Catherine had been carefully planning to marry off her daughter Margaret, a Catholic, to the Protestant Henry of Navarre in order to quiet the religious uprisings. In exchange for giving Henry strongholds throughout France and the potential of his son being heir to the throne, Catherine expected he would agree to marry inside our cathedral and accept his wife's religion. Catherine believed such a wedding might bring peace to France and end the violent wars that pitted citizen against citizen.

I always wondered about a God who wanted his flock killing one another over the ways that he was worshipped. But men are monsters all, and something in them wants to force others to see the world the same way they see it. More people had been killed in my lifetime over that eternal need to be right than any other battle.

Over the years, I'd had clients purchase poisoned garments or tinctures to add to food to exact revenge because they had been cuckolded or deceived. Those were reasons I could understand for taking action. Stealing your wife, your gold, your land, your belongings. Promising fealty and then taking it away. Yes, anger. Yes, revenge. But kill because my church has pomp and yours does not?

No, I was not that naive—it was really kill because you want power over me. Well, power or no, the queen had come up with what she thought was a reasonable way to quell the mobs.

Margaret, though, had other plans. The willful princess was carrying on a dalliance with Henry de Guise, whose family was at the heart of the anti-Protestant sentiment.

One afternoon she'd come to my shop and asked for a special fragrance. "Something that will make me unforgettable, René," she'd said. And then whispered, "Unforgettable to a lover."

Although she hadn't used his name, I'd known who the lover was. Margaret was careful, but the court was rife with gossip. I'd even seen her, in the Tuileries, with de Guise when Catherine was not at court.

I concocted a blend of honey and lilacs and tuberose with a hint of cinnamon. She wasn't a fair, fragile woman but a bold one with thick dark hair and blazing eyes. *The scent worked well for her,* I'd thought.

Henry de Guise must have thought so too because Margaret sent her lady back for refills every other week for a month. I'd been pleased that my handiwork was successful.

Isabeau had told me that she, along with other ladies of the court, sometimes spied on Margaret through a crack in the floorboards. I was hardly shocked. Hadn't my queen done such a thing? Spied on her own husband with his mistress?

"Margaret is wild with her lover," Isabeau told me. "Their lovemaking sessions last sometimes three or four hours. She's willing to do anything he wants, and apparently he wants quite a lot. He likes her to dress up for him in costumes."

The stories circulating court were quite explicit. One night she had dressed like a nun, and he took her while she wore her habit. Another time she'd dressed like a soldier. Yet another like a poor milkmaid. And his appetite, Isabeau said, was equally matched by hers.

"She is obsessed with him and his attentions, and sometimes she asks him to walk back and forth, naked, while she sketches his body." Isabeau blushed. "One of the ladies found one of those drawings. It must have slipped under the bed. It was of de Guise naked and fully erect. Can you imagine what a prize that drawing is? She will be able to blackmail the princess Margaret for whatever she wants with it."

On that fateful day that changed our lives, Margaret had invited de Guise to her rooms, and they were once again playacting. She had taken a

405

crown from the royal vault and was wearing it with an ermine cape that belonged to the queen. Underneath the fur, she was naked. They were in the midst of their theatrics, enacting a scene where he played a nobleman come to beg for the court's help.

De Guise was naked, kneeling in front of her, and she was teasing his cock with a gold bejeweled scepter when the door burst open, and Catherine and Charles IX burst in along with a retinue of guards. De Guise was grabbed, ushered out of the princess's room, out of the Louvre and thrown onto the street, his clothes following.

Meanwhile Margaret's screams, it was said, could be heard throughout the palace. She kept shrieking the duke's name, over and over, as they took him away. Catherine slapped her daughter and called her a whore. Told her to be quiet, but still Margaret screamed. Charles took over for his mother and beat his sister, cursing her all the while.

It wasn't moral outrage that inflamed Catherine and her son. Margaret was interfering with their political campaign. The queen's plan required her daughter be a virgin princess, so the affair was putting the Navarre union in jeopardy. Even now I cannot blame Catherine for her fury. She wasn't an evil potentate. My lady just wanted peace in France and an end to the fighting. It was a noble wish.

"Your selfish ways are putting my efforts at risk. You cannot give in to base, fleeting desires," Catherine shouted at her weeping, naked daughter. "You are a princess who will one day be the queen of Navarre. Your behavior is not befitting the Crown."

As Catherine lectured, the king flogged Margaret with a leather whip, lashing her cowering form. One of the ladies said that Charles was flushed and appeared excited by the thrashing, until, finally the queen ended the beating.

"Margaret is being kept locked in her room for several days and nights," Isabeau said when she related the tale to me. "It may be weeks."

"Why are you crying, Isabeau? Is the princess that badly hurt?" I asked.

"She has deep welts that could scar. Her women are applying oils to them."

I nodded. "They came to buy them this morning. I prepared them not knowing what they were for. Now I know why they seemed so subdued.

"Her skin will repair itself. Don't worry," I said to Isabeau. "I didn't know you were so close to Margaret, but she will be all right. A princess can't fall in love with whomever she sees fit. Surely you understand that."

"I didn't think they would beat her."

"I'm surprised about that too, but she'll recover."

"But they've imprisoned the princess for falling

in love with the wrong man. For doing what I have done, don't you see?"

I didn't, not really. "No, why is this distressing you so?"

"Because it's my fault." Her voice was barely above a whisper.

"Your fault? How on earth can this have anything to do with you?"

"I told the queen about the assignation. I bribed Margaret's ladies to tell me as soon as Henry de Guise next came to the palace and they were together. Once I got word, I went to the queen, and offered her the information in exchange for permission to marry you."

I was stunned by Isabeau's confession. "Why didn't you tell me what you were planning?"

"You would have talked me out of it."

"Yes, I would have. Guilt and deception are terrible things to live with. Now you are burdened."

"I did it out of love for you. So we can be together. So we can marry and I can bear you a legitimate son."

She had turned on a young girl who was in love out of love for me. The irony of it stung.

"I don't need to marry you in order to love you. We can be together here at court until you become free."

"But you are so unhappy at what I do for the queen. I see your face when Catherine has need for me. I can't bear what it does to you."

Had my jealousy made Isabeau do this? Was the blame mine? Why had I been so weak as to let her glimpse into my soul? Why hadn't I been able to control my feelings?

"And for all this what did the queen say? What is to be your reward?"

"She said the information was indeed important and should be rewarded, and she would give us permission to wed as soon as she has resolved the debacle with Margaret and has her married to Navarre."

I took Isabeau in my arms and let her cry herself out. Her emotions were a tangle of contradictions. Guilt and concern over Margaret's condition. Excitement that we might soon be free to marry. Relief that she might be done entertaining and spying on men for the queen. For the first time since we had met she had confided in me what a burden it was to cajole Catherine's enemies into bed, to lure them into telling her their secrets, to read their letters when they were sleeping, to be frightened that at any moment she'd be found out.

Isabeau often panicked when she thought about being discovered, so Catherine had given her a script in case it occurred. The queen had even coached her on how to deliver it. But Isabeau worried what would happen if she wasn't a good enough actress. If the man in question became suspicious. She was a spy, and spies were killed and their killers went free.

I was not so sure of myself that I didn't wonder sometimes how much of Isabeau's attraction to me was a means to an end. If we married, she could leave the palace and Catherine's flying squadron. Many a man might have done the job, but I was the one she met. That I was a favorite of the queen, a perfumer with wealth, was convenient, wasn't it?

But none of my doubts matter now. The question of how much of what Isabeau did she did for love and how much she did because she was a savvy political operator doesn't change how I feel.

That night, I held my love in my arms, and every tear that dropped from her cheek to my chest smelled like lilies of the valley so fresh they still trembled on their stems in the breeze. I let Isabeau cry so I could inhale those fresh, impossibly blooming flowers. The princess was locked in the Louvre, in pain, with welts on her back caused by this woman I loved. Isabeau had taken a terrible chance, but it appeared as if she had succeeded and soon we might be together. No fleeing to Germany or Spain. We could remain in Paris and Barbizon. I could continue my work, and the queen would shower us with her blessings. For the queen had said that Isabeau had saved France.

"She's right," I said. "You very possibly have saved France. If the queen does wed her daughter to Navarre, you will have helped assure that union. Now, we just need to be patient," I said. "Catherine's word is as good as gold."

About ten days after Margaret's incident, a member of the queen's retinue visited me in my shop on the Pont Saint-Michel. I didn't recognize her, but I paid that no mind. There were over three hundred and eighty-five members of the palace staff. At least one third were ladies who waited on the royals.

This woman had lovely red hair and was very pale. She said her name was Bernadette de La Longe and asked for lotion for her own skin, which she said was unusually dry. I showed her my best creams, made with olive oil from the recipes I'd learned in Santa Maria Novella. Nothing new I'd ever concocted bested those formulas.

Bernadette rubbed some into her skin, liked how the milk felt and said she would take a bottle. Next, she asked for a fragrance, requesting a lemon scent similar to the one the queen wore. I presented her with a light citrus-based perfume that had heliotrope and lavender in it. After trying it, she said it was exactly what she wanted. And then she hesitated.

"Is there something else you need?"

For a moment she didn't answer, just perused the array of bottles and jars on my shelves as if she were searching for one in particular. Then she stepped closer to me and, in a whisper, said she'd heard I sold other things.

"I do, my lady. There are creams that heat your skin and make you more receptive to a lover, others that warm his parts and give him pleasure. There are scents that can be used as aphrodisiacs and others that are repellants. Just tell me what you are looking for."

Still, she hesitated.

"I've heard every kind of request, so there is no reason to be modest."

"It's not for me but for the lady I wait on."

She was being careful not to mention the queen, I thought.

"Yes?"

"She is in need of a way to prevent a crime from being done."

I nodded. There was nothing at all unusual about the request other than her discomfort in making it.

"You make shrouds, do you not?" she asked.

I knew many people called the poisoned undergarments I sold shrouds, for indeed they were, but it always made me uncomfortable to hear them referred to that way.

"Yes. I do. I would need some idea of the gentleman's size if possible."

"It's actually not for a gentleman."

"For a lady?"

She nodded.

"Well then I would suggest a pair of gloves. That's what the queen has purchased in the past."

Bernadette seemed flustered. I was sure she was worried about bringing back the right thing.

The queen had previously bought several pairs of gloves impregnated with poison. I was aware of the pain they would inflict and the discomfort the wearer would feel. I knew that death was inevitable and always felt a terrible burden at being involved. But not so much that I didn't continue to supply her with what she required. She was my mistress. And so I told Bernadette the gloves would be ready in two days' time, and after she left I set to work.

The most complicated part of the process was the care needed to ensure I didn't injure myself. Breathing the fumes of the solution I was soaking the gloves in could be deadly. Frequently, I had to walk outside and get fresh air into my lungs.

Serapino had taught me the dark arts of his trade so I could protect myself if need be. He warned me the poisons were to be used only on those who were evil or threatened me. He had clear and precise rules for what was acceptable to God and what was a crime. I had been raised by this monk whose greatest desire was to salvage the human soul. And yet here I was. A man whose hands were stained with the blood of other souls.

As I poured the mixture of corrosive sublimate, arsenic and cantharides over a pair of lovely gloves, I did not think of the feminine arms that would pull them on. To wander there was to invite disaster. I had accepted this part of my job a long time ago and had inured myself to it.

Why now was I having a sudden attack of conscience?

Because of Isabeau. She had softened my hard shell. I couldn't help but see people now as creatures beloved by someone. Each of Catherine's victims—no, to be honest, *our* victims—had left behind a husband or wife, a child or mother or father. There was mourning and grief, the gnashing of teeth and falling of tears because of what I did.

That night Isabeau came to my store, and the darkness in my heart lifted when I took her in my arms and smelled the roses blooming behind her ears and the lilacs on her breath. I remember she was playful, and that her mood was lighter than air.

"What is so wonderful?" I asked her as I poured her wine.

"The queen has given us a date in December upon which she will host our marriage ceremony."

A sense of well-being suffused me. I had never yearned to be married before I met Isabeau and was a bit surprised by how much it appealed to me and how I longed for the months to pass so we might be wed.

The ceremony was to take place at Sainte-Chapelle. God would find that ironic, I told Isabeau as I took her to bed. "We are sanctifying, in that church, the sins we committed there."

"Oh yes, our sins," she teased. "With all that we see around us there is no question that us coming together and finding pleasure with each other should be considered a transgression."

"This kind of pleasure?" I asked as I rolled her onto her stomach and traced the line of her spine with my tongue and felt her shiver beneath me.

Of all the lovers I had taken, no one had enjoyed the act as Isabeau did. She reveled in my touch. Preened like a peacock. Our sexual union was not a dark secret but a honeyed one, rarely conducted in the pitch-black of night but rather in the golden tones of late afternoons or by candlelight. I can close my eyes and see her now, laughing with a joy that was in itself the most erotic sound, her arms open to me, her nipples hardened, her skin blushing rose and that smell emanating from her and coming up and surrounding me.

It took two days for the gloves to dry. When Bernadette de La Longe returned to my store, I handed her a wooden box and gave her instructions.

"The gloves are wrapped in leather, like a gift. Neither you nor your lady should unwrap them. She is to give them to her intended victim without touching them. And when she gives the gift, your lady should suggest that the woman try them on. That way she will ensure that the gloves will be used by the person they are intended for—rather than a manservant or lady's maid who might accidentally be injured. And then your lady should entertain her guest and ply her with wine and cakes so that she doesn't take off the gloves too quickly. The skin needs to start to absorb the potion."

Bernadette reached for the box.

"Do you understand? It's very important that no one else touch the gloves for any length of time."

"Yes, I understand. You were very clear, Maître René."

And then Bernadette de La Longe opened a silver mesh purse and counted out my payment. Each piece made a hollow sound when she placed it on my desk. And after she left I couldn't pick them up to put them away. Not for many hours. I kept staring at the tower of coins and thinking how cheap it was to buy a murder.

Chapter 37

THE PRESENT
TUESDAY, MARCH 25
BARBIZON, FRANCE

After a few hours of restless, nervous sleep Jac had woken, showered, poured herself a cup of black coffee, and by ten AM was back in René's lair, curious to see how the concoction was coming along. She wanted Griffin to arrive. To learn what the next steps were. To find out if this magician's potion held any promise. And then to leave here for good.

Jac sniffed the brew. It was heady and very different. It was truly another century's smell. The aroma of another era. She wanted to call Robbie and tell him what she'd done—and for a moment forgot that she couldn't. She was caught up short. How could she have actually failed to remember that he was gone?

Because I'm not.

Was she hearing Robbie's ghost? Or was she just starting another imaginary conversation in her head?

No. You're talking to me, Jac. To me. To Robbie.
"Why now?"
You need me now.
"I need you all the time."
And you have me all the time. You always will, in one way or another.

She heard the smile in his voice.

"What do you mean?"
You'll find out.
"Tell me."
You have to find your own way into under-standing. But I'll stay with you until you do. Help you.

"Griffin wants to protect me. You want to help me."

You need both of us right now.
"But you're not real."

I'm as real as every feeling you've ever had for me. All of who we were and are to each other—you think that dies? That energy? That love? Oh, Jac, you still have a long way to go.

It would have sounded like he was chastising her, but his tone was so warm, so caring. She felt cosseted. Didn't want him to go.

Don't worry. I'm not going. Where you are is where I am. It's part of my job.

"What job?"

No more answers. Not yet. You are too impatient, ma soeur, ma belle soeur.

His endearment, calling her his "beautiful sister," brought on the sting of tears.

"I miss you."

Silly goose, you don't need to. I'm here.

And then she felt the most amazing thing: his arms around her. And she was smelling him too. Not the sixteenth-century concoction that permeated the lab, but Robbie, her brother, wearing the Scent of Us Forever.

You have to learn trust. You don't want to believe that because then you'd have to risk pain. But I promise. No pain is as terrible as wonder is amazing. As love is astonishing. Try, Jac, all right? Try to trust. Tell me you will.

She hesitated.

Tell me you will.

"Yes, I will try."

And then she was smelling only René's elixir,

418

and a powerful wave of fear crashed over her. Jac tried to sense Robbie's presence, but he wasn't there anymore. She sat and waited, but no matter how hard she tried to conjure him, he didn't return.

Chapter 38

With nothing to do in the lab, Jac was uneasy in the house. Griffin had expected to get there late that afternoon, but that left hours. Pulling on a sweater, she decided she'd get out and take a walk, maybe return to the folly, with its lovely broken stone arches and moss-covered statuary.

Jac was circling the ruin for the second time when her cell phone rang. Looking down at the LED, she saw it was Griffin and answered quickly. But the connection was bad, and she couldn't hear most of what he said. Frustrated, she disconnected the call, then punched in his number. This connection wasn't much better. She could only hear occasional bursts of words.

"Meeting . . . not conclusive. Bizarre . . ."

"What are you talking about?"

His answer was all the more confusing and frustrating: "And that Robbie was . . ."

"I can't understand. What about Robbie?"

She only got two words back. "Tests showed . . ."

Then more of the crackling, and the connection went dead.

Twice she tried to call back but failed. Where was he? Why couldn't he get a signal? But more importantly, what had he been trying to tell her? Griffin had sounded concerned. Why had he mentioned Robbie?

Jac walked up the uneven steps and sat on a cracked stone bench. There were clouds in the sky, but every few seconds the sun peeked through and shone down on her, warming her. She'd thought escaping the château and the laboratory might relieve some of her free-floating anxiety, but the opposite was happening.

Jac closed her eyes and tipped her face up to the sky. She took several deep breaths. Let them out slowly. Forced herself to use the relaxation technique Malachai had taught her.

The wind blew through the trees. She still had her eyes closed, and the wind sounded like weeping. It was unnerving. Jac had known heartache, but had never known what sound someone's heart makes when it breaks. She knew it now. She was hearing it. And it reached inside of her and pulled her out of her time and place.

Chapter 39

MARCH 25, 1573
BARBIZON, FRANCE

I did not see Isabeau for the next week. Soon she would be released from her duties as a member of the squadron, but not until the queen devised a plan for shifting the duke's attention away from Isabeau.

Whenever she was with him, I lived a kind of half life. My thoughts would wander from my work as I pictured them together. Wondered what she was saying to him. How he was responding. What he asked of her. Torturing myself, I imagined him touching her, kissing her, smelling her.

When I had first met Isabeau and we had begun to spend time together, she had been more open with me about her spying and how she conducted her affairs. In time, she had become reticent to discuss the details. Isabeau claimed she couldn't bear to watch my face while I listened or tolerate the barrage of questions I asked.

"Why do you punish yourself, wanting to know these things? This is what I have to do for Catherine. Soon it will be over, but until it is, be kind to me and to yourself, René. Let us talk of other things."

421

But I would insist.

"Did you entertain him with stories and dine with him last night?"

"Yes, and I made him laugh and flattered him."

"And did he become aroused?"

"Yes."

"Easily?"

"Yes."

"And did you look at him when he was in that state? Does he like you to see him undressed, the way I do?"

"No, I told you, he doesn't luxuriate in it. He isn't sensual like you are."

"Did he touch you?"

"My breasts."

"Did he hurt you?"

"No. I told you. He's never interested in me, only in himself. What I provide is just a momentary reminder of his own power and prowess."

Once she had answered my questions I would descend into a dungeon. No torture chamber was worse that the one I concocted for myself. No whip or rack could compare to the pain I felt as I imagined this woman with another man. Imagined his hands on her shoulders, gripping her. Imagined the jolts going through his body as his orgasm gathered and readied. Imagined his face thrown back in ecstasy.

In those moments I wanted to cut off Isabeau's hair. Smear dirt on her face. Anoint her with a perfume made from rotten eggs. Make her unappealing to other men so that Catherine couldn't use her anymore.

They were fleeting fantasies that shamed me then and shame me more now. But I am a man. And I didn't want another man soiling my garden. I feared every time she came back to me that I would smell him on her.

I never did. Never saw a finger mark or scratch on her skin. Sometimes I pretended that she only told me these stories to incite my jealousy. That she really never ventured out of the palace to see anyone but me.

But I knew I was lying to myself.

She was gone for a week, and then on the next Friday she arrived with much fanfare, rushing into the shop, full of excitement and delight. Catherine had just spent the last hour working with Isabeau, explaining the plan for replacing her.

"There is to be a dinner party, and the queen is going to offer the duke a virgin who is much admired," Isabeau gushed.

So taken was I with her news that I didn't notice anything unusual at first. Here was Isabeau telling me she was going to be free of the duke!

"No man is going to touch you ever again but me," I said, my words laced with my lust as I imagined it.

"And that makes you happy?" she teased.

"Oh yes."

"You look happy, René."

"I am."

"Would you like to be even happier?" She laughed.

I knew that tone, and it stirred me. "Yes, yes. Please."

And so she began to play her games with me. Isabeau turned her back and began to undress for me. First she unbuttoned her dress, dropping the green silk to the floor. Stepping out of it, she took off the chemise beneath it. Her bare shoulders inflamed me.

Then, slowly, she turned around. Her corset fitted right beneath her breasts, pushing them up, showing them off. The entire rest of her body was covered by underskirts, stockings, shoes, gloves.

All that was bare were her neck, her shoulders and her beautiful ripe breasts.

The sight literally took my breath away. I went to her and buried my face between her breasts. They were warm and smelled of the most fragrant apple blossoms I'd ever inhaled.

Teasing, she pushed me away and continued to strip. Taking off one layer and the next until her breasts and her pudenda were bare, but her legs were in their stockings and her arms were still covered by her gloves.

The gloves!

What was it? The way the candlelight fell? The way the sun shone through the windows as it set?

What was it that suddenly pulled all the breath out of my lungs and clenched around my heart, squeezing the very life force from me?

It wasn't possible, but her gloves looked so much like that other pair. I grabbed her wrist and inspected the stitching.

"Where did you get these?" I screamed as I started to rip the right glove off her.

Startled, she fought me.

"They were a gift."

"From whom?" I continued ripping.

"Not from the duke. Stop it, René. They were given to me by a woman."

The right glove came apart, and the upper portion fell away, but her fingers were still covered with leather. I began to pull her hand out. "From whom? From whom?"

"One of the other ladies-in-waiting. She said she'd been given them but they didn't fit her. She asked if I wanted them."

"Tell me her name." I had gotten the whole right glove off and now was working on the left. Still Isabeau struggled with me, pushing me off.

"What is wrong with you?"

"Who gave you the gloves? What is her name?"

"Bernadette de La Longe."

"Oh no, oh good Lord no. Isabeau, how many days have you been wearing them? When did she give them to you? Tell me! Isabeau! Tell me!" I was trying to rip the left glove off, but she fought back, treating me as if I'd gone mad. And I had. I had.

"For the last three days, I've worn them, yes."

"Each day?"

She didn't answer. Didn't have to. I knew it was already too late, but still I worked at the glove, pulling and ripping until all that was left were the fingers of her left hand, covered still in the fine soft kid that I had soaked in poison.

Chapter 40

THE PRESENT

Still reeling from the scenario she'd seen playing like a movie inside her mind, Jac blinked in the afternoon light. Weak-kneed, she struggled to stand.

There was more to understand. More she was meant to learn. She wasn't alone here. But it wasn't Robbie's spirit guiding her. Not this time. It was René le Florentin's. And she had to meet him in the shadow realm where he was waiting for her so he could show her the rest of his story. But how to force another memory lurch? She'd tried that several times and never managed. Maybe if she didn't try but just continued to explore the ruin— doing what she had set out to do . . . maybe . . .

Chapter 41

MARCH 25, 1573
BARBIZON, FRANCE

Isabeau became ill the following day. Her skin erupted with boils and lesions that caused her to scream out in agony. I never left her side except to mix up more of the poppy elixir to ease her pain.

On the second day of Isabeau's illness, Catherine visited. The queen told me how terribly sorry she was. She said she believed the duke had discovered Isabeau was a spy and had punished her.

"I will find out who he hired to do this for him," she said.

"I already know." I told Catherine the name.

Hearing it, the queen became even more distraught and shortly thereafter left.

Several hours later, Catherine returned, dragging her daughter with her. Several of the court's ladies-in-waiting were there, worried, trying to help, spending these last hours with one of their own. They moved aside as Catherine shoved her daughter toward Isabeau's sickbed with so much force that Margaret tripped and fell.

"This is what you have done, you slut, you

whore!" Catherine shrieked at her daughter. "Your handiwork. Look on it. Remember it. May it haunt you forever."

It is one of the few moments of clarity that I have from those last days.

The princess was wearing a gown the color of rubies, with rubies in her hair and her ears. Her cheeks were rouged, but the effect was ruined by streaks of tears that washed away all enhancements. Margaret got up off the floor and turned away to walk out of the room, but Catherine grabbed her by the arm and kept her there.

"Speak to her," Catherine ordered.

Margaret pursed her lips tighter together.

Catherine's fingers gripped her daughter's arm so hard they whitened. "How dare you take this woman's life because she was looking out for my interests? She was not the one fornicating with de Guise, you were. What Isabeau did allowed me to protect you and your future and the future of this country. She is a hero, and this is not how she deserved to be rewarded. Make your peace with her, Margaret, or I swear you will live to regret it."

The princess refused to speak.

Catherine demanded again.

Margaret remained silent.

Catherine slapped her, the sound echoing in the chamber like a cannon.

Margaret turned on her mother. "This lady betrayed me. She spied on me. And this is how one treats spies, Mother. Where do you think I learned that? From you. You dare call me a murderer? Well, if I am, so are you. And I will not apologize for doing what she deserved to have done to her."

Margaret wrested her arm from her mother and stormed past her and out of the room. The door slammed behind her.

For a moment Catherine just stared at the door; then she turned and looked at me. Her eyes were full of unshed tears. "I will deal with her, I promise you."

But it didn't matter to me what she did or didn't do to Margaret. Nothing mattered to me anymore.

For the next two days I did not eat or sleep or drink except when Catherine brought me goblets of fortified wine. She tended to me the way I and her ladies-in-waiting had tended to her in those terrible days when her beloved husband, the king, had lain dying.

Finally, on the fourth day, late in the afternoon, Catherine took my hand and told me it was time. "Now, René, I'll stay here but you must go and get your bottles and capture Isabeau's breaths."

"It doesn't matter. I'll never find the solution."

I had forgotten Catherine was my queen and my savior. She was just my friend in a moment when there was nothing any friend could do or say to ease the horror of what was happening.

Isabeau was being consumed, and all I could do

was give her draughts of poppy syrup to make her sleep. Her slumber was so deep it was as if she had already died. I could not bear to lose her any sooner than I would have to, and so I would hold the syrup back every few hours so that I could talk to her. But then she could only speak a few words until the pain took hold again, and the only sounds she could make were moans that tore straight through me.

Hours later, while I sat watching Isabeau sleep, Catherine returned to my chamber followed by two of her ladies. I paid little attention until the women placed my breath-collecting apparatus on the bedside table.

I stared with surprise. The queen had gone to my laboratory and brought the tools I needed.

"You have to do this, René. There *is* a formula, and you will find it, and when you do, you'll be able to bring her back . . . and bring my Henry back . . . and all the others whose breaths you have confined to the glass bottles."

I hadn't realized until that moment how much faith she had put into my laboratory experiments. Hope shone in her eyes. After all these years, despite his mistress, despite all that he'd withheld, Catherine loved her husband still.

"You must return to solving this puzzle, René. We've come so far and been together so long. I know how this hurts you. Believe me, I know how you feel, but you alone have the knowledge to

430

beat back death. You must summon your strength and fight. You are one of my soldiers, and these"—she pointed to the bottles—"are your spears and lances, your shields and your armor."

She was my queen. I knew I should obey, but I didn't have the strength. I didn't care anymore about the endless effort that in my heart I knew was futile. I'd worked on the experiments for years to no avail. There was no way to bring someone back from the dead through their breath. It was as ludicrous as the magic spells Ruggieri cast. Perfume and medicine were sciences, but this? It was just Serapino's dream.

As if she could read my mind, Catherine shook her head. "It's not a dream, René. It's possible, and you are the only one who can make it happen. I saw it in the bowl of waters. You will figure it out."

When I did not make any effort to work the bottles, it was Catherine who picked one up, held it close to Isabeau's mouth, and then corked it and picked up the next bottle.

I reached out and, God forgive me, pulled it from her hand. "No, it's too soon. She is not ready." My voice was harsh, but Catherine didn't chastise me for talking to her without the usual respect.

"She is, René, she is."

I looked down at Isabeau, then leaned over her. I inhaled, expecting to smell flowers blooming, to smell that magical garden that was my lover's body. But the scent was no longer of fresh flowers. I was smelling the stench of decaying flowers left to rot.

What was the secret to her body? How did she smell of flowers? Blooming when she was alive, dying when she was leaving this earth. What was the alchemy involved? I would have thought it was a trick of my grief had Catherine not mentioned it. She'd sniffed the air. Then looked around, searching for but not finding any source. Finally she'd asked one of her ladies to see if there were any bouquets of rotting flowers in the chamber.

I didn't bother to tell them they wouldn't find any. I didn't want to share that secret about Isabeau, not with any of them.

"René?"

I turned to Catherine. She was holding out a bottle.

"You need to capture her breaths."

But that would mean accepting that her end was near. I took Isabeau's hands and held them. I whispered to her, "Wake up, please wake up. You have to live. For me . . . for us. Oh please."

Isabeau didn't open her eyes.

"My fault, all my fault," I uttered.

Catherine put her hand on my shoulder and handed me a bottle. "It is not your fault. How were you to know that you were being tricked? It was a terrible thing that my daughter did to you, and she will be dealt with. But you can't blame yourself, my dear friend. You mustn't."

The words floated around me. I heard without listening. I was too focused on the rise and fall of Isabeau's breaths. Hard fought, every one. The queen had forced my fingers around the bottle. My hand was frozen in my lap. To reach out and hold the bottle in front of Isabeau's lips would be to admit the most terrible thing I could imagine.

She *had* to recover. I had given her every antidote I could think of. Every formula the doctors said might cure her. None seemed to be working. Maybe more mercury?

Being alone had never frightened me, but that was before I had known Isabeau. I had gone a lifetime without grieving. Now I would spend the rest of my days mourning my loss.

Isabeau's breathing demanded I listen. Refused to allow me any illusion. It was growing more and more shallow. The stench of dying flowers was growing in intensity.

Beside me, Catherine took another bottle and held it up to Isabeau's lips, and after she exhaled, Catherine quickly corked the bottle and replaced it with another. Four times I watched in a stupor as she did the job I had once done for her father-in-law, then her husband and lastly her eldest son. Four times I cried out to her that it was too early—that she was wrong—that Isabeau was recovering.

The fifth time I tried to grab the bottle away, and it fell to the floor and broke. Surely the sound of shattering glass would awaken Isabeau. Surely she would open her eyes now and smile at me and show us that she was going to get better.

Catherine reached for another bottle and waited for the exhalation and then corked it and reached for a sixth.

There was no color in Isabeau's face anymore. I couldn't see her chest rising or falling.

She had stopped breathing. Which was her last breath?

But then I saw Catherine cork that bottle and reach for a seventh.

Isabeau was still alive.

There was something I had to tell her.

Leaning down low, I whispered, "It's my fault. I did this to you. I made the gloves. They were soaked in poison. My own tricks were used on you. I am sorry, my love. I am so sorry."

I buried my head in her neck, the faintest heartbeat sounding in my ear. I needed her to understand and to forgive me. To absolve me. But I had waited too late, hadn't I? She couldn't hear me anymore. The drugs had walled her away from me. Isabeau was so deep into her dream state that my voice couldn't penetrate it. I knew it, but still, I couldn't give up.

"It's my fault," I screamed. "Isabeau, it's my fault, please forgive me. Please, I didn't know. I didn't know who they were going to give the gloves to."

Panicked, I listened. Yes, her heart was still beating. Her breath was still coming. "It was my fault!" I shouted again. "Please, tell me that you forgive me."

And then suddenly the scent of dying flowers was gone, and the wonderful perfume that I had smelled the first time I met her suffused the air. Isabeau's garden was blooming around me. Inhaling deeply, I took in her lavender and lilacs, her lilies and violets, her orange blossoms and jasmine. I took in her wondrous roses. It was not words, but it was a gift. It was absolution.

Catherine picked up the eighth bottle. Gently, I took it from her fingers and held the cool glass up to the parched, pale and chapped lips that used to be red with blood and life and laughter. I held the bottle and let her breathe her last breath, and then I corked the bottle. Still holding it tightly in my fist, I fell to my knees, laid my head on the bed, and then, for the first time since I was a boy and watched Serapino breathe his last, I, René Bianco, master perfumer, who twice in my life had helped someone I loved to die, wept.

Chapter 42

THE PRESENT

Later, Jac wouldn't remember what propelled her to walk to the center of the ruin and then drop to her knees and start feeling around on the worn marble floor. But when she touched the edge of the tile, her fingers began to tingle, and she knew that she'd found what she was searching for. Even if she still didn't know what it was.

The tiles weren't large, but they were heavy. Each stone had withstood the elements for hundreds of years. She used a broken rock with a flat edge to pry up the first tile. As she lifted it up, a whoosh of air that smelled of dampness and dust, age and decay came with it. She'd smelled air like this in the caves in Jersey and Greece, in the catacombs in Paris and Rome, in excavations in Egypt and Cyprus. This was ancient air. Jac was certain of it. It had the aroma of centuries of fermentation and rot.

Jac shivered. The pull was stronger than it had been before. She felt certain, after all these hours of working in his laboratory, looking at his notes and staring at his handwriting, that René was here waiting for her.

She removed the tile. Underneath was a metal grid that fitted snugly over the opening, holding it in place. She started in on the next tile. And then the next. Once she had removed twelve of them, four across and three down, she removed the wire grid. Using the application that turned her cell phone into a flashlight, she examined her discovery.

Small and narrow, the limestone steps were spotted with moss and lichen. There was life here where there was also death. Serge had been wrong. This was no folly. This ruined structure was a chapel, and she was gazing down into its crypt.

Jac was careful descending the slippery steps that were barely wide enough for her feet. But that wasn't what caused her the most consternation. It was the smell of putrefaction rising up to welcome her. Of sadness and loss. She felt as if it had been waiting for her . . . for a very long time.

Reaching the low-ceilinged enclosure, she looked around. This was no rough-hewn dirt burial chamber. The cream-colored marble walls gleamed. Gold candelabras glowed. On each wall were mosaic scenes of Elysium. The brilliant squares of turquoise, sapphire, emerald, topaz, ruby and amethyst took her breath away.

There were nine tombs filling the space. Three rows of three. Against each wall were marble benches. Examining the one closest to her, she saw it was inscribed with names and dates.

Jac walked down one aisle, up the next, then down another and—

There was a skeleton propped up against a tomb. Jac approached. His feet. His torso. His rib cage. His arms. His hands. In his hands . . .

How was this possible? Jac thought she was seeing things. Walked closer. Knelt.

In his bony hands was a single rose. And for one crazy moment she smelled its perfume. Impossible. But she did. Jac was inhaling its sweet, heavy liquor. Seeing ruby red petals and verdant green leaves. Impossible. And then the flower metamorphosed in front of her eyes, and he was holding only a dried-out flower. Leaves and petals and stem all the dark ochre of death.

Jac looked down. Her flashlight had caught something glinting there beside him. It was a shape she knew. There were bottles like this upstairs, each seven inches high, made of thick pale-blue glass with a dark residue in the bottom. But unlike those upstairs, this bottle was missing its carved cork.

There had only been ten of these bottles in the château, but there were twelve silver bell coverings. Melinoe had said Robbie had broken one of the bottles. The other had always been missing. *This* was that missing bottle. Jac was sure. This was the twelfth dying breath.

But where was the cork? Why was the bottle opened? Jac searched the ground and found the small innocuous stopper under his thighbone—discarded. He hadn't needed it anymore. He must have had another plan. Jac picked up the bottle and looked inside at the dark and opaque substance coating the bottom. At the dark streaks on the side.

Was this residue the same elixir she was trying to replicate from his formula?

Had he come down here and opened the bottle and inhaled the breath? But why would he have done that? Whose breath had René drunk?

Yes, it was René. She was certain these were his bones. She felt it the same way she felt Robbie's presence. She had been seeing the ancient perfumer in her mind for days now, living out his story despite trying to shut it out, and she knew it was him.

Jac's knees ached on the unforgiving stone floor. She stood. She hadn't yet examined the sarcophagus. The red jasper marble was beautiful, with streaks of gold and black shooting through its surface. On the side closest to René was a plaque. Jac leaned closer and shone her light on it. Read the words. Shivered. Read them again. Reached out and touched the cold, cold stone.

She felt it sigh. Impossible, but it had. As if it was relieved to finally be giving up a long-held burden, a secret that needed to be told.

Her name was carved in small precise letters and painted with gold leaf that was still vital and vibrant.

Following that inscription was a series of roman numerals. Jac translated them.

1537–1571

Was Jac looking at her own tomb? Was everything Malachai told her true? Was everything Robbie believed right? Once upon a time, had Jac lived as Isabeau? Was that woman's soul now Jac's? Was the soul of the man who had laid himself beside Isabeau's coffin alive in Griffin North?

Was it possible that Isabeau and René, Jac and Griffin, were all connected through time?

Even though she was still asking, she knew the answers deep inside of her. The cycle was endless. There was no denying it. Through centuries, Jac and Griffin had found each other and helped destroy each other. But that left her where she'd been in Paris. She couldn't let it happen again. The thought made her tired. Maybe she should just give in and allow fate to play out. Even if it meant tragedy again. At least then it would be over.

She put her face, her burning skin, against the cool stone coffin. There was so much sadness here. So much loss. In the air the smell of the rose was still viable. Jac inhaled. Impossibly, this was the scent from the single flower that René had brought down into the crypt to give to his lover when he finally saw her again, not in life but in death.

Or did the rose have yet another purpose? Was it a message that had waited all these centuries to be delivered? Was it intended for today? What was it René wanted her to know?

Chapter 43

Griffin found Jac sitting on the stone bench outside. In her hand was one petal that had fallen from the dried rose. Finding it on the floor, she couldn't help but take it. She'd had to touch something René had touched. Had to connect to this man who had loved so much he'd chosen to die rather than live without Isabeau any longer.

"Jac, I'm sorry, this isn't going to be easy, but I know how he died," Griffin said.

"You remembered?"

"Remembered?" He gave her a quizzical look.

Jac realized they were in different times, different eras.

"I'm sorry. You mean Robbie! You found out?"

"It's part of what I was doing in Paris. What I wanted to tell you. I asked Marcher not to call you. I thought it would be better . . ." He took her hands. "I had an idea when you told me that you'd found out Robbie had broken one of the antique bottles, and I asked the pathologists to test it out. Robbie died from the mixture of breath and elixir he inhaled. The lab identified an ancient toxin that is several hundred years old."

It took a moment for Jac to take in what Griffin had said, then asked him if they were sure. He said they were.

"If it is true, why wasn't the lab able to identify the poison before now?"

"It's so old, no one thought to test for it. And then, when I suggested it . . . I don't know. It was just a guess."

"No. It was something you remembered," Jac said.

"I don't understand what you're talking about."

"You told me that you once asked Malachai to hypnotize you so you might remember some of your past lives, and it failed. But I think you can have a memory without knowing that's what it is. While I've been here, I've been learning about Catherine de Medici's perfumer. And of the romance he had at the end of his life. I think it was *us,* Griffin. I think you were René. I was Isabeau. And it's another tragic chapter of our past. Another incarnation where you died because of me."

And then she told him the story she had pieced together.

"René got permission to bury Isabeau here and continued to work on reanimating the dying breaths. And then, realizing what he had spent his life creating was toxic, he swallowed Isabeau's breath."

"He committed suicide?" Griffin asked.

She nodded. They were both quiet for a few moments.

Then Griffin leaned forward, put his arms around her and kissed her. Offering comfort, and taking it at the same time. It was, Jac thought, a sacred kiss in a sacred place. And below her, in the crypt, she was certain that the man and the woman who'd lain there, together but separated for so long, knew somehow they were reconnected.

When he pulled away, Griffin's face was filled with resolve.

"Jac, you know you need to leave here, don't you? There's nothing in Barbizon for you but danger—from the breaths—from Serge and Melinoe. Clearly she's obsessed and doesn't have boundaries. Back in Paris we can talk this through. I don't doubt the story you are telling me. But I do believe with everything in me that you are getting the meaning of all this wrong. You and I are not doomed. How much do you know about the cult of Dionysus?"

"A lot."

"Okay then. How many lives did someone live before they could go to Nirvana?"

"Three lives over three thousand years."

"You know Melinoe was the name of a priestess of the Dionysus cult?"

She nodded. "Of course. She and I talked about that. The goddess of the underworld and ghosts."

"If you give any credence to fate, then now her job is done. Fate's delivered you to the place where you could learn about your third incarnation. And now that your past is known, it can be dealt with. In the last couple of years you've remembered three of our lifetimes—the first dates back to the ancient Egyptian era. Your three thousand years of being reborn are over. Now it's time for our version of Nirvana. No one ever said it can't exist here on earth. I believe we can learn from the mistakes we made in those other incarnations and put them behind us. Maybe we were never strong enough before. There was an ancient perfumer who loved a noblewoman but allowed their affair to take place in secret to protect his position with his queen instead of declaring his feelings. There was a French perfumer who went to Napoleon's Egypt to chase a dream instead of staying home in Paris and being with the woman he would love forever. And now we know there was an Italian perfumer who cared too much about his power and wealth to give them up and leave the court with Isabeau. They could have gone to Germany or Spain and had a fine life. Or even stayed in Paris and kept his store open. But he wouldn't give up his position.

"In this life, we've already been given chances we've squandered, like they all did. But not anymore. We're going to grab this chance."

He kissed Jac again.

Intellectually, she didn't know if she understood what he was saying any more than she understood what Malachai had explained about her ability to remember other people's past lives . . . but it didn't matter. Everything Jac felt told her that Griffin was right.

As she let the kiss absorb her, a slight breeze blew around them. In her mind she saw it winding around, silver ribbons binding them. She saw the Greek goddess Moira standing inside of a marble temple, the Aegean Sea gleaming blue behind her. Moira was watching her sister Fates at work; Clotho was spinning thread, Lachesis weaving it into these silver ribbons that were tying Jac and Griffin together through time.

When they pulled away, Griffin asked her if she would show him what she had found. Together they descended into the crypt.

Jac watched Griffin look at the skeleton slumped beside the sarcophagus. He squatted down and examined the rose and the bottle and looked into the man's empty eye sockets. And then he did a strange thing. As if in some kind of ancient greeting, he reached out and touched the man's right hand.

Jac thought she saw glimmers of silver ribbons encircle Griffin and René. Invisible connectors were everywhere.

Griffin stood and began an inspection of the tomb itself. He ran his fingers over the plaque engraved with Isabeau's name and birth and death dates.

Jac wanted to ask him what he was feeling, but at the same time she didn't want to speak while down here. As if to do so would disturb these dead. But as Griffin spoke, when she heard what he said, she knew the dead would not be disturbed.

Taking Jac's hand, he said, "For them we're going to right all the wrongs." And then, for the third time that afternoon, he leaned forward and kissed her. There was no passion or longing in this embrace. Just a promise.

"Love," he said, "like energy, never dies. You lose people only in the moment. But time is a long road that circles back. At some point the missing turns into love and returns. It's returned now."

Jac felt the underground burial chamber growing warmer. The chill she'd experienced down here before was gone. The sense of dread and depression was lifting. The scene of René beside the coffin of his new wife was still tragic, but now it was also beautiful.

"It's time to go," Griffin said.

He was right. It was time to go. It was finally all

right to go. What had needed to be learned had been learned.

Jac went first, and Griffin followed. Then together they replaced the wire mesh grid and the tiles on top of it. On their knees, they spread the dirt and debris around the opening so it didn't appear that—

"What are you doing?" It was Melinoe.

Jac and Griffin both looked up at the same time.

She was standing on the steps to the ruin. With a gun in her hand.

Chapter 44

"Oh goodness, I'm so glad it was you. I was taking a walk and heard voices and thought you were intruders." Melinoe put the small silver pistol back in her pocket. "What were you doing?"

Jac quickly lied: "We were examining the stones for some kind of carvings or impressions. Just trying to date the folly."

Jac watched Melinoe assess what she'd told her. The woman took little at face value, but there was no reason for her to doubt Jac. What she was saying made sense. Besides, what else would they be doing? No one knew about the crypt. In fact no one knew the folly, fancily built to look like a ruin, was a true ruin of a real chapel.

"We're going to have drinks soon. Would you like to join us for dinner, Griffin?"

As they all walked back to the château, Jac thought that over drinks would be a good time to tell Melinoe what Griffin had learned. While they were all together having a glass of wine, she'd explain there was no reason to continue on with the experiment now that they'd learned the breaths were lethal.

At the house Jac excused herself to freshen up, and as she headed toward the stairs, she heard Melinoe offer Griffin the opportunity to visit the wine cellar and pick out a bottle from the collection.

When Jac returned fifteen minutes later, there was no sign of them. She headed toward the cellar.

"Griffin? Melinoe?"

There was no answer. She saw the laboratory door was open and walked in. Empty also. She took a moment to check on the formula she wouldn't need to finish now. It smelled wonderful. Ancient and rich. She imagined what adding the ambergris to it would do. How it would round it out. For a moment she regretted that she'd never smell the final composition.

The cellar was large, and she walked its perimeter, thinking Melinoe was showing Griffin some corner even Jac hadn't seen. Or that they were bent over a dusty bottle of Bordeaux. But then why wouldn't they have answered?

She made her way back upstairs and to the living room, where Serge mixed cocktails every evening at six PM.

He was there lighting a fire and looked up when he saw Jac. His face was pale.

"Are you all right?" she asked.

He nodded, but it was halfhearted.

From behind, she heard Melinoe enter the room. She'd changed for dinner, and her pink silk sheath rustled as her high-heeled shoes clicked on the marble floor when she crossed the room.

"I need you to make sure everything is secure," Melinoe said to Serge.

He nodded and left.

"Where's Griffin?" Jac asked.

"All in good time," Melinoe said.

Spinning around, Jac tried to identify what she was smelling. It was the scent of fear. It had come from Serge. Something was wrong. Jac was certain of it. Instantly cold shivers of panic took over her body.

"Where is Griffin?"

"Jac, I need you to finish what you came here to start."

"Where's Griffin?"

"Doing a little banking for me."

"What does that mean?"

"He's my security deposit on the formula. When you complete it, you and he can leave."

"What are you talking about? Where is he?"

"This house has secrets you haven't found yet. Yes, there's René's laboratory. And the crypt. Those are your discoveries. But you haven't stumbled on the charming medieval dungeon. They had them in the Middle Ages, you know. Very elaborate ones. Ours is the size of a bedroom. With all sorts of medieval wonders. Would you like to see?"

Jac knew that Melinoe was eccentric and dangerous. Why hadn't she realized how foolhardy it was to stay here? She knew the answer. Jac had wanted the elixir as badly as Melinoe. And now? What had Melinoe done?

"Is Griffin there?"

"Insurance that you'll finish what you started."

"Why wouldn't I? You don't have to threaten me or hurt Griffin—I'll finish the formula," Jac lied.

Melinoe stood. "Correctly? Or you'll corrupt it?" She walked to the door. "Aren't you coming? Don't you want to see where Griffin is?"

As Jac followed Melinoe, she watched the light reflecting off the silver heels on the other woman's suede boots. It was something to do to keep herself from screaming. There was no reason to panic yet. This was just some strange game Melinoe was playing.

They walked through the first floor to the kitchen into a pantry where Jac had not yet been. Off that was a hallway.

"This was where the kitchen staff lived,"

Melinoe was saying as if it were a normal evening and she was showing her house off. "The rooms were small, but at least they were warm—all of them have small fireplaces."

The dialogue was ridiculous.

"And here we have the staircase that led to the cold storage below."

Like the steps to the wine cellar, these were narrow and not easy to navigate.

One flight down and it was chilly. A second flight down and it was cold. They must have been on the north side of the house, where the sun heated the stones the least.

"In olden times, food was kept down here because of the natural chill, which they exaggerated by building thick walls.

"Now through here . . ." Melinoe opened a thick wooden door that creaked as the hinges moved. "We believe this part of the château dates back to the mid-twelfth century, before the current building was erected. This cellar was part of an older structure replaced by the château in the fifteenth century. As was the custom, the builders followed the previous footprint, even utilizing the old foundation."

A short hallway ended at a rusted iron gate. There was a key in the lock, but the gate was open. Beyond it was another staircase.

Jac held back. She smelled something foul.

"Come," Melinoe said, grabbing Jac by the arm,

fingers digging into her flesh. "We're almost there. Just one more flight."

Jac descended the staircase. For some reason she found herself counting the steps. There were sixteen of them. She was freezing now. Her teeth were chattering. A combination of cold and fear.

At the bottom of the stairs was a second gate. This one was closed. Behind it was a circular room ensconced in darkness until Melinoe swung her battery-operated lantern on a small section of it.

Jac gasped.

She was looking at a medieval Judas chair—triangular-shaped with a very pointed tip that impaled and either rectally or vaginally raped the victim forced to sit on it.

Melinoe swung the light to illuminate a different section of the torture chamber. Here was another chair, this one covered with spikes. Once you sat down, the pinpoints penetrated your flesh—all over your back, arms, legs—left there long enough, you'd bleed to death.

Melinoe revealed another corner, and Jac saw a head crusher—used mostly to extract confessions. A horrific, inhuman device.

Then the light moved again, illuminating a wooden stockade similar to what witch hunters had used in Salem. Griffin's head and hands were coming through center and side holes. There was a gag in his mouth, which seemed redundant.

They were so far underground, Jac couldn't imagine his screaming could have been heard by anyone upstairs.

"This is crazy!" Jac felt for her cell phone—then remembered it was in the bedroom charging. But even if she'd had it, there would be no signal this deep underground.

What was she going to do?

"Please understand, I don't have any interest in hurting your friend. Just finish what you started and complete the formula. Once you have, I'll release the locks and both of you can leave of your own free will."

"The formula is useless. The breaths are poisonous!" Jac cried. "Let Griffin go."

"You have no proof that the breaths are poisonous."

"We do. My brother died from an ancient toxin. He must have inhaled the breath by accident when he broke the bottle—"

"Your brother was visiting laboratories and asking chemists to make up synthetic ingredients. Whatever poison killed him must have been something he commissioned. There's no proof it was from one of my bottles."

Jac couldn't take her eyes off Griffin. "You can't do this!"

"I don't have a choice. I know you are planning to leave, and I can't let that happen. I'd finish the formula myself, but I'm not an expert and we don't have enough of the ancient ingredients for me to make a mistake. I need you. I have no choice, so you have no choice."

Melinoe wasn't sane. There would be no reasoning with her.

Across the room, Griffin looked at Jac and shook his head, no. He always knew what she was thinking almost before she did. From his expression she knew he had zeroed in on the thought that had hit her so hard she'd gone weak and almost fallen.

They had not broken the karmic circle after all. Griffin was going to die, and it would be because of her. Because Jac had involved him in this madness. It was her fault again.

She'd thought about this over and over for the last two years. She had loved this one man without reason and without hesitation since she was seventeen years old. Through her own crises and losses, through years of never speaking to him or knowing where he was. When she wasn't with him she felt she was only half a person, in limbo. When she was with him, she was complete in a way that embarrassed her. In a way that a woman with a career and friends and family and success is not supposed to feel. She was tied to him. At some distant point in time, their souls had imprinted on each other and they'd never been able to cut the threads of fate that connected them.

Death had only separated them from each other for a time.

And now here they were. Playing out the same scenario. Jac was tied to Griffin. And that bond had been his death sentence over and over again.

It would end now.

"Yes," she said. "Yes," in a flat voice. "I'll finish the formula," she added, knowing that she might be signing her own death sentence if the experiment went wrong. "But you have to let Griffin go."

"It's almost been twenty-four hours. We'll have dinner and then you can complete what you began. And then when I have what I brought you here for, you and Griffin will be free to leave."

Chapter 45

"Dinner will be in a half hour," Melinoe told her when they were back upstairs. "We never finished our drinks, did we? Shall we now?" she asked as if it were just another night.

"I need to go to my room first. I'll be down shortly," Jac responded, trying for the same tone, saying it as if she meant it.

Drink with them? Have dinner with them? Finish the formula now that she knew the breaths were poison? Jac felt as if she'd landed inside a surrealistic dream.

There had to be a way to get Griffin out of the antiquated dungeon where Melinoe was holding him hostage. Jac walked down the hallway to her room and stepped inside. She'd just do the most obvious thing and call Detective Marcher in Paris. Or was it better to start with the local police? Barbizon was a small town—the police were only a kilometer away.

Her bag was on her bed where she'd left it. She reached inside for her phone. It wasn't there. Of course not—she'd plugged it in to charge it before she'd gone downstairs.

She ran to the desk. The cord was there and at the end of it—nothing. After searching frantically for a few minutes, Jac had to accept the obvious. Melinoe had taken Jac's phone.

Panic sent surges of adrenaline through her like shocks. What to do?

There were other phones in the house, of course. In the library there was a telephone on the desk. Another in the kitchen. She'd just need to get to one of them. Just go downstairs as if she were planning on having drinks but detour to the kitchen. First, she needed to brush her hair, straighten her clothes, wash the dust off her hands and face. Present a less agitated exterior.

In the bathroom, looking at herself in the mirror, Jac saw a version of herself she hadn't seen since Robbie had gone missing in Paris almost two years before. Her eyes were bright with fear, and her face was pale. She looked petrified. And she was. Melinoe was insane. She'd stolen from a museum and killed one person so far to achieve her goal.

Practicing Malachai's breathing exercises for a full minute, Jac tried to calm down. She wasn't going to accomplish what she had to if she was in free fall.

She needed to get to the telephone. Steal one minute and summon the police. Just one minute. If she could visualize her next moves, it would help. In her mind she watched herself head downstairs and then, instead of walking right—toward the living room, where she was expected—she hugged the wall and slunk to the left. Moving quickly but avoiding any rash movements, she got to the kitchen. Looked for the phone. Then pictured herself walking over to the phone—on the wall by the window.

The last of the evening sun was fading. Twilight was pushing it away. In Paris and New York the night was full of promise. But here in the château, isolated from other houses, from the town, this encroaching darkness was full of anxiety.

Jac opened the door to her room and walked out into the hallway. It was dark, and she wondered why the housekeeper hadn't come around to turn on the lights yet. No matter, it was better this way. Shadows were perfect hiding places.

She reached the stairs and began her descent,

praying Melinoe wasn't going to come out and head up to her room at that moment.

Each step was a challenge. Jac's heart was pounding. The simple trip down one flight of stairs was taking too long. But the fear was stretching out every minute.

This is how you live forever, Jac thought. You torture the seconds with worry, you anticipate everything that awaits you, you trouble time, and it becomes an agony of isolated, unconnected moments.

At the bottom of the steps, Jac repeated what she'd pictured herself doing. Instead of heading toward the library, she went left and then down another darkened hallway and found her way to the kitchen without incident.

The smells here were a reminder of normal. There was a chicken roasting in the oven. The aroma of chocolate wafted in the air. A hint of vinegar. Rosemary. Bread baking.

But there was something wrong. It was dark here and empty. There was food cooking, but where was the cook?

The door to the pantry was open, and Jac began to shake, thinking of Griffin down below where she stood now.

Stop, she told herself. Just stop thinking. Use the phone first, then you can go to him. Once the police are on their way.

Jac walked across the room toward the phone,

plucked the handle out of the cradle, punched in the emergency code that was the same all over France. This nightmare would be over in minutes now. There was nothing Melinoe would be able to do—

Holding the phone to her ear, Jac waited to hear the ringing.

There was nothing but dead silence. Hadn't the call gone through? She depressed the connector button. Let it go. Listened for the dial tone. Depressed the button again. No dial tone. What was going on?

The cook stepped out of the pantry. When she saw Jac, she looked startled.

"Can I help you, mademoiselle?"

Jac explained she needed to use the phone.

"Mais oui," she said, nodding sympathetically, "but it isn't working because of the power outage."

"But the stove?" Jac asked.

"The stove is still going because it is gas."

"How long ago did the power go out?" Jac asked.

"About a half hour ago."

"Do you have a cell phone?" Jac didn't have any time to waste now. The power outage couldn't be a coincidence.

"I do, mademoiselle, but Madame borrowed it. Perhaps you might ask her?"

Jac nodded. Felt a wave of exhaustion. Melinoe had made it impossible for Jac to call for help. There had to be another way. Of course—it was so simple. Almost absurdly easy. Jac would just leave. Walk out the front door, take one of the horses, and ride into town to alert the police.

There were doors and windows everywhere.

"Other than the front door," Jac said to the cook, "is there a back entrance to the château?"

"Of course, it's through there." She pointed to a hallway.

Jac ran. She reached the door in seconds, but the handle didn't turn. She looked at the lock—it needed a key. Back to the kitchen.

"Do you have the key?"

"How stupid I am, of course it is locked. When the power goes out, the house is locked. Madame fears that with all the valuables here, an electric crisis could be manufactured and then the thieves would take advantage of the dark to take what they want."

"How does it work—if there is no electricity—how does the house stay in lockdown?"

"I do not know," the cook said. She was a thin, older woman with a heavily lined face.

"Can I get out through a window?" she asked the cook even though she was sure of the answer she was going to hear.

The woman shook her head. "Not without Madame unlocking it by hand. I'm not sure how it works, but when I came here she told me about it, and once a month she tests the system to make sure it is in good order."

Chapter 46

"I was looking for you, dear," Melinoe said as she entered the kitchen. She was wearing a white tunic and white leggings and had pearls in her ears, on her fingers and twisted around her wrists and throat. Iridescent and gleaming, the jewels made her seem to glow in the dark.

Carrying a lit candelabra, she cast a long, twisted shadow on the wall. Her eyes had an almost unearthly glint.

A she-devil, Jac thought, with those white wings on either temple and her wild Medusa hair fanning out and falling below her shoulders.

"Serge and I are waiting for you in the living room for cocktails. It's a shame about the electricity, but we can dine by candlelight."

With the most gracious of gestures, Melinoe hooked her arm through Jac's and led her from the kitchen. At the door she looked back at the cook. "Lisette, we will dine at seven thirty as planned."

"Oui, madame."

Melinoe didn't say anything to Jac as she escorted her out of the kitchen, down the hallway and into the living room, where a crackling fire and several wall sconces fitted with candles served to enliven the room. It was as if nothing were wrong here at all. The scene was no different than when Jac had first come to the château except for all the knowledge she now possessed.

Serge was standing at the bar, mixing a pitcher of what Jac knew were martinis, and the stirrer tinkled against the shaker with the same tiddly-wink noise it had every night. So normal except . . . except . . . nothing was the same.

He turned, pitcher in one hand, glass in another, and poured. Then he offered the glass to Melinoe. As he did, Jac noticed that his hand shook just a little. He was worried. Stealing a hunk of ambergris was one thing. But now they were involved in a murder and kidnapping. He poured another glass for Jac and handed it to her.

She met his eyes and noticed they were slightly glassy.

"Do you feel all right, Serge?" Jac asked.

"I think it's just a head cold coming on. I'll be fine."

"Are you sure? You look like you feel worse than that."

"He'll be fine," Melinoe said with slightly too much emphasis on the last word.

"Of course I will," Serge said as he poured himself one of the cold drinks and then sat down beside his stepsister on the couch. Melinoe reached out and stroked his hand. Soothing him as Jac had seen her do before. Then Melinoe leaned over and kissed him on the lips. She was a monster of seduction calming her pet. Jac could smell the sultry perfume she was wearing even halfway across the room. Serge's eyes half closed. His hand faltered. A tiny bit of the liquor sloshed out of the glass and soaked into his slacks. Melinoe whispered in his ear. He straightened. Took a sip of his drink.

"Aren't you going to taste it?" Melinoe asked Jac.

She took a sip.

"Is something wrong?" Serge asked Jac.

It was crazy. How could he ask? Didn't he know? *Everything* was wrong. How could she sit here and drink this drink and pretend that things were normal? That her lover wasn't being held hostage two stories below them? She wanted to scream. To take a chair and try to break one of the windows. She stood up. The glass fell on the antique Aubusson rug.

"Oh dear," Melinoe said, looking down.

The glass hadn't shattered. The rug had prevented that. But the stem had broken off.

Jac reached for it, but Melinoe got to it before her. She gave her an odd look—as if trying to gauge whether Jac had been planning to use it as a weapon.

"What a shame," Melinoe said as she carefully picked up the other half of the glass. "These are Baccarat from the 1920s and very hard to find. I only have a dozen . . . only had a dozen . . . now I only have eleven. There's really no reason to be nervous, dear. After dinner you'll put the final touches on the formula and all will be well."

But how could it? Would Melinoe let them go when Jac suspected Melinoe of stealing, of murdering Bruge? Or did Melinoe have alibis and explanations? What would she say? That locking Griffin in the stocks was a misunderstanding? That Bruge's death was an accident and she'd only taken the ingredients to protect them? No, Melinoe wasn't going to just let Jac and Griffin walk out of here. It was up to Jac to figure out a way to save them.

Serge coughed, and Jac glanced over.

"Jac?" Melinoe said her name softly, kindly. "Let's not wait any longer for dinner. I know you're impatient to retire to the laboratory."

Jac tried to stall. "There is no reason to finish mixing the formula. Now that we know about the pathologist's report from Paris—"

The stubbornness shone in Melinoe's eyes as she interrupted Jac. "You are drawing conclusions without proof. The formula will work," she said with unwavering determination in her voice. Melinoe was surveying the room. There was lust in her eyes, and her painted lips had parted slightly. She looked at her collection as if she were gazing on a lover.

Her glance caressed each Renaissance painting and sculpture, the rare jade and cinnabar carvings from Japan, and each piece of fine French Louis XIV furniture. Melinoe picked up a Fabergé frame that held a photograph of her with her father and stroked the smooth turquoise enamel, running her finger up and down one side.

"We can return. I know we can. And with René's method we can arrange to return when and where we want. I need to come back so I can stay with my beautiful things."

Serge coughed again. "Jac, what pathologist's report from Paris? Is this about your brother?"

Melinoe stood up quickly, still holding the frame. For the first time since Jac had arrived at the château, Melinoe seemed flustered.

"Enough conversation about nothing," she said. "Jac, perhaps it would be better if I had your dinner brought to your room. And then afterward you can go to the laboratory."

"So I'm a prisoner too? What will you do to me if I don't agree?"

"Prisoner?" Serge asked. "What the hell is going on here?"

"You don't know?" Jac turned to Serge. There was no question he was ill. A fine film of perspiration slicked his face. His eyes were glazed.

He shook his head.

"Melinoe has Griffin locked up in the dungeon. It's my incentive to finish mixing the formula."

Serge coughed. "And why do you need incentive?"

"Because Griffin got some results back in Paris. It seems Robbie was poisoned. He died from a rare and ancient toxin—a kind that has not been known—"

"No!" Melinoe shouted. "The report is wrong. I can prove it."

Serge looked at Melinoe. "I want to hear what Jac has to say."

"No! It's all a story she's made up so that she can keep the elixir for herself and not share it with us."

"That's ludicrous—why would she do that?" Serge asked.

"For money of course!" Melinoe said.

"The elixir has no value. It turns the breaths to poison." Jac turned to Melinoe. "Please, release Griffin and let us go."

"Once you finish what you started."

"But the breaths in the bottles are lethal," Jac said. "When René added the elixir to them they became—"

"Enough talk." Melinoe stood up. "Jac, I need you to come with me now. We'll go to your room. Lisette will bring up a plate of food. I insist. And Serge, please don't interfere." Melinoe's face was white with rage.

"Jac, don't go anywhere," Serge said and turned to Melinoe. "We've made terrible mistakes chasing your dreams, and we can't make any more. I've helped you. Been part of it. But this has to stop."

He coughed again. And again. "Let's go to the library," he said and took Jac's arm. "I want to hear what you have to say."

"No." Melinoe ran at them, pushing between Serge and Jac, using her body like a missile. Serge grabbed her and held her at bay. It was the first time Jac realized just how small and fragile Melinoe really was. Her energy and charisma had made her seem so much bigger. But now, even sick as Serge was, she was powerless against him as he pushed her back into a chair.

"What is it that you think happened to your brother?" Serge asked Jac.

"Griffin said the forensic team believes the breath and elixir mixture is somehow active. Trying to use it to reanimate a soul will only result in someone else dying. It's not a solution—it's a weapon."

Serge turned to Melinoe. "You knew this?"

She didn't respond. He looked back at Jac.

"My stepsister knows about this?"

"She overheard me and Griffin talking about it."

"When?"

"This afternoon."

"Are the doctors sure that—"

Before Serge could finish his question, Melinoe was on her feet, shouting *no* and then again *no*.

Jac and Serge turned in time to see Melinoe, the candelabra in her hand, her arm lifting into the air.

467

Chapter 47

Serge pushed Jac out of the way just as the silver objet d'art came hurtling at her. She stumbled and fell. The candelabra crashed into the wall. Lit candles rolled everywhere. Serge rushed to stamp them out. First one and then the next. But he couldn't get them all at once.

Suddenly it seemed small fires were bursting out everywhere . . . the curtains . . . the rug.

It was happening too fast. The air was too dry. The fabrics too old.

Jac rushed to help Serge, who was batting out the fire along the bottom of the curtains.

"I've got this. You get the one on the rug," he told her between coughs.

Melinoe began a frantic run around the room, gathering up treasures in her arms.

"I think we got them both. It's all right now," Serge said. His coughing was worse. From both the effort and the smoke.

Melinoe was still rushing around the room, grabbing objects. Taking pictures off the wall.

"We got the fire out," Serge said to her.

She turned to look at him but appeared confused. As if she didn't understand what he was saying. She struggled with an armful of treasures she could barely hold. Her pockets were stuffed with a jade figure and the Fabergé frame holding the photo of Melinoe and her father. She'd ripped her tunic getting it inside, and a flap of fabric hung down her leg, ruining the perfect outfit.

Serge went to the door. "We need to get some air in here." He tried the knob, but it wouldn't budge. "This damn power outage," he said and reached into his pocket for a key. Using it, he opened the front door, and a burst of chilly but welcome air blew into the room.

"Do you have the keys to the dungeon too? Can you get Griffin out?" Jac asked Serge.

"Yes, of course. Let's go."

Before they'd taken a dozen steps, Jac stopped. Sniffed the air. Fresh smoke. She spun around.

"Oh no!"

Serge turned too.

One of the candles must have rolled too far away for either of them to notice it. Now the curtains by the bay windows were burning. The rug beneath them had caught fire too. And as she watched, the wooden frame around the window burst into flames.

"Get out of the house," Serge shouted at Jac. He threw her his phone. "Call the fire department."

"What about Griffin?" Jac insisted.

Serge coughed again. "I'll get him—you go outside and call."

Jac hesitated. "We need to get Griffin—"

"I'll get him," Serge shouted. "You call."

There was the sound of something cracking. Jac looked up. A fiery piece of molding was plummeting toward her. And then someone—no, it wasn't someone—it wasn't hands—it was a force—shoved her out the open door.

She lost her balance. Breaking her fall with her right hand, she felt a stab of pain, but that didn't matter. The molding had fallen right where she'd been standing. It had to have been Robbie who'd pushed her out of harm's way, but there was no time to focus on that now.

Jac dialed the emergency number. While she waited for someone to answer, she looked through the doorway. The fire was traveling through the house, and the dining room was alight with flames.

"Where are you?" asked the voice on the other end.

As she recited the information to the operator, she heard Serge's shouts.

"Melinoe, leave everything, just get out of the house."

Jac watched Melinoe push him away and return to collecting artwork. And then Jac lost sight of both of them as gray-black smoke enveloped them.

The operator said they'd send fire trucks immediately and instructed Jac to stay outside and wait for the fire department. Not to go back inside under any circumstances.

But Griffin was inside, in the dungeon. Jac ran around to the other side of the house and tried the kitchen door. It was still locked. What was she going to do?

Looking down, she spotted a rock. The kitchen window shattered but remained intact. Jac pushed against it, but it resisted the force. Damn. Melinoe had really made the house impenetrable. Peering in through the cracks, Jac could see the kitchen was relatively free of smoke. The fire hadn't reached back here yet. She pictured the stairway. Even if the fire reached the kitchen, could it travel down that stone passageway? Was there anything to catch on fire there? But what about the smoke?

Jac ran back around to the front door. Maybe she could get through if she—

As she passed the library windows, she peered in. The glow was intense, flames licking at the window. All the books were burning. All those wonderful books.

She could feel the heat coming off the house now.

Where was Serge? Had he reached Griffin?

Even if he hadn't, the dungeon had to be safer than anywhere else in the house. The smoke would rise, wouldn't it?

Where were the fire engines? What was taking so long?

Someone was coming from around the side of the house. In the fire's glow, Jac could see the cook, Lisette, covered in soot and coughing. She ran to the woman.

"How did you get out?"

Lisette pointed and told her Serge had opened the kitchen door and helped her.

"Where is he now?"

"He went down to the cellars," she said and then began to cry.

"How bad is it in the kitchen?"

"There's smoke everywhere, but I don't know."

Jac ran to the back entrance. Smoke was pouring out of the open door, but she didn't see any flames. The cook had followed her, and together the two women watched and waited.

"With all the artwork and valuables in the house, why isn't there some kind of fire protection system?" Jac asked.

"There is," the cook said. "But when Madame Cypros shut off the power to the house, it must have shut down too."

"She *shut off* the power?" Jac asked.

Suddenly a loud cracking came from inside. The château's stone walls wouldn't burn, but the many ancient wooden beams crisscrossing the ceilings were a banquet for the fire. Jac pictured the tapestries leading up the landing to the second floor—all so old, ripe for a first spark.

The cook said something, but Jac couldn't hear her over the roaring. It was so loud now. *Like an orchestra from Hades,* she thought.

Suddenly, through billowing smoke, Jac saw a figure emerge. She held her breath. It was two figures, Serge helping Griffin. No, it was the other way around. Griffin was helping Serge.

Jac felt relief wash over her. *Griffin was alive.*

She ran to them.

"He's really sick, we need to get him help," Griffin said.

"No, I'm all right," Serge said in between coughs. "I have to go back and get Melinoe. She's crazy. She won't leave her collections. Doesn't she realize they are just things . . ." He was trying to catch his breath.

Serge started to head toward the door, but Griffin held him back.

Just then Jac heard the sound she'd been listening for: in the distance, fire engine alarms.

"I have to get to Melinoe . . ." Serge was trying to break away from Griffin. "They are just things . . ." A sob broke from his throat. "Just things . . ."

"Let the firemen get her," Griffin said. "You're not in any shape to go back in there."

"I have to. She's my . . . She's my . . ." Serge coughed again. "She's my life."

"But she made you inhale one of the dying breaths." Jac had guessed it when she'd seen Serge's glassy eyes, first heard him cough. "She overheard what Griffin told me, and she asked you to inhale one of the breaths, didn't she?"

Serge didn't respond. He was still struggling to break Griffin's grasp.

"How can you willingly risk your life for the woman who put yours in danger?" she asked.

Serge stopped fighting Griffin for a moment to look at Jac. In his eyes was an expression she knew and understood. It didn't matter what Melinoe had done. It wasn't what she felt or didn't feel for Serge. It was about what he felt for her.

Then, with a burst of strength that Griffin wasn't prepared for and couldn't stop, Serge broke away and ran, stumbling toward the house to find Melinoe. She was all he knew. All he'd ever known.

And just as the fire engines arrived, Serge disappeared into the firestorm.

Jac, Griffin and the cook stood in the chill night air and watched as the firemen made every attempt to gain entry to the house, but the entire downstairs was engulfed in flames. The most they could do was shoot powerful arcs of water into the Château La Belle Fleur, into the rooms filled with priceless paintings, sculpture and objets d'art.

Minutes passed without any sign of Serge or Melinoe.

Serge had told Jac once that he was to blame for Melinoe's father's death and despite that she'd saved Serge's life. That she had loved him despite what his life had cost her. That was what he owed her.

"She loved me that much," he had said.

And hated him that much too, Jac thought as she watched the fire's glow and smelled its terrible and powerful aroma.

Griffin, Jac and the cook continued to wait.

Finally the firefighters got the conflagration under control and were able to enter the house, but Jac knew that when they came out, neither Serge nor Melinoe would be with them.

Chapter 48

MAY 16, 1573
BARBIZON, FRANCE

As was befitting a lady-in-waiting, the funeral Mass for Isabeau was held in Sainte-Chapelle. The very place where we had trysted. Where we were to be married. I thought she would have enjoyed that. Her sense of irony was as keen as mine. It had been five days since her death, and I had barely slept for working on my formula. More than ever, I had to solve the puzzle of Serapino's notations. I had to bring Isabeau back to me.

I was not grieving as I thought I would. Not in mourning, for I was not really alive. I too had died that night. Now, I was a ghost who needed to accomplish one thing and one thing only: to figure out the elixir.

Catherine herself came and got me when it was time to go to the Mass. And then sat beside me, her arm linked through mine—abandoning protocol to be with me and shore me up.

I knew that she was doing this for me, but she was also conniving and clever, and she knew that now I had an ever greater incentive to work out the formula, which she wanted as much as I did.

I had given the priest the incense for the Mass. I'd taken myrrh and frankincense and added rose oil. A last bouquet for my Isabeau so that she would leave the world on the wings of a perfume that she loved. Now, as the priest swung the censer, the church filled with the holy scent, and the chanting sounded like tears falling, steady and constant.

The Mass was long and the church was hot. The fragrance I'd made mingled with the odor of the men and women in the court who were not as careful to bathe as Catherine and her ladies-in-waiting. The stench was vile and grew more disgusting as the Mass continued until it seemed some kind of monster, there to haunt me. I brought my scented handkerchief up to my face and buried my nose in it, and as I did, I caught sight of Princess Margaret sitting across the aisle.

Her skin was pale, and she looked ill herself.

Weeping, she appeared bereft. I was not so foolish as to think it was about Isabeau. The court was rife with the rumor that the princess had lost her prince. Henry de Guise had been betrothed that morning. He was soon to wed another.

I wished I'd felt some satisfaction that Margaret was suffering, but her pain didn't mitigate mine. Just mirrored it and made me all the more aware of the scope of my loss. Of the magnitude of my misery.

Watching Margaret, I suddenly wondered how she had discovered it was Isabeau who'd spied on her. Who had told her? Did it even matter? It was Margaret who had ordered the gloves, who had exacted her revenge.

Except it did matter, and I thought of little else during the next few days as I accompanied Isabeau's body to Barbizon to the tomb where Catherine had given me permission to inter her. And I continued to think on it as I returned to my laboratory in the Louvre, to resume my work on the formula.

My third night back, close to midnight, the door that connected my lair to the queen's chambers opened. Of course I expected Catherine. She had been checking on me often, treating me more like one of her sons than one of her servants.

But it wasn't the queen; it was Cosimo Ruggieri. His sly smile was on his lips, amused, it seemed, by my surprise.

"What are you doing here?" I asked. "That is a private entrance."

"I came to offer my condolences."

"Really?"

"Yes, really. I don't enjoy watching people suffer."

His eyes said the opposite. All of our adult lives, this man and I had been in competition. Somehow I couldn't believe that now his heart was breaking for me.

"What do you want, Ruggieri?"

"To help you find the answer to your puzzle."

Yes, this I could believe. He was a magician. Of course the idea of reanimating dying breaths would appeal to him.

"Catherine has asked me to assist you. Two of us working together are twice as likely to find a solution."

I didn't want the help, but I so longed to find the answer, to bring back my Isabeau, I allowed him to assist me.

And so began a series of days when the rancid charlatan worked in my laboratory, trying out various ridiculous ideas. First he tried using the water bowl that Catherine was so adept at, to see if he could see the solution there. Then he sought it through smoke seeing and crystal gazing. He put one of the bottles in the center of a pentagram and went into a trance. He wrote pages of copious notes. He suggested using essences and oils that I had never heard of and believed he was making up. In short he exhausted me and stole time that I might have put to some use.

We had been working together for a full week before I gleaned his motive. I had gone out to get some water, and when I came back, Ruggieri was bent over my book of fragrance formulas, studying them.

"What are you doing?" I asked.

"Just curious about your methods."

"Since when have you become interested in perfumes?"

"I'm not actually interested in them as perfumes but as possible portals that we can travel through to reach other levels of thought."

"Stairways to other times?"

"Yes, if you will. I made a relaxing potion for Margaret that enabled her to see into the future. It was no different than all the other relaxing potions I'd made her, so I wondered if it was the combination of my potion and the perfume she was wearing that had affected her so."

There was something about the way he said the princess's name that alerted me. Who can say what it was? To this day I don't know. But my skin prickled, and I felt shivers of cold up and down my arms.

"What was the perfume she was wearing—one of mine?"

"Yes, I believe so," he answered.

"Can you describe it?"

For all his brilliance Ruggieri didn't know I had any ulterior motive and described the fragrance, quite well I thought.

"Jasmine and lilac and lily with a bit of pepper, I think."

Yes, I had made that fragrance for Margaret and given it to her just the day before she'd sent Bernadette de La Longe to me to obtain the poisoned gloves.

And then I remembered something that Isabeau had mentioned that at the time had not seemed important.

When Isabeau had gone to Catherine to tell her about Margaret's planned assignation with de Guise, there were other people in the room. I hadn't asked and Isabeau hadn't told me who they were, except Isabeau had mentioned that the queen had been reading the water bowl when she had arrived. And the queen used it while Isabeau was still there to see if there was anything else she could glean about her daughter and de Guise.

I did not accuse Ruggieri there and then. He would just deny it. Instead, the following day, I went to see the princess, pretending to show fealty.

Margaret was seated at a desk when I was shown in. I presented her with a new scent, which she accepted with pleasure, though she was some-what subdued. Since the marriage plans of the duke de Guise had been announced, Margaret's manner had become listless. In time, she would recover to some extent, but never again was she the wickedly beautiful and vibrant girl she had been that summer.

As I watched, Margaret uncorked the bottle, sniffed at it and applied it to her wrists. For a moment I wished again that I'd poisoned this perfume. I'd been dreaming of doing just that. Only my loyalty to my queen had prevented me. One death had been enough. Isabeau was gone, and killing Margaret would not bring her back. Only I could do that by finding the formula. And to do that it seemed I needed something no one could give me: divine intervention.

"This is lovely, Maître René. What is in it?"

Margaret was even more interested in perfume than her mother and in time would bring other perfumers to the court who would create a business in Grasse. I've watched it grow these years, from the sidelines here in Barbizon, and it is impressive.

I recited the list of ingredients.

"Well, it's lovely, and I thank you."

I bowed. And then asked: "If I may, Your Highness?"

"Yes?"

"I have a bold question."

"Yes?"

"Since they were my gloves that your lady-in-waiting gave to Isabeau Allard . . ."

Margaret flinched. This was highly inappropriate of me, but the princess had known me for her whole life.

"What is it you are asking?" Her voice was pulled tight. The cords on her neck stood out.

"Can you tell me how you learned that she had spied on you?"

"It was a guess." Margaret looked down at the bottle I'd brought.

"I know you better than that. You are too intelligent to make a guess and act on it. Please indulge me and tell me how you found out?"

"Why do you want to know, René?"

"Because they were my gloves . . . because she was your mother's lady-in-waiting . . . because I wish I could have prevented what happened to her and to you."

She smiled. The princess was far more beautiful than her mother, but only on the outside. She was selfish in ways Catherine had never been and could never be. Or so I believed.

Leaning forward, Margaret put her hand on mine. "I appreciate that, René. It was a terrible day. My life . . ." She broke off. "It was Ruggieri who told me, who exposed the little bitch."

There it was. I had my answer. The answer I had suspected. As I walked back to my laboratory, I wondered what I could do with the information. The magician was important to Catherine. I couldn't be the one to tell her of Ruggieri's deception. But I could expose him in other ways. Take away what he loved and cared about. Do to him what he had done to me.

The one thing that mattered to Ruggieri as much as Isabeau had mattered to me was his position in Catherine's court. And so the next day I set off to visit the astrologer Nostradamus, who had come to the Louvre before. He'd read the queen's charts and forecast her husband's death. She'd told me then how impressed she was with him.

I brought Nostradamus back to the Louvre. The queen, delighted to see him, gave him an elaborate suite of rooms and visited with him for hours.

It was torture for Ruggieri. But as it turned out, that wasn't enough for me.

So I planned. And waited. And finally I made a discovery that enabled me to exact my revenge.

As I write this, six years have passed since Isabeau died. Six years since I left the Louvre and moved here to Barbizon to devote all my time to finish the formula to bring back the dead through their souls.

Last month, finally, I believed I'd solved the puzzle that Serapino had labored over for so long. I mixed it into all the breaths I had collected. And then a strange thing occurred.

I keep a hive to harvest honey, and four bees became trapped in one of the test bottles. I noticed them in time to free them before they suffocated. But the next morning I found four dead bees on the stones. What did that mean? When inhaled by an infant, the elixir was supposed to bring the dead back to life, not do harm.

But what if I was wrong?

I returned to Paris and, without telling Ruggieri, enlisted him to help me learn more about what Serapino began and I had finished. I would expose him to the mixture. If it was harmless, Ruggieri would live to an even riper old age and I would have to devise another method to exact justice.

But if I was right and it wasn't harmless . . .

I never meant to play God, but that is what I did. Now, as I look back, I don't regret my actions even if others will deem them wrong. I was an old man who fell in love with the scent of a rose. And the hope of smelling Isabeau's gardens again was worth all risks. Even if I spend the rest of my days in hell, I do not regret my efforts.

The mixture I'd created had indeed turned out to be the opposite of what Serapino and I expected. The combined breath and elixir, if kept in a tightly closed vessel for a month or more, produced a poison, a lethal weapon.

It took four days for the illness to take hold of the magician and fell him. I watched the demise of my nemesis with satisfaction. Visiting him often. Checking on his progress. And then the night came when the end was near, and Ruggieri knew it as well as I did.

"You have done this to me, René, have you

not?" Ruggieri asked, his voice faint, his lips dry and cracked, his body bloated, his skin yellowed.

I did not need to answer. He already knew.

"But you've exacted your revenge on the wrong person." His smile was evil.

I visited his sickroom to take satisfaction in his illness. He had been responsible for me losing all that mattered to me. But now it appeared he was the one taking satisfaction.

"I don't believe I have. 'An eye for an eye,' Ruggieri," I said, quoting scripture.

"Then it's your queen whose eye you must go after."

"You talk nonsense," I said stridently, even as a shiver traveled down my spine.

"All this time you believe that I acted alone? That I went to Margaret on my own? Did you underestimate our mistress to that degree?" These were the ramblings of a dying man. Ruggieri didn't know what he was saying.

"What nonsense you speak." I shook my head.

"Catherine arranged everything, you fool. She could not risk one of her spies leaving the castle and sharing all the secrets she knew. The gossip of Margaret's affair alone would have destroyed Catherine's plans to marry the princess to the Protestant. All of Catherine's efforts and secrets were at stake; the future of France was at stake."

And then Ruggieri laughed. Despite his sickness and his weakened state, Ruggieri laughed and laughed, taking pleasure in my surprise . . . and . . . my devastation.

Catherine had been responsible? My queen?

Yes, I knew she was a Medici. A determined ruler and a powerful force. Yes, I had seen her connive, spy, destroy and even kill. Had I not aided and abetted her with my poisons? We had spent over four decades together, and I had given her everything she had ever asked of me. But I had never imagined that in the end she would be the one to take from me the only thing I had ever longed for.

Hours later, I watched Catherine's astronomer and astrologer, her magician, die from inhaling the breath of a long-dead nobleman mixed with a fragrant elixir.

Nothing can bring someone back to life. Nothing can reanimate a breath. The secret, which is not so secret after all, is that the people who we love live on in our hearts, in the beat of our blood. The memory of Isabeau lives in every single breath I take. And on my deathbed, as I take in her last breath, she will be there with me, as alive and vibrant and wonderful as she was on every day that I knew her.

The dead do not have to be reanimated; they live as long as someone who loved them is alive.

Chapter 49

THE PRESENT
MANY MONTHS LATER
PARIS, FRANCE

Something woke Jac. Reaching out, she felt the space beside her. Cold. Empty. She listened. All was quiet. Opening her eyes, she peeked at the digital clock on her bedside table: half past two. Sliding out of the bed, she shrugged into her robe, padded out of the bedroom and walked down the hall toward the nursery.

More than three centuries of children had spent their infancies here in the L'Etoile mansion on the Rue des Saints-Pères. Dozens of them, including her grandfather, her father and her brother.

And now, Jac thought, her son would grow up here. Perhaps, like the generations before him, he too would fall in love with the world of fragrance and choose to devote his life to creating beautiful scents and evocative dreams.

The door was opened. Brahms played on the baby's music player. The only illumination came from a night-light teddy bear. But it was enough for Jac to see by.

Griffin had fallen asleep in the rocking chair, his

ten-week-old son on his chest. The baby wasn't sleeping, though. His eyes were wide open as he watched Jac approach. On his little face was a peaceful, almost bemused expression. As if he were saying, So much for *him* putting *me* back to sleep.

Jac reached down and lifted her son out of her husband's arms. The baby snuggled into the embrace with a contented murmur. Holding him close to her breast, Jac walked over to the window seat and sat down.

Rocking the baby to the music, she looked out on the moonlit garden. From here she could see the maze and follow the path to its center, where she and her brother used to play hide-and-seek among the fragrant boxwoods. At the maze's heart sat two stone sphinxes Robbie had named Pain and Chocolat—after their favorite breakfast croissant. This is where she had finally scattered Robbie's ashes and let his last breath float away in the breeze.

From here, Jac could see the glass doors to the workshop where her grandfather had created so many wonderful perfumes and where her father built the small perfumer's organ for Jac and Robbie. Where they had played at being perfumers for hours, concocting impossible scents.

All the generations of L'Etoiles had left their mark here. Here, all around Jac, was history, passion and life and death. It was part of her and now it was part of her son.

She rocked the baby in her arms. This tiny baby who she had so much love for already. Across the room, she glanced at his father. Griffin had been right. They'd had a destiny and a choice: to fear the future or learn from the past. To accept that not everything can be understood except this—except what she'd finally learned—that love was real. It hurt and was work and it failed sometimes, but Serge had shown her: it's the most real thing we can experience and know.

Jac bent her head to her son's. Her lips touched his fine brown hair that was just like his father's. The baby had his father's dark-blue eyes too. And his mouth was the same shape as Griffin's.

But the baby's smell . . . she inhaled it again . . .

Her brother's ghost had not revisited Jac after she'd left the château. She'd waited for his presence to reappear, but after she'd felt that push out the door, she never sensed him again. He seemed to have abandoned her. And so she had been forced to mourn him and feel all the grief and sadness she'd avoided and finally accept that he was gone.

Until that night, in the hospital, the first time the nurse put her baby in her arms. Suddenly a warm golden glow filled the room. Jac knew it was Robbie. And in that embracing light, when she'd bent her head to kiss her infant son, she noticed something extraordinary.

It was impossible for a newborn to smell like

anything but baby powder and mother's milk. But her baby did. He smelled of the scent she and Robbie had made up when they were children, the Scent of Us Forever. Cinnamon, carnation, patchouli, a little pepper and some jasmine. Spicy, dark and mysterious, it was a treasure hunt of a scent full of the mischievousness of childhood.

Jac knew her long quest to understand reincarnation had finally ended. She no longer needed explanations or proof.

We don't need a magical elixir to reanimate a dying breath and bring someone back to life. We don't need meditation tools or ancient formulas or hypnosis. The secret, which is not so secret after all, is that the people who we love live on in our hearts, in the beat of our blood. The dead live as long as someone who loves them lives.

Her baby's soul was alive with Robbie's soul. Reincarnated with her brother's love. With her mother's and her grandparents' love. Alive with the love of those who were gone and who she missed so very much.

And her baby's soul was alive with the love of one person who was not gone at all but sat, still sleeping, in the rocking chair.

She looked over at Griffin.

Jac settled back and inhaled her baby's smell once more. She would tell Griffin soon about the scent . . . wanted to share it with him . . . but for now it was her secret. Hers and Robbie's.

Author's Note

As with most of my work, there is a lot of fact mixed in with this fictional tale.

Officina Profumo–Farmaceutica di Santa Maria Novella, one of the world's oldest pharmacies, was founded in 1221 in Florence by the Dominican Friars who made herbal remedies and potions. The first "Eau de Cologne" has been attributed to the pharmacy's 1500s citrus and bergamot scented water created for Catherine de Medici.

René le Florentin was indeed apprenticed at the monastery and there created scents and creams for the young Catherine de Medici. When the fourteen-year-old duchessina traveled to France to marry the prince, she took René with her. He and Catherine are credited with bringing perfume to their newly adopted country.

René's perfume store in Paris was as described, and along with perfume he was credited with inventing creative poisons like the ones in the book, which his queen and her subjects used on their enemies.

Catherine de Medici, her aspirations, issues, superstitions, family, reliance on Cosimo Ruggieri and René le Florentin, her reign and the customs of her country are presented here as history portrays them.

Cosimo Ruggieri was suspected of all the nefarious activity René suspects him of in this novel.

There was in fact a secret passageway from Catherine's room to René's workshop, and their use of it was documented. Despite how much we know about their relationship, there is very little known about René le Florentin's personal life. He is rumored to have fathered several children but was never married.

Isabeau is a fictional character, but there was a "flying squadron" of women who were trained spies for Catherine.

The history of perfume and the fragrance industry past and present is based on research, and I would like to thank Victoria Frolova for her invaluable help. It was she who introduced me to both momie and tutty—real ingredients used in the Renaissance.

While there is no Phoenix Foundation in New York City or anywhere, the work done there by Dr. Malachai Samuels was inspired by work done at the University of Virginia Medical Center by Dr. Ian Stevenson, who studied children with past-life memories for more than thirty years. Dr. Bruce Greyson and Dr. Jim Tucker, a child psychiatrist, continue Ian Stevenson's work today.

As for the theory of the dying breaths: We don't

know where this concept originated or if anyone in the Renaissance suspected such a thing was possible. But it's not a far stretch from the well-documented and centuries-old alchemical search for immortality to the breath concept.

We do know that in the twentieth century, automotive magnate Henry Ford and the great inventor Thomas Edison, who both believed in reincarnation, supported the idea that in death, the soul leaves the body with its last breath.

Edison's dying breath, collected by his son, Charles, is in fact on display at the Edison Winter Home in Fort Myers, Florida.

Acknowledgments

My name is on the cover of this novel, but it takes a team to bring a book to life.

For the third time and with even more gratitude, thanks to my editor, Sarah Durand, who is truly an author's dream, and to Judith Curr, whose support means the world to me.

To Lisa Scambira, Hilary Tinsman, Ben Lee, Daniella Wexler and everyone at Atria Books whose hands this book passed through—your hard work and creative thinking does not go unnoticed.

To my agent, Dan Conaway, who is truly my knight in shining armor, and everyone at Writers House—I am so proud to be on your roster.

I also want to thank the readers, booksellers and librarians everywhere who make all the work worthwhile.

And, as always, I'm very grateful to my family and friends, especially my father and Ellie, the Kulicks and Mara Gleckel. And most of all, Doug.

Center Point Large Print
600 Brooks Road / PO Box 1
Thorndike ME 04986-0001 USA

(207) 568-3717

US & Canada:
1 800 929-9108
www.centerpointlargeprint.com